ALICE CHILDRESS, actress, director and playwright, was born in Charleston, South Carolina, and raised in Harlem. Her play WEDDING BAND was produced by Joseph Papp's Public Theater. Other plays by Ms. Childress include TROUBLE IN MIND, which won the Obie Award for the best original off-Broadway production; WINE IN THE WILDERNESS, presented on NET; and THE FREEDOM DRUM. Her young adult novels, A HERO AIN'T NOTHIN' BUT A SANDWICH and RAINBOW JORDAN are available in Avon Flare editions.

A SHORT WALK

ALICE CHILDRESS

A BARD BOOK/PUBLISHED BY AVON BOOKS

AVON BOOKS
A division of
The Hearst Corporation
959 Eighth Avenue
New York, New York 10019

Published by arrangement with
Coward, McCann & Geoghegan, Inc.
Library of Congress Catalog Card Number: 79-14262
ISBN: 0-380-54239-0

First Bard Printing, March, 1981

BARD TRADEMARK REG. U.S. PAT OFF. AND IN OTHER COUNTRIES,
MARCA REGISTRADA, HECHO IN U.S.A.
Printed in the U.S.A.

OP 10 9 8 7 6 5 4 3 2

To my daughter Jean

One

One morning, in the middle of the year 1900, in a two-room shack in Charleston, South Carolina, Bill James has a comforting breakfast of mackerel and hominy grits. Jesus looks down from the wall with compassion, down from his frame of pink and blue seashells. Bill is lean, good looking, and keen featured. His skin is dull, velvety, almost blue. Gently puffed lips glow grape-purple against strong white teeth. In one knotted, work-hardened hand he holds a newspaper, in the other a piece of fried fish. He shakes his head slowly, with great authority. "Etta, this world is somethin, first one thing, then another."

His brown wife peeps over his shoulder, pouring another cup of coffee, leaning in close, enjoying the odor of Dr. Alimine's Flower Pomade. She thinks of telling him how good looking he is, but says something else.

"You like to show off, don'tcha? Just cause you can read. You oughta be thinkin' 'bout buyin another paper. All that news happen so long ago till folks done forgot."

"I'm gonna buy a new one when new things start happenin. No point in buyin the same news every day, a waste a money."

Etta takes off her apron and picks her best black skirt free of lint. Looking in the speckled, cracked mirror hanging under Jesus on the wall, she smoothes thick, bushy hair and rolls down her sleeves. "Bill, what kinda eyes I got?"

"Gingerbread eyes and stand-up ninnies."

"Shame, shame, no way to talk on the day of a funeral."

"Yeah, it is. You got pretty little feet and a nice round boonky."

"Stop talkin underneath my clothes. No shame."

"Got dimples in her cheeks, all up behind her knees and everywhere."

Her eyes light with love. They think love thoughts about how good it is to be together, how good it was each time they had it, touching hands beneath the covers even when they weren't having it. How good it is to be black and brown in a morning glory-covered house; to have mackerel and grits on a four-eyed stove; to own plates, cups, spoons and an iron bed with a big, comfortable mattress.

"Billie-boy, ain't it time we 'dopted ourself a baby?"

He lowers his head as if examining the workboots, turning his feet this way and that. "Well, folks oughta have they own chirrun and—"

"Look like we ain't gonna have any of our own. Looks like I'da got that way in five years, but no sense in accusin Gawd."

Bill carefully folds the newspaper and places it in the sideboard drawer. "Folks should be kinda well-off when they think bout taking in a stranger-chile."

"We's well-off. Ain't many people got as much to show as we got. Not a meal goes by that we don't have food left in the pot. There's bedclothes in the drawer and a pump in the kitchen. We got pots, pans and dishes. How much can a baby use?"

"They don't stay little. They grow up."

"Let her grow if she wants to. That's what babies is for, for to grow."

"I gotta go to work. We gonna dig ditches behind the mill road. . . ."

"And I'm bringin Murdell's baby back after the funeral."

"But you dern well can't do it less I give the word."

"Give me your word."

"Look like Murdell's mama would keep it."

"Mrs. Johnson's gone so cripple till the next door people have to do for her."

"How come the next door people don't keep the baby?"

"Cause they got nine of they own. Haven't you been sayin and also silent-wishin for me to have a baby?"

Bill pops his knuckles and fine beads of sweat appear on his forehead. "I don't know how the baby look."

"You got eyes; come see."

"I can't look at the chile, then say I don't want it. That's rude. Bet they name it somethin I wouldn't like. Did they call her Murdell?"

"No, and you must never speak ill of the dead."

"Not speakin ill, just don't like that name."

"They gonna let me name her."

"You did it already?"

"I thought of a name and they callin her by it, but she's only three weeks old—we can change it."

"What yall callin her?"

"Cora, after your gone-to-glory mother who was born in slavery. Cora is a sound that's short, sweet and easy on your mouth."

He turns away to hide the pleasure in his eyes, having a

hard time of giving in, giving up and taking in the stranger-child. . . . "That baby is half white, Etta."

"But she's so sweetly brown, like coffee and condense milk mix together."

"But even so. . . ."

She cups his face in her hands. "Please, sweet daddy, do it just for me?"

His knees go weak. "Sure, for you and for me, too—but where will she sleep?"

She pulls his shirtsleeve, leads the way to the tiny bedroom. Squeezing her roundness past the washstand, she reaches under the bed and drags out a wooden box lined with cotton quilting. Bill stamps the floor and the walls tremble. "You ain't fixin to put our Cora to sleep in a Octiggen soap box!"

"What's wrong with that?"

"I wouldn't want nobody to visit and see her in a soap box. She suppose to sleep in a cradle."

"There's no cradle finer than this."

"Baby won't be able to see. She'll be thinkin the world look like the inside of a soap box."

"She won't catch no drafts."

"And no fresh air, either."

"Well, our Cora can sleep in the box till you get a cradle. Bill, we got us a baby."

Her face is so alive with happiness he has to reach out and take her in his arms as she cries out joy and relief. One hot, salty teardrop falls on his throat and trickles over his chest. Desire moves through his body and he is ready to lie down with her. She feels him stir, clings to him, kissing his lips, nostrils and eyes, nuzzling her nose into the hollow of his neck, wetting his face with her crying. He moves the soap box from the bed to the washstand and pulls back the patchwork quilt.

"Ain't this a damn shame . . . and I was all ready to go to work . . . a damn shame."

Unbleached muslin sheets are cool to warm bodies and this morning is the best of all times, a moment with them tight together in it, and the new baby waiting, and the Octagon soap box ready on the washstand. A sweet twenty minutes, the two of them one within the protection of drawn shades and friendly walls; with the sound of bees humming as they rob morning glories for honey. Bill rubs purple lips across her throat and whispers down the golden corridor of her ear.

"Ain't this a shame, a damn shame, and I gotta go to work. . . ."

People gather at the Johnson house to take one last look at Murdell Johnson before following her narrow casket out to the colored cemetery. Sad-faced little children stand around the front yard, starchily dressed in their best bits of finery—limp, threadbare hair ribbons, hand-me-down dresses, thrice-patched knickerbockers and overalls. One little girl pulls at a tall, skinny woman's skirt. "Miss Odessa, can we go back in the house and look at the daid again?"

"No, yall have looked several times before. Oh, children, I tell you, this life is for suffering." She waves a black-edged handkerchief, stretches out gaunt but graceful arms and showers boys and girls with clear, silvery, cultivated words. "Be good, live righteous, for we know not the day or the hour. Kojie, lad, you are the tallest, so when we start our march to the graveyard please lead the way for the little ones carrying bouquets."

The long-legged tan boy stands at attention, one hand respectfully held behind his back. A sharp crease is ressed in each pants leg of his denims. "Yes, Ma'am, Miss Odessa. Can

I get you someth*ing?* Maybe a cool, refresh*ing* dipper of water from the well?"

Odessa rewards him with a sad storybook smile and gracefully flutters her handkerchief. "Kojie, I do declare, you're going to someday be somebody of importance. You prove to us that color is nothing and the heart is all; as the French say, '*Couleur n'est rien, le coeur est tout.*' I'll have a dipper of water, God bless you. Let us all try to lift our race and remember to put *ing* on the end of our words. Death is indeed hard, children, we know not the day or the hour." She sweeps over to the rickety bench where paper flowers of every description are piled high; some old, some wilted, others heavily waxed, a few bright and new. "Oh, how good and sweet of kind friends to lend their flowers. Let's arrange them in small bunches to be carried by our angels. Yes, we know not the day. . . ."

"Stop all that drat goin on!"

Odessa and the children look up to see Addie scowling down from the porch. Addie—fat, red-brown, with black ribbons braided through her straight Indian hair neatly criss-crossed behind her shoulder blades. Odessa slowly unfolds the petals of a red paper rose.

"We're not making noise, Miss Addie."

"Then how come we can hear you talkin bout nobody knowin the day or the hour? Murdell's mama is quiet now, but if you'da heard her this mornin it woulda chilled the blood in your very veins. When she saw her child laid out she went to screamin and shakin. Her breath drawin in and out was like death rattles."

Odessa ties a pink streamer around a dusty cluster of waxed sweet peas. "Poor soul, life will test you—will test us all. What is it all about? That's the question, and who's to answer?"

Addie shakes her braids. "Don't let a little schoolin turn

you fool. Gawd knows what it's about. He's movin, workin his will and payin no never-mind to what niggas understand."

The children clutch their flowers and search Odessa's face for answers. She says, "Handle bouquets with care because we must return them to owners after the procession." The children stare, waiting to see if she will dare answer back.

"I'm teaching these children not to use the word *nigger.*"

"Well, I ain't no chile."

"But we shouldn't tell them not to say it and . . . and say it ourselves."

"And you shouldn't correct me before chirrun."

"I had to, I'm sorry."

"When white folk call us names I notice that nobody is ever on hand to correct them."

Odessa draws herself up even taller. "We can't be responsible for what they say but we can set the proper example."

Addie sucks her teeth, making a popping sound with her lips, picks up a tin pail and heads for the pump. "Oh my, we gettin so muckty-muck and dicty. Well, whilst yall play with flowers, I'm the one that's cleanin up. Schoolin and learnin ain't worth a poot in a china pot."

"May we help?"

Addie shoves her away. "No, go play with your flowers." She turns up the front of her black cotton skirt and pins it behind, showing a snowy petticoat patched with a bag from Webster's Rice Mills. "Fact is," she grumbles, "you right. It ain't nice to say 'nigga', but I don't be sayin it like white folk. I just say it dry-long-so. When they say it, it's to hurt." She presses down on the pump with both hands; there's a low, gurgling sound as it gives up a thin stream of water. "Fact is," she goes on, "I don't expect to hear chirrun sayin that word. First one do is gonna get a fast backhand slap in the mouth. Yall hear?"

The children nod solemnly out of respect for Addie. After

winning the battle with the pump, she squares her shoulders and picks up the pail. "Yes, chirrun, there's many a thing we got to learn cause life will test us. We know not the day or the hour and things like that, so you listen to Miss Odessa, cause she don't have to spend her time on no dumb chirrun. Long ago she could have shook the dust of Carolina off her shoe sole and gone Nawth where streets are pave with gold and sprinkle with diamonds, where all a nigga—a *person*—has to do is bend down and scoop up a bountiful fortune."

A little girl with wide, flaring nostrils suddenly holds them together and whispers. "Pewie, pewie, here comes the dog-nanny man."

Kojie snickers, then righteously scolds her. "Shouldn't say that. Suppose to respect grown people. Ain't she, Miss Odessa?"

"Yes, children, be very kind."

They watch the old man slowly pull the familiar sack up the street. He stops to sweep up something with a whisk broom and a small shovel, then empties it into his crokersack.

Addie sucks her teeth and spits. "Gawd, that poor man stink. Dog-nanny smell is all through his skin."

Kojie puts on a sorrowful expression and shifts his weight from one foot to the other. "Why he pick*ing* it up like that, Miss Odessa?"

"Mr. July is in the fertilizer business. He gathers—collects—er—dog droppings, then he dries them out in the sun . . ."

Another boy, with long fuzzy hair, leans over to Kojie and says, "You oughta smell his yard."

Miss Odessa pinches the boy's ear and goes on with the explanation. ". . . then he sells them over at the fertilizer mill so they can make fertilizer, which is then put in the earth to make the lovely flowers grow."

Addie shakes her head with grudging admiration. "See

there? White folk so smart they can even make money outta dog turds."

Mr. July rests his sack in the middle of the road and, cap in hand, approaches the gate. "Mornin, Miss Addie, Miss Dessa, just stop to pay respeck to the daid. Won't come in, ain't fit to come in, but wanta give this fifty cent piece." He places the coin on the gatepost.

"I hope you don't think we're going to let you leave without looking on Murdell's face!" Odessa protests. "Shame on you, Mr. July!"

He straightens his shirt collar and breaks into a snaggle-toothed smile, eyes glistening with appreciation. "That's kind of you, but makes no sense for me to come in the house while I'm out workin this way."

Addie places her hands on her hips and moves closer to the gate. "Mr. July, go look on Murdell's face."

Odessa flings the gate open. "Mr. July, Murdell had a high regard for you. Go in, present your respects and your money, look on her face."

He enters the yard, easing past the gate with delicate hesitation, three steps forward, a half step back, advancing and retreating, bowing to Odessa, the children, and even to people who aren't there—his walk a mute but grand apology for his station in life.

Miss Addie darts a barbed wire look at the children, threatening to butt heads if they laugh at him. She follows at a less-than-comfortable distance from July.

Murdell's mother, mumbling prayers, is seated to one side, in front of the varnished oak coffin. A few months before, a stroke had lifted and twisted one corner of her mouth, leaving her right arm uselessly dangling by her side. She wears forty-five years like seventy. Wisps of dry, snowy white hair show from under a black cotton headcloth. The good left hand drums out a tattoo on her knee. Odessa leads Mister July to the coffin. The corpse is a picture of regal, peaceful calm, laid out in a lavender voile dress collared with white hand crochet. Her jet black hair is a billowing storm cloud against the lavender lace pillow. Murdell . . . sixteen, darkly beautiful with the near-yet-far-away look of youth in death.

Mister July fears he may disturb her immaculate rest. A knot of pain forms in the pit of his stomach, grows larger and works its way up to his throat; shoulders shake and scalding tears run down his cheeks. He tries to hold back sound but it pours out in a hoarse torrent. "Ease, Gawd, give us ease!"

He places the half dollar in a glass bowl on the table at the foot of the casket. Murdell's mama holds out her good hand.

"No, Ma'am, I been workin."

"Why you wanta act sometimey?"

He gently shakes her hand. "Gawd move in a mysterious way his wonder to perform. He never forsake the orphan. Most forty years done pass since the last day a bondage, so Murdell's baby gonna someday walk where we now can't go, live to say what we can't, gonna taste the sweet years to come. Her life will live easy."

He leaves the way he came; three steps forward, a half step back, nervously twirling his old, weatherbeaten hat, smiling and bowing to those there and those who are not, begging pardon for his existence. "Thank yuh, thank yuh, yas'm, indeedy, scuse me, beg pardon. . . ."

Odessa says goodbye at the gate. "We are fortunate to have kind friends in the hour of sorrow."

Mr. July whispers a secret. "This work a mine ain't no bed-a-roses, but I gotta be m'own boss cause I don't like workin for white folk in a direck way. They too mean, treated me so bad at the lumber yard, cuttin down my pay. They keep the white and lay me off when work slack. I held my tongue in check so much till it was givin me pains in m'chest."

"We know, Mister July, we know."

"Yas'm, this ain't no bed-a-roses, but I ruther pick up behind dawgs than work for white folk."

More people arrive for the funeral, scrubbed with brown soap, neatly dressed in their darkest clothes. They stream through the gate carrying imitation palm wreaths trimmed with bows of white ribbon, fresh cut garden flowers, bunches of wild purple clover, yellow dandelions and pots of ivy. Women carry agate pans and ironstone jars of food. Men are wearing white cotton gloves and purple satin badges stamped in gold—First Colored Brotherhood Lodge. They walk solemnly, holding the right hand behind the back, their heads respectfully bowed. Some stand on the porch speaking in whispers.

"Where is Murdell's mama's brother? You'da think Sam would come home for buryin his niece."

"He's travelin with Rabbit Ears minstrel show."

"What he doin in a minstrel?"

"Go out in a parade, be buckin and wingin to advertise—in face black."

"His face black enough."

"But that's how they do."

"Yeah, black it and make the mouth white."

"Got a pretty wife name Francine, I hear."

"Rabbit Ears travels through Georgia—Chicago even."

"You think Gawd like that?"

"No. They do better to pray."

Etta James hurries through the gate carrying her best gray agate pot and a newspaper-wrapped bundle. "How's Murdell's mama? I brought mulatto rice and clothes to take home the baby." She has a hard time keeping up with Odessa's long strides as they head for the kitchen.

"She's holding up. Relatives came from Edisto Island to

take her back. They'll keep the baby until you're ready."

"I'm takin Cora today. People don't like to give up children after havin 'em awhile."

"If Bill is ready."

"He is ready."

The minister's face looks like dark, crumpled cardboard; a face in perpetual mourning, lit by black diamond eyes staring out on a world just beyond his understanding. In his heart he carries a burden of guilts: once, long years ago, laying with his best friend's wife; once stealing a pair of secondhand shoes; hating his old slave master; looking at a white woman's nakedness as he went about the business of carrying wood to her house; refusing to lend a brother five dollars the day before he lost his life under the wheels of a freight train; the sin of longing for such worldly things as a gold tooth, a horse and buggy, a Prince Albert coat and a gold ring with a cat's-eye stone. Reverend Mills is ever at war with himself to win the battle against sin and desire, against the feelings within, the churning thoughts which keep him wondering how the flock can look to him for guidance. But he is winning the war, and daily turns the other cheek and goes about his humble way, trying to deal with unreasonable colored and white folk, taking low when backed into a corner. Yet there is sin in it too; he feels the acid drops of hatred eating into the core of his heart—a heart which skips and flutters. The inner struggle has etched a pained, resigned and bewildered look in his eyes. People say, "Reverend Mills looks like a picture of a saint—a black saint."

He stands behind the coffin studying his congregation—crowded elbow to elbow in the small room, spilling out to the porch and looking in at the windows. He squares his shoulders and tries to feel like Moses or Daniel as he fights the fear inside and wonders, What is death? He longs for a secret word that, once spoken, could bring peace instantly. He lifts his arms, holds out roughened hands, flexing gnarled fingers that will never wear a gold ring with a cat's-eye stone. "The Lawd giveth, the Lawd taketh away, blessed be the name of the Lawd."

The congregation agrees with light groans and sighs.

"The grim reaper strikes like a thief in the night. Every time you look in the jaws a death, ask yourself: Is my house in order?" The little flock grows fearful, they avoid each other's eyes, look at the walls and the few floral pieces. The men smooth their white gloves and purple badges. They are uncomfortably sorry for the times they have quarreled, fought, lusted after strangeness, sinned against the flesh. They feel defiled, rejected, inferior and stupid from worldly sin. Their misery is cold, stiff, wooden. They lick their lips and swallow saliva to ease dry throats. Each thinks his or her sin is the ugliest or the heaviest to bear, all except Miss Emily. She knows God forgave when she lost her sight. She has paid her sin-debt with blindness. She serves the term in hell now and there's nothing to look forward to but the happy-ever-after of an eternity filled with the blazing promise of everlasting joy.

"Glory! Praise his name!" Reverend Mills folds his arms and eases into preaching. "Gawd is tired a sin. If Gabriel was to blow today, where would you stand?"

Silence except for a few sighs mingling in the air with the smell of dying clover.

Murdell's mama closes her eyes, reliving the memory of her daughter's confession about a day long ago when the girl stood admiring herself in the white folk's looking glass, trying on the woman's clothes while they were all gone off to a wedding party. The son returned home early as she was trying on his mother's cambric and lace wrapper.

"I got no business doin this. They back?"

"No. I left. Why do you always run?"

"We not s'pose to be friends."

"Don't you get lonesome . . . workin out in service, goin home only once a month?"

"It's lonesome bein the onliest colored."

"I'm lonesome, too."

"But you ain't been sent away to strangers."

"Why do they send you? Fifteen is too young to be alone . . . with strangers."

"Poor people gotta send girls off so's they get room and board."

"Doesn't your family worry bout you?"

"No use. They say to be good and to pray."

"But it's still lonesome."

"Uh-huh."

From that day on they were friends and soon forgot to think about past or future—the only time was now. The first loving was to be the only "sin" but they continued to meet; young bodies, heads and hearts caring without caution, blind to the rules and laws of planned, separate living. One night he crept to her room; after loving, sleep stole over them. The morning sun beamed in the attic window and lighted them cheek to cheek, arms entwined, damp with love, deep in peaceful slumber. His mother awakened them. They sent him away to visit a distant aunt. She was sent home to her mother, four months pregnant, with eight dollars back pay.

Murdell's mama turns away from her mind's eye vision, shivering with the thought of how hot hell must be. "Do, Lawd, have mercy on my only chile! Birth fever took her and she done pay with her life. Mercy, Lawd! Have more mercy!"

Her suffering moves Reverend Mills to hasten his sermon onward, to open the flood gates, to ease heart's pain. "But I tell you, my Gawd is a good Gawd-a!"

Two or three amens come from the people in relieved

recognition of soothing rhythm, the sweet sing-song promise of forgiveness. Faces eagerly turn to the preacher to drink in the crystal water of forgiveness.

"I say my Gawd is a good Gawd-a!"

Murdell's mama matches the rhythm of his "Gawd-a" with "Ah-yes-amen-a." The people take it up as their chorus and join in at the next turn. "Ah-yes-amen-a."

Now Mills fully enters the preaching pattern. "Sometime seem like there's no place to turn-a. You look up the road, nothin to see; look down the road, there's nothin but trouble, trouble, trouble-a is everywhere and the road is blocked-a!"

There are shouts of agreement as souls wrestle with trouble, guilt and forgiveness. A woman's shoulders shake as she sobs from some deep, scarred, silent place within her bosom. But there will be no full relief until the leader gives a special word, a signal to release a tidal wave of emotion.

"Have you been a-hungry-a?" Dull starvation moans.

"Have you been a-homeless-a?" The heels of the dispossessed rap out a staccato sound against the bare wooden floor.

"Have . . . have . . . have you been a-friendless-a?" A "Yay-Yay" from the lonely.

"Sayin Lawd, I don't know which way to turn-a?" Feet stamp and the flowers on the dead girl's breast tremble.

Mills' voice lifts and hammers ever harder, word by word, note by note, gaining ground on its way to heart's ease. "But I'm a witness! I say I'm a witness! My Gawd is a good Gawd-a. He never made a cross-a heavier than the cross-a carried on the shoulder of-a Jesus Christ-a, the king-a the world-a!"

They shout approval, urging and hastening him on. "Speak the word! Don't hold back!"

Beads of perspiration drift from his forehead, swelling veins pulse in his temples. His voice grates and thickens as he gulps in air, sending it back out in words as if a giant spirit hand pumps them from his chest. "Bowed in sin-a, bowed with trouble, poor, lost sheep-a, lost in shame and sin-a! But Gawd, my great Gawd-a, my good Gawd-a—praise his name-a—that same Gawd-a that knows every secret corner of a sinner's soul-a—that Gawd-a is a forgivin Gawd-a—and this day will he forgive, forgive, forgive-a all our sins-a!"

Forgive, there is the word; now hearts unlock and tears spill grief. A strapping young woman faints with relief, a man holds her up, the good boy Kojie runs to fetch a dipper of water. An old ex-slave grandfather gropes his way out to the porch. "Thangs to Jedus, thangs to Jedus."

Murdell's mama waves her good hand, riding the high wave of God's forgiveness. She sees the Almighty holding a great set of scales and using a pile of stones to balance her good deeds against the bad. He adds up all the clothes she has washed, the floors she has scrubbed. God smiles, shakes his flowing white hair and counts out each of her hungry days, every lonely hour of widowhood, then throws an extra heavy stone on the credit side because she has never owned a new coat or hat or new anything else in all the days of her life. God smiles as he adds more and more to her credit. She has labored hard, suffered a stroke, seen her only child die in the bloom of youth; she has no money except for the coins of charity in the glass funeral bowl—but, yet and still, she has loved God through it all. She watches the Almighty turn to the sin side of the scale, holding up one gray rock which is Murdell's sin. God studies that stone, then flings it away; it breaks apart from the force of his anger, smashing itself into tiny little pieces of star stuff . . . and the golden gates of heaven open wide to receive Murdell's soul.

Reverend Mills laughs with joy and proudly gives God the glory, paying the last tribute while the congregation hums "Nearer My God To Thee". "All who knew her loved her—she was kind, she was not perfect—and none of us are. The

Lord giveth and the Lord taketh away, blessed is the name of the Lord."

The lady from next door brings in the baby and hands it to the minister, across the dead body. He says, "Mother, rest easy. I now place your child in the lovin care of Mr. and Mrs. William James. From this day forward her name shall be Cora James and the couple will raise her as their own."

Etta raises her hand and pipes out a rehearsed pledge. "Before my Maker and all gathered in witness, I promise to care for this child and love her all the days a my life." Cora yawns and continues to sleep.

Etta carries her in her arms, slowly walking all the way to the cemetery, following the white-gloved pallbearers. Four boys from Jenkins' Colored Orphan Band play cornets and beat bass drums, booming and blowing a triumphant dirge through the cobblestoned streets. Murdell's mama rides in a carriage for the first time in her life—a black carriage drawn by a black horse decked in black plumes, knotted tassles, fringe, wooden beads and a purple satin collar around his neck. Six foot-mourners walk and weep before the congregation. They all pace straight on, moving with measured tread, taking no notice of distractions.

A four-year-old white boy stops playing hop-up-and-down-on-the-curbstone long enough to ask his older brother, "What they doin?"

The ten-year-old thumbs his belt in imitation of his father and tries to squirt spit through the side of his mouth. He wipes his chin and grumbles. "Aw, a nigger got kilt and they goin to bury him."

The little one gathers that this is something to be pleased about, that they should laugh or maybe throw something. He watches big brother to see how and when they will act.

An old white man with yellowed hair and pale parchment skin touches the big boy's shoulder. "Don't bother them niggers. Let em bury the dead in peace." The big boy shrugs and walks away, laughing at the old man's baggy, misfit pants. The little boy also laughs.

Mourners see her to rest in the colored cemetery. They stand in the chill breeze and cautiously draw their sweaters, shawls and jackets closer, trying to ward off enemy death, secretly wondering what it's really all about—if people really "die by threes", and who will go next? They finally turn away mystified, weary, emotion spent—and glad today is not yet their time.

Etta lingers at the foot of the grave to pray in private. "Gawd, this is the dead girl's chile . . ."

The gravediggers remove their caps and bow their heads.

"Dear Lawd, please don't strike me down 'fore I can raise her—that's all I ask you in the name a Jesus. Amen."

The gravediggers say "yay-men" and go to work filling the hole. Etta feels almost ashamed to be so happy—going home happy and proud to be a mother, the only way she can.

Two

Cora likes the solid feel of Bill's large hand circling hers as they walk along the street. She skips a few steps, looking up to watch his velvety dark face outlined against clear blue sky.

"Papa, after I'm five, what all I'm gonna do?"

"Oh, no tellin what 'fore all this is over."

"All what?"

"Life."

"What is life?"

"Life is . . . well I heard that life is just a short walk from the cradle to the grave."

"We walkin it now, Papa-la?"

"Yes-indeedy-ree, right this very minute we livin life and on our way to the future."

"What's future?"

"Whatever comes next, Cora, everything that didden happen yet." He swings her up on his shoulder. Low-hanging, leafy tree branches brush her face. She leans against him, breathing in Alimine's hair dressing.

"Girl, why you call me 'Papa-la'?"

"You always be Papa, but when it's nice, like now, then you turn into Papa-la."

"But what do *la* mean?"

"It's bein better than most people. One day I heard a fine 'la' sound and then I knew."

"Where did you hear it?"

"Inside a my head—'laaaaa'. The day you and me was standin on the side porch eatin grapes and you gave me the best ones and—you gonna laugh at me."

"No, I won't. If I do I'll gi'e you a dollar."

"You gave me the best grape and that's when I heard 'la'. I said it easy so you couldn't hear—'Papa-la'. You can laugh if you want and not pay a dollar."

"That's no joke. 'La' is one of the finest things I ever heard anybody relate. You can tell what you hear goin on inside a you—that's a gift. Thanks for tellin me la." He shifts her to his other shoulder as he hurries by the wrought-iron railing of the city park.

"I'm glad today's my birthday and glad we goin to Rabbit Ears Minstrel. How come Mama don't like minstrel shows?"

"Well, lotta buckin and wingin—she don't think it's fittin for nice people."

"But we think it is."

He laughs and chides her. "Girl, you talk too much."

"Papa-la, tell me what all I'm gonna be and do on my short walk."

"What short walk?"

"Life, Papa, life!"

"Well, you'll be a great lady."

"No, I mean zackly."

"Well, zackly you'll read and write."

"Like you?"

"Better than me. You gonna read and write up a blue streak."

In her mind's eye she sees the streak; it is very blue. She writes her way up the streak, then reads on the way down. The streak turns into a tree with blue branches, cool against her cheek.

"Why so quiet, baby?"

Looking over his shoulder, she sees a red, yellow and pink world on the other side of the fence. "I see flowers."

"A park."

"Who planted flowers?"

"The city. They hire men to do it."

"Let's go in."

"No, we goin to see Rabbit Ears."

"You said I can do anything I want on my birthday."

"We don't need to go in there."

"I need it, Papa-la."

"See that sign over the gate? It say 'WHITE ONLY'. We must not go in."

"You said I can do anything on my birthday."

He looks up and down the street. Not a soul in sight; the park is also clear. "We'll go for a hot minute, then right back out."

"Yessir."

They are in front of a large circle of flowers; the air is perfumed.

"Papa, is this heaven?"

"No, now let's go."

Around the turn, at the right of the gate, there is a policeman who turns red in the face at the sight of Bill. "Maybe you don't read signs, but you *know* niggeras not allowed to enter the park. Sign says 'WHITE'. You know what's on it even if you can't read atall."

Bill squeezes Cora's hand, the edge of his fingernail nipping into her thumb. The pinch means silence. Bill gives a hollow laugh and slightly bows his head to the policeman.

"Officer, wrong is wrong and we wrong. This devil broke loose from me and run to look at the flowers. I come to fetch her out." His fingernail presses deeper into her thumb but she doesn't feel it.

Patrolman twirls his stick. "You niggeras don't raise your pickaninnies to respect law. Spare the rod and they'll think they white."

"Her Mama gonna put some whuppin on her. I'd do it now myself but last time I almost kill her cause I'm too heavy-handed."

"Who you work for?"

"Mr. Ray at the phosphate mill. Been there ten years without trouble."

"How come you not at work?"

"It's slack time. Colored got few days off."

"Boy, what's your name?"

"Er . . . Willie."

Policeman waves them away. "Willie, you teach that gal that she's a niggera, the same as a boy and she got no privilege to break law and enter city property, 'specially the public park. Learn her at home or we gonna teach her out here. Understand?"

"Yessir, officer."

Policeman gives her a start by stamping his feet and making a break toward her. "I'm gon' gitcha and splitcha half-in-two!"

The sound of police laughter follows them as they hurry down the street. He releases her thumb. She looks back.

"Papa, he's gone."

"Good."

"Why you afraid of him?"

His voice is dull and heavy. "Sorry you had to see me make a liar outta myself . . . on your birthday. I could whip him without puttin half my mind on it, but they got the power of life and death. Five is young but it's time for you to know that white folks got the law on their side. They can and do jail us, they can even lynch. . . ."

"What's lynch?"

"It's killin and murder, and hangin from trees, settin bodies afire. . . ."

"Why they do it?"

"We the colored, that's why he say 'niggeras'; they the white, why we say 'crackers'. The rich white man run the courthouse, the bank, the jobs . . . and the poor white cracker is mean cause he don't run nothin and is scared we gonna cut him outta what little he do get holda. They glad for any excuse to kill us off. Cora, you five and you also colored. You can't go in parks, even some stores—lotsa places."

"Why they like that?"

"Because they cruel and uphold a mean rule. In slave time they use ta cut off our ears if we learned how to read and write."

"I don't wanta read and write."

"Well, that law is over now, but they still try to hold us back on every hand."

"Why they do it? Why they so mean?"

"Make em feel biggety and strong to see us suffer, to hurt and harm. Some people's bread and butter taste better if they know somebody else is goin hungry."

"Why we lettum do it?"

"They was even worse cruel back in slavery. My poor mammy went to the grave with whip marks on her back. They holdin us down now cause they fear we will someday pay back for the wrong they done."

"Will we pay back?"

"Yes-indeedy-ree—they pushin us to it."

They fall into a long silence. She walks primly beside him, hands hidden in her dress pockets.

"You gonna like the Rabbit Ears Minstrel, baby."

"Can colored go to it?"

"Yes, it's got colored acts. We related, in a distant way, to some nice people who work in it—Uncle Sam and Aunt Francina. You'll like that, Cora-la."

Her thumb still hurts but she slips her hand back into his. "Yessir, but let's not say 'la' anymore."

"Not ever?"

"Not today."

A white man stands in front of the tent at an open booth, taking in money and handing out tickets to the double line of people. The line stretches in two directions—one colored, one white. The ticket seller is a fat, red-faced heavy breather, loudly gasping and wheezing out the virtues of the show as his neck puffs in and out. "Step right up, folks! It's your one and only chance! Wheeeeeze. . . ."

Music blares from the tent as both lines impatiently push along to get inside. Cora sneaks glimpses at the white line. Most of them wear overalls and house dresses. She notices that those on the colored line wear hats and gloves—one man even wears spats and carries a cane. Bill hails his friend from the First Colored Brotherhood Lodge.

"Our people makin a fine appearance, Mr. Tuss."

Mr. Tuss leans on his cane, smoothes the lapels of his over-pressed navy blue suit. His hat is a brand new, pale gray velour, matching his spats with mother-of-pearl buttons. "Yessir, brother Bill, *they* wonders how we can do it. I borry this hat from my cousin John, but *they* don't know that."

"None a they business."

"Makes um mad to see that no matter how they do us, we still keepin our head above water."

"Right. How's the carpenter business, Tuss?"

"Poorly. I start not to come to this minstrel cause *they* done bout took it over. Used to be that colored thangs was for colored, but *they* done push they power to get all the best seats."

"So true."

"However, I come to Rabbit Ears cause we gotta seek pleasure sometime. But they don't have to paint us on the side of a tent, twice as black as we is and three times the size a natural."

"Well, Brother Tuss, this might be *call* a colored minstrel and colored might be in it, but who you think pocket the money?"

"Well, be that as it may, if somebody in this tent just whistle a tune and make me laugh, it'll be better than what I see and do from day to day."

The colored get pink tickets which admit them to the far left and the far right; the white hold blues which seat them in the center. The tent smells of damp mold, apple cider, popcorn and perspiration. The crowd begins to settle down after much aisle walking to buy orange belly wash in waxed paper containers, celluloid windmills, oil-sausage sandwiches, Rabbit Ears pennants, ice cream cups, pralines, hot boiled corn, peanuts roasted and crystallized. They crack and spit out sunflower seeds and yell show-off greetings to each other. Some have brought sardines in oil and mustard sauce—they keep busy rolling back can tops with the new-style opener keys. Biscuit boxes are torn open and they munch soda crackers with strong barrel cheese. Men pass bottles of hard cider hidden in brown paper sacks, also jugs of white lightning and medicine bottles of red-eye whiskey.

Newspaper lunch wrappers rustle underfoot like fall leaves as coloreds and whites have a mean good time of secretly laughing and whispering about each other, nudging the one sitting next to look over at *them*, the other kind.

"Yall see that poor, ole seedy cracker ain't got but the one tooth in his haid, yet and still, he chawin on a year-a corn."

"Yeah, he gummin it."

And the crackers laughing and winking at each other. "That pickaninny got a nose so broad it look like he got two noses on him."

A black man pops his fingers to his companion. "Study the back a that cracker's neck and you will see why they call em 'rednecks'—neck is crinkle and crease like a turkey gobbler's craw, baked out like whippin leather. Thass from scratchin at the ground while diggin in the noonday sun. They scroungy-necked like a woodpecker and thass why the cracker is also known as a pecker-wood."

Cora clings to her father's hand, feeling the excitement of danger around them, a scary memory to take back to bedtime, to be remembered in the lonesome dark. The sweetness of a peach ice cream cone brings coolness without calm—curiosity shoves fear into second place.

The eight-piece band of black, brown and yellow men quietly straggles across the stage. It takes awhile before the noisy audience even notices the tuning up of the large bass drum. Then tin reflector lamps brighten the stage to a red-orange glow. The children notice first; with the wild excitement of young discovery they pull at their mamas' skirts and their papas' shirt fronts. Grownups shake the clutching children loose from their clothing and scold with great authority.

The black banjo player stamps his foot down with a-one and a-two and a-three, gets the band started and nods time as he throws his big-knuckled fingers against the strings and lustily sings:

> Ahm-a here to tell you, Ahm-a here to say
> Yall gon have a good time today
> We gon shake it to the east, shake it to the west
> Gon shake it any way yall like it the best.

The band pours out a medley of gut-bucket sounds—quivering cymbals, crashing tambourines. One fellow deliberately makes suggestive toilet sounds by blowing into a gallon jug. The drum bangs emphasis as the piano player turns out a tinkling rhythm. A yellow boy with silvery thimbles on his finger tips scrapes a staccato beat and strikes sparks of fire from a washboard. A fat brown dandy with a slick city look jumps up and down on a tin washtub, playing it like a bass fiddle, plucking at strings held taut by a long stick running through the center of the tub.

Band sound drowns out all other. Excitement throbs and wings its way through the tent. The musicians take turns at screaming, shouting and yelling wildly. Listeners shiver and shake with pleasure—foot-patting and sweating up a damn good time.

"I love Rabbit Ears!" Cora exults in Bill's ear.

Black men in blackface come rushing from the flaps on both sides of the tent stage. They leap and kick up their heels as they run, shouting up and down the aisles, "Whoooo—eeeee, yow, yow, yow!"

One dressed as Mandy-the-cook wears balloons under his great, wide skirts. Two minstrel men keep flipping up the skirt, exposing baggy underdrawers made from flour sacks. Colored side and white side fall out laughing as Mandy screams in high falsetto, "Yall is some ruckstafructious gennamins! How dare you insurrect me for yall's pleasure!" Mandy is chased up one aisle and down the other, then stops running and glares at her pursuers.

"When yall gon ketch me? I'm runnin slow as I kin!"

Laugh follows laugh. The musicians play faster and livelier as Mandy turns to chase the minstrel men. In the midst of the slapstick fun, a tall white man with graying hair enters, walks to center stage and mounts an elevated platform. He is wearing a pale blue Prince Albert suit, white top hat, white gloves and shoes, a blue shirt with a white silk ascot tie and rhinestone stickpin. In one hand he carries a golden walking cane with a sparkling jeweled handle.

"Is he white?" Cora asks.

"Sure is."

The man leans on his gleaming cane and watches the minstrel buffoonery with casual grandeur. Bill tells Cora, "That's the famous Mister Interlocutor. He asks all the questions and gets all the answers. Talkin bout life, that's who it's best to be in this world—interlocutor, the top man. He runs the show and is the only one in it who never has to black his face. He calls the tune and says who is to speak, dance or sing. He says when to stand and when to sit. He wears the best suit a clothes and a diamond ring, is forever well-press with not a thread or a hair outta place. Mister Interlocutor is most nigh perfect."

Cora is afraid of Interlocutor. She clings to Bill's arm. "Papa, hold me tight 'fore white folks take away our breath. Mama say a cat can take a baby's breath—steal its breath and make it dead. I bet Mister Interlocutor can take breath better than a cat can do."

Bill takes her on his lap, locks his arms around her and laces his fingers together. "This is all in fun. That's a false and fearful tale."

Mr. Interlocutor clicks his heels together; the music dips,

lowers and fades into silence as he stretches out his arms and lifts them high. The jeweled cane glints back sparkling echoes of flickering light. Behind him is a half-circle of thirty chairs. The group of blackface minstrels take their places; each man stands in front of a chair, silent, a picture of solemn dedication through greasepaint. Each carries a tambourine held across his chest with the left hand as if displaying a badge of honor. No one makes a move. The white center and the two black sides of the audience sit forward—not a sound is heard under the tent. Then Mister Interlocutor calls out like Moses from the mountaintop, "Gentlemen, be seated!"

The gentlemen sit in their half-circle, waving tambourines in a jangling salute, fluttering red, white and blue streamers through the air. The audience applauds sight and sound. The "end men" play spoons and clack long flat bones between their fingers, hitting them against their thighs, clattering sticks, whirling canes, strutting like drum majors. They take turns rising from their seats and doing fancy walk-arounds to display the fine fit of their clothing, the bright flash of rolling eyes, buckdancing steps, group marching, shouts, shimmies, shivers and shakes. While one dances, the others stamp feet and the drummer beats fast cymbals—up-down, up-down, up-down. The stage is alive with clashing color and movement. The bass drum becomes the one and only note—boom, boom, boom, boom—holding and hypnotizing every one in the audience to move their feet in time, to stamp, rock and sway with revival rhythm. All are one except for the well-to-do whites sitting at the rear of the white center section. They neither yell nor stamp. They are there for a double purpose—to be amused by the audience as well as the show. They expertly know how to stare through and past the poor with an air of disinterested courtesy.

The well-to-do gentlemen excel at presenting strong appearances. All with small receding chins wear full, bushy beards; those with large chins flaunt magnificent moustaches and sideburns. All assume the same studied, half-amused, tolerant expressions. Once in a while one glances toward a lady and speaks in tones of hushed concern: "Too much noise for you, my dear?"

They covertly glance toward left and right aisles. Rear seats on both sides are occupied by the black and white sporting crowd—pimps, fancy-ladies and assorted hustlers. Both tawdry groups pay more for their back seats in order to be near the well-to-do.

Cora begins to understand. Her father's arms cannot shut out the many colored and white meanings behind the cross-currents of looks and laughter. She begins to decipher the true language of their world—realizing that words do not always mean what they seem to say. She notices. There are many things to be noticed at a minstrel show. Black people buy ice cream after the poor whites have first go at it, rich white people don't eat food sold in public.

The black-fancy women are decked out in yards of lace and satin, they are over-powdered and perfumed. When Mister Bones or Rastus tells a joke, the laughing black fancies toss themselves about, intentionally showing off a shaking bosom or a calf and ankle for white men to see. Some use laughter as an excuse to rear back and slide forward in their seats, drawing attention to shapely bodies outlined seductively in thin, silky material. All carry purses full of folded papers with their professional names and addresses:

Sugar Cane . . . 2 Jameston Road (Ring three bells)
Balila . . . 8 Cummings Court (side entrance)
Honey Dripper . . . 22 Adams Junction (Enter John's Alley)
Elouise . . . 1 Landover (white trade only)

• • •

During a burst of laughter, a paper flutters out in the aisle. A white gentleman quickly drops his Panama, scooping up the address as he rescues the broad-brimmed hat.

The white fancy-women tip the candy butchers to pass their notes because the coloreds have picked up the practice of note dropping. The well-to-do women keep a casual but close eye on the white sports; they are certain no white man known to them could possibly be interested in intimacy with a black—unless, of course, she might be an octaroon or mulatto. They never speculate on where mulattos and octaroons came from in the first place. The candy butcher makes good side money by pressing cards into the hands of gentlemen, cards accepted and pocketed without the blink of an eye—whether they will be used or not. It is good for a man's reputation with other men if he has a collection of these cards to show over after-dinner brandy and cigars. *White* fancies, of course:

> Miss Smith . . . Privacy and good taste . . . Over Tearoom.
>
> Miss Mary . . . Cultured . . . Business Men's Hotel Lounge.
>
> Miss Olivia . . . Blue House near the Battery.

Up on the stage, Mister Interlocutor calls out. "Mr. Bones, that is a fine little boy you have; he is very polite." Mr. Bones pushes back his top hat and scratches a thought from his scalp. "Yassuh, but ain't nobody ever accuse him of politeness fore dis."

"Well, yesterday I saw him in a candy shop. The Irish proprietor, being a kind, benevolent and goodly fellow, told him to take a handful of sweets from the candy barrel. The little fellow said, 'Naw Suh, ah ain'ta gonna put my hand down in that bar'l—*you* gimmie a handful, boss, if you please, Suh.'"

"Ho-ho!" laughs Bones. "Dat wassen polite, dat was smart. Little Referimus is slick. He know dat de sto'keeper's han is bigger dan his! Hee-hee, hee-hee-hee; haw-haw, haw-haw-haw!"

Poor blacks and whites shout with laughter and throw in approving comments: "Thass smart! Ummo remember that!" "Yeah, say his han was bigger!"

Cora laughs whenever the coloreds laugh, but she is not yet certain about what is funny. The show romps on with darkey jokes and Jew jokes and Irish jokes—all kinds of jokes except well-to-do-white-folks jokes.

Waves of laughter wash over the crowd. They barely recover from one surge of hilarity before another knocks them down and drags them out into a fresh sea of belly laughs. Once in a while some of the poor patrons turn to check on how the well-to-do whites are taking things. The moneyed usually manage to keep their faces composed in subtle expressions of pitying good will. But whenever a surprise joke catches them off guard and they break down from smiles to outright laughter, the poor are pleased. Prosperous public display of pleasure is a promising sign—hope for a better future. The crowd can momentarily enjoy the soothing thought that someday they may be accepted, perhaps even welcomed into that secret society of the very fortunate. The door may open a crack and they'd at last squeeze in and unravel the mystery of how and where the money flows—and why some folk have it and others don't.

Bill holds Cora close as he smiles and thinks the same hopeful thoughts as the rest. The well-to-do in good humor promises even greater progress to those on the bottom rung—the colored.

Conversation floats around Cora's ears and fear flies away. Now she knows it is only on-and off-again; colored and white are sometimes scared, sometimes funny and sometimes mean—but she's glad to know that all of it isn't scary like cats stealing the baby's breath.

Minstrel jokes give way to festive dances and more walk-arounds. A black quartet steps forward as Mister Interlocutor announces, "I give you our darktown troubadors who will render, for your pleasure, the immortal songs of that colored man of humble genius, James Bland. Ladies and gentlemen, we offer you 'Carry Me Back to Old Virginny.'" The quartet renders, and when they hit the line, "There's where I labored so hard for old Massa", the well-to-do ladies gently blow and wipe their noses with cambric, linen and lace. There's not a dry eye in the section. Mr. Interlocutor steps forward at the closing strains and holds up a hand in a no-applause-please gesture. "We now offer another Bland tribute to our beloved Southland: 'In the Evening by the Moonlight'."

The singers lead the company in unfolding the story of how slaves entertained each other at the end of the day, with Aunt Chloe telling stories to "the pickaninnies and the coons." Tears fall fast and free. Then the quartet shuts off the water by switching to a strutting pace with "Oh, Dem Golden Slippers". Dark dancing ladies prance forward and shake knee-length lacy skirts, kicking and high-stepping beside the tambourine dandies. A tall copper boy solemnly places a glass of water atop his head and jigs his way across stage to the delight and admiration of the crowd. He waves his arms, shrugs his shoulders up and down, wiggles his hips, keeps a steady slap-slap of shoe leather hitting against the boards—not a drop spilled. The dancers stop dancing, the singers break off in the middle of a note. The jigger removes the glass; then, leaning back, places it on his forehead. The band plays a subdued melody as he carefully slumps to his knees, stretches to a prone position, slowly arches his spine, cautiously works his way back up to a kneel, then stands first on one foot, then the other, breaks into a final flurry of bucking and tapping, removes the tumbler, and finishes with a deep bow.

Mr. Interlocutor leads the applause as the music changes to a strolling beat. The tent rises to give the dancer a standing ovation, and Cora shouts praise. "Papa, I'd like to spend my whole life in a minstrel show!"

"You just might, darlin, it be that way sometime."

"What's Mr. Interlocutor sayin?"

"He's callin for the Olio."

"What's that?"

"Play actin. Watch and see."

The scene is announced: "I give you 'Chief Boo-Roo of Kookalanki', a story of justice in far-off darkest Africa; the story of Chief Boo-Roo and his two daughters, Ross-a-jass and Rosalinda, in an adventure with Rastus and Mister Bones in the jungle."

The chief is fat-bellied and ferocious looking with a bone through his nose. He wears long drawers, spats, grass skirt and a bent top hat. Ross-a-jass acts wildly wild by glaring and rolling her eyes. She pokes out her bottom, bouncing it up and down with each step as she looks over Bones and Rastus with a hungry eye. Rosalinda, quiet, lovely and shy, remains sedately in the background.

"Cora, now be sure and watch Bones and Rosalinda," Bill said.

The story, told in advance by the Interlocutor, is that Rastus and Bones went to Kookalanki to discover gold for America and also to free all good Africans from the cannibal rule of wicked Chief Boo-Roo, who keeps snarling out, "Oom-golla-wugga, me hungry, me evil." After tricking Boo-Roo into permission to dig for gold, after much suggestive dancing by five African maidens, after joke telling, pratfalls and general fool-play, Boo-roo's fierce warriors angrily bind up Rastus and Bones, demanding that one of them marry crude Ross-a-jass, or else be made into "coon stew". Both refuse and are promptly thrown into a giant black cardboard kettle. The spurned maiden slices huge onions and carrots into the coon-stew pot.

Now, all in a twinkling, there is no longer a minstrel show—as the wicked chief's daughter, lovely Rosalinda, steps forward to plead in song for the lives of Rastus and Bones. She is deep bronze and satin smooth of complexion. Her eyes are large, dark and compassionate; lips maroon and heart shaped. She wears a dress of dusty pink chiffon drapery edged with metallic gold lace. The neckline is cut modestly low, the hem sweeps the ground, golden sandals with sparkling jeweled clasps peep from under the gathered skirt's fullness as she walks. One musician bows to the waist in gracious salute and hands her a mandolin shimmering with rhinestones, dripping pink and rose streamers.

"Papa, when I grow up I wanta be that lady."

"Cora, you can't ever be anybody but yourself."

"Can only be me?"

"That's right."

Many amber lights are held high by minstrel men to light the rare beauty of Rosalinda, who has somehow managed to wander out of paradise and find her way into this tawdry show. Head held high, she serenely stands above and beyond the ugly limitation of a patched tent and the double-aisled world of colored and white. Her hair is a flow of shining, crimped waves caught up in a soft, fluffy circle atop her head. Fine gold earrings swing a dozen diamond chips from pierced ears. Musicians play exotic sounds in restful tones as lovely Rosalinda gracefully commands the stage, gently strumming simple notes on the mandolin.

The best cotton picker in three counties folds his black hands and breathes appreciation. "Yay, Lawd."

Colored women murmur approval: "Like a dream."

"Lookin like somethin, don'tcha know."

"And not actin uppity."

Poor whites shift uncomfortably in their seats. Two sun-reddened women groan out fears and opinions. "Sure wooden want her to come in and do no day's ironin for me."

"Know it. When you look up she'd be done got your husband."

"Indeedy—they hound after a man till they break him down, so I been told."

A few poor white men in overalls inhale and exhale through clenched teeth, but most are not interested in Rosalinda. They can see she doesn't play any one-hour-pitty-pat, that she rates herself high on the ladder.

"Now I tell you," one says to another, "she come from that strain a nigger that push theyself into thinkin they good as us, if not some better. They can't be broke in for nothin useful. Be like ownin a racin mare that's plenty fast but won't run less she *feel* like it—a case a the servant turned master. She'll end up ownin you. Them lively ones is another story, but a thoughtful, uppity darkey is a everlastin, damn thorn in a white man's side."

To save Bones and Rastus from Boo-Roo's wrath, Rosalinda sings out in a clear, sweet soprano: "Let them be free, let them be free; Oppression, dear father, is slaver-ceee. . . ."

The well-to-do white ladies sit up at attention, straighten blouses and hats, fan vigorously, pull in waistlines to look even smaller. They turn stoney-eyed as they overhear a few hissing whispers from their men.

"We better come back tomorrow and see this alone."

"She's an untouched peach—a juicy, Georgia peach."

The well-to-do ladies send forth scathing comment and scornful laughter: "Dear Lord, please save us from nigger airs."

One woman speaks in high C. "Pity em if you want but I stopped that, specially with that kind. It was fun before this, now it's turned into nothin atall."

"It's out of place."

"And what's all this singin about freedom? They *are* free, aren't they?"

"They mean back in Africa, Lorina, not here."

"The song doesn't fit right."

"Feels like she's singin at us. We oughta register a complaint with the management."

At the end of the song, respectful applause comes from the colored section, with a bit of timid, polite clapping from others. Rosalinda shrinks a little, Chief Boo-Roo of Kookalanki forgets his lines, Rastus and Bones are very ill at ease in the pot, and Ross-a-jass is so worried by the coolness of the audience that she stops looking mean and evil and forgets to stir her paper carrots and onions with the four-foot wooden spoon. Boo-Roo gets himself together and commands in a loud voice, "Proceed! Cook dem darkies down to a low gravy!" The joke falls flat; they have lost their audience.

Someone from the poor-white center throws a paper cup half full of orange drink that splatters over Rosalinda's dress. There follows a hail of cups, wooden spoons and half-eaten fruit and sandwiches.

"Let all run that wants to run, Cora. We stay put where we are, so's not to get trompled."

Rastus and Bones leap out of the pot and pull Ross-a-jass and Rosalinda offstage. Someone knocks Boo-Roo's hat from his head with a well-pitched stick. He stoops to pick it up and is hit in the face with an open sardine can. Blood spurts. He gropes for the exit. Only the band remains through a downpour of garbage. The Interlocutor takes center stage, holding an American flag in one hand and a Confederate in the other. The band plays Dixie. The sporting crowd, black and white, and the well-to-do duck out the back exits. Poor coloreds busily salute the flag under the watchful, patriotic eyes of poor, saluting whites.

A canvas backdrop unrolls to reveal a life-size portrait of General Robert E. Lee. This brings a faint cheer from middle section, but the show is over with the disorder. The poor line up outside seeking a return of money because the minstrel has been shortened, but all in vain since the box office has disappeared. A few white stragglers stand around pitching mudballs and debris at the tent walls. The colored leave slowly, murmuring warnings to each other: "Best get home fore mo' hell breaks loose."

The crowd pushes, jamming and elbowing through the tent flaps, hurrying down separate but equal dirt roads, on toward the places where they separately live. Behind them follows the sound of the minstrel band: "Be it ever so humble, there's no place like home." Some flee slowly, white turning away from black with stony stares. Coloreds pretend not to see whites, as they scan the sky for signs of rain or search the earth for ruts and puddles. All are melancholy, minds heavy with the thought of money gone and little left for food during the week. Each group ponders—there they are, the others, near at hand for a quick killing. White could wipe out niggers—wham!—just like that, and there'd be the end of trouble. Colored could murder redneck crackers—each one "do in just ten"—and then free at last!

But thoughts are thoughts and the next day is Sunday. Most must go to church, some even have baptizing, there's collection to be taken up and hymns to be sung in the choir. Some must stay home to cook for six children on a pound of peas and a pound of rice, or turn the sick from side to side. Some must empty slop pails, or fight bedbugs, or just get drunk and fight, or beat the hell out of a wife who is either loved or hated more than anyone else in the world. Heavy-hearted footsteps hasten away from minstrelsy and foolishness. Sullen remarks fall between kindred; the cranky, accusing conversation of tired, unhappy merrymakers.

"Git offa my foot."

"You the one! Why you walk in fronta me?"

"Didden wanna see this show no-how."

Dust flurries behind them, voices dying out in the late afternoon breeze. Hate words and tiredness and fear sounds left hanging in the silence.

Bill and Cora remain in the emptying tent hoping the actors will return. None do.

"Let's find your Uncle Sam Johnson and Aunt Francine. He was Mister Bones and she was poor little Rosalinda."

At the back of the big tent, he carefully leads her over strange ground, loudly asking questions of whites so they will not mistake him for a prowler or a thief.

"Which way to Sam Johnson, please?"

Within the space of this day Cora has learned why her father raises his voice in that certain way around whites. Papa's voice keeps them safe from harm. She joins him in explanatory loud talk.

"We gonna see Uncle Sam, huh, Papa?" She knowingly looks sweetly cute and humble under her poke-bonnet straw hat, holding her head a bit to one side—like Papa. She has early learned about the colored and white of life and about interlocutors, and the unexpected dangers to be found in the best of minstrel shows.

Bill notices. "Cora, what's the matter? You not yourself."

"No, I'm you, Papa."

"You better be yourself, cause one a me is more than enough. I have given away a whole lotta myself today."

"How can you give away yourself?"

"I'll tell that another time."

They turn another bend and there, standing in front of a dressing tent, are Mister Interlocutor, Mister Bones, Chief Boo-Roo and the lovely Rosalinda, weeping into her lace handkerchief while Mister Bones holds her in his arms. Mr. Interlocutor's shirt is open, showing torn gray underwear. Without a top hat he looks shorter. His hair hangs toward his eyes in straight, slick pieces. He no longer seems perfect; he is angry.

"That's the death a that number. We don't need two daughters for the chief. After this, he got one and that's Ross-a-jass, cause the customers like her. Just Ross-a-jass—fore we all get kilt. I know yall tryin to put on the dog, but you gotta remember, dammit, Rome wasn't built in one afternoon. People comin here for some wide open fun. Any gal that can't shake it for the money—she gotta go!"

"My wife does not shake it," says Mister Bones. "She's not a shake dancer."

"She can learn," answers Mr. Interlocutor. He notices Bill standing to one side with the child and decides to reprimand him, too. "Now, what do you want? No hirin today and no money back."

"Just here to visit Mr. Bones—Sam Johnson—if he has the time."

Mr. Interlocutor heaves an impatient sigh. "From now on, all he has is time. I'm sorry, Sam, but business is business.

Think bout it thisaway: when you put on a act like Chief Boo-Roo and throw in a Rosalinda singin goddam light opera . . . well, hell, we're kickin Rabbit Ears to a early death. I know you two are man and wife, but we can't use Bones and Rosalinda less she can shake it like the rest, so maybe it's time for yall to collect what's comin and move on." Mr. Interlocutor walks away feeling injured and imposed upon.

Chief Boo-Roo holds a handful of bloody rag to his face while laughing at his wound. "Yessiree, stuck my fool face out there just in time to stop a tin can! Lawd was sure with me or else I'da been hurt worse. I hardly felt this 'cept when I packed the salt down in it—salt is a burnin purifier, you know. No use to be mad. There's always a bad apple in every barrel. Yessiree, stuck my face out just in time. . . ."

Mr. Interlocutor is now out of sight, and Boo-Roo fades to a stop. For a few moments nothing is heard except noisy roustabouts taking down the big tent. When the pause grows too long, Bill and Bones greet each other with the Lodge handshake. Sober introductions all around. Chief Boo-Roo speaks his heartache without laughter. "Glad to meet you, brother. They not willin to see us in the finer acts. When we talk sense and reach a little higher it distresses their very soul. Sam's lady, Mrs. Johnson, does not have whatcha call a comic voice; I wrote the sketch so's she could shine while us comics push the fun part. But I guess it's too soon behind slavery; they not ready for us to play more than the happy fool."

Cora is afraid of the bloodstained rag held to his cheek. He waves farewell to the company and slumps away to nurse his torn face.

In the dressing room, Bones and Rosalinda are husband and wife, Sam and Francine Johnson. When he removes the blacking from his face, Sam's brown complexion seems very light. He has a real mouth instead of a white circle, his voice is deep and not at all rasping and high-pitched. He tries to comfort Francine. "You the best, my darlin. This been a hard show to play and harder yet to watch, so our visitors might could stand some refreshment."

"Yes indeed," says Francine. "I'll fix tea while Cora tells us all about herself."

The child removes her hat and exposes neat braids and ribbons. She curtsies like her mother has taught, holding out her dress hem and putting one foot behind the other. "My name is Cora James and I . . . I'm colored."

"You know that so soon?"

"Yes'm."

Still wearing chiffon, lace and golden slippers, the lovely minstrel lady makes tea on a two-burner kerosene stove and graciously serves it in thin, blue china cups. There is also a plate of lunch biscuits and ladyfingers. "Cora," she says, "I am colored, too, and I'm only a pretend Rosalinda, but someday a Rosalinda will truly sing. Perhaps you will be the one."

"Can I call you Miss Rosalinda?"

"No," says Bill. "This is your Aunt Francine and that's Uncle Sam, not Mr. Bones."

"I beg to differ," says the lovely lady as she pours for Cora. "All girls have a Rosalinda inside of them; she's there waiting to sing or teach school, to do something fine before the world."

"I can be Rosalinda?"

"I told her that couldn't be done," Bill says.

"Well, someday when she becomes her best self, she'll be Rosalinda, in a manner of speaking. Cora, do you go to school?"

"Etta gonna send her to private, with Miss Addie and Miss Odessa. They startin a school."

"Today is my birthday, Miss Rosalinda."

They sing Happy Birthday and peace replaces trouble.

"Well," says Uncle Sam, "Mrs. Johnson and I now gonna quit travelin and see if we can't make it here at home. She's a good seamstress and I can turn my hand to odds and ends."

Rosalinda kisses Sam's forehead and regrets the passing of his career. "Such a shame—Sam is truly a great comedian."

"Well," Sam says, "we can't always be what we wanta be."

Cora asks a direct question. "But, Uncle Sam, you're gonna stay colored—you can be that, can'tcha?

"That's for true!"

Three

Miss Addie's School is an old four-room cottage. It has an inside kitchen pump, an outhouse and a fig tree in the yard. Clumps of carrots sprout helter-skelter. On the inside everything is crumbling—the plaster, the woodwork and the floors. Doors stick. The stove has three iron legs, the fourth is a stack of bricks; the stove pipe is rusting at the joints. Dampness and mildew smell is in the wallpaper. There's a small rickety porch and lots of healthy, fast-growing weeds. The yard space is the best part.

Odessa tries to praise the place. "Well, at least we have a piazza."

Addie laughs. "This pile a rotten wood can't be call a piazza. Call it a miracle, cause it's standin and holdin togetha with only the help a Gawd. But what you ain't got, you does without. After all, hard times will make a monkey eat red pepper."

Nothing dims their hopes for the fine future of "The

Onward and Upward School for Colored Children". Here youngsters from four to seven learn their basics before going to the public school for colored, where they will face strange, white teachers. Some may never get the chance to go to school again.

Addie tests the weak porch rail so that Odessa will not see the pleasure and pride on her face while she grumbles. "Make sure that none a these chirrun is so young and little that they mess their pants, cause I ain't the one that gonna be washin diaper and cleanin backside while you standin round recitin A, B and C and countin one, two, three."

The parents come in and scrub the school with Pearline Soap Powder, whitewash the fence, make curtains from bleached flour bags and do everything possible to make the school ready.

At first the cost is fifteen cents a week, but it is too dear and they cut the charge to ten cents for those with more than one student in the family. Miss Addie keeps a kettle going on the back of the stove; in it she cooks an Indian stew called "sofka" which is odds and ends of what's on hand—beans, a piece of pork, a potato, beef and lamb scraps, a few okras—all nicely seasoned. The children faithfully empty the pot every day, hungrily eating things from the sofka which they hate to eat at home. Parents and well-wishers donate supplies—a bunch of greens, a cup of rice, two turnips, a few bell peppers.

A line of nails is driven into the wall behind the entrance door. There hang sweaters, jackets, scarfs and other hand-me-downs to use when weather turns cool or damp. In Odessa's closet are socks and shoes of many sizes, rescued by houseworkers from the best of white folks' throw-aways, to be given to those who cannot buy new clothing—just about everybody.

Parents supply pencils and note pads, or slates which can be used over and over until they are dropped and broken.

There are very few textbooks, and none may be taken home. The larger children look after the smaller, wiping hands and noses and keeping general order. Some elderly men and women report to school every day that health allows. They sit in the sunny yard baking pain-ridden bones as they lean forward to hear the recitation of ABC and the calling out of multiplication tables—always applauding the six-, seven- and nine-times when properly rendered.

Blind Miss Emily is the sewing teacher and shows the girls how to turn worn collars on men's shirts, face hems, take in seams and fit neatly-made patches. The littlest girls rip basting stitches and thread needles before learning to sew; they also pick up pins and clean lint from material. Miss Emily can thread a needle by touch if it has a large eye.

On Tuesday, Mr. Tuss teaches boys how to make fishing poles and how to fashion benches, cabinets and baby cradles from scrap lumber. The old people feel free to call out corrections without the teacher's permission.

"Hey there, yall stop that noise."

"Don'tcha be sassy!"

"Um gon knock you down, then tell your Ma!"

"Yeah, so she can knock him again."

Cora watches and wonders what it must feel like to be grown and old, wonders where and how "old" began. She cannot believe they have ever been young. She thinks old people must have started as old babies, hidden out of sight until they became big enough to come out and be old in front of other people. Seven years is a time of deep thinking, also a time for looking in mirrors, noticing her reflection in pails of water and rain puddles, finding out about eyes, hair, and face and color.

In the dark of night, at bedtime, before sleep, remembering the overheard and whispered conversation of grown people, she begins to believe that colored people must have done some terrible thing and white was going to punish them all, without stopping, until they knew they were wrong and stopped being wrong. But no one seemed to know what it was that could or should not be done, and so they all kept guessing. At home, around the supper table, she listens to Papa and Mama trying to find answers:

"Bill, trouble is, colored race don't pull together."

"No, trouble is, we don't apply ourselves."

"Our people don't know how to save a penny."

At school, Miss Addie and the old folks make other guesses: "We too far from Gawd, done forgit Gawd."

"Trouble is, we don't have 'nough knowledge."

"We like crabs in a barrel; one hold back the other."

"We oughta look at the Jew and see how he do."

"Look to the Chinaman—first thing he do is open his own business."

"Trouble is . . . us."

No one mentions any troubles which lie outside of themselves. No matter how many times they hear and see the word, the children are not encouraged to mention "white".

All classes are held in the yard when weather permits. Children sit on stumps, logs or boxes. The elderly take their daily places in a row of chairs against the fence. The fig tree bears two swings made by carpenter Tuss who knows a great deal about seat balance and rope knotting. There is a plentiful supply of cool, sweet well water with gourds and tin dippers for ladling.

One precious textbook passes from hand to hand as they take turns reading aloud: "See Ned. Ned has a cart and a pony. Ned's cart is red. Ned's pony is gray."

Cora interrupts the lesson. "Is Ned white?"

Miss Odessa gently corrects. "Does it really matter, dear?" The old people fuss and grumble.

"Chirrun should speak when spoken to."

"Trouble is, we busy askin stead a doin."

Blind Miss Emily says, "Sho, Ned is white. What else he gon be in the white folks' book? You ain't write a book, is you? Ned gotta be white and his hair yaller and his eye gon be blue. Cora, you so dumb you gotta ask? Oughta know what Ned is without goin to school. Even the blind see that."

Miss Addie pokes out her mouth, sucks her teeth to make the "chups" sound and laughs until her shoulders shake and tears run down her cheeks. "Yeah, Cora, like Miss Emily say, Ned is white and so is his mammy and his pappy. Only thing don't look white is his pony—and he gray, which is almost white. You just learn to read what's written down and pass your test on that. Remember the worl'-famous sayin: 'Curiosity kill the cat'."

Cora joins in the laughter and throws out her father's famous answer to the saying: "Curiosity mighta kill the cat, but *satisfaction* brought it back!"

They make her stand at the end of the fence, in the hot sun, to think about how to behave in decent, unquestioning company. A boy named Cecil suffers for her while she enjoys herself watching red ants crawl in and out of a hollow log. She wonders how the drat teachers would feel if Jesus, the son of God, came down from the sky, snatched the book from whoever's grubby hands held it and gave it back to her. She imagines her friend Jesus pacing up and down the yard, sad-eyed like on church fans, making her enemies keep quiet while she reads about Ned and asks every question she wants answered. She sees them fall down on their knees before her pal Jesus. They beg his mercy and forgiveness. Jesus gives them a tongue lashing.

"Trouble with you colored people, you don't know how to listen to this child read and ask about Ned!"

Cora is pleased at the sight of all groveling and bowing with their bottoms high in the air, while she and Jesus ignore them and laugh and talk. Jesus also commands that they let her take the book home.

An old woman looks up from hem-sewing just in time to see Cora smiling. "You, Cora! You fulla the natural devil and got plenty stubborn in you. Gon hang to havin your way all your life—got that kinda mind that locks down on what it thinks."

Miss Addie surprises all with a word of praise. "Sometimes I think trouble is . . . we don't lock down as much as we oughta."

It was a rare treat to go out with the teachers. Cora was excited at the idea of going to see a Jew, with Cecil along also. Someone had told Miss Odessa that the Jew was a very wise man who owned a bookshop near the old slave market; secondhand books could be picked up for little or nothing. They went to King Street, past the old slave market and up a narrow side street to the Jew's shop.

"Miss Dessa, we truly gon see a real live Jew?"

Miss Addie thumps the top of Cecil's head and pinches his ear. "Never say 'Jew'; thassa insult. How you like somebody to call you black?"

"I don't guess I'd like it, mam, but I am black and a Jew is a Jew."

Cora smoothes her blue polka dot dress and explains. "Cecil, that's called manners. We suppose to say 'Mister' and 'Miss' and 'Yessum' and 'No sir'—no matter if people be Jew, colored, white or Chinaman. We never mention what anybody is."

Miss Odessa agrees. "That's right; courtesy and kindness, regardless of race, creed or color. Color is nothing, the heart is all—as the French say, '*Couleur n'est rien, le coeur es tout*'."

• • •

The Jew's shop is dark and narrow, the front window barely large enough to hold glass. Inside is little more than a hallway, with barrels, boxes, baskets and shelves of books so crowded there is little space for walking. Two hanging kerosene lamps weakly glimmer on books that are better examined by daylight at the doorway. In the back of the shop are odds and ends of secondhand goods—pots, pans, picture frames and smoothing irons. In the narrow window is a fly-specked sign: COHEN BOOKS AND USED ITEMS.

The bearded Jew wears a hat and sits in an old oak armchair. "Something?"

His bookshop has the smell of old stories on crumbling paper; history, geography, biography, bibles, novels, coverless magazines and split-back church hymnals. There are books from far away places, gathered and regathered by sellers; books about love and murder, about places called the Isle of this and the Isle of that. There are opened medical books with pale pink, blue and green pictures of human insides revealing sick and healthy livers, hearts and lungs, lots of color plates of ruddy sores and enlargements of worms and monster-headed invisibles blown up to visible. There are also sheets of notes to be read and played into music. There are dictionaries of words in German, French, Italian and all languages spoken; and pamphlets and folders and maps of the world. There are books of poems like those read by Miss Rosalinda—written by Keats, Shelley, Robert Burns and the Brownings—and a scant few paperback booklets holding the words of men and women "of color" and put into print by abolitionists and Quakers. There are special books filled with money pictures, butterfly pictures, pictures of ships in full sail on the ocean. The Jew wears thick eyeglasses with silver rims. Cora thinks of him as the Interlocutor of Books.

"Something?"

"Just looking, sir," says Odessa.

"Take time. No hurry." He can see they are the genteel poor coloreds, the intellectual poor, the hardest sale to make—and women at that. Colored men feel somewhat obligated to buy if he has spent a great deal of polite time with them. Women poke and pry through dozens of things, reading and whispering to each other, then may end saying, "Not today, we'll come back another time, thank you."

He figures these two might buy a bargain speller or arithmetic; a thirty- to fifty-cent sale. He gives them his full attention. "I have the best spelling books and arithmetics. Look and if you don't see, ask."

"Sir, do you have any poetry or perhaps a play? Shakespeare, or maybe a pageant?"

"This you're interested in?"

"Yes, a present for our elocution teacher."

Cohen walks from baskets to bins, collecting. "Shakespeare I got; poetry I got; pageants—only a few. Here's a Christmas pageant about three wise men, also an America pageant about why we love America. Not much call for pageants."

Odessa takes the *Complete Works of William Shakespeare*, shows it to the children. It has a blue, split leather binding with much gold-leaf scroll work—a fat volume with more gold edging the pages. "Children, isn't this a lovely book?" Cohen worries a bit as Cecil holds the brand new *Complete Works*. The boy's hands are so very black he can't tell if they're dirty or not. But when Cecil lifts his fingers there is no smudge; the page is clean.

After consultation with Addie, Odessa selects the America pageant, a blue-back speller and a map of the world, then casually asks, "How much is the Shakespeare?"

Cohen thinks of asking full price, then cutting some off or of cutting profit right down to pennies. He really wants them to have it and, after all, people are not waiting on line to buy

Shakespeare. "It's worth over one fifty, but take it for a dollar."

"Do you have one that's damaged?" Odessa asks.

Miss Addie chups and gives opinions while Cohen wonders what to do. "Shucks, we got to crawl fore we walk. If we give Miss Rosalinda the pageant, why she have to have Shakespeare, too? One book is a storm of plenty."

Cora's eyes follow Cohen over the path he wears from dictionaries to travel books. She notes how weary he seems as he studies the problem at hand, biting his lip, nodding his head from side to side, then back and forth.

Cohen is thinking of a son up in Philadelphia who does not write often. He wonders if the *Coloreds* know as much as he does about love and loneliness. He likes to be kind and generous, if it doesn't put him out of business. He thanks God that he was not born black, then says, "The profit I've taken out, and there is no damaged copy. It's a good buy."

Addie sees it's a valuable book but she firmly believes that all Jews are secretly very rich. She has heard that each and every Jew, even a very poor one, is given a five thousand dollar bank account on the day of birth, which gift he collects, along with gold and silver presents, when he reaches the age of thirteen. She has also heard it is good practice to "Jew down" a Jew from the first price he gives. "Mr. Cohen, can't you do some better than that?"

"Can I cut below no profit at all?"

"That's for you to say and us to guess at."

"If we take the books we selected," Odessa asks, "will you let us copy something out of Shakespeare?"

He nods agreement, sure she doesn't mean it. To his surprise, the fancy-speaking one takes a notebook from her purse and begins to copy.

Addie decides to really show off. "Odessa, why don'tcha have Cecil read us a snatch a that Shakespeare?" Cecil's mouth drops open. True, he's the best reader in school, but Miss Odessa always gives him time to mull over something first. She tries to rescue him. "Oh, perhaps this is not the best time."

"Read us a snatch, Cecil," Addie commands.

Cohen knows she wants to show off smartness to prove themselves bright. He goes along with the game. "Well, if he reads it, I'll give you the book for thirty-five cents." As soon as the words are out he is sorry, because the boy looks trapped and stricken.

Cora butts into grown folks' conversation. "He can read it. Cecil can do anything."

It has turned into an important moment. Odessa points to a place and hands the book to him. "Try this, Cecil."

His voice is hesitant and low as he picks his way through small print. "Tis better that the enemy seek us: so shall he waste his . . . his means, weary his soldiers, doing himself offence while . . . while . . ."

Cohen blurts out the word, "Whilst!"

Cecil speaks louder. " . . . whilst we, lying still, are full of rest, defense and nim . . . nim . . ."

Cohen takes over again. " . . . and nimbleness! Excellent, now do it over and go on through."

Cecil reads without stopping. "Tis better that the enemy seek us, so shall he waste his means, weary his soldiers, doing himself offence, whilst we, lying still are full of rest, defense and nimbleness."

Cohen wipes sympathetic sweat from his brow. "Correct."

"He'd a got it all by hisself if you hadn't a jumped in so fast," Addie complains.

"The boy did fine," he says. "Not only is Shakespeare now thirty-five cents but the America pageant is free. Cecil is smart. A boy like this will become a doctor or something else fine for his people."

Addie reaches into the deepest part of her handbag and brings out the money. Odessa repeats her thank you. Cecil is stunned and silent in awe of his own ability.

Addie places the books in her sack before Cohen can change his mind.

The shopkeeper is now filled and renewed with generous energy. "Here, take also stationery which is good for writing on one side." He thrusts a ream of paper into Cecil's arms. The letterhead reads, "Mississippi State Farm for The Indigent Insane."

Cohen explains, "I get broken lots of miscellaneous and there's sometimes blank paper. Maybe, thanks God, they went out of business, so cut off the top print." He reaches into a dusty bin and hands out more odd books. "Discover, discover—some books don't sell but they are very good, so you discover." They joyfully say their manners and leave with almost more than they can carry.

Cohen goes to the door to watch them vanish around the corner. Looking up and down the street, he wishes for some kind of change; perhaps his boy coming to visit from Philadelphia, perhaps a mailman with a letter asking him to come north. The street is empty. A breeze blows in from the sea and ruffles the papers. He closes the door.

Cecil walks ten paces ahead of the teachers, his arms filled with books, his mind with the triumph of winning, and the fine good feeling of women looking at him with admiration. Cora must half-run to keep up.

"Cecil, my legs are shorter than yours and I'm gonna drop my books or fall."

He stops and issues firm orders. "Place your books toppa mine. Now hold my arm and you won't fall."

She does. She suddenly loves Jews and must find out more about them. "Cecil, are Jews white?"

His body feels so light he fears his feet may leave the

ground and he'll go floating off into the early evening sky. Even the books seem weightless, because of reading and winning. And now Cora is asking him a question, as if she is certain he knows the answer. He must find an answer. He squares his shoulders and deepens his voice. "Well, it's thisaway: they are and they are not. They not like us and they not like white. They Jews, and that's a whole nother matter. However, be that as it may, I like Jews myself." He is surprised that he knows so much about it.

Cora looks right in his eyes. "I do too, Cecil and I . . . I like you very much." His face grows hot and his heart beats faster. They are in love.

Four

It took a few years before Reverend Mills was persuaded to allow concerts and other programs to be presented in Haven Church, and it made trouble, just as he thought it would. Sam and Francine Johnson, better known to the young people as Mister Bones and Miss Rosalinda, led the cultural and social affairs. They started out with readings on church history, then Christmas programs; next came piano and violin concerts, scenes from plays, and now a patriotic pageant rewritten by the Johnsons to include spirituals and inspirational material for the choir.

> Patrick Henry said be free or dead
> Free, free we will be
> While we have breath, have liberty or death
> With God on our side, stand tall with pride
> Free, free, free, forever and ever free
> and so we sing . . .

Oh, freedom, oh, freedom, oh, freedom over me
Before I'll be a slave, I'll be buried in my grave
And go home to my Lord and be free . . .

Some will read from Shakespeare and there is to be a lively dance by Sunday school members. Certain people begin complaining that the show is going to look like a high class minstrel act, but most of the parents are happy because they want to see their children shine for a day. So much costume making is going on at Miss Rosalinda's house that she is late finishing garments for her regular dressmaking customers.

Every minute is taken up with preparation and the church doors are seldom closed. Cora, at thirteen, is as brown as the back fence from taking elocution lessons in Miss Rosalinda's yard, saying, "I am a fairy queen, my name is Titania . . . and I come to you from *A Midsummer Night's Dream*."

And then Cecil steps beside her to say, "Tarry, rash wanton, am I not thy Lord?"

After a church rehearsal, the Johnsons had to change Cecil's speech to "Tarry, rash one, am I not King Oberon?" because an usher had complained about using the word "wanton" and had also objected to any person calling himself "thy Lord". Cecil explained that the word "Lord" meant other things than God. The usher had to be restrained from thrashing him. The speech was changed.

Cora recites her part over early morning grits and while walking to Avery school; her lips are always moving: "Therefore the moon, the governess of floods. Pale in her anger, washes all the air."

Her father delights in hearing her through it. "Say it again, daughter, tell Papa bout the moon."

One Saturday Reverend Mills unexpectedly calls an emergency meeting and sounds a warning. "Congregation, some high-up white folk have heard bout this pageant and they now in touch with us by letter, hand delivered." He clears his throat and roads:

Haven Colored Church
To Whom It May Concern

We hear you are giving a highly unusual program of a political nature. The undersigned have taken a keen interest in what the coloreds of Charleston do in the line of self-improvement and wonder why we have not received any kind of special invitation. As you know, some of us, in the past, have contributed to your scholarship fund for trade school and normal education. We feel this entitles us to request that you reserve a section for a dozen white guests to view your performance. In any event, count on us being present on Saturday evening next. In sincerity we are . . . Mr. and Mrs. Treadle (associated with Board of Education), Mr. and Mrs. Hawley (associated with Roper Hospital), Mr. James Weaver (associated with Charity Funds of Charleston), Miss Emmaline Swift (member of Emergency Food and Clothing for Indigents).

Mills mops perspiration from his forehead. "I don't know how news of what we do in this little church can travel so fast, but I do know this letter got a angry sound to it. The program is for us, but with them walkin in on it, we got a problem. Now, we all have a bleak idea bout what they do and do not like." He pauses for their support and agreement.

"Yes, indeedy-ree."

"Some tale-bearer done run tell em what we doin—one a us!"

"Yeah, a finger pointer been talkin to his master or mistress."

"Oh, yeah? Don't look at me jus cause I work for white. Who else I gon work for? Yall got a job for me? I ain't tole nothin!"

Reverend Mills signals for silence. "We are now open for discussion but not disorder. Brother Anderson?"

Kojie Anderson takes the floor, standing tall and looking far more prosperous than any others present. He holds up his hands as a sign of peace and a request for attention. He is twenty-one, married, and the youngest member of the Rock of Ages Advisory Churchmen's Committee, also Chairman of The Overseas Mission Fund; but above all, he holds down a steady job as an assistant to the white custodian of the city jail where he mops, cleans, runs errands, fills out supply forms and contributes many other odds and ends of service. On his time off he is impressively neat and wears prosperous symbols—hand-tailored suits of conservative cut and a gold pocket watch. He is the first member of his church to hold a city post. The church had proudly given a pulpit announcement of his appointment, and the news notice was repeated four different times in the monthly bulletin.

Many young men enviously wondered how he had managed to get a regular job in an all-white situation. Some guessed it came from the connections and influence of his wife, Lilly, who was at least eight years older than Kojie and had worked as a first class cook in the right kitchen for ten. When her father—Reverend Mills' brother-in-law—died, he left her the full benefits of his life as an independent hack driver—a five room house and three acres of land. Lilly had married young Kojie just when everyone figured she was doomed to remain a maiden lady. She turned out to be not only Kojie's wife, but also his business advisor. Kojie, a colored man on his way up, stands before the congregation, ready and eager to display his flair for leadership, and also to do a pre-arranged favor for Reverend Mills.

"Brethren," he says, "we can all sing together but we cannot all talk together."

"Tell um, Kojie Anderson!"

He puts on a grieved look to show the gravity of the situation, nods his respects to Reverend Mills and gravely asks permission to speak. "May I?" The meeting speaks approval.

Reverend Mills gladly signals Kojie to carry the ball because he knows where he is going with it—knows that the unfortunate white-folks'-attention-getting pageant is going to be kindly squashed under the gentle, guiding, popular hand of a young man who aims to become a deacon as soon as possible. Mills is pleased to have such a fellow on hand to bring them safely through a retreat, with honor intact.

Kojie walks down the carpet-covered aisle and goes into action. "Friends, as you know, I am a graduate of Shaw Boy's School, and also of Horatio Institute." Women wave their handkerchiefs in a general salute to education. A few men call out "Amen." Kojie adds, "I don't say that to be boast*ing*, but am merely present*ing* myself as somewhat know*ing* of whereof I speak—merely that."

A Sunday school teacher comments to his elbow neighbor. "I like how he say 'merely'. The man can talk."

Kojie draws circles in the air with his left hand and straight lines with his right index finger to illustrate the complicated depth of his thoughts. Often, at the end of a sentence, he brings one fist down on the palm of the other hand to suggest a period or an exclamation mark. If he uses the word "road," one hand draws a road; if he says "clock" he traces a circle in mid-air. When he reminds his listeners of his great gift of intellect, he points to his head; in this way he gives a constant illustration of the spoken word, meanwhile never forgetting to stress his *ing* endings. Pauses are timed and spaced into the unfolding speech, giving him long moments to look skyward or earthward in search of an elusive phrase which might be ripe for picking.

"Brothers and sisters, we got to crawl before we walk. Even Gawd a-mighty took seven days to complete this earth!" He sweeps one hand across the surface of heaven and arches his arms to illustrate the circular shape of the world. ". . . with its highways and byways, with its mountains and valleys. Gawd was not ashamed to take his time. He could have snapped his fingers and been done with the task, but not wish*ing* to do that, he did it not."

The organist calls out, "Gawd do like he wants to do!"

Kojie ventures further into the subject at hand. "But, just 'cause he made one thing first, it did not mean he was not going to do the next thing next. Some things he made on the first day, others on the fourth. Do you follow me?" He points to his head and pauses for encouragement—and gets it.

"There's a time for everything!"

"Can't put the cart before the horse."

Kojie rocks back and forth on his heels in imitation of Reverend Mills. "When the white man starts look*ing* in on what we're do*ing* as we are are about to do something new, it behooves us . . ."—He likes saying "behoove" and plays with the sound of it—" . . . it behooves us, I repeat, *behooves* us to examine the situation and maybe even make a change of plan. Some of us must have the foresight and intelligence to pilot the ship of race progress through stormy waters."

Reverend Mills wants no misunderstanding about who is doing the steering. He coughs. Kojie hears the signal.

"Lord, I'm truly thankful that Reverend Mills is the captain of this ship, and that I have health and strength to be one of his humble assistants."

Cora touches Etta's arm. "Mama, what is he talkin about?"

"I don't know. Kojie Anderson got so much edjication till I don't know what he be sayin. I do see Lilly lookin pleased as

Punch. That woman is thirty if she's a day—oughta be ashamed."

"But, Mama, he's the one callin off the pageant."

Etta agrees sadly. "Uh-huh, and you can bet everybody's gon go right along with him."

Bill pats Cora's hand. "Reverend Mills is the one eggin' him on."

Kojie draws more imaginary pictures in the air and uses longer sentences and varieties of words—patience, strength, Godliness, caution—then winds up with, "Sometimes we got to show more sense than they do. White folk might think they know it all, but oft-times we got to do the think*ing*. Our old folk have a say*ing*, 'Every shut-eye ain't sleep and every goodbye ain't gone.' Which is to say that we got more on our mind than most may think. Our old folk did not have my Shaw School and Horatio Institute education, but they had what we call 'mother wit'—the sense you were born with, the best kind a sense in this world. Thank you, Lord!" The meeting rallies to his aid.

"Mother wit!"

"Hallelujah! Thass what I got!"

Kojie pushes on to certain victory. "We're going to pretend sleep *momentarily;* that is, for the time being, forget the Freedom Pageant, and be about the business of pouring oil on troubled waters, until this cold wind shifts and blows in another direction. But since our interested white friends have invited themselves, we got to somehow welcome them. After all, we don't wanta be rude to those who might do us a favor here and there. Even if they may be rude to us, we will not be rude in return—and er . . . uh, I must admit they have at times been rude."

"Yes, indeedy-ree," Bill speaks out. "They couldn't get no ruder than slavery. That was the longest spell of rudeness anybody ever hear about."

Reverend Mills laughs good-naturedly, but hurriedly calls

for the vote. "All in favor of callin off the pageant for the time bein?" The majority votes to call it off. Kojie returns to his seat with relieved blessings from most of the congregation. The "Amens" come to a halt.

"Don't let them do it, Papa," Cora says.

Bill takes the floor. "Yall have just killed off the joy a the children. It ain't right. Brothers and sisters, let us work our own will and not let outsiders shape our minds by mail. They run the whole city, but don't lettum run Haven Church."

Reverend Mills rises from his motheaten, purple-velvet pulpit chair and settles the discussion. "Well, I agree with brother Kojie up to a point, but us old heads have to remember the young and give em somethin to go on. Also, I might add, we can't tell white folk not to come cause we have called off the program." He rears back and forth on his heels before giving the final solution. "True, we won't do the freedom pageant at this time, but let us at least put on a 'My Determination' program."

"Amen."

"Gawd bless."

"That's right."

Cora throws hostile glances in Kojie's direction as she thinks of how in a few minutes he has destroyed weeks of hard work. She is ashamed of the congregation.

Outside, on the sidewalk, Bill pays respect to Miss Rosalinda and her dead dream. "Look like they never will let 'Rosalinda' sing. First it's the crackers and now it's our own. Somebody's always on hand whenever you try to make a upward move."

Rosalinda sighs out her weariness, "They pursue us, even into our humble little retreats; there is no rest for the weary, no hiding place."

Etta and Cora are alone in the kitchen, cleaning up after

supper. Believing that it's dead bad luck to go to sleep with a grievance on your mind, Etta tries to clear the air. "What will you say for your 'My determination'?"

"Nothin. I don't wanta do that."

"Been so long since I heard one till I forget how it goes."

"A ought is a ought and a figger's a figger, everything's for the white man and none's for the nigger."

"That's not a 'My Determination', it's some brash remark you repeatin behind your father."

"Mama, a 'My Determination' is somethin we put on whenever white people visit our church. You recite a poem or a verse from scripture, then end by sayin, 'I'm a child a Gawd and my determination is to serve him in life as a . . .' Then you stick in the name of some trade like cook, baby nurse, or some such, and end up sayin, 'and help enlighten and uplift my people.' Have to call ourselves backward to get some applause. I hate white people!"

"It's wrong to hate, also a drat waste a time."

"Even when they hatin us first and stoppin everything we set out to do?"

"Cora, you big enough now to learn how to put a latch on your mouth before you get your papa or some other colored man in trouble. He's upstairs feelin sick cause he didn't fight Reverend Mills and Kojie. He almost resigned from church because a this Shakespeare and My Determination."

"I wish he had. I'da gone with him."

"You think I'm a fool, but you can learn as much from me as from that Rosy-linda and your daddy. Most times you gon have to handle things for yourself—ain't no man, black or white, standin by to smooth your way. Anything hurtcha, go to another *woman* about it and then decide what to do. We got to do it and you no better than the rest of us!"

"Times oughta change. Reverend Mills, Kojie, Papa—all of em better stand up and fight."

"Just last week a fella was lynched for doin that—hung and then burned!"

"Mama, what has that got to do with puttin on a pageant?"

"*Everything* has to do with it. The very ground we standin on throbs like a wounded heart cause the devil himself is unchained in this land where they makin prosperity outta misery. Challenge that and you'll be dead."

"Maybe there's a time to die for whatcha believe."

"There is, but we not to pick the time for somebody else; let each decide when and where. I'm a Christian, but the day anybody come here after me or mine, that's the day I take the loaded shotgun outta the back shed. I can't back up but so far. My home is the last stop on the Jim Crow line."

"At least we oughta write to the President of the U. S. A. to tell the people to stop lynchin. Do somethin besides pray."

"People been doin that. The president and the newspaper say the same thing, like many good nature white people: 'we deplore'. 'Deplore' don't help. Murderin rascals don't care bout deplore. All whites don't behave in a nasty manner, but they draw they curtains and keep quiet cause they as scared a each other as we are of them. If Bones and Rosy-linda make trouble, then we gotta see it through. While they recitin, we all be fightin."

"But they do want somethin better."

She had hit Etta's tender spot, the secret resentment against those who had the little bit of education she lacked. She attacks them through clenched teeth. "They goin crazy! They want this, want that, but nothin they get pleases em more than five minutes. They wound up like a tight clock, tickin off noise bout 'progress', but I'm hearin the alarm before it even go off. Nothin we crave is worth the one thing we got, life and breath. Don'tcha think I want things, too, just like the edjicated?"

"I never hear you say, mama."

"Many a day I'm walkin round with a rusty nail in my heart."

"I'm sorry, Mama."

"Not edjicated, but I know a thing or two, daughter. All them church women was after your papa, but I'm the one got him. Some of em, like that Odessa with the big eyes, could read, write and speak geography, history and poetry, even algebra. Well, they lost out to me."

Cora laughs. "How come, Mama?"

"Cause I set my hat to get him for myself with smiles, kisses, love and apple pie, that's how. I made him look at me. Every tub gotta stand on its own bottom."

"Mama, people need things. I'm goin to school, but there's nothin to look forward to like whites got."

"White folk are not my main concern, except for them havin the ku-kluck and like that. Nothin they have do I truly crave. True, we need a piece a cash to buy necessaries. But in my secret mind I'm longin for a place where this 'white' business is not to be dealt with. I'd like some dark, good earth where we can plant seed and grow food—peace and quiet and a chance to bathe in the salty sea—where we don't have to jump up durin the night to cry out—'What's that, who's there?'—cause we'd know it's just the breeze blowin, or the friendly voice of a good, kind neighbor."

"Mama, I'll find a place like that and take you there."

"Someday, Cora, but not soon. Learn to wait. Women must wait."

"You sound like some a the white teachers at school."

"Well, there's a lot you can learn from them without expectin to do all they do. On the other hand, they don't know it all. For an instance, they haven't yet figure out how to live forever, thank Gawd, else they'd give us heaven and keep earth for theyself. But Gawd's judgment is this: every soul must one day surrender all it has gathered from the earthly harvest; even these borrowed bodies must be paid back to the dust. Ain't no pockets in a shroud! So, who's got what?"

"Even so, I can't be satisfied with the crumbs."

"Cora, learn to bend and let some storms pass."

"Waitin for storms to pass makes me feel ashamed."

"You'll soon be a grown woman."

"I think it's gonna be awful hard to be a *colored* woman."

"The good Lord never made a finer group. We are his knife blades and he hones each of us on a different sharpenin wheel—until the fiery sparks fly. He makes us scream and cry against the grindstone, but in that way we become keen, able to cut deep into the shape a things. You recite that 'My Determination' and just bide your time. Your day will come. Now blow out the lamp."

"I hate the dark."

"Don'tcha worry bout darkness. You hold my hand and we'll find our way. C'mon, follow me."

Cora puts a "latch" on her mouth and painfully passes through grade school by writing down only the answers given in textbooks. She wins a silver medal for memorizing, a blue ribbon for tracing a perfect silhouette of a carnation. Near the end of eighth grade, a teacher named Miss Harley gives the class an assignment to deliver a short talk on "Further Opportunities for Colored People". Cora wins the box of candy.

> Further opportunities for coloreds are teaching in rural needy areas, preaching, undertaking, cooking and baking; child care, practical nursing for Christian homes and establishments, volunteer and overseas missionary work in the service of the Lord. I am a child of God and my

> determination is to someday become a teacher in order to uplift and enlighten my benighted people.

Miss Harley cries as she presents the box of chocolates. The box cover is decorated with the smiling picture of a white lady leaning forward in a lowcut evening gown, a pink satin ribbon pasted in her wavy brown hair.

It is the best candy Cora has ever tasted, even if all the pieces are gummy under the chocolate covering. "That's cause they're nougats," she explains, "the box says nougats." Papa kisses her for winning a prize. When the box is empty, she places her silver memorizing medal inside and keeps it on the mantle to show to company and remember winning. She also has a framed certificate to show she is a graduate of eighth grade.

Five

I didn't really know we were poor until now. A war is happenin overseas and somehow it makes things more high-priced here. Hard times are harder for us Negroes. We now say "Negroes" because it is a better title and means *black*, while *colored* also means Japanese, Indian, Chinese and others who are not white. I find it hard to say "Negro" because I'm not used to it. Cecil says I must learn to say it, because our position sets us apart from other coloreds, because we were brought captive from Africa to be sold and used as slaves—not like immigrants who came to get jobs for pay. Papa is awfully angry about immigrants and goes on so about them.

"Alla these Poles, Jews, Eye-talians, bullet-head Germans and Irishers . . . they pourin in by the boatload. None speakin clear English, but the first distinct word they learn to say is 'nigger'. They fast find out it's best to scorn and mistreat us if they wanta get along with the ones who mistreat them. They get off the boat smellin like stale grease and then steal every piece—a job we once had: coachman, barber, seamstress, baby nurse—even that's gone now. Also, they're not citizens yet but got the privilege to ride first class and go in the front doors while we who citizens still Jim Crowed by law."

Me. I don't believe there's any war. We sure don't hear guns in Charleston Harbor. But there's plenty warships dockin. Cecil and I go down to the battery to see them and get the chance to talk to each other alone. After Cecil's father died from a weak chest, his mother soon followed from cancer. People say it in whispers cause cancer is a curse from God and the person who gets it must have done some terrible wrong. We don't say "TB" either—it's kinder to say the person is in a "decline" or has consumption.

I miss school where students talk any and everything with each other, not just about illnesses. Some passed around drawings of what men and women look like underneath their clothes, show how babies are made and where they come from out of their mothers. I couldn't believe my parents would perform such filthy, low acts as those pictures. Some boys also drew pictures of a man's thing and used to tease us girls by rubbing one of their fingers in and out of a hole in a piece a paper. We came out of eighth grade knowing a good deal.

Cecil was turned over to Mr. Jenkins' Orphanage. Many homeless Negro boys were wandering the streets beggin and stealin. So, this musician by the name of Jenkins started the first Negro orphan home. His wife and friends teach orphans how to play musical instruments and do carpentry and shoe repair. Mr. Jenkins soon had so many to feed he went to the city and asked for money. They gave him three hundred dollars a year, and when that wasn't enough, he formed a band and they went on the street corners to play, then pass a tin cup to beg. People give cause they really do sound good.

When that band plays, washerwomen take their hands outta soapsuds and go to the corner to listen. The hungry forget about miss-meal cramps and barefoot children hop fences and run over hot cobblestone to see and hear. Cecil really knows how to beat on a drum.

One day Mama wondered why I didn't come out when they played our street. "Come on, Cora!" she called. "It's Jenkins' Band!" She came inside and found me sitting on the kitchen floor.

"Somethin's wrong with me, Mama." I had tried to stop the blood with my petticoat. My dress was soiled and I had cramp pains.

"Poor child, how long you been this way?"

"Since this mornin. My bed is soiled."

"Why didn't you say somethin?"

"I was ashamed."

"Don't be. This just means you a woman now."

"I am?"

"Yes. This gonna happen every month."

"For how long?"

"Bout forty years."

"Oh, Mama, no."

"Happens to all; you not the only one."

"Even to Miss Rosalinda?"

"All females—none can escape."

She tied a narrow strip of cloth around my naked waist. "I'll share my bird's-eye diapers with you. Care for them because there's no money for more. Be watchful to make sure you fall sick every month around this time." She folds one of the diapers into a long strip, passes it between my legs and tucks each end under the strip of belt, one in front, one in back, held in place by safety pins.

"Now," she said, "that's how you fix yourself. When this one gets too wet, put on a fresh and wash this out, first in cool water, so the stains won't set, then use hot soapy water after. Don't hang your napkins out on the line with other clothes, but dry them behind the stove where nobody will see. We don't let it be known when we have our monthly sickness. It's not nice."

Jenkins' Band was playin "Onward Christian Soldiers" while Mama talked. I felt like a Christian soldier beginnin a forty-year journey.

"Cora, don't let boy or man touch you down there, cause you now able to have a baby and you don't want any till after you married. It'd bring disgrace. They sometime put girls out the church for that. Nother thing—most men won't marry a girl who had a baby for somebody else. A man wantcha to be a virgin, untouched by any before him, understand?"

"Yes, Ma'am. Mama, I hurt."

"Ginger tea will ease cramps."

I guess Cecil wondered why I didn't show up to watch him beat the drum.

Cecil has an aunt named Looli. She is his mother's half-sister but not very close to the family. When she heard about him bein in the orphanage she went to get him. After all, he is her kin. Jenkins and some of the church people didn't want Miss Looli to take him because she had what they called "a reputation". She went to the police chief to see that Cecil was turned over to her. She got him.

Since I'm gettin older and Papa is gettin sicker, Mama is changin her tune about life and livin and bout not wantin after things. She's also critical about who I know: "Cora, you will soon be fourteen and in South Carolina that's the age a consent—you can get marry if you want—so be careful to know the right company. Nothin much good can come outta Squeeze-gut Alley where Cecil's Aunt Looli lives. Nothin there but them on the last go-round and the sportin roughs and rowdies."

"Cecil is there, Mama."

"Well, maybe he better stay there, poor soul. The child is a orphan, and got a aunt who ain't fit to raise a ear a corn much less a boy. I'd like you to have a chance at somebody a little higher on the scale—if not a doctor or a preacher, at least a businessman of some little property."

She's changin. I go right on meetin Cecil down by the battery. He doesn't care too much where he stays cause he plans to put up his age and join the navy.

"Cora, they takin in more Negroes and there are trainin camps at Augusta, Georgia, for soldiers. And the navy's gonna have a machinist school for Negro boys, right here in the city. They supply free blue uniforms with decorations for the sleeve."

My heart is sinkin at the thought of him goin away.

"On the other hand, I might get a job on the Clyde Line. They got passenger ships runnin between New York and down here. You work and live on ships and wear white coats, dark trousers and black bow ties."

"I like that," I say, but I'm wonderin how he can plan to go places without a thought about leavin me behind. Glad to run off without a backward look, and me carin for him till my throat is tight and my heart feels sad. I can't tell it, so I try to hold him back another way. "Cecil, don't leave your poor Aunt Looli. She must love you very much or else she wouldn'ta gone to the police to get you outta Jenkins home."

"She's all right, Aunt Looli, but her and my mama wasn't none too close cause Mama didn't like wild kinda livin and Aunt Looli got her some *ways*. You wouldn't know bout it, but some women got more than one man and don't have a husband—know what I mean?"

"She has two men?"

"More'n that."

"Three or four?"

"Aw, I don't be countin." His voice drops to a whisper. "She also have a lotta friend-girls drop by and they be sayin things you'd think a lady wouldn't know. Be drinkin whiskey and sayin how much money they get from men, just laughin. Aunt Looli got another rent house down the way in Squeeze-gut Alley and she and the friend-girls go there and stay up all night. She don't get home till most time for me to go to school, and she be drunk."

"Oh, Cecil, does she beat you?"

"No, she don't do that. She stagger round the kitchen fixin grits and side-meat, even can make biscuits while drunk. She give me plenty to eat and I got my own room. She say, 'Boy, don't do like I do, do like I say do.' And she tellin bout what a good education she gon see that I get and how she gonna make up to me for any sadness she give my mama. Cora, I ask her how come she could make the police do what *she* say to do steada them listenin to Reverend Mills and Mr. Jenkins. She pop her fingers and say, 'Ole cracker police better do what I say, or else! I got holda them where the hair is short!'"

"Cecil, I'd like to meet her. She sounds like a lady who doesn't wait for storms to pass."

"Squeeze-gut Alley ain't nothin but a lotta poor people and lotta bad people."

"We're poor. Papa is laid off mosta the time and he's sickly, too. We have very little these days."

"You better off than you think, so I'll keep meetin you by the battery to watch ships. Aunt Looli got money most times and she treats me fair, but she's a tough lady—one time had a fist fight with some other ladies . . . er . . ."

I help him explain it. "Mama says she has a 'reputation'."

"Yeah, that's what you call it. But keep what I say secret between us. If a person was to say somethin ugly bout her, in fronta me, I'd have to fight cause she's my blood kin, no matter what."

"Would you fight for me, Cecil?"

"Sure, Cora, I really would."

I pick a bit of lint from his sweater, since that's the only proper way I can put my hands on him. I'm glad his aunt is takin care of him and not afraid of anybody, not even the police. I wish I could live in Squeeze-gut Alley, right next door to Cecil, livin without waitin for storms to pass.

The rice, lumber and phosphate mills cut back Negro help to bone-bottom. Even in the dirtiest jobs, only a few are left working on half time. People hope for the U.S. to declare war on Germany because they say war will bring prosperity—and those who go overseas will leave jobs open for those not going.

On payday, talcum-faced prostitutes, drenched in cologne water, gather near the mills at knock-off time. High-life has become a tougher but more profitable business. Men have more forgetting to do during hard times. Madam Loolie urges her friend-girls to apply themselves. "Yall can make some good hay while the sun is *not* shinin. Steer them to my place on payday. Talk it up; gotta sell more than tail these days. Tell em we got free meals, a git-box blues player and lotsa laughs."

The girls work hard at it. They saunter up to working men as if they know them and lay out the tempting offers: "Want a free chicken dinner, daddy? We givin it way, sugar, when you buy a double-shot or deal some trade. Don't haveta overdo your spendin, baby, I know you know when to stop. I'm awful nice company, sweet papa, give it to you any way you want."

Family men push on home with their pay, but week by

week more of them "drop by" Squeeze-gut Alley to have one sociable drink. It's a rare fellow who gets out without leaving his entire pay. One drink is never enough—nor two or three—and by the fourth, the roughest hustling woman looks like the Queen of Sheba on her way to see Solomon. The back room is always waiting, with a red-shaded lamp, pink paper roses and a big brass bed. Looli proudly proclaims her place is for family men, mainly because family men are now the steady workers; the drifters are leaving town, riding the rails to Chicago, Detroit, Baltimore and New York.

Renegade husbands try to ease out of Looli's after spending a couple of dollars, but she takes care of that. "What'sa matter, honey, scared a your ball and chain? If I had me a good lookin nigga like you and even *thought* he wanted another woman, damn, I'd go out and find one for him. You too much man to belong to one petticoat all the damn time. You work like a dog, baby, so have yourself some fun. We not hurtin anybody. Whatcha think the folks at home gonna do if your ass drop dead from overwork? I'll tell you, they gon live on, daddy, just live the hell right on."

She always gets the same answer. "Damn right."

"Who wears the pants in your house?" That's Looli's clincher. "Who the hell is the man?" Ever the same answer. "Me! Me, gotdammit—don no black bitch better mess with me no time! Um the man!"

Some of the friend-girls try to be pals to the customers, sort of wives away from home—listening to troubles and sending a fellow on his way still holding a few dollars for the long, bitter week ahead. Looli dresses them down about it when the house is clear.

"You girls that's so understandin, I'm soon gonna throw yall in the street. If you gotta understand somebody, understand me who has to run this place and also raise up a boy-child. If a lonesome nigga come here believin I got nothin to do but rise at the cracka dawn, buy food, sweat my titties over a red-hot stove, feed him for free, let yall rock him in my bed—then send him outta here with a pocket fulla money to give some other bitch, he's either a fool or a goddam crook. Rob em, yall! Take what the nigga's got or walk on out with him, and see how far you'll go and how long you'll last!"

Through the meanest alleys and dead-end streets, men reel home drunk, angry with themselves, their complaining wives and the ever-hungry children. They stalk and stomp through the place called home, handing out cursings and beatings to those who look to them for the food, shelter and clothing they can't supply. The start of a new week brings sad repentance and secret vows to stay away from places like Looli's—for awhile.

Some wives learn to go to the job and meet weakening husbands on payday. The street girls jeer at them.

"Can't hold a nigga without comin down to get him? What I got waitin for him, he'd run home all by hisself, just to see if it's still there!"

"Why don't you 'wives' hang black crepe on your pussy? It's dead, done died!"

Stray words lead to a fight. Men have to separate two women from hair-pulling, snatching at earrings and splitting pierced ears as they roll in the gutter.

The boldest of the family women go to the white bossman of the mill and ask his aid and protection for the children: "We almost starve last week, Sir."

"Sam would'n go through his pay if them women didden drunk him on whiskey."

The white boss sternly calls in the culprit, smugly gives him a lecture on sobriety, threatens to take his job, then hands his wife half of the pay after warning Sam, Joe or whoever not to lay a hand on her. Then the white boss goes forth to buy his own weekly nooky, white or black.

Etta condemns evildoers, but disagrees with the legal women who plead in public. "I couldn't make myself go to a bossman and beg for my husband's pay. How is some outside man gonna run us? That's steppin back to slavery. However, who knows what we'll learn to do if we have to? I'm blessed, my husband puts his family first, but you can't get blood out of a turnip and there are so many saints and sinners out there fightin each other just to make a livin."

Short money can't stretch but so far. She teaches Cora how to pinch pennies and cut corners. They waste not and yet they want. Sausage meat mixed with cornmeal serves for three dinners instead of one. Once in a while Etta takes the girl out to Edisto Island by boat to visit relatives and come back laden with sweet potatoes, groundnuts and greens—and a standing invitation: "Come back to the country, the Affikan ways, shake the dust of the city off your shoe sole." Etta pleads with Bill to listen.

"Cousin Tandy and Cousin Flower say this city life be too mean and cruel. Bill, them country people got plenty everything except fancy clothes and house and furniture—and not much cash money either. But they growin and raisin they own food . . . smokehouse fulla hams and what all. They help one another through sickness. Christian means somethin over there on the island."

"Yeah," he says, "but no edjication goin on. Ain't no high school. Here we got Avery and maybe times'll pick up so we can send her off to that Tuskeegee."

Six

Every day Cora meets Cecil at the battery to count how many ships are in the harbor and to wave welcome at any Negro sailors coming ashore. On slow days, they watch the water reflect sunlight as Cecil tells hushed stories about those who come and go at Aunt Looli's—how she pays money to a policeman, but how he arrested her anyway and also kept the money. But the judge set her free because she showed him the poor, motherless child who would have to do for himself if she was jailed—Cecil. He hadn't liked it at all.

With more poverty and new wickedness unfolding on every side, Bill holds to his belief in the final triumph of good and the better future for the Negro race. He sadly wonders why neither idea provides comfort to other workmen around him, certainly not when there is the present excitement of strong whiskey and new bed partners.

Bill and other true believers gather at lunchtime to speak up for clean living and warn the younger men about diseases brought home from houses of ill repute. The younger men secretly laugh when they notice it is Bill who scratches at his crotch even though he never goes sporting.

"Oh, oh, look like crab lice done found a new home."

Bill doesn't have any kind of lice, yet the itching becomes unbearable. He hates to spend food money on a doctor, also he believes that doctors make people sicker, and have the sick come back too many times for the sake of money. He tries vinegar-and-water spongebathing, drinks ginger tea and sprinkles salt in his shoes, but he stays thirsty and his genitals keep on itching and throbbing. Discomfort finally drives him to the Hospital Clinic for Colored Men.

The white doctor sees two or three patients at once. "Sorry, boys, but we're short-handed and have a full house today. Drop your pants and hold it out."

Men giggle until their shoulders shake, as though the order is a clever joke.

"Pull it back, boys." Doctor looks no more than twenty-eight, eyes gray, hair brown. He treats the patients with a kindly but iron hand. He looks at Bill's penis. "Where you been puttin this, uncle?"

"No place, sir."

"No place!" doctor laughs. "Maybe that's what's wrong with it, why it got angry and swole up on you. You suppose to *put* it someplace." The others echo his laughter, slapping thighs, looking at the gray-eyed doctor with polite admiration. The doctor asks for answers. "Ain't that right, boys?"

"Yassuh, you sayin what's true."

"Sure is."

Bill is angry inside, but like the others, wants to stay on friendly terms with doctor. They fear to displease a man with the power of life and death. Bill thinks how fitting is the word "patient", how a patient must indeed show patience—especially a Negro patient. He tries to smile but the corners of his mouth will not go up. The doctor asks Bill to remain after he dismisses the others with prescriptions. The doctor feels sad because this poor fellow is pretty well shot, with no chance of being saved for very long. Bill reads his face. The doctor takes pride in his ability to speak *their* language.

"Uncle," he says, "you got the sugar diabetes; thats why your pecker is in this state. By the way, ever spit up blood?"

"Sometimes."

"What kinda work you do?"

"Phosphate mill."

"Quit it. Your lungs sorta weak. I wantcha to pee in a bottle for me and bring it back tomorrow. Got to be the first piss of the day." The doctor has a hard time looking into the eyes of the dying. He stares at the wall and scribbles a prescription. "You understand?"

"Yes, doctor."

"Meanwhile, from now on, drink nice, fresh milk, eat lean meat, fish and fresh vegetables. Leave off salt pork and starchy food like biscuit and cornmeal, understand?"

"Yessir."

"Get this filled on the medicine line. Don't go near sweets—no candy, cake, pies, whiskey, wine or any kinda alcohol. This prescription might spruce you up. Don't forget the urine specimen—er, the bottle of pee—first piss of the morning; don't forget."

Bill has the prescription filled and refilled at the drugstore but never returns to clinic. He goes to see a Negro doctor named Burns, but his face also reads a hopeless message. He gives up doctors and leans on the prayers and advice of friends and well-wishers who have known sickness in their families. They bring herbs, leftover medicines, licorice root, liniments and various good luck things like High-John-The-Conqueror and black hickory nuts to be carried in his pocket. He goes on doing the best he can.

• • •

The daily newspaper carries front page pictures of all ships scheduled to stop in Charleston Harbor. Cecil and Cora cut them out to paste in notebooks. They soon know each one by heart and pretend they own them.

"Cecil, we each have thirty ships. Your Aunt Looli sure buys lots of newspapers."

"Men leave the paper, and I pick it up."

"We're lucky she knows them."

"Kojie Anderson been hanging out round Squeeze-gut Alley since his wife died."

"What would he be doin there?"

"Maybe was just somebody look like him."

"I should think so."

Bill struggles to make time every morning, getting up earlier and earlier because it takes longer to wash, dress and walk to work. He tires easily and is almost grateful when he's cut down to two days. They get used to shorter rations and falling behind on the bills. Etta swallows her pride and goes with Cora to collect free flour and lard from city charity. There are two lines, the same as in the railroad stations. The "white" line gets five and three—five pounds of gray flour and three of stiff lard. The "colored" gets three and one. Bill is hurt, angry, cranky and ashamed. Etta often snaps at Cora about nothing—things like wasting hot water: "You learn to wash dishes cleaner in the first water, so you don't have to use so much for the rinse. We ain't got but so much wood and coal!"

Bill hates to hear her go on this way, but he keeps quiet because he is empty-handed. A real argument breaks out when Etta takes a laundress job with a well-to-do family.

"You now workin for the same people who broke the heart of Murdell and her Mama," Bill tells her.

"Them people gone, new bunch now, but it's all the same. Let the dead past bury the past. We can't live offa air puddin and wind sauce."

"Stayin alive is gettin to be too damn shameful."

"I work for whoever got a job to offer. Doctor done say your health gon fail if you don't eat fresh vegetable and orange."

"Let it fail."

Mumbling and grumbling slowly becomes a part of daily life. Cora endures going to a store where the grocer resentfully grants "credick" while licking his lips and staring at her bosom. Etta starts dipping into a wine bottle. One evening Bill snatches it away from her.

"Every day you scrubbin the skin off your hands and every night drinkin wine. Not right for a decent woman to be smellin like the twenty-five cent illegal you buy from Mr. Tuss. Yeah, he even ask me about it. 'Brother Bill,' he say, 'I hope my wine is helpin your chest like Etta say.' I ain't tell him that you, the woman, is the one doin the drinkin."

Etta's anger matches his. "Yeah, I'm drinkin. Every day I have to wash all kindsa clothes, the monthly bird's-eye and also them towels they use for they pleasure. The well-to-do have a way a doin like anybody else. I stand there with a stick, pokin sweaty underwear in a boiler fulla scaldin water. I don't need nobody to tell me what kinda job it is! There's many a woman in our church who prayin they get the same job. Nobody can make it without a dollar, so don't talk bout the little taste a wine I'm takin to settle my nerves. You just eat them good oranges I'm bringin home. A orange is a orange no matter where the money come from."

"You quit that washwoman job! They call it laundress when it's servin the well-to-do, but it's washwoman just the same. I'll go steal or else pick up behind the dawgs like Mr. July! Etta, you a Christian and you know Gawd don't like ugly!"

"Then why don't he rain down some oranges and a few pennies to rub one against another? You a man and Gawd is a man, so yall answer me that, gawdammit!"

He grabs for the wine bottle, a push leads to a shove, a pan hits the wall, then they are scuffling.

Cora, in bed, hides her head under the quilt. A dish shatters, a glass breaks and then—muffled sobbing. Bill pours the wine down the sink and takes Etta in his arms. Kind words. Cora comes out from under the quilt, knowing Saturday night storm will be followed by Sunday calm.

Lying on her cot, watching moonlight spill across the room, Cora knows the sweet, sad feelings of girl-becoming-woman. Her thoughts stray from parents arguing about oranges, money and dirty clothes. She thinks of Cecil and ships, and of someday becoming rich enough not to care about money. She and Cecil will make lots of money and go halves, and send some back to Mama, Papa and Miss Looli.

In the morning, Etta pats her daughter awake. Cora stretches lengthening limbs and enjoys the sound of Papa's fragile laughter and the music in her mother's voice. Etta is shy again, flirting with her husband. "Awwww, stop now, behave yourself." The house is filled with the tantalizing smell of one sausage apiece, grits and coffee. Her mother calls her a second time. "Get up, gal, rise and shine, we gon be our natural selves today!"

But the sweet, happy times are fewer and farther apart. Things that happen to outsiders worsen and touch their lives, plowing deep, dark scars of memory.

One day, a man across the street who always said "Howdy-do and good afternoon" for years—this very same man chases his wife out of the house. She spouts blood from a dozen fountains pierced in her body with an ice pick. The woman runs screaming to the middle of the street, crying out his name, "Buckley! Buckley!" Her fluttering, dark hands clutch at the stained bosom of her dress, trying to dam the flow. She screams and whirls through a terrible bloody dance as he weeps and stabs new fountains. She weakens, quivers, droops nearer to the earth and stumbles back toward home. There, on the porch steps, she becomes still—a crumpled little scarlet heap, under the branches of a fruit-filled pomegranate tree. The man drops the bloody pick as people move toward him—too late. He gathers her up in his arms, senselessly trying to call her back to life, "Dinah, don't leave me!"

The dead wagon comes to take her away. Police arrive in the Black Maria and take him to the jailhouse—weeping, bloody, alive and yet dead.

Cora dreams it over and over and ever after hates pomegranate fruit because it brings back the memory of love turned to murder for some mysterious reason. She wakes wondering if it had to do with not having money, or perhaps who slept with who, or maybe the price of oranges, or the colored and white signs, or three and one surplus . . . or some other such thing.

Seven

My father sleeps late one morning. When he tries to get up he falls. Mama is at work. I help him back to bed, give him a sponge bath and put brown-paper-and-vinegar poultices on his forehead and wrists to cool the fever. His sickness moves on to worse. Daily, his eyes grow bigger, his face narrower. Our church prayer band comes by twice weekly to rally with him. Members of the First Colored Brotherhood Lodge take turns sittin with him through the night; each gives my mother a twenty-five cent piece before leavin in the morning. Temple sisters and neighbor ladies bring broths and medicine along with prayer, but he remains sick, getting sicker.

Mama tells him good-news stories about the phosphate boss patiently waiting to put him back to work on full time, about Edisto Island relatives and about a cousin Estelle up in New York—all beggin us to leave Charleston and live with them. There are constant messages of cheer from church members, prayers embroidered on linen, plants potted in tomato cans—every day a gift. Each mornin I look in the sickroom, fearin death may have taken him while I slept.

Late in the day, sunbeams fall across the table beside his bed, sparklin through green and blue medicine bottles, makin pretty lights, a table of jewels. I try to prepare him for the hard night to come: "Papa, drink a little eggnog so you'll be strong again."

"I'm dyin, daughter, but don't tell your mama till I'm closer to the end."

Kojie Anderson is turnin into a good, true friend durin these days. He does his night duty as a lodge brother three times as often as the others. He is now twenty-five, a widower, and still wearin a black armband for mournin. He is just as serious and proper as the older deacons. He gives dependable surprises, never failin to bring some treat—a palm-leaf fan for the sickroom, a nightshirt for Papa and delicacies for Mama and me. When we try to thank him, he won't have it.

"Now, now, my sisters, are we not one in God? Didn't I go through the sorrow of losing a beloved one? Don't I know suffering?" He raises his arms and eyes toward the ceilin in Christ-like blessin, placin one hand on Mama's head, the other on mine. He is so dignified. Kojie Anderson has turned into a most distinguished and unusual person. Every other night or so he sits with Papa, each time leaves a new quarter, taxin himself more often than any other member. Mama is moved to tears by such free-handedness. "We can't take and take from you. It's not right."

Kojie just smiles. "Don't you know, my sisters, you are making it possible for me to serve the Lord and do good in the memory of my late wife?"

"All right, Kojie," Mama says.

The way he looks at me—more than just respectful—I know he likes me and wants me to like him back. Everytime he leaves, Mama goes over his best points. "Kojie is full of sound ideas and worthwhile answers . . . and he never comes empty-handed. His dear, sweet wife left him well-fixed, too. He's on his way up."

Doctors, prayer band, charms and medicine, special food—nothin helps my father. We plan to go to a special healin meeting. The healer's name is Mountain Seeley. He is able to cure uncurables right before everybody's eyes. Mr. Tuss told us about him. Since we can't carry Papa to the meeting, we are to take a piece of his clothin because the spirit of the afflicted person becomes a part of any garment he wears.

The last healin service is tonight at a large church, the True Zacharias Gospel Tabernacle. Brother Seeley goes from town to town, performin his miracles. Ministers of low-membership churches are glad to have "The Mountain" visit and draw a crowd. I hear they split the collection. Several gentlemen travel along with him as his disciples and servants to run his business affairs. Reverend Mills and our members are not supposed to believe in The Mountain, but faith takes a different turn durin sickness and we are forced to believe in miracles.

The pulpit and walls are decorated with old crutches, braces, canes, eyeglasses and large cane-back wheelchairs—things people don't need any more since they are no longer sick or crippled. A disciple tells us we can make one wish as we place a quarter on a table for the entrance fee. Naturally, me and Mama have the same wish; a healin for Papa.

Mountain Seeley is tall, lean and hunch-shouldered, about

six-feet-four in his Cuban-heel shoes. He wears a handsome, dark, chalk-striped suit, a double strand watch chain, and a diamond horseshoe stickpin shines in his silky black necktie. One of his front teeth is gold, with a diamond set in the center. His smile is bright, his voice raspy and deep.

"My friends, you may wonder and ponder on me, the man you see before your eyes. I am only a mortal man. My mama named me 'Mountain' so I'd grow, strong and mighty! I'm a healer, but I still ain't God—I'm a man!" He rears back, rocks his shoulders from side to side as the gaslights shine on his dark face. "Only a man, but a man of God!" He puts his hands on his hips and leans back and forth. A woman screams, others shout. Ushers and disciples turn stern looks on them. Mountain scolds. "Oh, I can read some sinful minds. Yall better cut loose from hot desire and get closer to God! I also can read doubters, can tell what you thinkin! You wonderin how come a man a God is wearin diamonds, gold and fine clothes! But didn't sweet Jesus wear the finest garment? Yeah, He did! He wore Hisself a handwove, seamless suit a clothes! Yeah, and drank wine! Had Hisself a little taste a toddy now and then." He laughs. The sparkling tooth makes him look very handsome and prosperous.

He hops up and down and claps his hands. "I use to be scared to *shine* for God, to *heal* for God, but I ain't scared no more." He struts back and forth and shows off his clothes. "I learned that to look good is to heal good, then you feel good! A servant is a-worthy of his hire, don'tcha know. God pays me and he dresses me. Yeah, He do. Now let's move on. The good book say that if the mountain won't come to you, you's to go to the mountain. Well, go no further, your Mountain is here! I'm gonna heal tonight, if you believe!"

Gospel singers clap hands as they sing a special number. "Heal me, I believe. Heal me, I believe . . ." Me, Mama, everybody, we sing along with them.

Mountain Seeley points from one to another of us. "All you who sorry for the dirt you rollin in, raise your hand and lemmie know you wanta wash it off with the healin blood a Jesus! Sinner, show your hand!" Mama takes my hand and holds it up with hers. She jumps to her feet, pulling me up beside her, shouting to Mountain: "Have mercy, heal my husband! I ain't gonna drink no more wine! Not gonna offend His holy name!"

Lady ushers come over to cool my mother with a cardboard fan that says "Compliments of Mickey Funeral Home." They hold smellin salts under her nose. "Please Mama," I beg her, "hush so we don't miss the healin."

Reverend Mountain goes on. "Brothers and sisters, I feel there is a man in this temple who is unable to speak. Brother, whoever you are, I promise you a healin! No matter whatcha got—TB, sugar disease, cancer, St. Vitus dance, whatever it is—with God all things are made possible! Come forth sinner, blasphemer, fornicator—I will cast out your devil and heal!"

A man stands and stumbles forward in the aisle. His shoulders are stooped and he drags one leg behind him.

"Ah-yah-yah!" he cries. "Ah-yah-yah!"

People draw away from him as he staggers and flings himself from side to side, falling forward until he crumples at the feet of Mountain Seeley. The man is really speechless except for that "Ah-yah-yah", which he says over and over. Mountain reaches down and snatches the cripple to his feet and shouts, "Heal him, heal him, heal him, Lord!" The cripple cries out, moans and *speaks*—he stands up straight and *speaks*, "Hallelujah! Praise Gawd! Praise His holy name! Hallelujah, thank you, Jesus!"

No longer does he "Yah-yah"; his voice is clear as a bell. Someone throws a bunch of dollar bills at Mountain and they flutter around his head. Gospel singers dance and clap their way into the aisle. Half the congregation is up pushin and shovin toward the pulpit, holdin out dollars, throwin them up to Mountain. We're all cryin—I believe, I believe, I believe!

Mama can't get through the crowd which is elbowin and jammin the way, but I can. I grab Papa's shirt from her and hold it over my head; in my other hand I'm wavin three dollars to get Mountain's attention. He's lookin dead-straight at me as I push past all in my way. A woman grabs my shirtwaist, tryin to get ahead. I won't let her. The blouse tears but I keep goin, she grabs at my camisole and leaves me half naked to the waist—no matter! I shout over the heads of those in front and I'm holdin Mountain's eyes with mine, "Heal my father! I'll work and give you money for the resta my life!"

Mama gets close enough to pull the rough, wild woman offa me, so I can reach Mountain. I'm there, wavin the shirt for blessin. He takes my hand, pulls me forward and I fall at his feet. He bends down and caresses Papa's shirt. "A-heal and a-heal and a-heal!" And then I feel his hand touch my breast, rubbing the nipple with his thumb. I lie still and let him do it, fearin he'll not give the healin. Rubbin makes me feel—in my stomach, the backs of my knees, between my legs. I know this is not a part of the healin, but I try to believe just in case it is.

"Heal," he says. "Be healed."

I'm hopin and prayin it'll be like he says. I pull up by graspin his arm. The disciples rush in to protect him.

"No touchin, sister."

"Hands off the Mountain."

"Power needs no touch."

Out in the street, Mama wraps me in her sweater and we rush homeward. I can't wait to see Mountain's healin magic. Surely Papa must be sittin up in bed, wonderin why the health and strength is suddenly flowin back inside of him. We keep sayin it as we hurry along—I believe, I believe, I believe, I believe.

Kojie meets us at the door. "He had a hemmorhage. I cleaned up and . . . Oh, sisters, I'm so sorry."

Papa's face is ash-gray against the white pillow case. His eyelids flutter, but he is asleep. I am angry with Mountain. Mama cries. Kojie strikes up a kindlin fire and makes tea. "You have to let go, sisters. You're praying for a healing miracle, but God and Brother Bill got other plans. Cora, stand strong and put childish things behind you."

Bein a woman is more than Mama said, more than washin bird's-eye cloth to secretly dry behind the stove. It's bein afraid, alone and not knowin the true from the false, or whose word to take.

Kojie pours tea and opens a tin of biscuits. We sit at the table sippin and wonderin. Lord, do tell, now I feel the light touch of a hand restin on my knee. I reach under the table to remove it. Kojie takes my hand in his and rubs the center of my palm with his finger. I try to pull away but he holds fast. The flesh behind my knees quivers—and a tinglin creeps up my thighs. He doesn't miss a word Mama says and never drops one of his *ing* endins.

"Miss Etta, never stop counting on me as a friend, or thinking of me as a son; lean on me."

Mama is nicely comforted by Kojie's sweet cream wafers and his offer of protection. "Kojie, you are my son, sent by Gawd in my hour of need."

I now know that, if I want it, I can have a five-room house with acreage, garden and fruit trees and a man's steady pay envelope comin in. I can see Papa restin out in the garden, both he and Mama sittin in the shade a my own vine tree. I smile at Kojie and gently smack his hand off my knee.

• • •

My father never had much time to himself before the illness. Now he doesn't have to go to the mill, to church, to lodge meetin, or anywhere else. He lies flat on his back starin at the ceilin, and talkin bout the Charleston slave market. "Cora, these days, Negro women go there to sell quilts and baskets, but that place is still my bad dream." He wakes durin the night and cries out about the noise in the market, his mother on a platform while men call out her price.

Kojie gives pain pills to get him back to sleep. I could have gone to Avery High School on scholarship, but it'll wait till next year, when Papa is better. Mama works and I must nurse him through this bad time. It's almost like goin to school. He talks about all sorts of things and I spend most a my wakin hours sittin on the foot of his bed.

"Papa, you lookin better."

"I'm dyin, Cora."

"Don't say that."

"I'm dyin—let's not fall out about it. Don't act like death is somethin I thought up. Help me straighten my affairs."

"Yes, Papa."

"Is my burial policy paid up?"

"It is."

"Good, now is not the time for it to lapse."

I get my copy book and write down things as he tells them. "See that your mama don't let the undertaker get everything. He put away old Miss Emily for seventy-five dollars, plus fifteen for the grave. That'll leave yall with seventy-five clear. It can last two months if she's cautious. Don't bury me in my good suit; give it to Mister July so he can go to a funeral steada hangin round outside."

"Yes, Papa."

"I leave you with this piece a knowledge: don't let the slave market have every bit of you . . . understand?"

"Slavery's over."

"Only in a way a speakin, daughter. The law still pushes us to back entrances and separate lines. But while you standin separate just keep tellin yourself that Jim Crow law is nothin but some bad echoes from a old slave market."

"It doesn't make me as mad as it use ta."

"Hang onto 'mad'. When you stop mindin, that's when they got every bit a you and have fulfill the purpose of their meaness, which is to turn us into wrung-out, tuck-tail dogs; whatcha call 'defeat'."

"I'll never act like a tuck-tail dog."

"They don't wantcha to *act* like one—they wantcha to be one and act like you not."

Outside of the sadness, I like the talks. Other people don't seem interested in what we go into. If they are, they keep quiet about it. When I ask folks to tell me what they think about life, it makes them uneasy. Mama says, "Love Gawd and keep goin, that's all I know." Cecil declares life is first one thing and then another. I can't dispute that, but it doesn't get down to facts. He laughed at me and tried to prove his point with a silly joke. "First it's one thing, right? Well, if it doesn't get to be another . . . you *died*."

Papa gives answers. "Well, honey, I still believe life is a short walk from the cradle to the grave and it sure behooves us to be kind to one another. We are born, then we begin to take notice. Noticin is not enough, so we try to find teachers to point out what we fail to notice. We begin to catch on to how things are done. We suffer some, then think we know it all . . . so that leads us to make mistakes. All such errors make us doubt our own minds. As we go along we learn not to judge people too hard but you gotta be careful who to give your deepest heart and thoughts to, because you'll carry alla those people inside for the resta your days and that can either tear you up or else make it go smoother. But with all our best figurin, somethin keeps goin wrong and we begin to think too little of ourselves. Well, trials keep comin, finally we begin to catch on to how to live . . . but by that time life's almost over."

"Papa, tell me what to do. What's right for *me*?"

"You can find a good husband or else go back to school to get a education. Failin that, you can lend your free service to some tradesperson in exchange for learnin the trade. Get Miss Rosalinda to teach you to sew. You have to have some money knowledge and can't rely on Shakespeare's moon and poems to put bread on the table."

"That's it, Papa, I have to learn how to earn my own livin without a bossman."

"I got nothin to leave my family, but I wantcha to know I don't like it. When I'm gone, please go to the old slave market and address yourself to it, say, 'That's all you gonna get, my father is the last. I'll be no man's slave, I belong to myself.'"

Durin this illness he puts things better and clearer than ever. I pat his hand, rub his head and pour paregoric in a great big spoon. Paregoric is a fine medicine, makes people able to stand illness. Papa loves it. Soon as he gets one spoon, his mouth is open for another. Even when paregoric has him addleheaded he still makes sense.

"Another piece a knowledge, Cora. Watch out for Kojie. People call poor, dead Lilly a cradle-snatcher cause he's so much younger. But Kojie was at least thirty-three when he was born. He sweet-talk Lilly into marryin. Your mind is as good as his and the only one you'll ever have for full-time use."

My notebook is fillin up from all these things, but we push on because the time is short and we can't discuss in front of Mama. Death is a forbidden word far as she's concerned.

"Bury me in my lodge badge and apron, with the tassel-cap on my head. You keep the gold and crystal drinkin cup with the emblem on it. Someday, if you have a boy child, it'll be on the mantlepiece, so when people ask, he can say, 'That was my grandfather's.' My pocket watch is only gold-fill but your mama will take pride in it. She's also in charge of all else that is mine and has the entire say-so in the final arrangements. You could tell her that my favorite hymn is 'It is Well With My Soul' and not 'Nearer my God to Thee', unless you think it might distress her too much."

There's no way to stop him talkin and paregoric brings out crazy kinda things, more than anybody needs to hear—"And as far as you not bein our own child." . . .—tellin me that kinda stuff till my head feels like burstin open. He'll say some, then go back to it and say more, then forget all about it. Feels like I'm dyin right long with him. I look at walls and out the window and down on the floor, everywhere but in his face cause I don't wanta believe such lies . . . yet knowin it's true.

"Papa, I don't belong to you? I'm not blood kin?"

"Course you belong to us."

"But if somebody named Murdell was my mother and some white man . . ."

"Don't tell Etta. She don't want it told."

"Papa, you scarin me."

"Truth must be told. You belong to yourself more than to any of us. Nobody is to own alla your secrets, even if they did adopt—not even me. Give me some more paregoric, please, and more pain pills."

"There's only a few pills left, you must have had four today."

"Etta and I couldn't have any of our own, you been my heart and hers. But alla your business belongs to you. Right is right."

"Yes, Papa, right is right."

The churchwomen are here to fold my father's hands, to close his eyes with pennies. Every mirror in the house is covered so his spirit won't be trapped and lose the way to the Hereafter. They pray for his soul as they lay out the suit, shirt and tie for the undertaker. The children carry messages to the neighbors and the rest of the congregation. Churchwomen wash, cook, dust and scrub the floor, always scrubbin toward the street door to drive away any evil spirit that might visit the house and claim the dead. As they work they tell good things about my father.

"Never had a harsh word, not a one."

"Was a good provider. Had not a selfish bone."

"You'll not see his like again in a hurry."

Kojie returns with the undertaker and his assistant. They carry Papa out in a long basket covered with canvas. I try to follow; the women hold me back.

I tell them, "Take the canvas off. Don't leave him in the dark. No canvas, please."

Kojie puts his arms around me. "They have to cover him, darling, because it is now raining."

Miss Odessa peeps at the street through drawn blinds. "Heaven is weeping," she says. "That's a good sign."

Miss Jenny holds my mother's hand. "We know not the day or the hour."

People, more and more people, bring sympathy. I go in his room. His bed is freshly made, as smooth as glass, empty lookin, as if he's never been in it. Kojie follows and neatly puts away bottles, spoons and medicine glasses.

"Cora, it's for the best."

"Everyone says."

"We can't question God's widsom, dearest."

"I guess not."

"If you need anything remember I'm here, sweetness."

"Thank you."

"Not only in this hour of sorrow, but from now on."

When no one notices I go out the back door, down to the battery to find and tell Cecil. He tells me he's sorry—then we start countin how many ships are in harbor, testin to see if I remember the names and numbers. I know each navy ship, the merchant marines and the tankers. When we run out of ships, we count every sailor wearin a white cap, and when that's done with . . .

"Cecil, since you told me about your Aunt Looli, I'll tell a terrible thing Papa told before he died. I'm not theirs. My mother's name was Murdell, my father was some . . . some white man."

"I know."

"How do you know?"

"I heard it from other people."

"Well, I guess he was right to tell me if everybody else knows. Don't let my mother know that I know—it might hurt her feelings. I feel like I belong to nobody atall."

"Mr. James shouldn'ta told you."

"It was the paregoric . . . I don't wanta go back home yet . . . to all those people knowin more bout me than I do almost."

We walk past the flowery, White-only park where I once read up and down a blue streak. We walk beyond houses with double verandas, upstairs and down; past larger places smellin of gardenia and lemon leaves and magnolia; past piazzas with porch swings. Houses become scarcer and green is more. We pass a white man on the road, he waves to us, smiles, then goes in a pretty house.

"Dirty, lowdown thing might be my father. For the resta my life I'll be wonderin which one a them mistreated the mama I never knew—the one named Murdell."

"Sure sorry he told you," Cecil says.

"It was the paregoric."

We sit down to rest on a log. He tries to cheer me up. "Guess what? A frienda my Aunt Looli promise to get me a job on the Clyde Line that runs between here and New York. Just be runnin errands and carryin trays. Pay is small but I get berth, board and tip money. Call it 'cabin boy', then I'll work up to waiter or steward."

"I'd like to do it, too. Do they take cabin girls?"

He looks at me like I lost my mind. "No, they don't, Cora. Girls suppose to do girl things."

We walk on. There are now fewer houses, We leave the road to cut through a clover field. I wish he would put his arm around me, I need it, I need it. He must hear me thinking. Now we lie on the grass in the sweet smell of clover. He kisses me. Oh, I need it—not Mountain's rubbing hand, or Kojie's finger on my palm, nor the "credick" grocery man bumping against me as he weighs out sugar and rice . . . oh, but this good feeling—Cecil's arms around me. Someone belonging to me while I cry about Papa gone.

"Don't be mad with me, Cora."

"I'm cryin cause Papa's dead and soon you'll be leavin on a ship and I'll be left alone."

"I won't leave, if you love me . . . I'll never go."

The sounda my heart is in my ears. He fumbles with the button to undo my shirtwaist and it pops off.

"I'm sorry, my darlin."

I can see Mama's face even clearer than Cecil's dark eyes lookin down into mine. I don't want to get in trouble, but I kiss him back and close my arms around him. It's all clothes, buttons and wigglin. His necktie is across my face and there's no way to move it without askin and I'm ashamed to ask. My leg is crooked and I try to straighten it.

"Cecil, I don't want to get in trouble."

"I won't do anything, I promise, just want to be against you—been wantin to touch you for so long . . . must be forever."

"Cecil, did you . . . did you ever do it with anybody?"

"I don't wanta tell. Must I?"

"Yes, you must."

"Uh-huh, a lady one time stayed a week at Aunt Looli's. She kinda made me, y'know?"

"Me, I never did. Cecil . . . I can't."

"I promise not to go inside . . . promise." His hand goes in under the camisole and I'm thinkin that it's fortunately freshly ironed and lacey. His hand moves over my breast and I want him to break that promise. He's kissin and kissin. His face is wet with my tears, his mouth is wet. He touches my stomach. I do care so much about him. My dress is up and his hand is between my legs . . .

"Cora, I love you, do you love me back?"

"I do . . . I'll love you, Cecil, for the resta my life."

Strangers are laughin. We sit up and try to fix our clothes. Three big white boys starin at us. Cecil helps me to my feet and we start back for home. I hold my blouse together as we go. The boys follow. I hurry faster.

"Don't run," Cecil says. "They'll catch you." He's right. The boys move as fast as we do. Out of the corner of my eye I see they are poor and mean-lookin. They shout nasty remarks like they're talkin to each other, but want us to hear every word.

"I been told that black nooky is somethin every white, red-blooded Amurkin boy oughta have for hisself, at least one time."

"Yeah, long as it's new nooky and not any that a black buck nigga's been pokin in."

"No matter, just rinse pussy off and it's good as new."

Cecil holds my hand tight and talks, not makin sense but tryin to make better time. "If I get the ship job—hurry now, Cora—walk just a little bit faster—I'm sorry bout your father but we do have to take life like it happen—hurry little more." The boys don't like us hurryin. I feel like a insect must feel runnin from a foot that's bout to smash it. They comin closer, talkin louder.

"If I was to stick my pecker in her, oh, boy!"

"Bet she got a fine juice-box!"

"I'm gon ram it home and make her holler!"

"Oh, do it, sweet Mister White Man!'"

"Gon stick mine in her right ear, that's what."

We're still a good block away from houses and people. I'm gettin outta breath. Cecil says, "Break away and run for one a them veranda houses. If they chase you, holler loud, but they won't cause I'm goin the other way. More likely they'll follow me. He squeezes my elbow, gives me a push, and I pick up my skirts and run. Cecil goes the opposite direction and sure enough they chase after him. He keeps goin, takin them away from me.

They corner him back in the wooded area where they first saw him. It is early evening now; each white boy thinks of being somewhere else, half wishing they had gone on about their business and didn't have to think of what to do with the nigga boy, but full well knowing they must do something for the sake of white honor, now that they have him.

Cecil looks into three pairs of icy eyes—brown, gold and blue—hopefully studying them for a sign of kindness or weakening of purpose, some slight sympathy. Brown-eyes and Blue-eyes look meaner: Gold-eyes turns away from his gaze, leading him to think that this lookaway-boy might save him from the wrath of the others. He tries to pray inside of himself as they study him.

Brown-eyes wonders what it must feel like to be the nigga, particularly this one who let himself be cornered and caught all for the sake of some wild-ass nigga girl. Blue-eyes wonders what it will feel like to torment a living thing. The hopeful look on the nigga's face is making him angry. Gold-eyes resents the nigga having on a pair of salt-and-pepper knickerbocker pants, a white-on-white, long-sleeved shirt with a necktie, and black oxford shoes with shiny brass cleats on the heels and toes—a nigga trying to look like some well-off person, trying to act better than white when he's really dumb, black, ugly and stupid.

"We gonna cut your cock off," he says, "unless you git down on your knees and beg us not to do it."

Blue-eyes takes out a penknife and opens the blade. "And I got this to cut it off with. Gonna dig your nuts out and carve my 'nitials in your coal-black ass."

Cecil pauses for a brief, thoughtful second, then falls on his knees. "Please don't hurt me."

"Nigga, you spose to say 'Mista'," says Brown-eyes. "Bet if I kick your teeth in you'll talk mo betta."

Gold-eyes kicks Cecil on the backside and sends him falling forward on his hands. "Speak up, nigga!"

"Mista, if I did somethin wrong, I'm sorry."

"Yeah, you did somethin wrong—you was born, you black fucka!"

"Did you put your prick in that pretty nigga gal's pussy?"

"No, Mista."

"We saw you!"

"Tell us how nigga pussy feel. Did you git some and shoot off in her fore we got here?"

Now all three are holding knives ready. Cecil says, "No, sir." Gold-eyes lifts Cecil's chin with the tip of one foot. "Stand up, don't lie to a white man!" Cecil, fearing a kick in the face, cautiously rises to his feet, trying to figure which one to go for when they jump him.

Blue-eyes slips a knife under his belt and Cecil's pants fall down. "Let's see what a black pecker looks like." At the points of three knives they make him drop his underwear and expose himself. They pour sandy soil and pebbles inside his drawers, they command him to crawl and call himself dirty names, they make him sit up like a begging dog, parroting their words back to them.

"Please, white man, won'tcha please piss all over me?"

One at a time they wet on him; his flesh burns like fire wherever urine splashes, but chill evening breeze instantly cools until he is shivering cold. He wishes he had a weapon. When it is Brown-eyes' turn, he decides to outdo the others.

"Open your mouth, Nigga, open it wide, so I can piss in it."

Cecil's body refuses to obey his mind's cautious order. He quickly thinks of all he'd rather do than die—He'd like to see Cora again, work on a Clyde Line Ship, see New York, get a diploma, even keep living at Aunt Looli's——just to grow older—there are so many things to do if you're alive, but he can't open his mouth.

Brown-eyes and Blue-eyes are becoming fearful and tired of the game which is getting out of hand. The first hour had been fun; now it is becoming more than what they want to do. Anger is ebbing away.

"Aw, kick his black ass and let him go."

"I got me some other things to do."

But Gold-eyes stays with the moment, can't turn back. He takes a small fishhook out of his back pocket, unwinds the string wrapped around it and swiftly stabs it into the captive face. The hook penetrates an inch above Cecil's top lip, just underneath the left nostril. Blood spurts.

"Caught a nigga fish. Watch me haul it in."

Cecil inches forward to save his mouth from being torn open, pleads through warm blood dripping over his lips as Gold-eyes tugs on the string, "Please, yall . . ."

Blue- and Brown-eyes back away, glance at each other and silently agree to call off the game. "Hey, what'sa-matta, Royal? He ain' nothin but a skinny-ass, puny nigga."

"Fuckit, come on!"

"Nough's nough—that's nough, Royal!"

Gold-eyes yanks the line before they can reach him; one hard pull and hook tears through flesh leaving the lip wide open. Blood flows over Cecil's teeth and gums, pain throws him to the ground as Gold-eyes spits out blind hatred. "Ya goddam nigga mouth is open now, nigga mouth!" He leans down to reclaim the bloody hook from the dirt. Cecil reaches up, pulls him down and grabs Gold-eyes. Hands clawing, feet kicking, teeth biting through blood—hanging on to never let go, clawing his nails down the front of Gold-eyes' face.

"Git this nigga offa me!"

Cecil's teeth sink into the boy's ear. Brown-eyes throws advice to his captured friend. "Use yo' knife, Royal!"

But Cecil has Royal's knife and he plunges a deep gash into the cheek of his tormentor. They flail in blood and dirt as the others tug to divide them.

"They're over there!" The sound of Cora's voice and feet breaking through underbrush sends the strugglers apart, and the white boys flying away.

"Come on, Royal, it's a ganga niggas!" The trio runs down the road at top speed. Looli's harsh voice is sweet to Cecil's ears. "Cecil, where the hell you at?"

A white man's voice joins hers. "I'm armed. Anybody in there is to come out!" Only Cecil is there . . . bloody.

The white man is called Mister Rooster because he works the railroad roundhouse on the five A.M. shift. He lifts Cecil, carries him to the wagon, and they take him a half mile away to the back door of Dr. Kinley's office, the white doctor who treats Looli and her friend-girls when needed. He stitches the raggedly torn lip together and does not charge a fee: "I'm white and the culprits are white, but this is terrible. Decent white folk deplore this kinda thing. Yall should ask the police to take a hand."

Looli doesn't agree. "No, doctor, and I'll thank you to report it to nobody atall."

Mr. Rooster agrees. "May's well leave it be."

Outside, Cora questions Looli's wisdom. "The doctor wants to tell the police. Maybe we oughta let him, no matter what."

Looli straightens her. "Just as long as I got to go round to the back door of the doctor's office, that's just how long we don't need him whistlin for police. Come trial time, me and Mr. Rooster would have to stand witness, you gon have to account for yourself—and one a yall might back down from what they got ready to lay on you. Plus that, Cecil done half kill a white boy."

"Anyway," Cora said, "I'm glad Mister Rooster was at your house when I got there."

"Yeah, and hush up bout that, too, or you'll make more trouble than we got."

The doctor had stitched Cecil's mouth and put a dressing over it. Fists on her hips, Looli preaches instruction. "Yall two not child no more, you man and woman. Where I come from, people your age gotta chop wood for theyself, cause nobody gon haul your load." She looks Cora over with kindly pity. "Girl, when I was your size I was supportin my poor old mother and two full grown men. Now I'm raisin and supportin this black fool here, and his mouth is stitch together like a patchwork quilt cause a havin a hard head and thinkin he can do what he please. Yall oughta know better than to walk in a strange white neighborhood; oughta know they ain't plannin to bake niggas no cake, or hold a welcome party for you. Cecil better learn to carry his own blade or somethin better, just in case. You girl, grow up and catch on to how to care for yourself."

"I will," Cora said.

Eight

Now and then I go down to the battery, but it's no fun since Cecil ran away to New York. If only he worked on the Clyde Line, at least I'd be able to see him when they dock in Charleston. He sent me a nice postcard of the Brooklyn Bridge but it didn't have a return address. One day I watched to see if he might be one of the Negro sailors gettin off a navy ship, but that's not really possible because it would take time for him to get the trainin part—even then his ship might not come into this harbor.

I do not want to move out to Edisto Island. I've seen enough on visits. Mama keeps praisin the country life and tryin to win me over. "Cora, they are good people, so don't sit in the seat of the scornful."

However, matters not what I want; we're packin and gettin ready to go. It's makin me very sad. There's snakes out there and no runnin water and no street lamps—everybody goes to bed at sundown to rise at four A.M. They sit in church all day on Sunday. I never have seen anything else to do except play jack-stones, and I'm too big for that.

Not sittin in the seat of the scornful, but they are also strict. "Chirrun should speak when spoken to." I told Mama's relatives that I am sixteen and no longer a child.

Cousin Flower said, "If, at your age, you married, then you a woman. Long as you single, you's a chile. And sixteen or no sixteen, next time you answer me outta turn, I'm gon give you a backhand slap in the mouth, which is somethin I been itchin to do ever since you come in here after your father die, with your clothes tore cause you ramblin with that little black nigga that done run off to the north. You in no way was showin respeck for the dead."

Mama's cousins, Tandy and Flower, told her not to let me live on here in the city, even though Miss Rosalinda has offered to take me as dressmaker-helper.

"Drat that," Cousin Flower says. "This womanish gal ain't belong to no Miss Rosey-Linda. She belong to you and my nephew-by-marry, who is now dead and gone. She family to us and not no Rosey-Linda. Nother thing: Rosey-Linda useta show her body on the stage. Gawd'll punish alla us if we lead our kinfolk inta temptation."

I can understand Mama goin to the island. Doin other people's housework is too hard for her—she's not used to it. She needs the peace of the country. All she wants these days is church meetin and rememberin past days with Papa. I think of him nightly, and talk to him: "Dear Papa, my name is Cora James and my determination is not to live out on Edisto Island." He knows I'm not scornful. I want somethin grand and wonderful to happen for me; it never will if I live out in the country. But it's time to go and I can't defy Mama because Miss Rosalinda says she will not take me in unless it's with my mother's consent.

Watchin old Tandy and Flower dip snuff does make me

feel kinda scornful. I don't think it's proper for seventy-year-old twin ladies to dip snuff sticks in a can, then mop that brown stuff over their teeth and gums. They like the way it stings and itches, say it feels good and keeps their teeth from hurtin. I feel scornful bout their spit cans, too. It's disgustin to see people do that. Mama says rich folks do the same, only they use brass spittoons. But the rich don't call to me, "Cora! Bring the spit can!" The twins always have to have one at their feet even in the parlor or on the back porch. They never remember to move it when they move, just call me.

Mama is packin the last of our things. Tandy and Flower are helpin, foldin away curtains in the boxes, closin down our humpback trunk. The twins are strong and able. Flower moves that trunk and Mama can't even budge it. Tandy says, "Plowin a straight line'll give you good muscle."

Well, my determination is also not to plow a straight line, or a crooked one. Tandy has six holes through each ear and wears as many pairs of earrings. Flower doesn't wear jewelry, but her mother had cut six half-moon scars in each of her cheeks when she was just a baby. She says, "This is my carry-over from old, Affikan ways."

Mama says those scars have magic power to harm or help a person. God bless the dead, I remember Papa once said he wished they'd use some a that power to get the race outta the tight bind it's in. These cousins had enough power to walk from the docks to our house with bundles on their heads. They plan to go back the same way they came, only totin more. Tandy is a midwife/nurse and Flower is on the church trial council where they try wrongdoers who have not yet fallen into white folks' court—wrongs like stealin from one another, doin a wife some ugliness, refusin to help a neighbor, gossipin to cause harm and all such as that.

I don't want to go to the island and now there's only a few days left. Flower is busy shakin down ashes in the stove, makin ready to roast sweet potatoes. Tandy is busy with her snuff stick and Mama is takin down the shell-framed picture of Jesus on the wall. I'm slowly settin the table for supper and grievin in my heart about Cecil. Seems like I lost all that was dear when he had to go the same time as Papa. There's a knock on the door and who should it be but Kojie, bringin a armload of presents—six cans a snuff, a tin of sweet biscuits and half of a baked ham. Tandy shows her brown teeth in a grateful smile. They ask him to stay for supper; after all, he brought it.

Kojie is wearin a tailor-made blue serge suit, nipped in at the waist and smoothly fitted like Evangelist Mountain Seeley's. His shirt is blue striped pongee, his tie is white silk.

"You look so refined—" Mama says, "like you goin some place mighty particular."

"Well, Mrs. James," he says, "I have come on a very daring and important mission."

We all stop what we're doin and listen to hear about the mission. Kojie points to his sleeve. "As you can see, I no longer wear a mourning band. I have completed the time of grieving for my dear departed wife. Mourning is past and now I must return to the fullness of living, as God would have me do."

"Amen," says Flower. "Some mens don't wear a band after the funeral atall—some mens got no honor." Tandy agrees. "Gawd gon bless you, son."

He smiles. "Ladies, if I'm too bold, please stop me."

"Not you—" Mama says, "you never too bold."

Kojie holds up five fingers. "I have a five-room, well-furnished house, with a cellar, front and back porches, a yard and running water inside; I also have a steady job and several irons in the fire getting hot."

"Uh-huh," says Tandy, "heat-um up, son."

"They gon hot," says Flower.

"Ladies, I have come prematurely, I repeat, *pre* . . ."

"He means too soon," I explain to the relatives.

Kojie goes on. "I risk your displeasure by asking for the hand of Miss Cora James. I would deem myself the luckiest man in the world if you, her family, and Miss James herself, of course, would allow me to make her my wife . . . to become Mrs. Kojie Anderson."

None of us can think of a thing to say, so he goes on. "Naturally, the protection of my abode is also offered to her mother, Mrs. William James. However I . . . er . . . hear she prefers the quiet of the country. But, as I say, my home is hers for visiting or staying purposes." Our silence makes him say more. "During the days of your husband's illness, I grew more than fond of your lovely daughter, though I fear to use the familiar word 'love' in the presence of sensitive ladies."

"Well, Kojie," Mama says, "you have paid my daughter the highest honor. But she's so young and. . . ."

Flower cuts in, "Sixteen is two years past the age a consent." Tandy shows concern. "But marry is serious. What you think, chile?"

"If Mama says yes, I'm willin."

Mama shakes her nead. "No, willin is not enough. I have to hear the word love; that's what your papa and I had."

"Mama, he didn't say it, so it's not proper for me."

Kojie drops to one knee like a church usher havin the collection plate blessed. "I love you, Miss Cora James."

Tandy pats her foot for joy. "He sure say it, chile! Now it's your turn, if you wanta say it back."

I notice that he does look fine, and it's all like a scene from a lovely pageant—the kinda thing Miss Rosalinda tried to put on. Suddenly I feel God in the room. I have been prayin for somethin to happen—some miracle, a way to keep from movin to the island—prayin so hard to God and Papa. And now here comes Kojie just as the last articles are bein packed, provin that God truly moves in a mysterious way His wonders to perform. It is hard to say it when you're not sure, but I do believe I'm beginnin to love him—right this very moment. It's not like lovin Cecil—it's higher than that, there's somethin holy about it—and I know God does not want me to leave this man.

"I love you, Kojie Anderson."

Mama looks pleased. There is solemn handshakin all around. Flower brings out her bottle of blackberry brandy and we each have a little to mark the moment. Kojie puts a ring on my finger.

In respect of our recent loss and Mama's immediate plans, we were engaged for three days and married by Reverend Mills with only relatives present. I had begged Mama to stay in town with us, but she really wanted to go. "Cora, it's best for a couple to start out alone. You have made a fine marriage, but always know that wherever I may be, there's another home, if you ever need it. Daughter, you have done more than well. Talk about prosperity, you have fallen inta a tub of butter—and with a Christian."

Nine

The front of our house looks like a face. The scrollwork design over the door seems a moustached mouth, and it has window eyes. The roof is the man's hair, parted down the center and stickin straight out at the sides. My husband grips my arm, not even lettin go while he searches his pockets for keys.

"Kojie, dear, are you afraid I'm gonna run off down the road?" There are beads of sweat on his forehead. He doesn't let go of my arm until he lifts me over the doorsill.

A lovely painting is on our wall, an Indian paddling a canoe in the moonlight, a lovely scene in bright colors on black velvet. It glows in the dark, so lovely in its gold, oval frame.

"What a strik*ing* scene," I say, carefully using my *ing* ending because I do want to live up to Kojie's education and position in the community.

"That thing cost more than it shoulda," he says, "but the former Mrs. Anderson, like you, had a weakness for the arts.

She also, like you, was taken up with book reading and poems."

"Where are the books, dear?"

"Books are not for this evening, Mrs. Anderson. I gotta see bout some a this."

I feel sorta let down bein thought of as "some a this." At the same time I can't be too picky; he has given me more than I've ever had in life—a diamond engagement ring set in fourteen-carat gold, a weddin band and a five-room house. One day I'll remind him to keep up the perfect manners which made me regard him so very tenderly in the first place. But not yet.

"Mr. Anderson, dear, will you please step back outside and bring in my valise which you left on the porch?"

"I don't mind," he says, "but we're married and you're not to call me Mr. Anderson, or even Kojie—when we are alone. I want you to call me 'daddy' or 'sweet papa,' some kinda sugar name. But naturally, when you're speaking with outsiders you will say, 'my husband, Mr. Anderson, says thus and so'; I'll say, 'My wife, Mrs. Anderson, says this and that'." He holds my cheeks between his fingers. "Say it, baby, say Kojie-daddy. I want to hear that. Say it for me."

"Er . . . Kojie-daddy."

"That'll do for now. You'll sound better once you learn to express your full feelings." He brings my bag inside. He lights a kerosene lamp—such a lovely lamp with a flowered shade. He leads me through the house. "Sugar-thing, this is our bedroom set. It's genuine oak, so I've been told. The mattress is comfortable and the springs don't screech. You must wind that brass alarm clock every night and set it for six A.M., but not for the next two days, cause this is honeymoon time, and we're going to be making love." He pats my backside as he talks, but I keep remembering what Mama said about lettin him have his way. I make myself stand still for the pats, tryin to act married steada single. It's hard to stop bein single all of a sudden. Now he's talkin bout pork sausage. "Yes, indeed, every mornin I like a good breakfast—sausage, eggs and grits, with coffee and biscuits—cause custodian work at the jailhouse is demanding. A man needs something that sticks to his ribs." His hands are on my breasts; he gently pinches the end of each one. I smile. It would be rude to ask him to stop. He talks on, rubbin my stomach and reachin down further.

"Honey-love, once in a while I might ask you to switch my sausage to fried salt pork or smoked ham, just for a change-off. My back garden is full of pole beans, cabbage, collards and okra. Down cellar I have smoked meat hangin, so dinner kind of takes care of itself—just needs throwing together. Over there on the washstand is a pitcher and basin. First thing in the morning you fill that with hot water before you cook my sausage and things."

I'm standin in the middle of the floor, still wearin my new hat and the knitted purse is on my arm, while Kojie's hand is rubbin my private parts right through my best skirt. I'll have to teach him to do better. After all, Rosalinda said, "A woman must mold and shape a man anew."

"Kojie, dear heart, show me the rest of the house and let me rest my hat."

"Sure, baby, you can rest everything, right on down to the skin far as I'm concerned; but what did I tell you to call me?"

"Kojie-daddy."

"That's better."

He leads me into the parlor. "Sweetness," he says, "this is our horsehair furniture. A trustee at the jail sold it to me when his wife bought a set of over-stuffed, but this is better quality than the new kind. We'll keep this room closed off unless there's company, which won't happen often, cause too many niggers get on my nerves." He opens the door to a little room off the entry hall. "This is the catch-all. That's a pump organ but it doesn't work. The late Mrs. Anderson did her sewing and crochet in here; she liked to call it 'a retreat'."

"Yes, Kojie-daddy."

"Oh, you're learning fast, Sugar-tit. That's one a my secret, sweet names for you, cause you got such sweet looking little sit-up titties. Kojie-daddy going to find out if they sweet as they look."

Now we're in another room: a bathtub and toilet but no runn*ing* water. "Someday," he says, "when I can spell able, I'll put in plumbing pipes."

The kitchen is spotless: there's a cast-iron sink with a pump over it, a large cook-stove with a hot-water tank, beside it a huge box of wood and two scuttles of coal. The floor is bleached oak and there's a door right in the center. He leans down, opens the door and shows the steps lead*ing* to the dark cellar.

"Storage down there," he says. "Tins full of dried beans, rice, sugar and flour. Tins protect from rats,"

"Rats?"

"I set traps down there cause neighbor people keep chickens—they draw rats, y'know. But none's coming up here where Sugar-tit's with her Kojie-daddy."

He closes the door and locks it. "Baby, you have some of everything that a colored woman could want, and the best is yet to come."

I think of my poor father and how it's too late to give him garden vegetables, smoked meat and preserves. Kojie rubs my ribs. "Sugar-tit, let's get in our big bed."

I feel ashamed that I'm a little bit frightened. It's not even dark yet. I have never gone to bed before dark, except when I was a baby. "Er . . . Kojie-daddy, I . . . I'm hungry."

• • •

He's weary of this waiting, but he cannot, will not scold the girl during honeymoon time. She might be truly hungry. He well knows the signs of a woman running away from him, but after all, Cora is young enough to be the late Lilly's daughter. He remembers that he forgot to remove the dead wife's picture from its brass frame on the parlor table. He wonders if it made his new bride jealous. Sadly, he feels she is not jealous.

Things had gone downhill for him after Lilly's death. A few times his nature needs had sent him to a bawdy house, a different one each time. He never liked any of them, but it was better than approaching the church widows, grass or natural. They were all dead-set on getting married again and he hadn't wanted any of them for a wife. They were too old, stale, hardened, demanding and set in their ways. He recalls spending a shameful evening at a church sister's house, his pants finally off and his nature standing straight up and out while the old two-husbands-gone–bitch tried to wring future promises out of him. When he told her, nicely, that he wasn't yet ready for marriage because Lilly was still on his mind, she said, "Well, just keep her on your mind and jack-off."

Even that remark didn't cause his nature to fall, and there was the added shame of the moment when she handed him his trousers and said, "Better hop back in your pants before a cold draft gives you pneumonia of the balls." She slammed the door behind him before he got down the front path and out of the gate. He thought of that happening every time he saw the rude sister in church, wearing a starched uniform, quietly ushering people into pews on Sunday morning, looking too sanctified to say "damn", even if somebody was to haul off and hit her with a sledgehammer. He thought how few people know that a widow-woman can speak worse than a drunken sailor, if you get hemmed up in private with her. He is truly, gratefully glad to have an unspoiled, young girl-wife, even though it means teaching her everything, step by step.

I've called Kojie twice and he's still staring into space. There's a lot of wet newspaper around the ice in this box. I can't get any for the lemonade. I call him again. He unwraps the newspaper, chips off a few pieces for my glass.

"Baby doll, always keep my ice wrapped in paper so it won't melt away too fast. Also remember to look at your icepan underneath the box or it'll run over and ruin my floorboards. Also keep your shelves washed down so my box doesn't get a rank smell. If your ice runs out, keep the doors open to prevent mold, until I buy a new piece."

"Yes, Kojie-daddy." I take a long time over my bread, butter and cold ham, with small bites and long chews. He isn't hungry and drums on the table with his fingers until I'm through.

"Throw your burnable garbage in that can over there. I have a stone burn-pit out back where you can burn the burnables at the end of each day. Your cans and bottles go in the crokersack on the back porch. When it's full, we sell it to the bottle man—when I'm at home. Now, Sweetness, when you empty your garbage, always scrub your pail, line it with paper so it'll be clean and handy by the sink. One more thing—a surprise." He takes my hand and leads me out to the dimness of the backyard, down a narrow brick path to the outhouse. He opens the door and shows a nice clean toilet and seat. He pulls a chain. There's a rumbling sound; a flood of water tumbles into the toilet and reels round and round and out of sight through a deep, dark hole.

"That's my flush toilet. No hole in the ground for us. Nights we do our business in the house in the china commode, all private; then, next day, you empty it out here where it will not offend. Once a week give this bowl a good scrub with ashes, and always keep the bedroom jars sparklin. The first Mrs. Anderson kept a bit of cold water in the bottom of the jars so no icky sticks to it. Excuse me, I won't mention her again."

"That's all right," I say. "I'm not jealous."

He sighs.

It is bedtime. She undresses in the bathroom-to-be and puts on the pretty pink nightgown fashioned by Miss Rosalinda. The top is crocheted in ecru thread, with satin ribbon laced through and tied in a bow. She slips on her matching bedroom slippers with pom-poms. Her blue cotton kimona, a gift from Etta, ties to one side and is delicately stamped with butterflies and violets. She enters the bedroom trying to look like the Rosalinda of Rabbit Ears Minstrel, about to appeal for justice from Chief Boo-roo. She holds her head high, like Queen Titania in Shakespeare's *Dream*.

"Sugar-tit," he says, "we're not going to the President's Inauguration Ball."

He is in bed, propped up on two pillows, wearing a shortsleeved nightshirt. He whistles his admiration. "Just look what the good Lord done sent me. Walk for me, baby, walk round in all that ribbon. Tip it for daddy, tip it over there, then tip it back to me. Lord, if only the jailhouse gang could see me now!" He is happy.

She walks back and forth until he calls a halt. "Now, take off the pretties." She removes the robe.

"Baby, you too young to know, but you not suppose to keep your gown on. Don't want to ruin such pretty night-clothes. Take it off and hop in by your Kojie-daddy."

She strips naked and stands frozen to the spot. He enjoys the sight of her lean, tan body and assures her, "Baby, all you don't know, Kojie-daddy is going to teach you." He gets out of bed, his private part bobbing up and down under the long nightshirt. She pretends not to notice. He slips the shirt off. "Now, we're both naked together." He takes her to bed.

"Mr. Anderson . . . er . . . Kojie-daddy, please blow out the lamplight."

"Blessum bones, don't be scared. Daddy just wants to look at the liddie puddie cat down there." He props her knees up, gently pushes her legs apart, and holds the lamp closer.

"Kojie, please don't do that. It makes me ashamed."

"That's cause you sweet and innocent. Daddy gonna name down there 'pink candy'. Will you always keep the pink candy just for daddy?"

She closes her eyes and whispers, "Yes."

He touches her breasts, then feels his way back down to below, touching and touching, asking a flood of questions, while lamplight reveals the crevices and curves of her body.

"You ever let anybody touch it before me?"

"No."

"Ever show it to anybody?"

"Oh, no."

"Any little boys ever played with down there?"

"No."

"Any men?"

"No."

"You mean to tell me nobody ever asked you for any? Didn't that little black nigga name Cecil beg you for a little bit?"

"Of course not."

"Well, did you ever do anything unnatural?"

"What do you mean?"

"Sometimes girls go with each other. They rub against this part right here, or use the mouth."

"Please blow out the lamp. Let it be dark."

"Blessums liddie bones, you so shy." He examines her buttocks. "If girls have a baby it leaves welp marks on the belly and thighs."

"I've never had a baby."

"Can see that—you smooth as silk."

Lamplight flickers against his face as he pours out a proud store of first, second and thirdhand knowledge on new ears. "Sometimes even men go with each other in a unnatural way. They go with each other in this part here instead of that part there. They do that sometimes at the jailhouse." She flinches.

"Your fingernail hurts."

"Excuse daddy. That's for men who are called sissy. But your daddy ain't no kinda sissy. He's gonna go with this baby right inside a the pink candy. Kojie-daddy is all man."

He replaces the lamp on the night table, then hands her a large towel. "Put this underneath you so we don't soil our bed."

She obeys.

The instructions go on. "If you've been a good little girlie, this is gonna hurt some, and I'm beggin your pardon in front." Now he is gasping and groping, pushing against the wrong place, then finding the right one. It does hurt, from hips to knees. He sucks at a spot on her chest.

"Baby, that's a love bite, by tomorrow you gonna have a love-cherry mark . . . to remind you that your cute little tail is all mine."

She clenches her teeth together and holds onto the head of the bed, tightening her stomach to keep breath from being cut off.

"No, no, baby," he gasps in her ear. "Ease up, relax, hold me, talk. *Say* somethin!"

"I . . . I'm . . . sorry . . . I really don't know what to say."

"Say it's good to you—keep sayin it, sayin it, be enjoyin yourself."

She notices he has dropped his *ing* endings. Trembling from head to foot, she makes herself say it over and over, trying to say it well. "It's good, Kojie-daddy, it's good, it's good, it's good. . . ."

He goes wild with happiness, raising his head and calling out to the heavens, "Great-Gawd-a-mighty! Great balls-a-fire! Snow on the mountain-top! Shit! Fukkit, fukkit, fukkit! Whoo! Don'tcha worry, daddy ain gon ever stop! Aw, you pretty, wild-ass, candy-pussy, bitch!" He goes on and on making words and motion one.

She is soaked in his perspiration; the two bodies make suction noises. She moves and moves, determined to keep the marriage vow, saying it over in her mind—"*love and obey, love and obey, love and*"—suddenly she knows that her pain and shame is only God's just punishment for coveting Kojie Anderson's house and pay envelope, for using him to keep from going to Edisto Island. She should never have coveted a neighbor's goods, and now justice is being done and she is on her way to dyin. But just before her heart reaches the bursting point she is saved.

He gives a loud whoop, clutches the hair of her head with both hands, and loses all reason.

"Whoo, whoo, whoo, Lawd-Lawdy, woman whatcha doin to poor me! Look out, here I come!" He collapses the whole weight of his body on hers. "Yes, indeedy, indeedy, indeedy, you gon kill your poor daddy. Gawd knows it! They say a young woman can kill a older man. Oh, darlin, baby, I think I musta knocked you up. Yesiree, if that didn't do it, I don't know what will." When the gasping is done, he rolls her over and worriedly glances at the towel. "Woman, you sure had me fooled. Thought you was a virgin. Told me nobody been at it. Why you tell me that?" She moves away from his hand prodding her shoulder for an answer; warm wetness pours from her. His tone changes. "Yeah, blessums bones, there tis—that's daddy's little virgin. Was a virgin but her's a little woman now." He kisses her elbow and gives her backside an approving pat. "Now we gon rest ourselves so we can get us a little mo after a while. Second time won't hurt, but we gotta take it slow cause daddy can't keep up that fast stuff. Next time gonna be slow and easy like ole married folk."

The night wears on and time drags on the lines of his heartfelt song: "Sweet Christ! Great balls a fiery snow-water!" Long later, in the middle of rest from celebration, he falls asleep.

Her name is Mrs. Kojie Anderson, and her determination is to make the best of what she has, keeping herself only unto her husband for as long as they both shall live, to be a good wife, keep a neat house, and try to please him in every way. She gets up, puts on the butterfly robe and carries the lamp from room to room. She stops in front of the picture of Kojie's dear departed, wondering what secrets Lilly carried to the grave. She smiles from her frame.

Daylight streaks the sky, the first rooster crows. She thinks of her mother and the old lady twins; they are awake on Edisto Island. She wonders how many women know what she now knows, and never tell. Well, she won't tell, either. She'll make the fire, heat water, bathe and dress; then she'll cook sausage, grits and coffee before her husband awakes.

Ten

After a year of marriage she is still trying to make the best of things, daily reminding herself that she is more fortunate than many other women. The world outside of her father's house is a strange place. After each morning's work she rests in the yard, under the fig tree. She is kin to nothing and hardly knows herself these days. Some nights it seems as if she is standing aside in a corner of the bedroom, watching Kojie and Cora Anderson struggling through their evening connections. She listens to his sounds and cries, hearing her own voice trying to match them. Her body is there in the bed with him, but she is gone—to the corner of the room, high up near the ceiling.

She finds no right or wrong to being married, no good or bad—but there's such a constant doing and doing. There is a crucifix on the bedroom wall; over Kojie's shoulder she can see it by moonlight or sunshine, whenever they are "makin little love". She can see Jesus with her eyes open or closed.

His head hangs down, thorns bite into his temples, blood drops stream, his feet are neatly crossed and pinned down with a spike—blood drops on his instep and a flow of blood drips from his side. "Poor fella, what a shame."

She learns to pass through the ritual of love by thinking of what to cook the next day, or planning chores, or picturing how to lay out a piece of yard goods to make a new dress. Daytime, tired of thinking, she goes back to doing the many married things she has learned: crocheting edges on washcloths and towels, turning Kojie's worn shirt collars, airing bedsheets in the sun, putting down bread to rise, sweep-washing the porches with broom, sand and water, tending the garden, and figuring new ways to chip some money off the grocery bill so she can pocket a secret dollar for herself now and then. Kojie never hands over money unless he knows exactly what it is for. He also checks the grocery list. She buys three-fourths pound of beef and charges it as a pound. When dress goods are a dollar a yard, she marks it up to one-fifty. Soon she feels right about doing it, when she finds out that other women do the same—sort of a woman's private, good-natured joke, something to chuckle to herself about whenever a husband is unpleasant in some way or other.

She keeps her secret money in a Mason jar, under a floorboard, beneath the bed. It pleases her to think of silver dollars and dollar bills in her jar. Of course, if he ever becomes ill, she plans to give it all back to him, if it comes to that. But she knows it won't. She feels the money is truly hers because she has worked hard to earn every dime.

Some afternoons, it is her pleasure to sit at the front window, peeping through lace curtains, hoping to see someone pass on the street, to hear trees whispering to the wind, or the thunder of a coming rainstorm, or just to palmetto-fan the hours away until high noon heat is over.

Today she watches overtime. The colored chain gang is repairing curbstone. The street is alive with convicts wearing black-and-white–striped suits and skullcaps. Each man is linked to the next by a length of heavy steel chain. Large cannonballs are fastened to the chain to keep men from running away. They had arrived in a mule-drawn wagon, surrounded by picks, shovels, sledgehammers, and all sorts of rattling metal equipment. Another wagon contains cobblestone, cement, sand, tar and other street-repairing necessities. Two armed white guards sit high on the wagons to oversee the prisoners as they hammer and pickaxe the curb. The men sing songs of sadness and smothered anger, their voices timbred by hard work and mean living. Words to their music tell about "Leavin this hard row", and "Further on down the line", and "When I die who gonna haul this stone", and "My baby done left for New Orleans", and one-word songs full of feeling, even when the word is just a man's name. "Hey, Buster . . . Yeah, Buster . . . Well, now, Buster." The song troubles the heart. Overseer yells, "All right, boys, change that tune." They switch to ricky-ticky time: "Had me a gal name Eliza, what did I do but surpriza." Behind the curtain, Cora pats time with one foot and enjoys them almost as much as Jenkins' Orphan Band.

The sun climbs higher. They take off their striped shirts and work naked to the waist, gleaming wet with sweat. Once in a while a man raises his hand for permission to dip drinking water from a barrel, or go inside of a small tent to somehow see to other needs. She enjoys watching their bodies move in work rhythm, hearing the belltones of picks ringing against concrete. The overseer lazily smokes his pipe and calls orders. She counts twenty men on the team, different sizes and ages. An older man, dizzy from the heat, staggers and falls against the water barrel, knocking it over. After sitting him under a shade tree, the men ruefully watch their drinking supply soak into dry, thirsty earth.

The overseer knocks on the front door. She enjoys the excitement of answering and seeming surprised. The overseer does not know how to start. She is too young for "Aunty", too old for "sissie", and it's not fitting for him to call a nigra "Ma'am" or "Mrs." He decides to show respect and call her nothing.

"Afternoon. We got Charleston City prisoners out here makin a better-lookin street for you. They outta drinking water. Would you give em a couple a pails? It's awful hot today."

"Of course."

The prisoners look to the overseer, all yearning to be unchained long enough to fetch water. The overseer crosses the street and unlocks one man who is allowed to follow her into the house, carrying two pails. The overseer stands gun-guard on the porch.

The prisoner pumps water at the sink. He turns his head a certain way and the window light shines on—her father!—just like him, but darker, more Cecil. She notices how slowly he pumps, trying to stretch his few unchained moments.

"All the mens thank you, Ma'am."

"They're entirely welcome."

He is a big man, gentle in manner, moving cautiously as if he fears to startle her, carefully, so not to splash water on the floor. He cannot be more than twenty-three, eyes cloudy brown. She wonders what he has done to become a convict. He knows she wonders like all outsiders.

"I'm servin time for not havin a job or a place to stay. They call it vagrancy."

"I'm sorry." She blushes because he seems far too nice to be wearing a convict suit.

"I don't wantcha to think I harmed anybody."

"How much longer must you serve?"

"Six months; hope it's all city work. Time drags slower on a cotton farm."

The guard calls from the porch. "Ready!"

He starts out with the water, and she calls him back, "Wait a minute, Mr.—?"

"Sonny, I'm call Sonny."

"Wait, Mr. Sonny." She opens the kitchen safe and brings out one of two pies made that morning.

"It's sweet potato and enough for all to have a small piece."

Sonny nods, too surprised and pleased to speak. She follows behind him carrying the pie, waits on the porch while he delivers the water and returns for the gift. Some of the men tip their skullcaps in gratitude.

"You can keep the tin, Mr. Sonny."

"Thank you, Ma'am."

His smile goes with his name and she is wishing she had given both pies. Kojie turns the corner and approaches the front gate. Sonny leaves and passes him. "Scuse me, Sir."

She is sorry that Mr. Sonny's shirt is so broadly striped and sweaty with road dirt. Suddenly all of the prisoners seem to look tougher and very guilty. The overseer calls from across the road. "Hey there, that you, Kojie?"

"Yessir, Mr. Grady."

"That your little woman?"

"Yessir, my wife."

"Helped us out when we lost our water."

"Thank the Lord we could help." He hisses to her under his breath as he continues to smile. "Bitch, get back in the house and stay there." He strolls back to the gate. "Anything more I can do for you, Mr. Grady?"

"No, Kojie, we're goin on over to emergency duty on Calhoun Street."

He laughs as if Grady has said something amusing. "Well, if you need anything else, sir, that's what I'm here for." The chain gang divides the pie and exchange smug looks. They know Kojie is hot about the pie, water, overseer—and blind jealous of his pretty, young wife. They know that Grady and the other guard are not wise to the fact that the man behind the gate is mad enough to choke an alligator. When they start loading the wagons, one prisoner starts up a song.

> Cause I'm tormented with the flame
> Cause I'm tormented with the flame
> Stick your finger in the water
> Come and cool my tongue
> Cause I'm tormented with the flame

Cora is angry, too. "How dare you call me a bad name? My name is Cora James and my determination is to be respected!"

"Your name is Anderson, bitch!" Kojie strides through the house pulling down shades and closing inside shutters. He scolds in whispers. "Woman, you low-rate me before the scum a the earth, paradin your ass in fronta murderers and rapists. Them men ain't had none for months, maybe years—and you fannin it in their faces. You what they call a cockteaser. They don't want piece a no pie—they want piece a you! If each and every one of em had come in and jumped you one at a time, I couldn't defend you in court cause you teased em—opened the door and invited em into your husband's house while he was away. Convicts laughin cause they see how easy it'd be to get in my stall, take what's mine!"

"Dirty mouth, stop, stop it!"

"You a married woman, you are Mrs. Anderson. I hold a position in this city and you holdin me up for a joke!"

She covers her ears against insults and pours out her own held-back thoughts. "I'm sick a hearin how important you are. You never fooled my father with your fine airs. What in hell happens to your *ing* endings when you come in this door? You're a bossy, nasty-mouthed, sonofabitch!"

He slaps her and hairpins go flying. She is more angry than hurt, and taunts him further. "Tell me, did you beat poor Lilly to death? Or did you just work and ride her into an early grave? Nasty thing, ridin on me every night like I'm a goddam railroad train!"

He runs to a window to see if there are convicts, guards, or passersby. He fumbles with a shutter latch: the shade falls to the floor. But, no, they are gone—there's only a distant veil of road dust from the departing wagons. She tries to run into the almost-finished bathroom and shut the door, but he grabs an arm and half drags her back to the kitchen.

"Hard as I work and good as I been to you, you hold me up to public scorn? You ain't had but one damn pair a shoes when I married you!"

She squirms under his hand, tries to get away while talking back. "Well, now I got three and you welcome to take your two pair back!"

He grabs an agate pot lid and thrusts it in her hands. "Hold that so you don't scream. *Hold* it!" She clasps the pot lid, thinks there must be some magic relief or protection in it, some new thing she has never heard about. Perhaps a pot lid brings light to this situation. He forces her to her knees as she clings to the lid. She thinks of the Sunday School picture "The Rock of Ages"—a young woman grasping a cross rising out of a small rock in the midst of a dark ocean storm as she is about to be dashed into the sea. So she clings to the pot lid. Kojie hits her with his open hand, about the shoulders, on her back, avoiding places that show. Tears roll down her cheeks.

"Common-actin bitch, disrespectin your husband for the world to see!"

Profanities to match his rise to her lips, but she smothers them back for fear he will hit harder. Instead she turns into the tuck-tail dog. "Kojie, please, have mercy." She drops the pot cover to the floor where it whirls and spins before clanging to a stop. The power behind his blows is gone and she thinks the lid has reminded him that she can take no more.

"Cora, don't make me kill you! How come you not making a baby yet? Why you use to run off to the battery with that nigga, Cecil? Why you smilin at a sweaty coon convict like you never look at me? Why is a nigga woman so loose?" He wipes away tears of rage. She bathes her face at the sink and daydreams wild, terrible visions of pomegranates, blood and murder. She thinks of telling Reverend Mills and the congregation, telling them just as Kojie is about to take up collection, of telling his boss, of running away to her mother on Edisto, running away to Papa's cousin in New York. She decides to put more money in her Mason jar and do more thinking. Run—stay—what? Her head is full of pictures.

That night she sleeps on the floor in the parlor and he knows better than to touch her. In the morning he begs humble pardon. "Cora, forgive me, I promise never to raise my hand to you again."

She studies his face to see if he is crazy. "Kojie, why the pot cover?"

"It was something I saw my father do to my mother . . . that's all."

"Did you do this to Lilly?"

"No, I never hit her cause, well, I didn't too much care. But I care about you till it's drivin me crazy. I love you. Please don't hold this against me. Let's make out like it didn't happen. We can start again from the first; please, I'm beggin."

Her mouth speaks forgiveness but her heart will not. He

hurries home from work every night, bringing peace offerings—a box of chocolates, six yards of beaded lace. She thinks of something her father once said about keeping a part of yourself for yourself. She also remembers an unkept promise. One morning she walks away from her chores and goes down to the old slave market to whisper the words in his memory. "Slave Market, you've had all of me that you're gonna get. I ain't no slave. The rest of me belongs to me."

She returned home to water the garden and plan the future. Her mother will not approve of what she is going to do, the church will not—certainly not Kojie. The island women will hang their heads in shame, but on and on she plans to leave her husband. Every week there is a little more money in the jar. She puts up many new shelves of preserves, makes brandied fruitcakes for his Christmas, cleans the house until it shines, weeds the yard and irons all of his shirts. She does not want anyone to say she left his home in poor condition.

Eleven

Cora shifts the hatbox and valise as she shows an elderly man a scrap of paper. "Mister, can you tell me where to find this number?" He examines the address, purses his lips to show deep thought and great knowledge.

"Walk a few blocks thattaway, then follow the numbers on this side a the street."

"Do you know Mrs. Estelle Tobey?"

"No, daughter, this New Yawk. Nobody knows anybody else less they been knowin em all along—this New Yawk."

She follows the numbers and at last stands in front of 310, an apartment building which is a picture of old, decaying splendor. Two stone lions guard each side of the entrance. A stout brown woman with shiny, straightened hair sits on the stoop reading a newspaper.

"Lady, do you know Mrs. Estelle Tobey?"

"What you want with her?"

"She's my father's cousin."

"Look in the mailbox for names."

"Lady, I'm just up from South Carolina. She was to meet me at the station."

"Mmmmm, best look in the box. Big apartments here; lotsa roomers, lotsa names."

"Where are the boxes?"

"Down the hall, underneath the steps."

"There's no light back there."

The lady screams up toward the sky. "You, boy! You hear me? I'm callin you!"

A lean, lanky child sticks his head out of a window one flight up. "Yes'm."

"What you doin?"

"Polishin my shoes and ironin me a shirt fore I take a bath."

"Boy, you gonna wash all the goody offa you. Is such a thing as bein too clean. Throw down the young lady some matches so she can see a mailbox."

Cora smiles gratefully, but now the woman is humming to herself, eyes closed.

"Look out, lady!" He tosses the box at Cora's feet.

"Thank you. What's your name?"

The boy hangs further out the window. "It's Chalk, that's what." His mother says, "When he was a baby we called him 'Chalklit Drop', then later 'Chalklit', now it's cut to Chalk. But his name is Alexander Roxbury the Second, after his grandfather."

"Thanks for your kindness, Mrs. Roxbury."

"Wasn't nothin."

Behind the steps, she lights a match. A message is printed across the wall in red crayon—"Jerry loves Vilets pussy". A cat scurries across her foot, leaps through a door leading down to the courtyard, and the match goes out.

"Lady?" It's Mrs. Roxbury. "I mind my business, but

since you just come up here . . . well, Mrs. Tobey lives three flights up, in the front."

Estelle Tobey is adding onions and cayenne pepper to a huge pot of pig feet, ears, chittlins and snouts. Sugar, her thirteen-year-old daughter, is dicing potatoes into a stoneware crock. All six burners on the big gas range are lit, cooking peas and rice, collard greens and fried chicken. Cora's knock sends Estelle into a state of alarm.

"They better not be comin early! The party's for eight thirty—who's comin early?"

She sweeps her long straggling hair atop her head and fastens it with a tortoise shell hairpin as she grumbles her way to the door.

"Who's there?"

"Cora Anderson."

"Bless Gawd! Come in, darlin. Sugar, come meet your cousin! Sugar went to the station yesterday."

"I had to leave a day late. Kojie took time off and I couldn't pack."

"But you got away! I hope you didn't tell too many people where you can be found."

"None atall, except a letter to Mama, and she knows how to keep a secret."

They view her from all sides, admire the well-cut traveling suit, marveling over her dark brown hair and hazel eyes.

"Sugar, just look at that coffee-and-cream complexion. Ain't she pretty?"

"Yes, Ma'am. I'm proud to have us a cousin."

"Cora, Sugar's name is Ophelia, but I call her Sugar cause she's so sweet with her little, round, plump self. She gets nothin but A in her school work and can read all kindsa books—geography, fairy tales, anything you can name."

"Oh, Sugar, I'm also glad to be your cousin. You made 'A', just think of that."

"I also made a apron in school, Cousin Cora." She dances up and down for joy. "You gonna share my room."

"But for now," Estelle says, "go back to the stove and see that our livelihood don't burn." She leads Cora to a large room off the parlor. "Gawd has blessed me with seven sizable rooms. Cousin, it's downright hard to find nice apartments if you Negro. Most of us livin up North like sardines packed in a can."

"Estelle, this place is beautiful—very comfortable and rich lookin."

"Indeed, darlin, I try to have me some a everything that stores be sellin. Up here is just as mean as down home, only with no colored and white signs, but it's the same system. However, when life shortchange me in one way, I make up for it in another." She explains the room. "Yall got the front, street view, but not much to see except jobless people hangin round waitin for somethin to happen. The top part of the mahogany chest is for you, the bottom is Sugar's cause she's shorter. The vanity dresser; yall each take half for things like comb and brush."

Cora sits on the edge of the bed, crying and murmuring thank you. "I'm not sad, I'm glad. I'll get a job right away, you'll see."

"Worry not, just rest from your trip . . . and wash up—I know the Jim Crow coach is still the first one behind the engine."

"Yes, Ma'am, blowin smoke and cinders in my face for two days . . . right gritty."

"We got a great big bathroom with a overhead shower; also you got a nice washbasin right here in the room. Life is about to treat you better."

"I feel fine . . . except for what I've done to Kojie. My conscience hurts."

"Fret not. When they hear you're gone, there'll be six women ready to walk in and help him forget. Man does not mourn a gone woman but for a short while."

"Hope that's true."

"It is. Sometime they got another one even while you still there."

Estelle's parlor wallpaper is abloom with brown and blue cabbage roses. Side drapes of purple velveteen hang at the double window, held back by tasselled ropes. Gas firelogs knock the chill off the room. There is a large, three-piece, overstuffed set of furniture—straight chair, rocking chair and davenport—complemented by carved, Chinese endtables with marble tops. A huge sideboard is laden with sparkling cut-glass baskets, bowls and vases, reflected in the beveled mirror. A dark-red Oriental rug covers the floor. In one corner of the room is a player piano with a revolving stool and a matching cabinet full of piano rolls; in another is a standing Victrola and record cabinet.

Cora and Estelle are dressed and ready to receive the evening company. Sugar pumps out "La Paloma" on the piano.

"Estelle, you don't have to explain a thing to me. It's your house and I know you wouldn't do anything wrong."

"But I want you to understand that even though what I'm doin is against the law . . ."

"It is?"

"In a way a speakin."

Sugar stops pumping. "It's also against Christian Science."

"Hush," Estelle warns. "Cora, we have never set foot in a

Science Church but I bought this book called *Science and Health with Key to the Scripture* through a frienda mine who is a follower. It cured my friend of a bad heart just by readin it, so I bought it for Sugar to read to me. I do believe it cured my indigestion. I also bought her Grimm's and Hans Christian Andersen fairy tales, because she is bookish and should have some in the house even though she is a member of the public library."

Cora is eager to show New Yorkers she knows a thing or two. "Even down home they're talkin bout Christian Science. It was started by a lady named Mary something-or-other—correct me if I'm wrong."

"That's right," says Estelle, "Mary Baker Eddy." Sugar throws her arms around her mother. "The only thing Mama does wrong is sell whiskey." Estelle corrects her. "Illegal, Sugar—not wrong, just illegal."

Cora feels doubtful. "Cousin Estelle, without bein overly critical . . . er . . . well, is it really Christian to sell whiskey?"

"In all truth, Science and Health and all other faith, except Catholic, is set against drinkin, but I never read anything about sellin it. I'm just as close to the Lord as the next one, but if he didn't want us to drink alcohol, he wouldn't let the grapes and grain ferment. God also knows people get tired of abuse and hard work, and how they might need a little toddy to lift their spirits. I believe that's why whiskey is called 'spirits'."

"There's some sense in that," agrees Cora. "He also knows we're Negroes and I'm sure he doesn't expect us to starve just cause there's no jobs. Didn't our folk work all through slavery for free? How are we to take up the slack, to catch up with alla those years when white folks made fortunes while we stood in rags?"

Estelle leaps to her feet and paces the room. "Talk! The

Bible says, 'till death do part', but didn't you have to leave that Kojie?"

"Yes, Ma'am, I did, because the Bible also says, 'If thine eye offend thee, pluck it out.' Also says, 'Shake the dust of that city from your feet'. What can a poor woman do?"

"Cousin, you mean what can a poor *Negro* woman do. Well, baby doll, this one gives quiet parties for better class railroad dinin-car waiters, Pullman porters and select theatrical people, particularly those from South Carolina. It's not what you do, but it's how. Lotta folks here in Harlem give whatcha call house-rent party. That's some common, wide-open notoriety. Not me. I don't take in strangers from off the street. When the trains roll into town, my special guests come here to where it's refined, to enjoy home cooking in a clean, elegant home—a respectable place to have a friendly drink and meet the quiet side a show business."

Cora helps her to tell it, trying hard to become a new, responsible person, a full-grown woman out to make her own way without fear. "That's right, any work can be dignified and done without roughness."

"And I only rent my sleep-over space to old Pullman reliables who want to *sleep*. Those lookin for bedtime capers must seek elsewhere. You lend me a hand helpin to serve and I'll see that you always walk with some money—that's till you find work you wanta do. You welcome to stay here and welcome to go when you want. That's sincere, comin from a true heart."

"Estelle, I like to learn, I'm used to hard work and I'm anxious to keep my mind off thinkin about . . . other things. What do I do? I'm ready to start."

"Well, it's like this. I answer the door. Every soul that enters must lay a half dolla: on the silver tray—I see to that part. I serve the food; you can wait table and collect for that.

Sugar will show you the ropes till ten o'clock. Not until she goes to bed does the poker playin start. After all, she's a child."

"How much is the food?"

"Sugar, darlin, shut off that pianola and tell prices."

"Yes, Mama. Pigfoot plate is fifty cents, fried chicken is sixty. Cold souse, chicken and pigfoot combination is seventy-five. Pie or pound cake is a quarter."

Cora repeats and gets it all right the first time. "Estelle, I'm so glad to be here and I pray God continues to prosper you."

"Oh, I am blessed. Lord lets me pay my bills and save some over to send Sugar down to Tuskeegee someday, so Jesus can see that she meets a young doctor or preacher to marry."

"For a woman alone you do very well."

A few men straggle in between eight-thirty and nine. The older ones, tired from the Chicago run into New York, make arrangements to sleep overnight before making the run back. They wear large, engraved, gold watches, with chains strung across their vests, and solemnly check the time every few minutes. In the kitchen, Cora fills cut-glass decanters from a demijohn filled with caramel colored hooch. Plump raisins and prunes soak in the bottom of the vessel.

"Estelle, why raisins and prunes?"

"To mellow it, cousin. If you don't doctor it some, that raw, cutthroat hooch is hard to get down. Prohibition is a pain. My top-class gentlemen bring in their own bottle-in-bond. I charge them a one dollar house fee just for ice, gingerale and highball setups."

The Pullman men look like prosperous politicians, graying at the temples, immaculate in white shirts and dark suits. Their shoes gleam from shoe-parlor shines, pants are sharply pressed. As they sit down they pull up their trousers slightly at the knee to preserve knife-sharp creases. They greet Cora with cavalier grace—"My pleasure."—"My compliments."—"How do you do, Mrs. Anderson?" They make a ritual of smoking good cigars, first examining the band, then biting off the end, moistening it with the tip of the tongue, passing the cigar under the nostrils to test aroma. One nods to Cora: "Madam, may I?"

"Please do. A good cigar gives a gentleman a certain air."

Cora catches on to what's around her. She is born anew, another person. She has deliberately added about five years to her age. She is girlish and motherly, pleasantly shy and ladylike. Estelle is pleased with her. The gentlemen are on their best behavior; they are inspired to show off their knowledge for her education and approval. They imitate wealthy whites who ride in private drawing rooms.

"Yes, dear lady, there is nothing like quality. Today I brought in a railroad vice-president by private parlor car. At the end of my run, he slipped me ten dollars and ten Havana cigars. I graciously accepted them, of course, but in my lockaway I keep my own brand, 'Legitimas', primed and hand rolled right *in* Cuba, not exported Cuban tobacco which has been machine-made into cigars in Europe, then labeled 'Havanas'." He lights up a prized Legitimas and gently blows a curl of smoke. "My friends, this is Vuelta Abajo leaf from Pinar del Rio—the very best tobacco in the world."

The others applaud as Cora brings in the setups of cracked ice, gingerale and Saratoga water to go with the government-sealed bottled-in-bond.

"Not being forward, Mrs. Anderson, but you lend such charm, grace and class to the evening."

"Thank you, Sir, so kind of you to say so."

Another Pullman man boasts: "Of course, right here, down in our own Grand Points, Louisiana, we grow what is called Perique. It beats many imports." He hands his glass to Cora. "If you please, a splash of Saratoga."

A portly senior in the rocking chair shakes his head in disapproval of vice-presidents in private parlor cars. "I, for one, would rather handle the more general public than bother with a bigwig with a car to himself. Have to wait on him hand and foot and he won't come up with one tip to equal a full passenger train—that's a fact."

"True," says the tobacco fancier, "but then there's the contact. Sometimes it takes pull with one of the big white boys to get your son or daughter into the best darkie college, cause they're up there presiding on the board of directors." There's general laughter and a chorus of, "So true, so true."

They dine around a large mission oak table, compliment the cooking, the linen and silver which has been partially supplied by Pullman Company.

"Mmmmm, this souse is better than the double sirloin steak we serve in the diner."

"Your linen reminds me of the joke about this darky who stupidly invited his railroad supervisor to dinner. The boss notices Pullman towels in the bath, Pullman linen on the table—even the silverware was familiar. He finally was moved to say, 'Boy what time do you think this damn train is going to pull out?'"

They laugh at the old joke as if it's never been told before. Estelle is busy taking in fifty-cent pieces and putting away canes and fedoras as the theatrical crowd arrives. They strut in calling out, "We're here with green money and it spends!" "Put it all on the table, the big time is here!" One fellow, with heavily pomaded hair, stands his whiskey bottle in the middle of the floor and dances around it.

"That's a quart a genuwine Canadian. Save your hooch and enjoy the best. Nappy's gonna good time this evenin!"

Cora enters with a tray. Nappy looks at her and falls in love—"Oh, my." They eat and joke and drink and smoke while Sugar pumps the pianola. They harmonize "Sweet

Adeline" and "In My Castle on the River Nile". They roll back the rug and teach Cora the Cakewalk while Sugar pumps "Georgia Camp Meeting". Nappy gives her a highball; she likes it.

"Uh-huh, so your name is Nappy. Well, well, so this is New York. I like it."

Estelle sends Sugar to bed. The elder statesmen let their cigars go out and they retire for "some shut-eye before tomorrow's run". The young men cover the table with a woolen blanket to keep money from clinking and make ready to play cards until dawn.

"Nappy, deal and cut the game for me; see that the house doesn't get shortchanged."

"Okay, Estelle, soon's I get better acquainted with your cousin."

"Remember, she's Mrs. Anderson."

"Where's Mr. Anderson?"

"Down South."

"Then that's his bad luck. Cora Anderson, I'm Napoleon Ramsey, and I been waitin to meet you alla my life."

"How come I heard somebody call you Bill?"

"Cause I'm a 'Elk'. This is my lodge." He points to the blue-and-gold emblem on his lapel: "Improved Benevolent Protective Order of Elks of the World". People call all Elks "Bill".

Cora is enjoying her maturity, the new power . . . feeling so free. "Oh, Nappy, you say it so proudly. I know it must be something very important."

"It's more than just important. I got put in jail for wearin my emblem. The white Elks don't like us wearin it, cause they say it was theirs first. They wouldn't let us be members, so we started our own and sent off for the copyright, which they never bothered to do. So now they makin a court case. Judge took away my pin and let me go. Soon's I got out I bought me another—and a ring, too." He holds up his hand showing the second blue-and-gold emblem.

"You must love your lodge very much."

"I do, but I'm mostly talkin cause I want you to know all there is to know bout me from when I was born, right up to now, so you'll know what you're gettin into."

He winds the phonograph and puts on a waltz record, "It's Three O'Clock in the Morning". "Care to struggle around the floor with me?"

"Nappy, I don't know how to dance."

"Let's stumble along together. A waltz is a good excuse to hold you in my arms." They glide around the cardtable, away from childhood and wifehood, around and around.

"Cora, you move well, light as a cloud."

"I've gained ten pounds in the past year."

"Good, just right; no sharp edges. Know anybody else up here besides Estelle?"

"Cecil Green is from down my way, but I don't have his address. Do you know him?"

"If I did, I wouldn't tell. I'm not gonna help you find another man."

The cardplayers grow impatient. "Nappy, you cuttin for the house?" He turns off the music. "Come on, Cora, I'll teach you how to be a card dealer. Such knowledge, along with your pretty face, might able you to take over the world. "Ready, soon as I get more setups."

In the kitchen, Estelle whispers a secret. "About that Cecil Green—the Charlestonians up here don't have anything to do with him. That fool has turned into a full-time West Indian, what they call 'monkey-chaser', followin full speed behind a troublemaker named Marcus Garvey."

"Who is Marcus Garvey?"

"A little black fella from down Jamaica. Bought hisself a

one-way ticket to New York and got off the boat promisin to take Negroes back to Africa."

"For what?"

"To be royalty—kings and queens, lords and ladies—and to own all of Africa. Cecil is one a his right hand men. One damn fool in the service of another."

"Cecil is very intelligent."

"He goes out ravin and talkin on street corners."

"Cecil was always sensible and proper."

"Cora, Kojie Anderson was one mistake; don't look for another. Go watch Nappy deal."

Twelve

The past couple of years have been good to me, but I'm ready to move on. Kinda tired of it always bein party time. Parties are work when you're dealin twenty-one and poker and "cuttin" for the house—and findin a million and one ways to hold off men who wanta get too close. That's not easy. The hardest one to deal with is Nappy. He has done so many favors for me, hopin that I'll give in and agree to live with him. Couldn't meet a finer person than Nappy, but I don't really wanta live illegal. Anyway, I never wanta live with anyone I don't love again. I also sure don't wanta get in a family way for a man that's not my husband. Since I didn't get that way with Kojie, I'm believin maybe I can't have children. Only reason I ever sleep with Nap is just pure gratitude. His middle name is "generosity". I don't mind makin love with him but I sure can't afford to get knocked up over it.

Nappy taught me how to dance the "Soft Shoe", to sing, to

play chords on the guitar, and do straight-girl for his comedy number. He's trying to ready me for an act so we can go on the road together. To me, that sounds like the first step to "shacking up". He even offered to give me top billin on our very first job: "Cora and Nappy—Southern Song Stylists."

"Nappy," I say, "I'm afraid I'll get pregnant and be in deep trouble. I don't know what to do to keep from having children."

"I do. Don't I take care of you?"

"Oh, must be somethin else to do besides that."

"If I withdraw aheada time, and we don't go again, there's no way for you to get caught."

"I'd rather know how to take care a myself."

"Trust me, honey. Even if we trip up, I ain't goin nowhere. We both would be in it together, till death do part, like legal."

I'm kinda scared a that part, too, but I can't say it and hurt his feelins. On accounta him teaching me cards, I have almost two hundred dollars saved. I love to deal twenty-one—some call it Blackjack—cause it's a fast turnover and I get a tip on both ends—one from the house and one from the winner—so I stay ahead, no matter how the game goes. I can now riffle my deck in the air like a magician, and some gamblers tip me just to shuffle a few extra times. The heaviest bet-money I've seen is on poker. Five-card stud, that's the true-blue gambler's game. Lotta party folks like to play five-card draw and even seven-card draw, then they want wild cards; all that does is make the game cute and they can lose just as hard, only it might take a little longer. When they play what's called "Spit in the Ocean," I turn up a wild card, then stick it right on my forehead and say, "There's your wild card, Negroes!" When the pot goes over twenty dollars, I stick the wild card on my bosom, if I'm wearin a lowcut dress. But when some big, dead-serious bankrolls show up and wanta play straight five-card stud, I don't cut the fool—they don't go for capers. I show respect, deal slow and call clear. I can roll dice, too, but I never play. All I do is deal and call. It's a business with me.

Trouble is, I'm gettin tired of it. It is really not my determination to be a card dealer. I'd like to do something of importance for my people. My sewin is now pretty good, but it tears me up to make a dress for five dollars when I can earn that on one hand a poker. Estelle doesn't wanta lose me but she thinks I'd enjoy trying a show biz tour with Nappy. She's for me, really in my corner.

"But, Estelle, what is the TOBA circuit?"

"Well, cousin, it stands for a company, but my show folk say it means 'Tough On Black Ass'. Course, that's just a wicked joke. But it is rough out there, hittin Jim Crow cities, sometimes stranded with no pay. Still in all, those in it can't quit. They say if you smell greasepaint you hooked on show business."

"Goin out with Nappy's gonna lead to shackin."

"I know, but it's rough bein alone. My husband walked out on me, but he sure knew how to sex. I miss that."

"I need to miss it, after Kojie. Now I worry myself to death bout gettin in the family way. I put Nappy off mosta the time, can't rest easy until I see my monthly visitor."

"You gotta give up somethin, or else a man's gonna find another woman for a outlet. It backs up on him, makes him restless."

"I wish I knew how to take care of myself."

"I hear of a doctor who will put a gold ring in your womb—'pessary' it's called. You take it out just before your monthly."

"I'd die of shame just askin for it. Isn't there some other way?"

"Some women use a little silk sponge soaked in petroleum. They tie a string on it."

"And do what?"

"Push the sponge up inside, and leave the string hangin out, so you can take it out later. Then douche."

"Estelle, that sounds awful. What do I say, 'Excuse me, dear, while I put in my sponge?'"

"No. When you see him gettin all hot and bothered, just go to the bathroom and quietly fix yourself."

"And that works a hundred percent?"

"For some it works; the others get caught."

"Oh."

"Vinegar and brown soap and water is used for double insurance—also can douche with somethin called 'javelle water'—that's clothes bleach."

"But there's still a chance of a slip?"

"Certainly, that's how these abortion folks make their money. I had me two of em. Maybe you best have the doctor put a gold pessary."

Every time I try out for another kinda job I come back to Estelle's. It's mean out there. I've been to employment agencies one after the other, without findin much. Go see bout a job and they say right to my face, "We don't get much call for colored," or look past me, sorta shamefaced.

Today Nappy goes with me into a restaurant on One Hundred Twenty-fifth Street called "Childs". They won't serve us. Just let us sit here while they serve whites who came in long after we did. Nappy is sore with me for walkin in after he said, "I don't know about this place." What is that supposed to mean? I thought he meant it wasn't fancy enough. We're sitting here long enough to grow to our seats.

Finally Nappy calls over somebody who looks like a manager. "Are you goin to serve us?" Stringy-haired monster looked tender-hearted, then said, "I'm afraid not, sir." He hurries off like he's scared we gonna beat him, and he well needs a stompin to straighten his mind out. We sure didn't enjoy makin a tuck-tail exit. Most diners stop dinin and stare. Some seem shocked at our nerve, the nicer ones look down in their plates as we pass.

Tell you bout this New York! If we go to a Broadway theater, we're always in the same row with other coloreds—Negroes—because they herd us all together in one section, with not a sign in sight; they just put us where they think we're supposed to be. Sugar took me out to Rockaway Beach and damn if they don't have a Negro section without a sign. And if you move out of that section you may get hit with a rock. After we leave the stupid restaurant, Nappy says, "I like down home better cause at least them signs are honest and straightforward about the thing."

"All cut outta the same cloth, Nappy. Two faced sons-abitches sleep with us on the q.t., then punish us in public."

I'm annoyed with him and he with me. I'm damn tired of the same situation day in and day out. He's goin on and on about it, explainin what I know and carryin it further than that.

"I don't wanta go where I'm not wanted," he says. "My own are plenty good enough for me."

I'd like to take off my shoe right here in front of Weissbecker Market and give him a heel whippin. "With or without signs," I say, "I don't go in restaurants or anyplace else to 'be with' white or any other kinda people."

"Cora, you're too scornful. If you had said you wanted a nice meal, I could have taken you to a fine Negro restaurant in a private home."

"I wasn't lookin for privacy. Some of your finest 'Negro

places' don't want us, either—they're caterin to the other side."

"It's a tough row to hoe out here, baby. Our people have to first make a livin and take care a the race problem later. You might not be ready to go out on road tour, cause it's a lot tougher than this. Lynchers now stringin up a nigga a week. I don't wanta be one of em."

"No, I won't go, so rest easy, your life'll be safe. No need to defend me." I'm mad as hell, so is he. People stare at us. I turn away and start walkin east, almost kill myself bolting in front of a horse-drawn wagon as I cross Seventh Avenue.

Nappy is right behind me. "All I mean, Cora, is we'd have to ride Jim Crow on the road, find colored places to eat and sleep, and when there are none, we sit up all night in the railroad station. We can't go to the lunch counter in the station except where they'll put it in a paper bag so you can take it outside. You not gonna get to go to the diner on the train, and in the theaters we work you can't buy an orchestra seat. Our people have to use the separate entrance and go up in the peanut gallery. That's how it is and it all started long time fore we were born. But we gotta somehow find a way to live, so why fall out with me?"

He's right. In one of Sugar's fairy tale books there's a story about a sleepin beauty, a princess who has a curse on her. She falls asleep and doesn't wake up for one hundred years. A prince kisses her and the curse is over. She wakes up happy and as beautiful as the day she went to sleep. Of course, he must be eighty years younger, but time stands still for love. It's not a bad idea to go to sleep for a hundred years and wake up when things get better. I've almost forgotten Nappy who still walks beside me. At Koch's department store I look at the window display of hand-drawn shirtwaists trimmed with Irish lace. "Well, Nappy, I think I'll go in and look around. You're right, we shouldn't be short with each other because of this everlastin race thing."

"It's hard on everybody, Cora."

"No hard feelins."

"But your eyes sendin a cold message."

"I'm sorry."

"Let's still look forward to the road tour."

"The 'tough on black ass' circuit?"

"It's hard to believe, but we have a lotta good times on the road—have a ball."

"I'll think about it."

"Damn that restaurant. I might drop by Saturday."

"Sure, Nappy, any time."

The shirtwaists are no big bargain. They looked better on the dummy in the window than lyin on the counter. Also annoys me to look at the labels: "Irish lace". That manager had sounded Irish; however, my new white friend, May, *is* Irish. The first white I've really known and she's a joy. Everybody who lives in Estelle's building is interestin company, but May is extra.

She's married to a Filipino named Apolinario Palmas. He is short, dark and very handsome. It's hard to imagine her mother refusin to meet a man with a name like that—seems like she'd at least be curious. He's not pure Filipino but is mixed with Chinese on his mother's side. May met him on a Chinese boat excursion to Atlantic Highlands, a place where people go to have picnics. He is a watchmaker and repairer, but does that on the side. His main job is cook in a Chop Suey joint. May invited Estelle to bring me down to their apartment and Apolinario made a fine supper for us. Imagine a woman havin the good sense to marry a cook. He used to be in the merchant marine and decided to jump ship and stay here without a permit, even though the Philippine Islands are under American supervision in a way and jumpin ship is against the law. People oughta be able to go ashore and stay ashore anyplace in the world. But I don't make the laws, and those that do, don't do it worth a damn.

Apolinario is also an expert gambler. He knows how to mark a Bicycle deck with his thumbnail while the game is in progress. It'll do you no good to break open a fresh deck because he'll mark em again while playing, and so light and easy that you can't see a dent with your naked eye. But he knows what everybody's holdin. Estelle won't allow him in our games. He says that if he was washed up on a desert island, with not a possession in the world, he could gather stones or coconuts, invent some kinda gamblin game and soon own everything on the island, just win it all away from the rest of the survivors—clothes, medicine, fresh water, or anything else they might have. May looks sad when he says such things.

"Apolinario, my love, you are not so cruel. Why sound so hard and ruthless?"

Soon I began to visit May without Estelle. We confide in each other. May is my first close friend-girl of any race—my closest friend since Papa died. Like him, she also knows how to look at matters and trace meanings and feelings down to the core, knows how to do it for everyone except herself. It hurts her to be disowned by her mother. May is plump and ordinary lookin and so sweet, without being sickenin and sugary. Apolinario is crazy about her. They live on the fourth floor rear and I believe they are the richest couple I've ever known—nice furniture, beautiful lamps and vases, so many unusual things fresh off the boat. And they have such friends—Chinese, Filipino, Cuban, African, West Indian—seamen from all over the world. Men who left home to labor their way around the world. They know how to play tiles, mah-jong, Chinese lottery, twenty-one. They work hard and bet the races, the numbers—doin everything they can to get hold a some money. And they are good to their women.

The Palmas' apartment is a wonderland—beaded curtains at the doorways, windbells hangin in the kitchen and blue-and-white china canisters with tall vinegar-and-oil bottles, blue-and-white gingham curtains, flowered linoleum floor rugs, incense burners, a Chinese tea set with a gold-and-white dragon on each piece. Framed pictures of Filipino ladies, Apolinario's mother and sisters wearin transparent, puffed sleeves, seated on the front porch of a lovely place called Samar, Philippines.

"Apolinario," I said. "Why did you leave paradise?"

"To make some money."

One day May showed me a pack of letters tied together with blue ribbon. They were from her mother, looking like love letters but reading like pomegranate nightmares.

> Hello May . . . Still married to that full-a-pee-pee? A white woman that lays on her back for the pleasure of a oriental is a hore at heart. She lives in mortal sin and shall skip purgatory to live forever in eternal hell fire. Every day I burn a candle for your lost soul. Don't come near me until you turn your back on the sin you call love. You wallow in filth like a pig. If you have a child for this half man, it will be monster.
>
> One who once was yr mother.

"Why do you keep this?" I asked her.

"It is my mother." She cries and cries. "I sometimes do miss my own people. Apolinario is gone six days a week—all day until nightfall, up to his elbows in sliced onions. He doesn't want me to go out to work because that would make our situation look even worse. I clean and clean the house, remembering. . . . I guess I still love my mother, no matter what. Sometimes I miss Irish things. Everyone has *people,* Cora, not just you and Apolinario."

"Forget that woman," I say. "May Palmas, she is not related to you. It's all a big mistake. Sometimes we're related to others than the blood kin. Those closest to me are not blood."

"I know, but I hurt inside because she hates me so. When I am in Apolinario's arms her words write themselves across my closed eyelids. I need her forgiveness. She is this way because I married outside of the Irish—way outside."

"Ask the priest what to do. You're a Catholic."

"And so is Apolinario. The priest advises me to make peace with my mother. He says there must be some reason why God made us all different and wants to keep us each to our own. My poor mother; if she had ever been loved as I am, she could not write such a letter."

I remember thinkin, we all need to be loved that way; ask me. But most times we talk about makin dresses and trimmin hats. We went shoppin together to the lisle stockin sale, then spent what we saved on something else, then went to her house and drank liquor and sugar water the way the Haitians do. We play the Gramophone and danced to a popular record. There's a sort of West Indian Calypso called "The West Indian Blues":

When I die don't bury me
Don't call no undertaker
Throw me body in the Harlem River
And I'll float back to Jamaica

I come out of Koch's department store carrying the Irish shirtwaist for May. I feel good. It's the first present I've ever bought for someone white. The softly turned-back lace collar, mother-of-pearl buttons, fine tucks and pleats will go well with her pretty complexion and swept up goldy-brown hair. Oh, good Lord, I wish every white person in the world would turn into May Palmas!

Damn, now I'm walkin in the wrong direction, going further uptown on Lenox Avenue. I could take the open-air trolley, but it never hurts to know a city, or to walk off feelins bout what happened in Child's Restaurant and the silly argument with poor, dear Nappy. I'll just walk until I ease my mind, then turn back at One Hundred Thirty-fifth Street. Two girls are playing jump rope. They sing out a rhyme as they see how long they can skip without missing. They sing Calypso, like the rest of Harlem.

> All you children stand on line
> Get your tickets for The Black Star Line
> How many? And a-one, and a-two, and a-three . . .

A slender black man is passing by; he stops and grabs the rope. "You children are laughing at yourselves, making fun of what you don't understand, denying yourself, ridiculing your race." They snatch at the rope. "Let go, Mista!" He turns and I see his face—the mouth puckered into a jagged scar on one side.

"Cecil, is that you?"

"Cora James!"

"Anderson."

"The last time I saw you. . . ."

"We were in trouble."

"Well, we kept going in opposite directions until . . . we meet again."

She feels ill at ease because of what she has heard about

him following Garvey, but wants to know him again, to invite him over to visit—but maybe Estelle would not like it. It's fine to be next to him, walking further uptown together.

"Where are you headed, Cora?"

"Just walkin. Where are you goin?"

"To an appointment, but it can wait."

Recalling how he scolded the rope jumpers, she wonders if he's on his way to meet Marcus Garvey. Perhaps Estelle has been shortsighted in the summing up of Garvey—she hopes so. It is hard to read Cecil's face, to figure out what the years have done for or against him. She picks after information. "And what are you doin these days?"

"Working hard for an organization, a sort of all-round man for . . . for the UNIA—that's the United Negro Improvement Association."

Since he has not mentioned Garvey, she decides to be cautious. "It sounds familiar; I think I've heard of it before. Cecil, you look so well. Life must be treatin you kindly."

"At the moment, yes. When I first came, I washed dishes at a hash-house. Then there was a year—fourth cook on a passenger ship to Canada. I've learned a lot about living." He waits for her to tell what she is doing. He's heard stories about her working in an after-hour buffet flat called "Estell's". They say she's a card dealer, sells whiskey and hangs out with blackface comedians, buckdancers, Pullman porters and all sorts of characters. The hardest to understand is that her best friend is a white woman who lives with an Oriental, and how Cora is mixed up with attending parties where Chinese, Cubans and other aliens socialize. He always gave his informants terse replies: "I'm sure she'll find the right path in due time." Then there was that other story from down home—how she had robbed Kojie of money and then ran away from him after becoming his wife. It all sounded more like his Aunt Looli than Cora James—Anderson. So many times he had wanted to go and see her, remembering first love, but better judgement kept him away. He could not introduce her to Garvey, or any of the UNIA members. They had left loose living behind them, left white folks behind them, and now worked day and night for the unification of the Negroes of the world. They wake up glad while others mourn, they sing no blues; they are sober while others are drunk; they read, study and prepare themselves for a better earth while others shake tambourines for the heaven to come. Others dance their way to hell, singing and begging for white folks' approval. Well, for him, Garvey has come.

He looks down at the top of her head; the perky black straw hat shines in the sun. She returns his glance. Wonder of wonders, her face has not been touched by the life she lives. Perhaps people lie about her, out of jealousy. Garvey endures that kind of persecution.

"Cora, we are now passing Harlem Hospital."

"It's a fine building. My Cousin Estelle says colored people. . . ."

"Negroes," he corrects.

"Yes, Estelle says Negroes should not go in there as patients because they give us, the ones they don't like, the 'black bottle', some kinda poison to make us sleep forever."

"I've heard the same—and about surgical experiments. It may not be true, but it doesn't make one eager to enter. We must look forward to building our own institutions and facilities."

She notices his speech has changed, is sort of on the British side, and it occurs to her that this Garvey has come from the British West Indies. They sit on a street bench. He buys hot peanuts from the vendor and they feed pigeons.

He does not seem to be "a ravin fanatic" as Estelle said. His suit is nicely cut, but has been cleaned, brushed and pressed for too long—beginning to show shine. The unscarred side of his face is soft and kindly looking, all Cecil. The other side, where the scar lifts his mouth, is a new person. He waits to learn more about her present life, she waits for the full Garvey declaration. They go on feeding pigeons.

"Cora, I hate to say goodbye. My place is nearby at Fifth Avenue and One Hundred Thirty-third. Can you trust to spend the afternoon?"

"Yes. I've thought about you often."

"The same with me. I'll never forget."

"Cecil, I'll not pretend. I know you are a follower of the man named Garvey. It kept me from searchin for you. I don't wanta get mixed with that. And then you hadn't looked for me after leavin Charleston." She knows honesty has to be the best policy; after all, the last time she was with him he was feeling her naked backside.

"Cora. I left down home in a hurry and hoped to return in triumph. It didn't go that way. Then I heard about Kojie, the marriage. Since you've been up here, there are stories about your working in an after-hours joint and dealing cards and—but, truth be told, we've shared a good past and shouldn't let present circumstances divide us forever."

They exchange stories about themselves. He learns about Estelle and Sugar and May and Apolinario and Chinese seamen and Filipino musicians and about *Science and Health with Key to the Scripture.* She learns about Marcus Garvey, the United Negro Improvement Association, the poor of the West Indies, the history of Afro-Americans, The African Orthodox Church, the plight of South American cane cutters—and about Cecil and Cora missing each other. Causes, jobs and relatives temporarily fall into the background and man/woman takes first place.

"You're still lovely, Cora."

"And you're still the brightest scholar. Teach and tell me everything like my papa used to do. You should be our Garvey, our leader."

"Not so. Only one out of millions has the gift of leadership, even though many may have the intelligence. People would not follow me to the corner, no matter how sound my argument."

"Hard to understand that."

"Every once in a great while some magical person appears—and there may be gaping holes in his every proposition. He is attacked by the mighty, and often makes wrong decisions, but he always carries within a bright light, and so crowds follow. With and for him we bear scorn, ridicule and persecution; risk being killed for his beliefs. Our spirits are lifted higher and higher. And we follow him because we need his light to shine upon us—the strength of his belief."

"Cecil. I'm glad I found you again."

His three-room apartment is clean and neat except for stacks of books on chairs; magazines on the floor, back issues of newspapers, pamphlets and handwritten papers.

"Oh, Cecil, it's like Cohen's bookstore."

"But don't straighten, Cora, or else I'll never find things again."

He unfolds a rickety cardtable, hands her a cloth and paper napkins. "You set the table while I boil grits to go with our canned salmon—that's all there is. I'm unprepared for my honored guest because I spend my all on books. I'm a member of our debating society. We have some awfully sharp fellows—British trained *barristers*, no less."

"Tell about Mr. Garvey."

"Cora, the white man has held his bloody foot on our necks for so long, till now we think it belongs there." He punches the can opener into the can, sawing around the rim as he warms to his subject. "But now we face a new day. Garvey has planned our first Negro steamship company—the Black Star Line! Black captains, crews, sailing and calling on the great ports of the world—trading!"

Cora marvels at his fire but finds the story hard to believe. "How can that be? The ports are theirs. They own all the—"

"Damn to that *they!* We picked the cotton, *they* prospered. We laid the railroad track, *they* prospered. Now we are in the middle of this mockery called 'emancipation'. *They*— from here and overseas—*they* prosper. They have the mines, the banks, railroads, shipping, all and everything that they have stolen and invested out of slave sweat, cheated out of the past and the present. Every day further locks us out of the future! What have we reaped? Men hang from trees while we gamble, laugh, sing and dance!"

"But what else can we do?"

"Make our own way to manhood, force restitution for the goddam hundreds of years—time used to line their pockets with blood-gold while we built halls, hotels and arenas which they now legally withhold from we 'freed' people. My dear lady, *they* can't plant stones and look for a harvest of fruit. They promised us forty acres of land and a mule. I'm glad they never gave it. Where did the mule go? Same place as the promises made to the Indians after stealing every goddam piece a earth from under the red man's feet. Whenever someone takes back a gift, they got the gall to call him an 'Indian giver'. Now let that 'they' use some small part of their plunder to send us back from whence we came—Africa. I've bought fifty shares of stock in UNIA, Cora, that is the future."

He takes ten bonds from a drawer and fans them out on the table before her. She fingers the papers, enjoying his intensity as they crackle. She holds the bonds to her bosom. He tries not to think of her naked body in Kojie's bed.

"Cora, why in hell did you marry that Kojie?"

"He was good to Papa, I had no job, Mama had no money. Tandy and Flower came to take me with them, but I didn't want to live on the island."

"Enough said."

"But it wasn't fair to Kojie."

"Fair enough, considering his calculating ways."

"He's very ambitious, says his determination is to reach the heights in business."

"What kind of business?"

"Insurance. You know Negroes can't buy much from white companies. They say we die sooner."

Cecil laughs scornfully. "The race has one foot in hell, the other on a banana peel, and he wants to make profit on our dead bodies?"

"Oh, Cecil, don't be so hard on us. We have to profit on something or else just stand still and starve to death."

He moves the precious bonds and serves grits and salmon on the plates. "Sure," he says, "we've got plenty ambitious ones learning fast how to snatch a living from our bewildered poor. When it's time to pay out that insurance benefit, who gets it but the one called 'undertaker'. He takes us under, right? I heard of one Negro who got so big for his small britches, he stopped being a undertaker and changed himself into a *mortician*. Others raking in fortunes from preaching to washerwomen who turn over all they earn for the glorification of a white God."

She flinches and Cecil is suddenly sorry to have ridiculed her religion.

"Cecil, you don't believe in God anymore?"

"I do, but my God now lives in the African Orthodox Church. If God is not black, I don't know that I care to meet him."

"And if he is," Cora added, "I'd like to know why he's been puttin us through what you say and all that I know firsthand. However, I don't like to think of God bein any particular color."

"Most black folk don't, Cora, but white folk believe he's white." He lights a kerosene lamp, then switches off the naked electric bulb. A soft glow falls over the room. She smothers a desire to touch the wounded place on his lip. He is calmed by the amber light on her face. She thinks, "Cecil has bedroom eyes, like a dapper, street corner lover-man." She knows that love and sex will always be special no matter how many leaders come and go.

"Cora," he says, "God is somewhere within your lovely self and is not to be found in the churches of racist rascals. I hold but only one membership in anything—that is the UNIA. I lecture for Garvey and write for our newspaper, *The Negro World*. I am esteemed by our membership. I have a title, the Royal African Knight. I work very hard for you and the rest of my people because there is no way for me to go anywhere without taking along the rest."

"It's mighty fine to have grits and salmon with an African knight. Cecil, do you mind, very much, if I say blessin?" She murmurs grace; he studies the shirtwaist which barely shows the outline of her bosom. A velvet band belts her waistline. Her crimpy hair is center-parted, held in a bun by two tortoiseshell combs. He leans forward, trying to steal a look inside the front of her blouse. The faint smell of violet cologne sweetens the air—violet, almost like remembered clover. Her sleeve exposes the soft place in the curve of her arm, inviting his touch. He wants her.

"Cora, black paradise is coming true, just as sure as we are sitting here."

"Estelle says West Indians don't like us—they're very clannish. Monkey-chasers are foreigners like any others.

They work harder and for less so they can earn money to bring over the resta their relatives."

A dish bounces as his fist hits the table. "Monkey-chaser, be damned! Don't repeat fools who attack greatness!"

"Cecil, don't be angry with me. I'm only sayin what I heard."

"I'm sorry."

"Papa said my own mind was the only one I'd ever have for full-time use. But, God knows, I need another one to think for me while I take a rest . . . and depend."

"Cora, are you free of Kojie?"

"Yes, in my head, but still married accordin to law, with no way of untyin the knot. South Carolina doesn't grant divorce except for insanity."

"See how 'they' run our lives with laws?"

"Kojie's the least of my worries, Cecil. Estelle's way of life is wearin me down, yet it's only her kindness that has brought me this far. Through her I've been able to send Mama some regular money. Oh, God, sometimes receivers don't know how much money costs."

"Cora, I fear I've spoiled your appetite with political talk."

"No. I hate to leave, so I linger."

"Stay the night. I'll sleep on the floor."

"You don't have to sleep on the floor."

They talk, sing and play "My Determination", read poetry and recite King Oberon and Queen Titania, as if they are still children. He washes and dries dishes, shows no undue haste to tumble into bed; she likes that, particularly since she has almost asked him to make love. His body is narrow and wiry; the ribs can be hand-counted and his belly makes a little valley as he lies on his back. One thin arm around her, his voice caresses information. He is unable, even for the sake of love, to wholly tear himself away from the cause of his life.

She places her hands on the crinkly, crisp hair of his head, rubs his scalp, trying to cool his freedom fever.

"Life is complicated."

"Not now."

She is glad to be in his arms, touched by his hands, wooed by the praising of Garvey. Each learns the other's body well, as if this was not the first time. There's no shame, no shyness, no struggle, no sparring and awkward playing at love, no worrying about tomorrow or where this will or will not lead, no adding up of losses or gains, except. . . .

"Cecil?"

"Yes, love?"

"A foolish question?"

"Yes?"

"Shouldn't ask, but I was thinkin."

"Ask."

"Is there somebody else?"

"Now and then. If we see each other, we do; if not, it's all the same to her. And you?"

She decided he doesn't know very much about women; also decides not to add Nappy's name to Kojie's at a time like this. She kisses his scar, touches every part of the healed wound, memorizing the feel and shape of it.

"Cora, don't think back on that day."

"I'll never forget, baby."

"Say 'baby' again."

"Baby, baby, baby."

"Tell me again. Is there anyone else?"

"No one but you, daddy." Now she knows why Kojie wanted her to call him that. Such a short, sweet, trashy way to say "love". She also now knows why a woman shouldn't tell a man certain things, the truth in particular. Like Mama once said, seems every man wants to be the only sex part in a woman's life. Even if he goes with every woman in the world, he wants to be the first for each one.

"Cora, are you truly through with that Kojie?"

"Ran away from him like a thief in the night."

"Didn't ask that, baby."

"I'm as through with him as I am with last year's snow."

"Mmmm, good." He sighs and nuzzles his head between her breasts. "If he shows up, I'll beat him or shoot him—maybe both. You are my lady, mine alone. Don't lose weight."

"I'm your sweetheart."

"No, my lady. Remember, I am a knight."

"Yes, daddy, I know, I know."

They move on, rushing faster than they mean to go. There are no more world questions needing answers, no problems to solve, no living to earn, no white folk and black folk, no battles to be fought, no prizes to be won, only two hearts finishing the oldest race at the same time, together.

They plan the great future. He covers her shoulders with the washworn quilt and lights up a Chesterfield.

"Don't take any drafts, Cora. We have to stay well and get married."

"I can't get a divorce, honey. It's the law."

"Soon, my lady, we'll be making our own laws."

Thirteen

A crowd is lined up at 56 West One Hundred Thirty-fifth Street. The line stretches up to the corner and around it. People wait quietly. Some are well-dressed, carrying briefcases and portfolios; a few are down at the heels. A sober drunk closes his tattered coat, trying to smother the smell of sleeping off last night's moonshine in a basement hallway. He carries a paper shopping bag containing stale soda crackers, a soiled undershirt, and a two-page, handwritten, surefire plan to show Garvey how to take over the world. He needs to see the great man face to face to explain the idea.

A West Indian, bearing a tray of coconut candy on her head, waits to present it to Garvey, to beg that he use his influence to bring her brother up from Jamaica without awaiting government clearance. An abandoned woman with five children wants either a job or a free return-ticket to the Danish West Indies. A vendor happily moves up and down the line, selling meat patties and ginger beer out of an old, rickety baby carriage.

"Cecil, it's too crowded. Let's do it later."

"No love, we have what is called priority, and you are with me."

"I hate to shove ahead of others—it looks rude."

"Get used to it. Going ahead is not always arrogance; sometimes it is only necessary."

They move past the crowd into the hall. Cecil flashes a card to men who know him without it. "Go on up, brother." They pass through the barriers of guards on the first and second floors and then there is a waiting room filled with petitioners, old men rolling cigarettes and feeling proud that they have lived to see the day when justice is about to prevail. Cecil greets them with grave respect. They must wait a few protocol minutes before a large surly fellow opens the door to the inner office. "Garvey will now see you."

Cora remains in the outer room and waits. The others waiting smile at her, believing she must be someone truly great—or at least of some importance—to move to the head of the line. The walls are lined with pictures of well-known Negroes—Booker T. Washington, Frederick Douglass—and many of Garvey himself posing with important people. In one he is standing beside a bus with a sign—UNIA—several men holding the banner. The receptionist is a young woman with braided black hair gathered and pinned neatly into a bun. Cora makes conversation; "Can you tell me who is the distinguished lookin gentleman standing next to Mr. Garvey in this picture?"

"But certainly. That's Mr. Hubert Harrison, a learned scholar and organizer of Liberty Hall. It was he who first introduced Garvey to the American public. But surely you must have heard Harrison speak at one time or another?"

Cora studies the picture more closely, as if she had not

been able to see too well at first. "Yes, indeed, now I see it's Mister Harrison." She is ashamed of the pretense, but it does seem best to *know* something.

Cecil comes back and now Cora is tempted to turn and run downstairs, to escape to the safety of Lenox Avenue's subway. Cecil speaks in hushed tones, "Garvey is waiting."

Two men stand protectively near the man's desk. One has a bulge which could be a gun in his belt, the other holds a sheaf of papers needing Garvey's signature. The gunbelt man is counting money on a table laden with greenbacks. Several suitcases contain an overflow of more money. There's also a punchbowl filled with silver coins, a basket of checks, and money is spilled haphazardly on the floor. The "gunman" is opening a pile of letters with a knife. More money and money orders fall from the envelopes to the table. Wherever there is not money, there are magazines, pamphlets and books.

Mr. Garvey nods in her direction as he continues to sign checks and papers.

Cora wonders if she should bow or make a curtsy. Cecil has not told her what to do.

"Have a seat, Mrs. Green," Garvey says.

Cora almost falls in the chair. Has the man made a mistake, or has Cecil told him they are married? She doesn't want to deny or affirm. "How do you do, sir."

He is solemn but, for a moment, seems about to laugh. The moment passes and he turns away to sign the last few papers. Cecil catches her eye and winks for silence. Cora studies a fly crawling across the ceiling. She tries to notice nothing in particular. Money is everywhere and it's awfully hard not to see it.

She giggles foolishly. "Well, that's what riches looks like."

Garvey says, "My accountants are busy day and night, recording and issuing stock. What you see represents the savings of Negro laboring people. They don't often use banks, and seldom do business with checks. This hard-earned currency came out of cigar boxes and tin cans, from underneath mattresses, from the hearts of the people, to us."

"Yes, sir, I see."

"President Garvey," Cecil says, "may I present my wife, my Lady Cora, Mrs. Cecil Green."

"But, Cecil . . ." Cora starts to speak, but she is stopped by warning signals. The "gunman" looks stern.

Cecil slightly raises his eyebrows and goes on with the introduction. "Cora, I have the honor to present no less a person than our very own Marcus Mosiah Garvey, founder and leader of the Universal Negro Improvement Association."

Cora rises to her feet and to the occasion: "I'm honored, sir. Cecil has told me what you're doing for our people and . . . my determination is to study and learn more about it and, and. . . ."

"Well spoken." Garvey holds out his hand and she takes it. His handshake is vigorous. "Your husband is one of the few Negroes I know who happens to be a shade darker than I—and, of course, my complexion is midnight. Blackness, dear lady, is something which our organization regards with pride." She suddenly wishes she was darker, to be held in greater regard by this intense man because he means so much to Cecil.

Garvey seems to read her mind. "However, when African blood is in the veins, we all belong to the same company. And all in the race are brothers and sisters."

"I'm glad to hear it, sir."

Cecil says, "Someone told my lady that the UNIA has little esteem for American Negroes, that it is for West Indians."

"Well, either her informants are ignorant or mischievous."

The secretary enters carrying a pitcher of ginger-beer and a stack of glasses.

"Mrs. Green," Garvey says, "I approve of your going along with your husband. By the time you return from your trip, I shall have accomplished other business of importance in Canada."

"Congratulations, sir," she says, wondering what trip he is talking about and where, when and how long she and Cecil are supposed to stay in the mysterious place. Garvey's assistant stops opening mail and lifts his glass in Cora's direction. "To the honeymoon!"

All join in the toast. "Happiness!" "Long life!"

"May more victory come to the UNIA."

Garvey standing proves shorter and stockier than he appears when seated. "Why do you say 'may' we have victory? We shall have it, and that without hoping. Lady Green, early in life I came to the realization that I must wage a hard battle in order to gain a place in this racist world."

"Sir, I wish my father was alive to hear you speak. Many of our people down home need to hear you." Cora has forgotten her fears. "They would rally together under your leadership, if only they knew."

The secretary helps her to tell it: "All have to see and hear for themselves, just as you are doing. Mr. Garvey is not to be described—he should be experienced. And tell us, my dear, how long have you and Cecil been married? Why has he kept such a lovely secret?"

Garvey clears his throat; Cecil gives a quick answer. "Oh, er . . . two weeks."

The devil in Cora is irrepressible. "No dearest, it is now three."

"Well, it just seems shorter," Cecil stammers.

"Welcome, Lady Cora," Garvey says. "Cecil, why don't

you present the gift so all may enjoy it?"

Cecil reaches into his coat pocket and brings out several UNIA stock certificates. "Cora, my dear, you now own five shares in this organization. To you, from me, with love." Cora is obviously moved. "Thank you."

Garvey takes the shares from Cecil. "Sir Green, what kind of milk-and-water presentation is that? No, my lady, you do not merely own stock in an organization. You now posess five shares in the future. Madam, as a child, like many others, I felt no difference between white and black, but soon I was forced to see the injustices done to my race."

Cecil calls out, "Speak!"

"Madam, I was forced to see. I wondered where is the black man's government, our king, our president; where is our army and navy?"

"I understand, sir," Cora says, "that is what brought you to your great determination."

"Yes, Madam, to bring what was lacking into being. No, don't look upon these bits of paper as stocks, bonds, mere money shares, or any other flimsy material thing. With these symbols you will help pave the way to a new world of Africanism, where blacks are no longer content to be slaves!"

Cecil starts the applause, and from the waiting room, behind the closed door, it is picked up by those who overhear the message. Garvey throws the door open and straddles the threshold. Black, stalwart and proud, he speaks to all within hearing distance. "I hold in my hand shares in a universal government, absolutely our own! We are no longer to be black-white persons with the dream of becoming reasonably prosperous. No, we are to become a *power* and gain the full recognition and respect of all who now look down upon us! Today we are hampered by circumstances, but no one is *keeping* us back; we now hold ourselves down! Never mind boasting how educated you are—educated to do what?

Forever bow to the dictates of others? Fulfill your own destiny! Become a power, a power, a power, a power. . . ."

In the room outside, the word is repeated softly. A murmuring wave of sound soon sweeps down two flights of stairs and out to the street. ". . . a power, a power, a power. . . ."

Garvey paces in and out of both rooms, no longer addressing only those gathered, but calling to Africans, West Indians, South Americans, Fiji Islanders.

"Wake up! Promote the intellectual, commercial and national interest of this race of which you are a member—do you wish to live forever in degradation? No! Do you wish to be pitied? Show respect for yourselves. Look at my black face, my full lips—whoever you are, colored, mulatto, or black Congolese—I am your mirror! How long will you continue to ridicule yourselves? How long will you call yourself 'nigger'? Full grown men so greet each other: 'hello, nigger'. It feels comfortable to make fun of yourselves in that cowardly way. We say the white fellow must not call us 'nigger', but we choose to say it, fitting it into our lives like a shabby, greasy glove which easily slips over the fingers from constant wear!" He walks to the office window and waves the papers at the black world beyond. "Here is pride for those blacks who can remember themselves in the likeness of Toussaint and Dessalines. Go back, brothers and sisters, to that primitive start where you had the brightest and best of arts and sciences, and from that memory take courage to create an even worthier future. It is no dream; there is no 'maybe' or 'perhaps' about the matter. Believe it and live it and the kingdom will surely come at your command."

The listeners remain quiet. Garvey wipes his sweating face with a linen handkerchief. He thrusts his large jaw out, a temple vein throbs. He returns the papers to Cecil. "My brother, in *this* way I want you to present our shares."

Cora is smiling and crying at the same time.

The taxicab rattles and jostles them back toward Cecil's apartment. He draws her to him. "You see; you heard him for yourself."

"Cecil, I'm not thinkin of Garvey. *Why* did you say we're married? An outright lie! He didn't believe it. If we were married, wouldn't you have mentioned it before?"

"I did it for a good purpose and I can undo it if you want."

"No, leave it alone now. He'll wonder why I didn't deny it."

"Cora, remember how we used to count ships?"

"I don't like bein held up to scorn! I'll jump out of this taxi!"

"Claiming you as my wife is not my idea of scorn."

The cabdriver turns around, looking worried. "Only a family discussion," Cecil reassures him.

Cora murmurs, mumbles and complains as they climb the steps. "What am I doing following this liar back to his apartment? Why, why did you do it?"

He kisses her. "Cora, what's in a name?"

"And don't give me any of Miss Rosalinda's Shakespeare! There's no big to-do about a *man's* name. For the rest of your life you'll walk around with the one you were born with, always knowin exactly who you are from one end of your life to the other. You are forever Cecil Green. My real mother was Johnson, she died and I became 'James', then Kojie turned me into 'Anderson'. Now you say 'Mrs. Green', 'Lady Green'—I never seem to know who I am!"

"Cora, I want you to share the first voyage of the Black Star Line, under the UNIA banner. Garvey has purchased the *Yarmouth*, a British-registered freighter, the first seafaring vessel owned by Negroes."

"Cecil, truly?"

"No joke, my lady."

"I can't believe it."

"She sails to Cuba, touching ports through the West Indies, under the command of Captain Coburn, an African who is British-registered. But also aboard will be an American-registered Negro. Garvey is sending me—us—to promote friendly relations. Cora, at last, our own ship."

"The *Yarmouth*?"

"She is registered as that, but we call her the *Frederick Douglass* after our own—never mind the registry. I couldn't bother our leader about your marital situation. We must show respect if we are to travel together."

They stay up deep into the night, too excited to sleep.

"Cecil, has anyone seen this Black Star liner?"

"I haven't, but it's now heading for New York harbor."

"How many others will go?"

"Thirty-five—thirty-six if you go with me. We'll carry cargo to Havana, Jamaica, Barbados."

"What kind of cargo?"

"Whiskey."

"Oh, dear Lord, but what about Prohibition?"

"We will sail before the midnight deadline against shipping alcohol."

"Before midnight sounds just like Sugar's Cinderella book."

"On return trip we'll bring back fruit. Take away some business from the United Fruit Company."

"Oh, so much excitement."

"Cora, will you go?"

"Maybe someone is foolin Mr. Garvey. Do you think this ship will really come in?"

"I know it. Remember how you longed to be a cabin girl? Now you will sail away on our very own ship. No more counting other folks' vessels—this one is ours. Say yes."

"Oh, Cecil I want to, but, who are the other passengers?"

"A few like us who need something good to happen. There is one man, a black Cuban, who sold his business to pay his way here in order to book passage back down to Cuba on our ship."

"But if he lives there, he could have met the ship on that end."

"Understand it, love; he needs the magnificent satisfaction of sailing on the first black ship."

"I need it, too. I'll go."

Cora touches the scar on his lip. "Honey, the time of the fish-hook is over!"

"Remember how once you told me you wanted to be like Miss Rosalinda when she stepped out onto the stage at the minstrel show, beautifully dressed and singing? It's long past time. We leave in two weeks!"

"Cecil, how will I ever be ready? And what about you? Won't you need tie and tails?"

"Mine is ready: a dark blue uniform with red trouser stripes, a dress sword at my side, a white plumed hat, epaulets. It's Garvey's adaptation of the British field marshal's uniform, but no red coat and white trousers. Navy blue is more elegant."

"Be sure it fits well."

"Tailored to a 'T'."

"But let's not overdo and look foolish. All eyes will be on us."

"We can't look more foolish than British royalty, the Pope and the rest of those fellows in the Vatican. They overdo everything. Have you seen pictures of them? Lace, velvet, purple, gold, diamonds and emeralds."

"Even so, I don't want white folks to laugh at us."

"Cora, let them do what they will. We sail down to Cuba if

we have to navigate the *Frederick Douglass* through a sea of blood."

"Dear heart, I'm ready to go as Lady Green, your wife, as if we were legal."

"Don't you worry your head. A printer friend will make us a marriage certificate to represent white folks' permission."

The lady and the knight make plans. He talks of ambassadors and trade agreements. She has visions of herself, hand resting on his shoulder like pictures of ladies in the Sunday rotogravure. She sees herself standing at the ship's rail, holding her scarf in place against the fluttering wind. He proudly talks of alliances with other shipping firms, of promoting Black Star stock, of standing in a reception line with other black officers—The Earl of the Congo, the Baron of Zambesi. Cora wonders how much gold metallic lace she will need to trim the bottom of an evening gown.

She tosses and turns through the night; he sleeps with a smile on his face. She gets out of bed and wanders through kitchen, bath and living room, her head whirling with thoughts. Being Lady Green will be a great responsibility. She determines to help her Knight of the Nile to properly represent Marcus Garvey, Provisional President-General and Administrator of the Universal Negro Improvement Association. She determines to learn *all* the correct titles, to buy an etiquette book, to learn introductions, to find out what to wear at what hour—and to master every bit of it within the next two weeks. She clutches Cecil's robe around her, sits cross-legged on the living room floor, whispering into the darkness, "Papa, there *are* things wrong with it, the lying and living with a man. But I must go with the Black Star Line—I need it for my soul."

Fourteen

Everyone rallies to my aid, even the chief doubters. I stand in May Palmas' little bedroom, with nothin around me but love and assistance. Oh, I am blessed. Sugar, hands clasped together, looks at me as if I am the sleeping princess come awake after a hundred years. Cousin Estelle cools herself with May's Spanish hand-painted fan, while admiring a white-on-white embroidered silk shawl with hand-knotted fringe. May's best clothing covers the bed.

"I'm proud as a peacock," Estelle says. "Cora is the first person I've known to go anywhere they just didn't *have* to go—the first to take a trip just dry-long-so, cause she drat well feels like it."

"You see, cousin," I say, "Garvey turned out to do more than you expected."

"Sure did. That old monkey-chaser done stirred up a rich broth! Sail on, Marcus, sail on!"

I have to correct her. "Oh, Lord, Estelle, please don't ever let Cecil hear you call President Garvey a monkey-chaser."

"Honey, I know when and where to say what. I know how to walk with kings as well as talk with the common flock. And you, Cora, must learn how to flutter this fan, then hold it just so, so that only your eyes show over the top. Society ladies do like that."

I just love Estelle as she peeps over May's fan. She is so full of very fine virtues and petty little faults. Her cotton housedress is stiffly starched, too short, and covered with impossible green daisies. Sugar, the child of her old age, looks over her shoulder; in her I see Estelle young again without a line or wrinkle, without the salt and pepper hair creepin loose. There's nothin ill-fittin or wrong with the real Estelle. She is love and, as she says every mornin, "Look out everybody, here comes God's perfect child." She is. If I was an artist I'd paint my Cousin Estelle right now as she pats her foot and flutters May's fan.

"Cora," Sugar says, "there is a book called *The Language of the Fan*. I'll borrow it from the library again. It tells how to open and fold it, turning it this way and that so it means messages like 'meet me later', 'I admire you', 'ask me to dance' . . . and like that."

"Thank you, Sugar," I say, even though I don't plan to sit around sendin fan messages. Oh, Lord, what is money and opportunity? It seems impossible for all of us to enjoy something at once and together. Mama should be going on the voyage, and all in this room—all of the women who have so labored to solve each day. If I could I'd carry everybody—and if Nappy wasn't angry with me for runnin off with Cecil, I'd like to see him able to go. However, I must admit he took the news as best he could after I told him face to face. It woulda been wrong for him to hear it from others. Estelle said some men mighta shot me.

I don't want to take May's lovely shawl because she's never

used it herself. But she insists. "Take it, use it, that's what expensive things are for. Also take the eight-button white gloves. It's a privilege to have them go on the Black Star."

"She'll be sitting at the captain's table," Sugar says, "lolling in deck chairs, and may even get to ride a horse-drawn carriage in Cuba."

"Hush, Sugar," I say, "it's grand but scary."

Apolinario stands in the doorway, his eyes bright with interest. May caresses the pockmarks on his cheek—once he had smallpox, back in the Philippines. May's hand is pale against his brown skin. She is about two inches shorter; they are both short and look well standin together. I think of how I kiss Cecil's scar to comfort him for past pain.

"Cora," Apolinario says, "it's good to be going on a trip, but *why* are you going? You must know the government is hot after this Garvey, and Cecil is in the thick of it all. Have you thought of the risk?"

"Yes, Apolinario. My head is full of heavy thoughts, fearing that we might get arrested or that something may happen to the ship and we'll sink into the sea—some flash of lightning seek me out and electrocute my sinful heart."

"I know, I know." May understands.

"Then why go?"

May makes the sign of the cross and reminds him, "For love, Apolinario. Surely you know what love can make us do. Women do everything for true love."

Sugar giggles with embarrassment because May talks about love. Estelle whacks Sugar with the folded fan. I'm thinkin May has it wrong. What I'm about to do is not *all* for love.

"Apolinario, I'm going on this trip because some part of me has to belong to myself, no matter what the government thinks."

Givin a reason for goin helps me to understand Mr. Garvey better. Some might call him pompous and airish for usin bigger words than a thought might call for, but I know why he is what he is—and I know why some people make fun of the man. They think it out of place for a black to declare himself the equal of anyone on the face of the earth. They find it hard to forgive those who travel other roads than those laid out for them. Our own can also be mighty touchous bout who's to be the Negro spokesman for the rest.

Cecil is asleep in my arms. Soon, now the time is soon. I lie awake and string my thoughts together. The iron hand of the white man was upon Kojie. He made me pay for that in strange, hurtful ways—with a pot cover. My mind gets smart when I think quietly and don't have to argue a point with someone else. I don't explain very well. Often I laugh and say something silly when I really know the right answer. I'm sure there are others like me, doin and sayin the wrong thing even when they know the right answer. That's why Garvey is needed—someone to step forward and speak without fear of bein wrong or takin punishment. It takes tough courage even for a man to be his natural self. It's stranger yet for a woman to speak out. Maybe it comes from my talkin to Papa so much—mannish ideas, maybe.

Fifteen

The ship's whistle gives a loud blast, lettin the world know this is the beginnin of the Black Star Line. I can't find Estelle, May or Sugar among the crowd on shore. All Harlem is out and quite a bit of downtown is here at the One Hundred Twenty-fifth Street dock. The well-wishers are an endless field of black velvet faces, and hands wavin white linen handkerchiefs.

They shout up to our deck, "Happy Voyage!"

"UNIA forever!"

"Victory! Victory!"

I unfold the black, red and green banner I made out of silk—it is six feet long. The African colors billow in the wind—black for my people, green for African land, and red for the blood shed to bring us this far in progress. Those on shore go crazy with joy when President Garvey comes on deck to bid farewell and Godspeed to the captains. The president is quietly dressed in a dark business suit, but his men are wearin their fine, navy blues with gold braid. Lord, I'm proud of Cecil standin so handsome and lookin smooth as satin. I know the blood must be runnin through his veins like a stream after a rainstorm.

A stout yellow-brown woman stands beside me at the rail. She's wearin a new white uniform, also a wide smile. "Daughter," she says, "my name is Laverne Washington. I'm a Black Star nurse and have sold more shares of stock in this here venture than any other UNIA member, man, woman or child. This trip is my reward. Move over and let me share your banner, so I can wave my friends the kinda farewell as befits my station."

I say "Yes, Ma'am" and give her one end of the silk to hold. Laverne is more than stout, but very neat about it—corseted to a round firmness. We hold the scarf high over our heads and a gust of cold wind blows the material out. The crowd sends up a cheer.

"Let go, Laverne, let it go down to them!" It floats out prettily, like a blessing over the heads of UNIA members—down, down, down. Someone far back in the crowd catches and waves my flag. A brass band is playing. Countless banners are held up, streamers and confetti everywhere, a paper storm of red, black and green. There is barely standin room on the dock, and still they come. People and more people in every direction and they're all glad at the same time, like when Miss Rosalinda had our Baptist choir singin the "Halleujah Chorus" the Easter just before I left Kojie.

Garvey looks stern and properly proud. An eight-man royal guard clears the way before him; the same number follow behind. Captain Coburn and Captain Mulzac are with him, wearin their white uniforms under a bright winter sun. It is a cold February day but, no matter, they wear tropicals—we are goin to Havana. Such a fine sight to see, African and American captains, so well turned-out. The whistle blows again and crewmen walk the deck callin, "All ashore that's going ashore." Well, thank the Lord, they don't mean me. Garvey steps away from his guards and comes over to us.

Laverne curtsies as he takes her hand. "Mr. President."

"Represent us well when you touch the shores of Cuba and Jamaica," he says, "for, though I am not with you, there you will see my face as you gaze upon our brothers and sisters who are members. Reach out beyond them to further swell our ranks."

She presses his hand to her cheek. "Mr. President, it is done even as you say it. I am your humble servant."

He turns to me and I curtsy as she did. "I appoint you, Lady Green, Lady In Waiting to Madam Washington who is officially titled 'Countess of the Congo'."

"Thank you, Sir, I'll do my best."

"I have no doubt on that score. Aid her in every way. Extend organizational greetings to the First Ladies of government at social affairs throughout the Caribbean. Let them see in you the happy countenance of an American member of the invincible UNIA, while the countess presides as a born Jamaican returning in triumph to shores she once left as a pauper."

Tears come to Laverne's eyes. "Oh, my leader, I remember how I had not a decent shoe on either foot, and the straw satchel was half-stuffed with old newspapers to keep my few rags from rattlin round inside. I didn't want folks to know that I had not what to carry. The good Lord knows I even had to borrow the satchel from my mother's aunt, cause she was the only one I knew that owned a bag to carry. She had bought it from someone who went to a brother's funeral when he was killed in the terrible Kingston earthquake of nineteen and seven."

She weeps and turns to me for comfort. Garvey looks

away, givin her time to wipe her eyes. I put my arm around her shoulder. "Now they will see how well you have done."

"Take care of her," he says. "She deserves our love and highest esteem."

"Yes, Mr. President."

"Ladies." He bows his head slightly and goes off with his guards, back to shore.

I hear my name called. I look down and there's Nappy lookin up from the wharf. "Cora! Cora! Don't forget to come back!" I wave to him and blow a kiss. He waves farewell with—my silk banner. Such a dear, sweet, forgivin man.

Our cabin is comfortably roomy, with double bed, dresser, vanity and desk all bolted to the floor. The closet is narrow but my steamer trunk will take care of extra clothing. When will I wear this many things? Cecil bought me two nice pieces of hand luggage. He's in and out of the cabin a dozen times lookin for this and that, takin notes, changin his dress-clothes for a worksuit. The crew dashes up and down the corridor followin captain's orders. Once I manage to hold onto Cecil long enough to help me find the la-la, which is without a sign and just outside our door. It's quite nice—with a shower, two washbasins and a clawfoot bathtub almost big enough to swim in. There's a good-sized pitcher and basin on a commode in our cabin—blue china, and it's anchored down firmly within some kinda brass frame, which is fancily made like leaves and grapes.

I stand on the trunk and look through the porthole. Water is churnin by as we pass the Statue of Liberty holding her lamp high and clutching the lawbook. I try not to think about Jim Crow laws—for a moment I know what it's like to feel patriotic, and U.S.A. becomes my very own country as our black ship tugs past the white woman wearing her crown of spikes like Jesus' thorns. I would like Liberty better without her spikes, but perhaps there is an art rule that Liberty must wear spikes for a crown. I roll on my bed, stretch out my arms, and feel glad.

Cecil comes in lookin for another book and pencil, beginnin to "ship-talk" about the *S.S. Frederick Douglass* and sayin "hull" and "keel." He gives me a large envelope and hurries toward the door. "Meeting with Coburn and Mulzac about landing orders. Enjoy the ship, walk around."

"I want to go with you and . . . take notes."

"No other women will be there. You wouldn't understand it."

"I could learn."

"Sometimes men use strong language. Enjoy the ship."

Well, if I went it might be tiresome. Lord knows there's enough for me to do . . . takin clothes from my trunk and puttin them into drawers. Laverne might need me. Bein a lady in waitin must have duties attached. I hope so. I open my envelope and in it is a marriage certificate with the goldest seal and the reddest ribbon I've ever seen. It tells me we were married two months ago in Egg Harbor, New Jersey. The big, fancy penmanship can't be read, but underneath is printed "Judge Fast". I have a good laugh about the Judge's name which sure fits our needs. Well, Lady Green, who is not, sails on the *Frederick Douglass*, which is not, so I'll not say Anderson or *Yarmouth* for the rest of our trip. We're Green and Douglass all the way.

Laverne is across the hall and her door is ajar. She is seated in a leather chair, with both feet resting on the bed. The front of her unbuttoned uniform exposes a new pink corset.

"Countess, what's the matter?"

"Save 'Countess' for official days. You call me Laverne and I'll call you—?"

"Cora."

"I can't get these damn canvas shoes off my feet. The foot's swollen and the button won't unbutton. I don't want to break it off, cause then I won't have what to wear when we get to Cuba." The slippers are lowcut, with one strap across each instep. I try her buttonhook and a shoehorn, but she remains locked in tighter than ever.

"Laverne, let's cut it loose and get a workman to move it over a bit and sew it on again."

"Yes, cut, cut away, even if you have to take the foot with it, because I suffer." A scissors sets her free in a few snips. The shoe has cut through the silk stocking, into the flesh, and raised blisters.

"Thank you, darlin. That feels good."

I unhitch the top of her stockings from the corset and roll them off. The woman's poor feet gratefully expand.

"Now, darlin, kindly help me outta this thing they now callin a foundation garment." It is one piece from shoulder to thigh, the back laced as well as the front.

"Just undo the front so I can get myself back in it without aid."

Underneath is still another panel over the stomach, fastened by hooks and eyes. She draws in her breath each time I try to unhook. Once she has to rest and gasp for air; my finger is pinched under one of the hooks—black and blue. I curse the corset and want to cut it off, but Laverne won't hear of ruinin her custom-made garment. Her flesh is criss-crossed with welts and the shoulder straps have pressed deep grooves into her shoulders. Her breasts and buttocks finally ease free and she throws on a pongee wrapper.

"Whew, thank you, darlin."

"Don't ever get back in that harness, Laverne."

"I sure can't go to the captain's dinner with all of me shakin. And I'm not goin to miss it."

"Well, I'll help you lace it loosely. But there's no way to enjoy a meal in a corset huggin like a boa constrictor. I read in a book that it's bad for you."

"In a book? Child, this garment can tell you better than a book. Look here."

She holds up the hem of her wrapper and shows a gauze- and tape-covered spot on her thigh. "Honey, a whalebone worked through my old garment and rubbed a piece out of me. Been over six months and still nothing can rest too hard against the place; can't stand pressure."

I tell her how Mama had gotten heat rash from a one-piece garment, and how the skin peeled from underneath the crease in each breast from hot perspiration bein shut in too close.

"That calls for Fuller's Earth," Laverne says. "Buy it from the drugstore and put it under the breast, between the thighs, the buttocks—wherever the skin is pressed and irritated. But, what you gonna do? We sure can't look slack in our clothes."

"Just have to eat little or nothin and lose weight."

"Cora, child, anytime you don't see me eatin, I'm exertin self-control. I stay hungry before the meal and after—don't know what it is not to feel hunger. Anyhow, I'm glad we don't have to dress high-fashion until tomorrow, because my poor body is on the weary side. I'll just nibble here in my room."

"Don't you have any easy-fittin shoes?"

"But they look like they've seen far better days."

"No matter, they'll do for the captain's dinner. A long dress and a pretty hairdo will keep everybody's eyes up where they ought to be."

We begin to know each other. "Cora, I done a little of everything: the factory, general housework, baby nurse, looked after chronic sick, also was assistant to a undertaker—what they call 'female attendant', dressin the dead and all such. When Garvey come along I was past ready to join somethin, you hear me? Reason I had been doin first this and then that was because I wanted to find a good situation where I could serve and yet walk with my head high. I can't stand a job that breaks your spirit. It's not the work, it's how people treat you because you doin the work. They make it their business to disrespect you on accounta how you earnin a dollar. So, when Garvey come, I became first a Black Cross nurse; now I'm recruitin officer and saleslady for UNIA stock. Bless Garvey!"

I help her unpack right down to a hand satchel full of groceries. "Countess, do you expect the ship to run out of food?"

"No, my dear, but I don't go anywhere empty-handed in a dependent state. I always carry a few tins and a couple of jars; also I got Uneeda biscuits and breakfast teas. If we get into food trouble, remember I got what to fall back on—potted meat, sausage and all such."

"Anything else I can do for you?"

"No, my present plan is to crawl between these sheets. But watch out come dawn . . . I'll be ready."

"Good night, dear lady." I hang and straighten things in my cabin, turn back sheets and then watch patterns of froth through the porthole. Cecil returns to ask me to dine alone because he is adding up cargo money losses with Captain Coburn. I don't see how we can be losin when we just left shore. He doesn't have time to explain. I lie across the bed restin my eyes, waitin for him to come back. When Cecil opens the door, I awake and see early mornin light.

"Move over," he says. "We're so deep in debt already it's going to take a fortune to haul us out."

I help him shed his clothes, then get out of mine and hop

back into bed. He folds me in his tired arms and I kiss his crooked smile. "Garvey will manage," I say.

We hold each other, we kiss, we try to make love—we try, we try. I awake to full sun in my eyes. Cecil still sleeps—or can he be dead? He doesn't seem to breathe. I place my cheek to his nostrils and feel a faint stir of air. Poor fellow is worn out. But we are on our black ship, on the high sea. It is done, and we did it.

Laverne has been up for hours. She keeps me company and sponges my back as I bathe in the clawfooted tub. She tells about the other passengers: Señor Gomez, and a Mr. and Mrs. Balfour who are going to Jamaica, and a certain stuckup lady and her husband—neither wishes to keep company with ordinary people. I tell her about Cecil worryin about losses for the best part of the night and how I can't understand losses, and how Cecil wouldn't let me go to the meeting.

"No, Cora, they don't want us present, so I don't give them any bother, but I'm damn sure goin to find out what's what. First thing this mornin, I found me a friend in the kitchen. A waiter named Mac. Since he fetches and carries coffee and drinks, he has to hear what they say in those meetins."

"Laverne, one idea is that money is bein lost on this cargo of whiskey. Do you think the crew is drinkin it?"

"No, sugar plum, that's not it. Some them fellows back in the Harlem business office—they didn't charge the whiskey company enough to cover the cost of deliverin our cargo."

"We should turn round and give them their whiskey back, refuse to take it."

"Can't do it, lovey. A contract is a contract, and it is now Prohibition. The U.S.A. has gone dry as a desert bone. If we sail back into port with whiskey, Garvey will go to jail. It's called the Volstead Act."

"What's Volstead?"

"The law against alcohol. Them government slicksters

always thinkin up a new law. Law ain't nothin but a word. Them same ones that made 'law' now goin to make money by doin bootleg in the city and moonshine in the country—to get rich."

"I guess the fellows back in the office will have to learn how to do better business. Can't let everybody slick us out of our profit."

"Maybe some of the 'slickers' are right in the home office. Cheatin Garvey and UNIA while takin bribe money from some outside concern."

"But how could that be?"

"People got a way of passin money, greasin palms and doin each other in. But don't repeat what I say, because if I hear it again, I'll swear it's a lie."

"Never fear, but somebody should tell Garvey."

"Somebody will, in time, Cora, but let it not be you or me, cause menfolk don't want to get enlightened from ladies. They funny that way."

"Mac the waiter must not feel like the rest."

"Long as he's carryin a tray, that keeps him down with us. But if he ever rises up high, he'll go along with them and leave us behind."

"We live and we learn."

"That's right, dumplin, so be sure and keep me straight about what and what not to do when we get out into deep society."

"You lean on me and I'll lean on you, Laverne."

The dining salon is decorated for the captain's dinner. Coburn and Mulzac stand at the double entry, in full dress uniform. They greet the announced guests as they enter.

"Mr. Frank Johnston, Lord of Uganda, and Lady Johnston."

The titles seem most fitting now that we are off to ourselves, away from all who poke fun. Laverne and I stand with Cecil, waiting to be called. I remind myself to use *ing* endings and to move gracefully. The dining room has only ten tables, each set with snowy white linen and small flower bouquets. China and glasses brightly gleam by the light of a small chandelier. The floors shine with polish, and you can notice a faint smell of lemon oil furniture polish. On one wall there are two gold-framed pictures—Garvey and Frederick Douglass.

"Sir Cecil Green, Knight of the Black Garter, Lady Cora Green, and Madame Laverne Washington, Countess of the Congo."

Laverne steps forward in her long blue-lace formal; it sweeps the floor and nicely covers the buttonless canvas slippers. She gracefully tips her head in greeting, and I make my curtsey to Captains Coburn and Mulzac. A waiter leads the way to the captain's table, which is longer and wider than the others.

Laverne whispers, "It's Mac." Only his eyes smile; mine smile back. Names are written on cards and the Countess of the Congo is seated next to Captain Coburn, with Cecil on her other side. I am next to Cecil. The card at my left reads "Señor Geraldo Pastor Gomez". Next to it is his wife's, "Señora Felicia Garcia Gomez". There is a printed menu in front of each place.

THE BLACK STAR LINE
S.S. *Frederick Douglass* *(Yarmouth)*
CAPTAIN'S DINNER

Oysters Alexander Dumas	Wines
Celery Radishes	Pommery Sec
Okra and Tomato Carolina	Cliquot's
Red Snapper à la Creole	Hocheimerberg

Deviled Crab Gold Coast
Steamed Shallots
Virginia Ham with Turnip Sprouts
Roast Squab with Wild Rice
Chicory Salad
Georgia Peach Cobbler
Black Coffee
Caribbean Cordials
African Fruit Bowl
After dinner mints

There are less than fifty guests in the room, including the thirty-five passengers and officers. American Captain Mulzac presides at another table. Certain names and positions cause some changin around and rearrangin. Cecil excuses himself to go handshakin and backslappin.

"Good Lord, Lady Green," Laverne worries, "we have to nibble carefully to get through all of this."

"Countess, take just a dab of each, else we'll come down with galloping indigestion. And watch out for anything with 'a la'—it means *sauce.*"

Captain Coburn blesses the table for this trip and for the UNIA, then reads from the Bible, soundin more English than African: "Make a joyful noise unto the Lord, all the earth: make a loud noise, and rejoice, and sing praise. Let the floods clap their hands: let the hills be joyful together before the Lord; for he cometh to judge the earth: with righteousness shall he judge the world and the people with equity."

Amens and so-be-its travel from table to table. A champagne cork pops as three crewmen wearin red coats enter with guitars and mandolin. They make their joyful noise, and the dinner is on. The first toast is to the Provisional President of Africa, Marcus Mosiah Garvey. The men face his picture and raise their glasses, which are instantly drained to the bottom and refilled for another toast to the memory of Frederick Douglass. The music goes on and on, as does the dinner, with frequent toasts between courses—in spite of staunch Garveyites being teetotalers—to the ladies, to Old Glory, to the Union Jack, to the Cuban Flag, to black manhood, to black womanhood, to world trade, to Africa, to each nation on the African Continent, the Gold Coast, Zanzibar, Ethiopia, Chad, The Sahara. We salute the Ibo people and the Mandingo. Senor Gomez starts toastin his way through South America, the West Indies and the Canal Zone. Toasts come so fast that we must do it by small sips and swallows; no bottoms-up. Dinner is delicious. The captain says our chef served as officers' cook in the navy and bases his cooking know-how on the recipes of a man named Mr. Allesandro, who was chef for The House of Delmonico in New York.

Some dance between courses, the musicians lead us in singing "La Paloma" and "Sly Mongoose", which is not respected by Garveyites because of a few trashy words and general buffoonery. But the fellows substitute sounds for bad words and the men smile while we ladies look like we don't understand. I eat the "a la's" along with everything else. When we get past the roast squabs and chicory salad, the countess takes off her shoes and does a slow turn around the floor, carryin her weight gracefully, holdin out the ten-yard blue-lace skirt of her gown. The musicians switch to "The Merry Widow Waltz", and my dearest, beloved Cecil meets her out on the floor, kisses her hand and leads. Her lace swirls so prettily and I feel so high and happy. Someone tells me to be extra kind to Señor Gomez and his wife, because they are the Cubans who came up to New York just for the ride back to Cuba, and they speak very little English. We do a lot of smilin and noddin. He can say "beautiful" and "sankyou" and "jes" and "no". We all have a way of makin "ah" mean anything. And so, with my "gracias" and "si" we manage to carry on a fine conversation, with added hand signals and eyeball rollin. American Captain Mulzac is slim, light-complexioned and most mannerly. Cecil and the countess seem to move on air.

The wicked part of me opens May's hand-painted fan, even though it's not hot. I flutter it and safely flirt into the dark, meltin eyes of tall, dark African Captain Coburn. I am happy.

I enjoy sittin on this small canopied topdeck, since we've been cruisin through tropical waters. There's less grit up here. It's windswept and rain-clean, an awfully good place to lally-gag and daydream. It would be nice if the *S.S. Frederick Douglass* had more than one smokestack; it might look more impressive as we enter the harbor of Havana.

I get more service and attention than I've ever had in my life, but I don't have much money. There was never any when I was with Kojie, and lately there's been no need for it. I'm the kind of person who doesn't like to ask for money, or anything else. While workin for Estelle, I had money: men and poker players are generous with tips. I sent some back down to Mama in Edisto. I saved bills and change in a glass jar until Estelle took me to the bank and showed how to open an account. There's over a hundred dollars on my book. In the back panel of my steamer trunk there's another hundred. I feel good knowin it's there. I have sixteen dollars in my purse.

There's not a thing to buy on ship and my every need is supplied, but it bothers me that Cecil never mentions money. Each day I wait for him to offer me some. Each mornin, after he leaves the cabin, I look in my purse, under the pillow, on the dresser, thinkin he might leave something as a surprise so I won't have to mention the subject. I do want to buy presents for Mama, Sugar and Cousin Estelle, and May has been so good to me. Then there's money needed for trinket souvenirs and picture postcards. I like to have money in my purse even if there's nothin to buy. I'm beginnin to believe that when you sleep with a man there oughta be some cash around—not as pay, just as cash on hand.

Last night I looked in his billfold while he was dead asleep. There was only nine dollars. I replaced all of it. Maybe he hasn't collected his pay yet, or perhaps his money is in the ship's safe. He'll most likely surprise me with spendin money when we reach Cuba. Papa hardly had enough money to eat decent; Kojie had quite a bit but was awfully stingy. I have an uncomfortable feelin that nobody plans to give up much if they can help it.

Yesterday, crewmen on the lower deck were down on their knees shootin craps. I laughed to myself knowin I could start with a dollar and clean them out. Could do better yet if the game was changed to Blackjack. Lady Green would leave em all cryin cause they lost a month's pay in advance. Just a thought. Not a one of em would give you a quarter—the only way you'll get it is to trick em out of it. If they have a woman back home she won't see a penny by mail. I know a lot more than I used to. They'll gamble, drink and buy sex on shore. Or if they don't outright buy it, they have to buy treats for the lady they hope to get for free. Papa said one hope a woman has is a good provider. Well, my provider might just turn out to be me.

We anchor outside of Havana for five days waitin our turn to pull up dockside and unload the whiskey cargo. Seems the harbor can't hold but so many vessels at a time. A constant traffic of small boatloads of singin Cubans brings us baskets of fruit, flowers and rum. Many bring their life savings to purchase shares in the Black Star Line. Some pat the deck, kiss the railin; others wave to the smokestack. A pretty white boat brings uniformed messengers from President Mendocal himself. We are invited to a gala at the new Presidential Palace—a banquet held in our honor.

"Cora, stop daydreamin," Laverne says, "and go tell Sir Green that we are about to run out of stock certificates."

The best Cecil can do is show us how to issue handwritten receipts which state the bearer will get his printed shares by mail. These are not so popular, cause they don't look as classy as the printed kind with emblems, swirls and fancy penmanship; however, they sell anyway since something's better than nothin. Cecil has sent a wireless back to Harlem tellin Garvey to mail certificates cause the buyers want to frame them for hangin. I told Laverne not to figure any more change on half-shares because coin change is all in Cuban money. So we changed prices to round figures and this keeps down confusion. Now business goes faster.

Cecil, the captains and others are in constant meeting over ship's affairs, but I know just as much as they do, perhaps more. Laverne trickles the news down from Mac the waiter—what goes on at meetins and behind half-closed doors. There's goin to be trouble. This ship is eatin up every bit of cash we get our hands on through the shares. Salaries are behind and Cecil is gettin his pay in stock. He has a bag full of certificates. Some advance came in from companies makin deals to have tons of fruit taken back to New York; now they're mad cause we're behind time in pickin it up. Fruit rots.

"No, Green!" roars Captain Coburn. "We will not pick up passengers in the Canal Zone! You cannot give orders while this ship is at sea. I am the responsible person in charge of the *Yarmouth*, and you cannot change our course. You cannot order what or what is not to be repaired, and Marcus Garvey cannot indulge his whims by wireless. This vessel is a painted-over, rusty sardine can with rotten boilers. She's ready to go for scrap and the only way to keep her afloat is to make immediate repairs in every port of call—and that's expensive. I'm trying to push her along in one piece."

"We'll stick with Garvey!" Cecil shouts. "If not for him there'd be no ship—nothing but empty space where now floats the *Frederick Douglass*! When he says go, we go! If he says turn about, you are to do it, because we are all his vision. Would you like to be relieved of your post?"

"Not by you! And if Garvey relieves me, he will have to replace me with another British-registered captain, to match this ship's registration, and there is not another black one! It is impossible to take a hundred passengers from the Canal Zone to Jamaica. This vessel is for cargo, crew and thirty-five passengers. We will proceed directly to pick up the tons of coconuts we have contracted to deliver to New York City."

Crowds of visitors keep comin aboard. Some are country people, poor and ragged as jaybirds; some crippled and sick, believin that seein and touchin this ship will cure them of illness. They truly seem to perk up once aboard; eyes shine bright, voices grow stronger. They lower tin pails over the side and dip sea water to bathe their faces and hands in magic waters touched by Garvey's *Frederick Douglass*. Someone has spread the rumor that water near the ship has the power to heal. The poor people wear Black Star Line certificates in their hatbands or pinned to their clothing. Many now offer extra dollars for printed ones instead of handwritten receipts. Laverne's pockets are loaded with "Loteria Nacional" tickets given her by well-wishers who hope Garvey will collect winnings. Flowers are everywhere, on the hatches, the railings. The ship is in bloom with pink, red and white; the air is perfumey. At the end of the day, dockworkers come aboard with mandolins, guitars and drums. Young and old form lines and dance around and up and down on the decks. Some carry colored paper lanterns, lit by candles; whenever one catches fire it is thrown overboard, streamin down like a comet into the sea. They sing all night long and refuse to go ashore at dawn. Some have nowhere to sleep but on deck cause they came from far away places by train or bus. Many have walked for days from a district called Vuelta Abajo, Pinar del Rio. I recall they are names of places that make cigars for Cousin Estelle's Pullman visitors.

Lots of religious people are visitin aboard. They bless our vessel with prayer and song. The Catholics sprinkle holy water, the Baptists sing gospel songs in English and Spanish. Today the Voodoun, or Voodoo, also hold service on the lower deck. One señora explains that Voodoo is a religion which recognizes that there are powers of evil. These spirits are at war with good spirits and that is why we have things like war, pain and sorrow. One woman went into a trance; her eyes bulged, she trembled violently, then became very still. The sweet voice of a child came from her lips. Followers wept with happiness. They say the child's voice belonged to a little girl named Rosa. Rosa had the gift of second sight and healin. God took her to himself when she had given all the messages it was her duty to deliver. Now her musical little voice comes back through a medium, singin a song, blessin our ship, and promisin that someday we who are downtrodden will rise in the light. Every color shall then live as one—because of the Black Star Line.

I wept. The voice of poor little Rosa took me back to childhood and the Rabbit Ears Minstrel, and my papa's voice: "When will Rosalinda sing?"

Surely, someone will throw a tin can at our plans, bespatter the spirit of dead Rosa's lovely dress, pain will open Cecil's heart—and leave a deeper scar than the fish-hook that pierced his lip. It takes ice-cold courage to deal with a day just the way it unfolds, and I now have it. I also long to hear some spirit voice, but all I hear is the buzz of a bee stealin sweetness from a flower on the ship's rail.

Cecil cries out in his sleep at night, falls into fevers and sweats. In the morning, fever gone, he is off to meetings with businessmen who press to make fast shipping deals. The Black Star still foolishly offers bargain rates far below profit because it's black and in competition with the largest trading ships in the world. At three o'clock in the morning, Cecil sits up in bed, talking in his sleep; "Sweet Christ, how can we undersell the United Kingdom, The U.S.A., Germany and Japan? We're payin a goddam fortune to keep this wreck afloat, conducting business at a loss. . . ."

"Cecil! Wake up, honey, it's a bad dream!"

"I am awake. Oh, God, if only it *was* a dream. Somebody has signed us to cart merchandise at less than half of what it will cost."

"Tell Garvey."

"He says take what we can get."

"Well, do that."

"We're spendin investment money faster than it comes in. Cora, men can go to jail for these things."

"Stop signin papers. Tell Mr. Garvey—it is givin you bad dreams."

Cecil paces the floor and smokes cigarettes, lookin at me with pity for the fool woman I am. "Now is no time to show faint heart. Garvey is about to buy two more ships, the *Phyllis Wheatley* and the *Booker T. Washington*. The *Frederick Douglass* is paving the way, taking the beating so the new ships can build profit. Woman, we can't *afford* to lose faith at the first sign of trouble. We are now taking in more UNIA members than any time since the movement started. Cora, don't lose heart."

He's the one who wakes up screamin, not me. Well, poor man, I guess he's really talkin to himself. I hold him in my arms and give comfort, cause lovin is the only time that things go well with us. Except, lately, he doesn't feel like makin love and *can't* even when he feels like it. I put on my best lacey nightgowns, but anxiety about shipping and boiler repairs and back-to-Africa gives him a new bag of worries every day. It's cuttin us down.

Tomorrow we move into port. The company that ordered the whiskey has not yet sent anyone to meet us. Cecil says he'll have to track them down because each day in port will cost the UNIA money, since they have no insurance to pay for late deliveries. Cecil is losin his appetite and weight—a nerve jumps on the scarred side of his face and his smile is tight. This is no time to tell him I'm ten days late on my monthly—even with a pessary inside a me from Estelle's doctor. This morning I prayed before a statue, a present given me by a Catholic visitor. It's a very old Virgin Mary; her little, chipped face is nicely brown and she wears a wise smile. The señora who gave it said, "Santa Maria, Madre de Dios." Santa Maria must have heard many secrets like mine.

Up close, Havana loses its fairytale look. There must be ninety million Ford cars here, each tryin to run down a walker. We are met by government limousines driven by white-uniformed drivers wearin flashy gold braid. To clear the way, they honk their horns without stoppin. There is much salutin, wavin and greetin from those on the sidewalk. I'm thankful for Laverne because it looks like it's goin to be the two of us against the world. I woke up this mornin to find Cecil quietly weepin into his bare hands. There he sat, in full uniform, formal to the teeth, weepin—not at all like himself.

"Dear heart, don't cry. We'll soon be ashore."

"Cora, a longshoremen's strike starts today. We can't unload cargo—and we have to pay a daily dock fee."

"For how long?"

"As long as it lasts. We've given the crew short pay, and all my salary has gone into the fuel fund along with the share money we've collected."

"But, sweetheart, why do we need a fuel fund?"

"So the goddam ship can move! It burns coal! Christ sake, don't you know anything besides silk fans and lace on dresses?"

"I do, if you'd give me a chance to think instead of tellin me to shut up."

"Well, it's not your fault. Being married to that dumb nigger, Kojie Anderson, could not be a help to anyone's development."

"Well, at least the *dumb nigger* is not anchored in Havana harbor durin a strike, with no money for fuel."

"No, that coward is safe and sound, happily kissing white ass in exchange for money."

"Cecil, you shouldn't say 'nigger'."

"My worst has come to the surface."

"Send another message to Garvey."

"It's been done. He says to collect the funds due on the whiskey delivery."

"That's a fine idea."

"Also says go to the Canal Zone and pick up two hundred desperate souls ready and waiting to pay passage to Jamaica."

"Now I feel better. That's good advice. Do one step at a time. First get money from the whiskey firm."

"I can't find them—haven't talked to one motherfucker who's ever heard of them. The office is a thirty-mile train ride from here—that is *sixty hours* round trip."

"Can't we send a telegram?"

"What the hell makes you think telegrams perform miracles? They go out and you wait and wait."

"I still believe in God, Cecil. A poet named Paul Laurence Dunbar said:

> The man who is strong to fight his fight
> And whose will no front can daunt
> If the truth be truth and right be right
> Is the man that the ages want"

"Oh, Christ. Well, anyway, thank you, love."

"Cecil, I surely don't expect you to make it on just a poem. In this trunk I have better than a hundred dollars. You may have it all, except for a few dollars for my souvenirs. Don't say no; take it."

"I'm owed nearly two thousand in back salary. I'll pay back when I get it. Meanwhile, you can have my shares."

"Thank you."

"The Black Star Line is well over a half million in debt and fast going deeper in the hole. I don't know which way to turn."

"Just go on anyway, darlin. Walk proud; carry yourself like

a black man who is half a million dollars in debt. That alone makes you somebody in particular."

Every Cuban official, from Mendocal on down, has gone out of his way to give us the red carpet treatment. We have the best hotel rooms lookin out over Central Plaza, where a military band serenades our arrival. We have not had to spend one *peseta*, much less a dollar. Laverne and I have been showered with gifts—embroidered handkerchiefs, shawls, carved candles, perfumes, soaps decorated with imitation pearls and rubies, and boxes and boxes as yet still unopened. Someone has sent us a *duenna*—Señora Carrera—an elderly lady to accompany us through the shops.

In Cuba, ladies do not walk out alone or enter stores alone, or they will be considered loose persons who wish to be approached by strange men. Or worse yet, peasants tryin to pretend they are ladies. Señora Carrero speaks for us and tells the salesman what we want, even though we are standin by her side. It's just about impossible to even find a saleslady because it's not considered nice for women to deal with the public. You can't buy an underslip without facin the man in charge.

The *duenna* handles the money and receives the wrapped package. High class ladies do not carry packages and neither do they walk. The managers send guides, interpreters and salesmen to escort us to different counters. I notice that Cuban ladies are jeweled and dressed to the teeth, no matter if it's ten o'clock in the mornin.

I miss the privilege of goin for a walk. I miss Cousin Estelle, Sugar and May. I miss home. I want to go back to Africa, but I'm thinkin that if people in the United States weren't so mean about race and color and the lynch habit,

America would be a beautiful place to live. I'd never think of leavin. Fact is, when I see the American flag flutter and wave the words "star-spangled" rush through my heart and soul. But I grit my teeth and hold back my love, cause there's somethin pitiful bout lovin somethin that doesn't love you back—even if it is a country.

One thing I know, the presidential reception was a demonstration of plenty few people ever witness in their life. Once our limousines got through the crowds shoutin for "El Garvee", we passed a billboard advertisin "Lydia E. Pinkham Compound for Female Distress". The sign blocks some of the view and entrance to the beautiful domed palace; but once inside, we enter a world where every luxury abounds. For the first time in my life I am lookin at black, brown and white people minglin, talkin and dancin. True, there are fewer blacks and browns than yellows and whites, but just to see it! Black bushy heads and straight blondes, with such elegant airs! The gentlemen bow from the waist, the ladies incline their heads. When a señor wishes to dance with a señora, he asks her husband. We are greeted on receivin line by El Presidente and his family, then we enter the Champagne Ballroom. No one dances until El Presidente leads the First Lady around the floor, then they are followed by the top officials, our ship's officers and other honored guests.

"Cora," Cecil says, "this is where you belong—in a palace."

"You, too, Sir Green. If all else vanishes, I'll live on this for the rest of my days. Tonight goes with that other magic moment you gave me."

"And what was that?"

"When you read Shakespeare and won the book."

"I love you, Lady Green."

I'm tempted to tell my condition, but I can't. It'd spoil it—goin into the sad part bout not bein able to get a divorce, how we have no money, and this Garvey thing—I'd rather waltz.

"Look at the different colors! Have they overcome race prejudice here?"

"No, only somewhat. These are the privileged few. There's more black poor in Cuba than any other kind. They flood the street, begging or selling lottery tickets."

"Even so, they're ahead of us on race."

"When the Pilgrims landed in America, Havana had a hundred years' head start. Some of these folk have mothers and fathers out in the provinces—common field laborers, picking bananas before dawn, riding third-class on the trains. But, if they get hold of money they may ride where they wish. They seldom get it."

In the center of the banquet hall there is a huge lion carved out of ice. He slowly drips smaller durin the evening. Lion started out sleek and prosperous lookin, but he grows lean and sharp along the backbone. Waiters on either side of him hand-pump silver champagne fountains.

We've been docked in Havana harbor for nearly a month while Cecil, the Captains and all concerned search for the whiskey shipment owners. When finally found they won't pay for dock fees—only for the shipment. Cecil is encouraged that the *Douglass* is financially able to take on coal, food supplies and to do minor boiler repairs. I am homesick. I'm glad to get back on the high seas, even though we must follow Garvey's orders to pick up passengers in the Panama Canal Zone and take them back to Jamaica where they came from in the first place. Cecil has worried his waistline down to the last belt notch. Several back issues of the UNIA newspaper caught up with us. Cecil reads them with clenched teeth.

I talk it over with the countess. "Laverne, why does Garvey make friends with the Ku Klux Klan?"

"It's not friendly—merely proof that we do not wish to socialize, intermarry or work with whites. It is his way of sayin we're for separatism, and that we can give aid and comfort to each other on that score."

"I don't like unifyin with the Klan about anything. Why should Garvey pay a Klansman to come and speak at our meetin hall?"

"He simply wants the Klan Wizard to tell how they pledge to drive Catholics, Chinamen, Jews and *us* out of America. Then he believes that we will stop beggin for this damn integration thing. Let some of our dumb darkies hear it straight from the cracker's mouth."

"Laverne, you nor Cecil's gonna tell me how to think about this. If we wish to pay somebody with a different view, why not send for a speaker from the NAACP?"

Cecil slams his fist down on the writin table. "Yeah, one a them yaller niggers like DuBois. He's ready to march up and down Fifth Avenue to ask white folk to stop lynching! *Asking* the enemy to stop killing; wanting to stay on in America with those who hold us in bondage! Woman, are you crazy?"

"Booker T. was 'yaller' and Garvey loves him. I wouldn't buy a ticket to hear a Klansman insult me."

"Cora, we need a hard message delivered in person before you can believe you're not wanted in America."

"Maybe the cracker who stuck a fish-hook through your mouth is bein sent for to hook you again, and this time you'll pay him to do it!"

"Oh, shit, what do you know!" He dashes out of the door and slams it behind him.

I mumble at the closed door, "and fuck you too." I'm crying. Laverne gently takes up where he roughly left off. "No, no, my sister, you are wrong."

"Right or wrong, I can't be Cecil's echo. Why do I have to agree just to halfway get along?"

"You think you the first woman ever ran into such? Don't tell all you know. Learn to keep a few secrets."

"I've kept a few. I'm not married to Cecil. I deserted my husband. I'm two months gone with Cecil's child and haven't told him because I'm tryin not to send him stone crazy. Why the hell should I care what upsets him? When it's like this, they say the woman is 'in trouble' but *he* is 'trapped'. I still wouldn't pay a Klansman to talk to me!"

"Poor child, pregnant: that's why you're so touchous. Learn to trust your man, follow behind him, let him be a man."

"Laverne, followin behind others doesn't seem to work for me."

"Tell him about the baby and see what a difference it will make. From this day on you'll be his queen."

"I see plenty women with children bein mistreated. There's no magic in havin a baby, specially when you're not married to the father."

She massages my feet even though they don't hurt. Dear soul is givin out what she'd like to have for herself. I lift her feet to the bed so I can massage them in return as I let the kindly words wash over me.

"A woman should never argue, Cora. Got to hint your way along with a man. Believe me, in my heart I know a woman's place is truly in the home, raisin' the children."

"And yet you never married?"

"Darlin, some in my position will lie and say they never found 'Mr. Right'. Look good, dearie. I'm big-boned, stout and I ain't a tantalizin tan, nor that sun-kissed bronze. I'm sort of a muddy brown, so I got me a harder row to hoe. Them funny picture postcards—Oh, it seem so mean to call us 'mammy' and 'auntie', all because of the flesh, y'know?"

"I do know, Laverne, I know. When I was a child I went to

a minstrel show. Men stuffed balloons beneath their clothes, and wore big red bandanas to make sport of fat black women."

"Child, it ain't just in a show. The 'minstrel' is not confined to a tent. As long as I'm treated so bad on the outside, I don't care what goes on in a show, cause in that show they ain't showin *me* to the world; they're showin the world how *they* feel about me."

"You are right."

"I'd be glad to find peace as the wife in the kitchen. Women like me got to work harder than the pretty ones. Most of us can somehow get married cause a wife is the only way a dirt-poor man can get a lifetime servant, till death do part, to cook, clean and wait upon him. A poor woman, such as myself, got no way a-tall to find shelter from the storm but to marry. Even then, all too often, we have to also haul our backside out to clean the white woman's house, then hobble home to do it again for husband and children."

"Oh, Laverne, I wonder if God knows what we see."

"No need to bother God, ask man."

I mull over her words and mix them with my ideas. I don't care to be less honest than the countess.

"Would you call me nice looking?"

"Indeed so, Cora; that and more."

"Well, I haven't been treated any better than you. Some 'pretty' women lie more than the homely, pretendin like all is well. I left my husband, a good provider, because he beat me in private. I couldn't live with such a mean secret, and yet, for pride's sake, I couldn't tell it and wouldn't go to the Jim Crow court and tell the Jim Crow judge. Why should I go lookin for justice on that score while he's not handin it out on anything else? Couldn't have that outside judge smirkin and askin questions bout how come this and how come that."

Tears stream down my face. Laverne is cryin too.

"I know, darlin, Garvey knows too." She has almost rubbed a hole in my left foot, but double hookers of gin with grenadine give us consolation.

Sixteen

We are in the Panama Canal Zone. Standin here on the top deck, it looks as if we're now a passenger ship. People on the dock are crowded elbow to elbow, singin, dancin, prayin, beatin drums—five hundred passengers demandin to be taken aboard for Jamaica.

Their spokesman declared himself two days ago to Cecil and the captains. "Sirs, mosta these souls come here to work on the canal years back. Now who needs to hire a strong back? None! This is a sad place. They got a system call the 'silver and gold plan'. Us black have to stand on the silver line; the white on the gold, even in the post office. And a gold pay envelope got more pay in it than the silver, even for doin the same work. Now all we buyin shares want to get back to Jamaica. The United Fruit Company had to declare a holiday cause who is gon report to work with the Garvey come? Had to declare a national holiday. Ain't nobody gonna harvest while the Black Star is in port, and she can't leave port without those that's wild to go. We all goin."

They can't be talked out of it. They line up as far as the eye can see, they sleep on line, they chant and chant.

"Garvey, carry me home!"

"Back to Jamaica!"

"I'm gon ride the black ship!"

Cecil can't turn them back; they push their way aboard. They ignore Captain Coburn's plea, "Two hundred and no more!"

"Garvey say we *all* to go!"

"Take me aboard m'ship!"

"Gang way! Make room!"

A few drunk rowdies wave rum bottles in the air, dancin around straw sleepin mats.

"Garvey is m'king, mon!"

"To hell with Pa-nee-ma!"

Two hundred is impossible, so why not three hundred more? The Panama police are laughin, glad to see five hundred pieces of "silver" pilin into our hull. It is filthy below deck because the *Yarmouth* was last used by the Scots as a coal carrier.

"Cecil, what will they eat?"

"What they brought, added to whatever we have left over, and that's now damn little."

"What about . . . toilets?"

"Pails I guess, I don't know."

"Do we have enough pails for all these people?"

"Then some will have to shit in their hands!"

It's against some maritime law for people to travel this way, but each and every soul is goin or they'll tear the old boat apart plank by plank. Rain or shine, most will have to sleep on open deck and take turns goin below. Cecil tries to keep order. They like to bunch in front of hatches and doorways.

Laverne is worried. "Lord, I hope they don't tip us over. If all run to one side at the same time, we are finished."

"Oh, Laverne, look down there, see that poor pregnant girl. I could share our cabin with her and ask Cecil to move in with one of the men."

"And where will you be, Cora darlin?"

"In the cabin with the poor girl."

Laverne puts her hands on her hips and laughs. "That's where you wrong, because she *one* is not coming. There's no such thing as *one* West Indian. We move in groups. Pregnant or no, she ain't gonna budge without bringin husband, mother, father, brother, grandparents and neighbors. They'll take over, and your behind will be out in the hallway. However, if push come to shove, you can bunk with me."

Somehow w make Jamaica and many other ports. We are wined, dined and honored till our nerves are raw. We sell and sell shares and more shares. We spend and spend, and borrow from New York. The ship's boilers are repaired time after time. Short rations. We rescue a Japanese ship from trouble at sea and tow her to shore. Drinkin water runs low. The coconuts in the hold are rotting. The *Frederick Douglass*, listing a bit to port, steams back home to Harlem. Cecil is skin and bone and all too quiet. There's to be a quick stop at Philadelphia, then on to the big welcome parade. I'm weary. Only Laverne seems as bright as ever. I can't wait to get home. We've been gone two months.

Way up in front of us, behind two marching bands, Garvey rides in an open limousine. We turn One Hundred Tenth Street and slowly move up Lenox Avenue. Slow is the only way to go. People cover both sidewalks and spill out into the middle of the avenue and cross streets. They have come to witness the triumphant return. The Black Star Line has proved that black shipping can exist. Our provisional president is in full dress today: navy blue, with white ostrich feathers atop his hat. I'm glad our car is closed, so the crowd can't stare at Cecil's haggard face. There is only one sound—cheers and cheers, with no pause in between. Cecil's long, dark fingers feel like ice. I rub his hands but they take no warmth.

Laverne has asked to sit in the front seat with the driver. She waves to her friends in the UNIA. We look like success.

"Cecil, did you hear anything?"

"What?"

"Did you hear any news yet?"

"News?" He salutes those trailing beside our car, smile frozen on his face. I rub the center of his back and try again.

"Did you find out anything?"

"There'll be investigation and arrests."

"Garvey?"

"About mismanagement of funds."

"Hardly enough to mismanage. The ship eats fuel."

"And the British Secret Service is also on our tail."

"The British?"

"Something about instigating political unrest in their colonies."

I realize there's never goin to be a right time to tell him about my condition. "Cecil, I'm goin to have a baby. I was hopin not—didn't know how to tell you, been afraid to say—the way things are. . . ."

"No way to arrest Garvey without taking me. Where he goes I go."

"Cecil, I'm in a family way."

"It'll be midnight before I see him alone." He doesn't hear me. He sweats ice water. Cecil will not be of much help for awhile. Laverne throws kisses to her friends. The two of them are on separate paths. Nobody's goin in my direction. A crowd has been turned away at the doors of Liberty Hall. A path is cleared for our entrance but we must wait until Garvey and the other top dignitaries are inside and seated with guards.

Laverne calls back to me. "Cora! Cora! Someone is hailing you. There he is!" Nappy has taken off his cap to wave a greeting. Suddenly I can feel the ace of clubs sticking to my forehead and the ace of hearts on my breast—and my own voice in my ears bringing back memories: "All right, gentlemen, aces high, nothin wild, beat the pair in sight." Nappy has his stylish cap in hand to show off his straightened hair. It shines like patent leather: if a fly lights on it, he'll break his leg. He does look fashionable in that gray tweed suit with cap to match—and, do Lord, he's holdin up a sign on a stick: WELCOME HOME! Well, he's a dear man and a damn good sport if ever there was one.

"Cora, what do you want to do now?"

"Well, I don't know, Cecil. What do you think?"

"Probably you want to see Estelle after being away so long; or perhaps you might go to my place and rest until I get hold of your baggage."

"But what about the rally? What about Mr. Garvey's speech? I don't want to be rude and run off after the trip is over."

"Don't worry, he won't mind."

"I guess not. What about you?"

"We may be here until all hours. I'll give you my keys and hail a cab. You don't really care about speeches—and you see the state I'm in. Here are the keys, unless you're going to

Estelle's. In that case I'll keep them so I can get in. Here, have this—it's twelve dollars—or would you rather wait at my place?"

"Cecil, I'll go to my cousin's. She may be concerned about me."

"That's best the way it is now."

"And I'll hail my cab; it's broad daylight and no harm can come to me."

"Oh, no, I couldn't let you go alone."

"I mean it, dear. Bring my things over to Estelle's when you can; after all, so much of the stuff belongs to her and May. Make a good speech, love. One good enough to win a Shakespeare book. I love you, Cecil."

"I don't like you calling your own cab."

"It's all right, believe me."

Laverne's eyes are glazed but she remembers to give me a hug. "Did you tell him?" I nod and smile. "You see," she says, "I told you." She hurries into the hall surrounded by sister members who give me brief looks of dismissal. I am walking away from the Black Nationalist Movement, or else it's walking away from me.

May loves the statue of Santa Maria. I like it, too, but a Catholic will get more good out of it.

"And what did you bring for Estelle?"

"An embroidered nightgown, and ivory earrings for Sugar because she has pierced ears. This white silk tie for Apolinario; cigars for Estelle's favorite customers. . . ."

"And for yourself, did you bring back something for you?"

"May, I have a baby inside me."

"My dear, but why look so sad?"

"I am very sad."

"He doesn't love you?"

"He loves the Garvey movement more—loves it the way I'd like to be loved."

"It's different with that; it's not the same as man and woman."

"You don't know."

"Nappy is so glad you're back. *He* loves you. While you were gone he'd drop by looking moony and asking if we'd heard from you."

"It's hard to love when it's someone like me. I think of Kojie, then Cecil. I have too many ideas of my own. I'm stubborn. I'd love to be able to love someone 'till death do us part'. That's such a mean, long promise, but it's what love and marriage is all about—clingin until death hacks us apart."

"Then you haven't loved yet. It can be beautiful, it should make you feel good even when life is going wrong."

"When your mother sends her mean letters?"

"She is helpless in the face of my love for Apolinario. What will you do?"

"I'm afraid to have the baby. Do you know anyone who might help me?"

"Oh, Cora, don't ask. I don't want to help with that kind of trouble. You could . . . well, I mean you might. . . ."

"Die?"

"I've heard of it. There are people I know who could tell us about such a person."

"Nappy has asked me to go on a road tour—he's forgiven my leaving. I feel so sorry for him."

"But who's to feel sorry for you?"

"Me, I guess. It's wrong to take a life, and yet, if I don't, so many people will be hurt. May, you know I was just thinkin of a girl named Delores. She was a member of our church and they held a trial over her because she became expectant without a husband."

"What happened to her?"

"I don't know exactly, but she had several other children and there was never a husband. My mother said if a man whispered a kind word to her she'd drop her drawers in appreciation. There's something to that, I guess. A kind word goes a long way in a world where they come few and far between."

"Never mind Delores, Cora, you've got to think about yourself and what to do."

"I'm married, and this baby's father has other people and things on his mind. I'm broke. It's best to have something done."

"I . . . I'll ask around. You have to be careful because some abortion people are careless . . . it's dangerous. I wish I were pregnant. If you have it, Apolinario and I could say it's ours."

"May, there is no way that Cecil and I could make a baby that looks like it belongs to you and Apolinario."

"We could raise it for you in case you have to go to work."

"In case? No doubt that I must work."

"Why don't you talk about it with Cecil? Seems he'd be glad to do the right thing."

"What is the right thing? What does a man of honor do in a case like mine?"

Deep into the night we exchange terrible stories heard about different ways of having something done, stories about girls who take pills made of ergot, and about doctors who use instruments to scrape out wombs, stories about midwives who put in straws and tubes and packings to bring on a miscarriage so that a real abortion is not necessary. I recall Estelle mentionin a man who pumps air into the womb with a small bellows which serves the same purpose as the packin treatment. There are druggists who give black pills and bottled medicines to get rid of "the condition". Nothing sounds right.

• • •

They stand in the hall on the third floor and look back down at the flight of stairs that leads to the street, fresh air, and freedom from fear.

They speak in whispers.

"You're sure, Cora?"

"I said I was. Don't keep askin."

"It's just that I want to be sure that you're sure."

"I guess I'm sure. What do we say? I forgot what to say."

"We say we're 'Marie's' friends . . . and that's all. Three-D, this is it. Now knock."

"You knock."

"All right. Maybe she's not home."

The door opens and a pleasant-faced, motherly-looking woman invites them into a small, clean living room. The shades are drawn against daylight. Two pleated silk lampshades edged with bead-fringe cast a soft gleam over the waxed linoleum floor.

"Have a seat, ladies."

May elbows Cora to speak, and finally speaks for her. "This is Marie's friend."

"I know. Would you ladies care for a cup of tea?"

"No, thanks."

"No, thanks."

"I don't perform this service except for very special friends . . . and their friends—close-mouthed people."

"Yes, Ma'am."

"We know."

"It's forty dollars."

"Yes, Ma'am."

"I'm holding her money. Could we see where it happens?"

The woman leads the way to a small bedroom. There's a long wooden table beside the bed, and a small gas-burning stove with a pan of steaming hot water. The steam has coated the dresser mirror. The woman spreads sheets of newspaper over the table, throws a fresh towel over that. Below the table is a pail. Cora steals a look into the pan of hot water. Several metal things appear to be long scissors and blunt tongs. There's a short pointed instrument and a metal one like a soda straw.

"Don't look at the articles, daughter."

"No, Ma'am."

The woman hands her a blue wraparound apron. "Take off everything except your top underwear. Your friend will have to wait in the other room." May pats Cora's hand and disappears.

"May is holdin the money."

"Don't mention names. This is a secret. I'm the one takin the risk—jail and all that. But someone has to help those in trouble. I'm placin my confidence in you—my trust."

"I won't tell . . . not if I die from it."

"You won't die."

"Does it hurt?"

"Nothin much . . . like cramps. Over before you know it."

Standing there in the blue wraparound, she understands the words *alone* and *lonely* for the first time. The woman helps her climb on the table. She hears the newspapers crackling underneath her hips. The woman's hands knead into her stomach.

"How far along are you?"

"Close to two months."

"I don't touch anybody that's too far gone, so don't lie. It's your health."

"It's true."

The woman takes a belt from the dresser drawer, a long belt, a man's belt, wide and strong with a large buckle. Cora sits up.

"What's that for?"

"I don't have stirrups like a hospital; you know, the things to put your legs through?"

"Yes?"

"You have to hold steady while I work. I pass the belt around your neck this way, then underneath the thighs like so, and pull it as many notches through as it'll go. That way your legs stay bent up at the knee, like the hospital position."

"Oh, God."

"Be brave. Nothin happenin yet, shinin my flashlight, petroleum on my hands, just feelin. . . ."

Suddenly the word *helpless* is harder to bear than the word *lonely*. "Let me up from here. Let me up now."

"We gotta do what we gonna do, or else don't do it atall."

"Don't do it." She hears the clinking sound of metal against metal. Holding her head up she can see the gleam of an instrument.

"Don't put that inside. May! Come in here! Unbuckle this strap. Let me out."

May stands in the doorway. "Oh, Cora, does it hurt? Oh, dear!"

"I've changed my mind!"

"She's actin up too bad for me to work. Maybe you can calm her. She must be still."

"Unbuckle this belt."

"Daughter, I turned down others to give you this time. Look at all my preparation. Time is money."

"May, give her some money. I want to be unbuckled!"

The woman unbuckles. May gives her ten dollars and an apology. Cora trembles back into her clothes, the drawers on backward, the petticoat on the wrong side.

"This is confidence—I don't want trouble."

"Forgive me, lady—it's all my fault. I thank you for your help, but I can't do it."

• • •

"I'm glad you didn't do it," May says.

"So am I, but I still don't know what to do. Shall I jump off a bridge?"

"Here's a better idea. Let's open a bottle and have a good time."

"I've chosen the child's name, be it boy or girl."

"Oh, what?"

"Delta—it fits a child of either sex."

"Sounds like down south."

"I've put two names together, the last parts. My mother's name is Etta, so I take the 't' and the 'a'. Once I had another mother and her name was Murdell, so I take the 'del' part and add the 't' and 'a' to it—Delta! I bet no one else ever was named that. If I had money I'd go off somewhere when I begin to show . . . to peace and quiet and kindness, away from stares and talk, talk, talk."

Cora considers going down home, out to the Islands, but that would only make matters worse. A baby is a secret that gets bigger every day, and Kojie would know, and Reverend Mills, and Miss Addie, and Miss Rosalinda, and . . . all, all who had taught her beautiful things.

"Money is the answer."

She's been out on the road for four months, learned five comedy routines and several dance numbers—the Cakewalk, Charleston, Black Bottom, time-step and tap routines. She plays straight for Nappy's jokes. They call themselves "the funniest team this side of the Mason and Dixon line". No matter which side they're on they keep to the same slogan. Cora adjusts well to the road, Jim Crow trains, dressing rooms without toilets, theaters where *Colored* must go up to the peanut gallery while *Whites* sit in the orchestra, all happily enjoying "An All-Star Colored Cast".

It takes some doing to find places to stay. Nappy often leaves her waiting in the train station while he looks for rooms. There is seldom a Negro hotel. He stops respectable-looking people and asks them if they know of places. They send him to rooms for "respectable colored transients". There are rules against cooking in the rooms and laws against eating out in restaurants, even those in railroad and bus stations.

Third month out becomes a time of morning sickness. Cora can barely lift her head from the pillow for the nausea. The name of the show is "Shades of Dark Laughter".

In each new town, Nappy asks for an advance in the week's pay, not trusting to wait until the end of the run because theater managers have a way of crying the blues and handing out short money; more than once he has been stranded in the sticks without a dime.

Everybody says Cora is a real trouper, taking the hard knocks of show business and going on the boards without complaint. They also like the way she deals poker backstage and how she cooks a good meal over a can of sterno. They look out for one another. There are nights when they sit up in the railroad waiting room until dawn because they've come in too late to find a place. Cracker police search them out and say, "Vagrancy is against the law; yall move on." They walk together, in a group; they look out for one another.

Cora rubs her ankles. "Nappy, I can hardly hook my dress for the last show."

"Yeah, that's the name of it, baby, the *last* show. No way to let out your costume any more. You really showin now and TOBA time is crowdin you. Get home and take it easy until our baby comes."

"Our baby?"

"Sure, I tell everybody that's my child and he or she is gonna be named 'Delta'."

"You're a dear, sweet man."

"I know it. You rest and I'll do a single for awhile."

"When I come back, let's have our own show."

"I'd rather not have to deal with these tough bookers and theater managers."

"Let's call our company 'The Delta Show'."

"Would never do. From us, the public wants color in the title, but in a pleasant way."

"How bout—'Delta's Dark Sunshiners'?"

"There you go. Not a bad idea."

Seventeen

Labor is hard—over twenty-seven hours of pain meeting pain—in a place called "the labor room". She begs for water.

"No, mother, just wet your mouth and spit it out. Don't swallow."

Someone screaming in another room matches her screams. An old colored attendant is smugly satisfied by the sound. "Uh-huh, yall didn't carry on thataway when it was goin' in, didja?" White doctor enters snapping on a rubber glove to do the painful thing again, push his finger up her rectum.

"Please, don't do that anymore."

"It must be done, mother." His hand is large and his finger is a knobby round of steel pipe. "She's not ready yet."

For hours she has held back groans, feeling good about her bravery; but pain is about to tear her apart. Now comes the end of dignity.

"Kill me, kill me, please let me die!"

A stout nurse speaks with calm disapproval. "You're not

the only one. I've had two children and didn't carry on this way—two!" She wonders why the woman seems against her.

"Mother, you should pray. Try prayer."

"I've been prayin."

"You say 'Oh, God!' but you're expressing pain. Pray for God's help."

"Oh, God! God, help me!"

"That's not prayer; that's fault-finding."

Cora pleads again for water. The nurse places the pitcher out of her reach. The metal stretcher-table gives no ease to her aching back.

"My throat is dry. Let me stand, please."

The nurse leaves quietly on rubber-soled shoes. The voice down the hall cries out profanities: "Goddam you, Michael! Don't ever put your goddam hands on me again!"

Cora gets up and eases her heavy body down to the floor, gropes her way to the table, picks up the water pitcher and takes great gulps. Ice water spills down the front of her gown as she drinks. A student nurse enters, the one who "prepped" her by shaving off all the hair below and dying the skin red with mercurochrome.

"Mother, look what you've done!"

She flies out of the room with a rustle of starched white apron over blue-striped uniform. The apron is criss-crossed at the back and a scissors is tucked in the waistband. Cora longs to snatch the scissors and plunge it into her own bosom.

There is only one window, high up in the wall. She pushes the chair over and climbs to end suffering. There are bars on the labor room window—thick iron bars. The labor room is a prison. She grasps a bent bar; it does not give under her touch.

"Let me out!"

Nurses run in. "Mother, you're being a bad girl!" She makes plans to run through the outside halls, into the street, to beg help from strangers. They place her back on the rolling stretcher. They untie the back strings of the short hospital gown, put on a fresh one which is too small to fasten.

The doctor returns, snaps on another rubber glove and pushes his finger.

"Mother," nurse asks, "are you a Protestant?"

"No." She wonders what difference it will make. Another doctor comes in and goes off with the first to talk. A tall heavy-set Negro woman enters; she wipes the sweat from Cora's forehead with her bare hand.

"Cecil's downstairs, but they won't let him come up. No men allowed."

"Lady, help me, I wanta die."

"Can't letcha die, honey. I'm Looli, Cecil's aunt. Remember me?"

Looli turns to the doctors. "What yall gonna do? Her pains been together for a long time. What's to do?"

"I've seen them go longer than thirty-eight hours," the smiling nurse assures.

"Never mind what you seen. What's to be done for my niece?"

A priest enters wearing a long black dress and a white collar. Fiery red hair peeps from under the edge of his brimless black hat. "Daughter, do you wish to say an act of contrition?"

"No, please help me."

He waves his hand over her face, mumbles prayers she can't understand, places something on her lips. She tastes oil and salt.

Looli asks, "Cora, did you turn Catholic?"

"No. Please, won't somebody help me!"

The student nurse is shocked. "You said you are Catholic. He's giving you Extreme Unction."

"I didn't say Catholic—help me, please!"

"Well, you said you're not Protestant and we know you're not a Jew."

The nurse offers apologies to the priest. "I'm sorry, Father."

He turns red, says "Bless you, my child," and leaves.

Doctors move in. "We're going to help you, mother. It'll soon be over." They turn to Looli. "No more visiting; we're taking her in."

"In where?"

"The delivery room."

"What'll happen?"

"We'll take the baby—not a cesarean, just help with forceps. She'll be knocked out first."

The nurses roll her away. The woman down the hall screams on, "I hate you, Michael!"

In a large room full of white tile, echoes and metallic sounds, she is lifted from one steel table to another. Walls are white, ceilings white, glaring white light pours down on her face. Nurses tie her wrists to the table.

"Don't tie me."

"Behave, mother, we're helping you to do what you can't do for yourself."

They pull long canvas stockings over her legs, thigh-high and secured by tapes. Now they lift each leg, holding them wide apart to slip through steel circles dangling overhead. She is helpless. One doctor massages her belly, the other watches her vagina.

"Oh, don't touch me, please!"

"You're going to sleep now."

Someone behind her places a mask over her face; a heavy, pungent, sweet odor—tingling and pins and needles on her face. She breathes in deeply to get out and away from this.

"Slow, slow, breathe easy, mother."

• • •

The first thing she sees is a tall vase of white flowers on a medicine stand. The nurse is smiling now that the ordeal is over.

"Mother, do you know where you are?"

She looks past the flowers and sees another woman on a stretcher table, legs up, looking like an express train has run through her privates, leaving a great, gaping, blood-lined hole.

Cora looks down and is glad to see that her own belly is almost flat.

"Yes, I'm in a hospital."

"You have a lovely girl."

"Not a boy?"

"Do you want us to put it back?"

"Oh, no. What's the matter with that woman?"

"Nothing, she's just delivered. This is the recovery room."

"Do I look like that?"

"Not quite. You had sutures from inside the vagina and outside to the rectum. Cutting saved stretching."

"Is my baby alright?"

"Fine. Tired out and resting."

"It's good to be alive."

"It's not this bad for most."

"I'm glad."

The nurse passes a pink ribbon under Cora's head and ties it in a bow. "New mothers look so cute with ribbons, like little girls."

She is only one in a ward full of ribboned heads. Others can sit up, but she can't—too weak and too sore with sutures. The attendant brings her baby and teaches her how to nurse. Places the baby's mouth over the teat; nothing happens, it doesn't suck. The attendant gently squeezes little jaws together and releases them, again and again until a drop of milk is the reward.

"Keep it up, mother. She'll catch on by the second or third visit."

After the attendant leaves, Cora does what all other beribboned mothers do. She gazes into the baby's face, studies its open eyes, speaks to it briefly, then unwraps all the wrappings right down to the belly band. She examines each leg and arm, gently smoothes her hand over the stomach bandage, eases the child over to examine the back, all the creases and folds right down to the soles of the feet. She is very weak and it takes effort to ease the infant back into her wrappings. Delta smells of oil. She has two black-and-blue marks on her forehead which the attendant had explained. "Forceps marks; they'll fade away." It takes only two visits before jaw squeezing can be discontinued.

In the morning, before the breakfast tray, there is washup and then hygiene. Bedpans are eased underneath the mothers; the old, cranky attendant rolls in a cart of supplies.

"All right, ladies, open up."

They raise their knees. "Wider, mothers!" From a huge pitcher she pours a red mixture over their private parts, next sprinkles white powder from a can, then finally uses tongs to place a gauze-wrapped pad of cotton between the legs. "Hygiene for the mothers! Open wide for the hygiene!" From somewhere down the hall can be heard screams and groans. "What's goin on?" Cora asks.

The old attendant smugly laughs and repeats her only joke. "Another one in labor. Bet she didn't go on thataway when he was puttin it in."

Cora closes her eyes and says a prayer for the woman in pain. She'd like to tell off the attendant but instead follows the fear-manners of the helpless in hospitals—she quietly smiles.

Cecil calls every day at visiting hour. He's going through his own labor, controlling his anger about Cora keeping the baby a secret and going off with another man. He is secretly ashamed of how he has counted months on his fingers to make sure the child is his. It figures right, Looli had assured him, but sometimes a baby can be premature.

"Ain't nothin premature bout no eight pound girl," Looli had assured him.

He has made up his mind not to argue or ask questions. The woman has almost lost her life and it is his child no matter how she has behaved. He still feels love for her but does not trust himself in her hands. Cora, wearing a ribbon, looking like a girl again reminds him of the carefree days when they strolled along the Charleston battery. Her looks betray her actions—going off with some man to play at show business, sleeping with that man while carrying a child for another. Cora, with ribbons, has a legal husband in the south, she is a dealer for gamblers—with a face so smooth and sweetly innocent. This Cora, wearing ribbon, is the kind of woman a man has to kill or walk away from. He trembles inside as he talks of commonplace things, trying to make her smile, showing off the tiny yellow sweater and blanket.

"Looli says blue is for boys and pink for girls, but yellow will do for either."

"I'm glad it's a girl, aren't you?"

"Yes, they say girls are closer to their fathers."

He has a million questions to ask this female stranger, but he will not, nor will he mention the hell he is going through in the Garvey movement. He cannot bring himself to confess that he is broke except for the small money he places on her bedside table. "That's for a little ice cream and tips. Bet you were surprised to see Aunt Looli. Glad to say she's settled in a nice, respectable job since coming north."

Cora tries to keep her eyes from counting, but it is only one dollar and thirty-five cents. She decides not to hand it back.

"That's nice. What is she doing?"

"Maid to an actress in a Broadway show."

"I'm glad to hear opportunity knocks."

Cecil sits on in the visitor's chair, wishing he was well-off. Bad enough to owe her money and not have it to return. If only he had a steady income he could lay down the law and say how she must behave. Money could put and keep her in her proper place; it could also snatch Aunt Looli away from washing the star's underwear.

"Have you chosen a name?"

"Yes, it's Delta. Do you like it?"

"It's a nice sound. Does she have a middle name?"

"Not yet."

"Make it Garvey."

"For a girl?"

"Spell it G-a-r-v-i-e or just put 'G' in the middle—we'll know."

"All right. Her last name must be Anderson—Delta Garvie Anderson, until such time as my name changes again, legal."

He wants to slap her, but instead stands and looks down the corridor to see if Looli, Estelle or some other visitor will show up so he can leave. No one is in sight. He's glad Nappy is out on the road; otherwise he might have the brass-ass nerve to show up, and he'd be forced to beat him even though this whole mess is Cora's fault.

"Cecil, the baby's lovely, looks just like you."

"Poor child." He feels forced to take on responsibility, even though he may be on his way to jail along with Garvey, and there's still anger in his heart over her behavior.

"Cora, is there some way of undoing the thing with Kojie? My daughter's legal name should be Green, don't you think?"

"Divorce isn't allowed in South Carolina. Here in New York they have to catch one party in bed with an outsider—with witnesses—adultery."

He can't help thinking that it shouldn't be too hard to catch her in bed with an outsider, but he pushes the thought away. Kojie might agree to take on the burden of being the guilty party in exchange for the wife not asking any alimony. Maybe he will approach him as soon as he has some cash on hand. She reads his mind and hers jumps ahead of his talk.

"Even if he cooperates, it'll take money."

"I know that. I don't expect him to pay."

"No matter who pays, we'd have to handle it in another state. Anyway, I've promised to go on another road tour." She's trying to push him to the wall and he's willing to go there even though he knows she's being high-handed.

"Well, don't worry for now. I'd like to provide a home for you and the child."

"That'd be nice."

They both know the home is fading into a very dim possibility, and that these visits amount to just so many farewells. They both feel a sense of relief that they have not shown outright anger.

"Aunt Looli is staying in my apartment while I go down to Atlanta for Garvey's trial. The apartment, such as it is, is yours if you want it. Looli will help with the rent if you don't mind her staying on. I'm glad you finally called me, Cora."

"I was in labor and about to have our child. It was right to call you."

"You and Delta can have the bedroom; Looli can sleep on the couch."

"I'd best return to my cousin Estelle. There's more room, and she's at home to look after me."

"Sounds good. I'll send money when things smooth out. UNIA owes me a great deal of back pay. They're making a Federal case out of Garvey. He'll be tried in Georgia."

"I'm sorry they're gettin the best of him."

"It's rough, but the UNIA will triumph in the end."

Cora holds her tongue about the Klan alliance. She would

like to say "I told you so", but guards her words.

"And how is Laverne?"

"Organizing a busload of women to go down and sit through the trial to give moral support."

"I wish I could help her."

"It'll soon be over, then we can get back to carrying out the program—factories and bakeries, plants to make jobs for our people. Cora, there's little room for love until we solve this race hell, until it is resolved we suffer."

"I guess. You promised to bring me newspapers. I want to keep up with happenings so I can understand what you're talkin about."

"The papers are full of nothing but front page distress. Pictures of black men hanging from trees—lynched, bodies burnt. They cut off their—desecrate the bodies. I can at least let you enjoy motherhood without such gruesome sights."

"Maybe you should settle for just a plain job rather than trying to be head of a factory or manager of a steamship line."

"Cora, a short while ago, a Negro janitor killed a white woman. The next day almost every black janitor and handyman in New York City was fired from his job. There's no individual life for any of us."

"Estelle says people don't spend like they used to. The Pullman men are losin work, some are takin elevator jobs—college men."

"I'll run elevator if I must, but it's no damn solution to half starve on that."

"I could help you go back to school—some profession maybe. . . ."

"Didn't you say the Pullman porters and elevator operators are college men?"

"Well, some Garveyites have to take low, too."

"Never mind Garvey and Pullman porters. Tell me, why did you go off dancing and acting the fool for that buffoon of a man who calls himself 'Nappy'? Did you enjoy working in those dirty, dark little theaters?"

"I did it for money. No matter who saves the Negro race, I have to pay bills with money." She pulls herself up in bed, favoring the bottom which is still sore. "My determination is to get out of any trouble I find myself in! I can't get anywhere on this streetcar called 'the world' without havin to pass some man who's always the conductor. And most of the time I have to pay my fare by layin out on the flat a my back, just to get him to take me wherever he might be goin!"

"I didn't know you thought of me in that way. There was once love between us. So now it's gone?"

"Do you think Nappy would have taught me his routines and paid my bills while I was carryin another man's child for nothin!? For no soft bosom to lay his head on comes night, after he's spent the day grinnin for the booker and the evenin grinnin for the audience? Listen, paymasters don't like niggers who don't grin, and they hate nasty, bitter ones, so they're not ever gonna give you anything atall!"

"No, they're only willin to give to loose women. We all know that, lady!"

"No man gives anything away without a chance to get at some pussy!"

"You've lost your womanhood as well as your mind."

"Cecil Green, don't look at me with mean judgment in your eyes. How dare you sum up your Aunt Looli—'nice respectable job'. You have no right to add up any woman, much less me!"

"I expect a woman to be a lady, whatever her color or position in life."

"A goddam lie! Look in my eyes and tell the truth! Have you ever in life gone to a place where you can buy a girl, just long enough to get some relief? Have you?" She holds his gaze for a moment, he looks away.

"Woman, I can't indulge you in this kind of ignorance."

"I know you can't! Men who go to whores, make whores! So let your women—aunt, sweetheart and *daughter*—let us *be* whores. I ask you how is Laverne, and you tell me she's organizin a bus? That's not how she is, that's what she's doin!"

"I'll tell you how she is! She's a fine, decent woman!"

"So fine and decent until neither you nor those like you have asked her to marry. Why? The decent lady is too fat? Is she too dark? Does she look too much like Looli who made your hot biscuits while she was drunk? Likkered up to forget what she did all night for biscuit money?" Visitors and patients look toward the argument. Attendant and nurse hurry down the corridor as Cecil rises to leave.

"I walk away from your stupidity."

"No, you won't!" A gush of blood pours out of her as she leaps forward and grabs the lapels of his jacket. "You'll hear me out!"

"Your father must be turning in his grave."

"Let him turn, let all men spin till their bones rattle like the dice on Estelle's table!"

"Fool me, I thought you loved him."

"My mother died for love, second mother scrubbed clothes for love—and oranges! Mountain Seeley couldn't help me, white first-father didn't help Murdell, and you can't help Delta. You don't know how to love, nigger!"

Cecil grabs her wrists trying to escape her grip. The covers fall away and expose two shades of red on her flesh—blood and mercurochrome. Visitors call out in alarm: "Stop—leave her alone!"

"Let me go, woman, the past is past."

"No, it's not. They're gonna bring the past in here after you've gone, so she can learn how to suck my breast for nourishment!"

He slaps her as nurse and guard arrive to pull him back and hold his arms behind him. The guard keeps asking a question: "Lady, do you want to press charges?"

She is fighting them to take their hands away, to release him. "No, no charges, he didn't do anything! Leave him alone! Take your hands off! No charges!" The little yellow sweater is on the floor under the guard's feet. "Leave him alone, goddamit! Get your hands off!"

After he is gone, the student nurse brushes grime from the sweater and folds it back into the store box. An intern gives her a sedative. Another student nurse changes bedding, gown and padding.

"Mother, excitement makes you hemorrhage."

"I am not your mother!"

They take her temperature in search of post-partum fever. Temperature is normal. A man named Michael places his arm around his white wife who lies in the opposite bed. She wears two blue ribbons in her brown braids.

"Honey, I hate to leave you in this ward."

"I'll be okay, Michael."

At the nurses' desk, two black attendants exchange opinions.

"Woman just gave birth. Did you see that nigger hit her?"

"But did you hear her break bad when we pulled him off her? Go to help her and they both jump you."

"I've seen it time and time again. She's not gonna press no charges; they'll do it every time."

Eighteen

The country people of Edisto Island know how to have a natural good time, how to laugh, dance and sing God's praise in full, with nothing held back for the sake of whoever might be watching and making judgments. They have a grand way of walking with the old African stride. They know how to tend birth and when there is death they tend that also, and do not hurry the body out of the house into the basement of the undertaker's. Loving hands close dead eyes, bathe the body, lay out best clothes and dress the dear one for the last time. Those closest to the dead gather around the body and keep it company until earth time.

Cora arrives the day after Etta died. The weather has turned warm and the islanders do not believe in that "embalm" business, and there's no one nearby who would know how to do it if they did. They had washed her, stuffed openings with cotton, dressed her in an old-timey but fine dress of black silk and jet beads. Tandy said, "Ain't but so many darkies get lay away in taffeta. Flower's old white mistress sent it. Used to belong to her mother. Etta's face looks so restful. Cora, let us know when you wanta talk; we'll go outside."

Flower smoothes down the corpse's hair, stands back to inspect her work. "When Judgment Day come, Etta gonna rise up as the best dressed one in glory. Don'tcha think so, Cora? Why you so still? Don't she look natural?"

"Why wasn't my mother taken to a hospital?"

"No hospital is out here," Tandy says. "We'd haveta take the boat inta Charleston. She did not wanta die on the mainland. Etta was not one to quarrel with God."

"Yall just let her die from appendicitis."

"We forgivin you," Tandy says, "cause your heart is broke and that tongue is bitter, and you also been done had three glasses a wine. She had many a spell and we give the cold pack, but this last one turned inta crisis, so she was gone. Man born to die, and woman, too. She and Bill must now be walkin hand in hand. Hereafter is more better than here. Ain't that right, Flower?"

"So true, Glory be to Gawd."

She is alone with her mother. Etta's hands are gracefully crossed, one over the other. Lace and silk nestle under her chin. She is wearing black cotton stockings, but no shoes. Cora sits on the foot of the quilted bed, the cornhusk mattress rustles under her weight. She rubs the dead feet. "You are cold, second mother." She takes off her own patent leather theatrical shoes with steel-cut buckles. Etta's feet are smaller than hers; she stuffs newspaper in the toes, then the shoes fit.

The death room is stark, papered with newsprint. There is a green, tattered, drawn window-blind to keep out the twilight. A half length of curtain flutters as the October breeze creeps through cracks in the wall. Papa's picture is on the chest of drawers next to Jesus on the wall. Stuck in Jesus's frame is a snapshot of Cora and Delta at five, both stiffly standing on the corner of One Hundred Thirty-fifth Street and Lenox Avenue.

Death room smells of brown soap and kerosene oil. A lamp sends shadows flickering. The floor is white from many years of sand-and-water scrubbing. Cora examines every item her eye meets as she talks to a woman who can't talk back. A tattered straw hat hangs on a nail driven into the back of the door. One windowpane is missing glass, covered with a slat from a crate. Piled in a corner is a stack of baskets which Etta made, woven from marsh grass. The corpse lies on a quilt made of scraps of clothing which once belonged to Cora, Bill, Tandy and Flower; to Jenny, and Odessa and Mister Tuss, and Kojie and all those Etta once knew. The pattern is interlinking circles called "friendship". Cora recognizes pieces her mother saved over the years—bits of wedding dress, a baby coverlet, a tablecloth—memories pulled together and lovingly stitched in her last, fading years. She strokes a patch of her father's vest which nestles against a round of blue plaid, the dress she wore when Cecil was hurt.

"Mama, it's a beautiful quilt; so was your life. The slave market never got very much of you, cause you ran off far away from it. But hidin killed you—like the song says, 'There's no hidin place down here'. I sure ain't one to sit in the seata the scornful, but I can't bring Delta to live down here, to get little or no schoolin—not if she's gonna someday leave the country and go back to the city. I've been seein a lot more of this world than you and Papa."

People are arriving to view the body. Death has made them put down the tasks at hand, take time to greet each other with a kiss and a hug, take note of how children have grown, to look for and regret that eight-year-old Delta did not come down with her mama so that Etta could have her granddaughter at the deathwatch.

"I've never found a set, particular church where I belong; I know that was a fond hope you held for me."

She arranges the shroud sleeve on Etta's palm to cover a place calloused from the basketmaking. "On the road, I get to wander through the streets of strange towns and cities. Each time I pass a church I go in to visit and say me a prayer, be it Baptist, Seventh Day, Catholic—wherever a service is on or the door open, I enter. I talk with God the way I'm talkin to you and I leave my offerin, but I don't belong in any. None feel right. My foot has not touched homeground anywhere."

A voice calls from behind the closed door. "Cora, you finished talkin to your mama? People now here to view."

"In a minute, Cousin Tandy."

She kisses Etta's forehead. "I'll see you and Papa later."

The next morning they place the body in a pine coffin and nail the lid in place. Kojie is at the graveside to stand with Cora and place his arm around her shoulder. Those who know their story think he makes a fine picture. Reverend Mills, old as he is, has come out on the boat to say final words. Many of the colored sisterhood and ushers made the same trip, even though it means they can't return home until the following day. When the body is lowered into the grave, there is a splashing sound as Atlantic water washes over the coffin. Cora cries out, "My mother, the sea has taken my mother, the sea and death! The walk is over! She's home!"

Kojie pats and comforts her. "Don't grieve for her. Cry for us who are yet here. She is truly home at last." He is sincerely sorry for this attractive round little woman who leans on his arm; he is also grateful to God that he did not lose his mind when she left him—even more thankful now that he has met a fine "race woman" of property, one who owns beachfront and shrimp beds over on St. Helena's Island, one whose brother left her a house and twenty acres of farmland up at Monk's Corners. He can well afford to give comfort. "Cora, God moves in a mysterious way his wonders to perform."

Nineteen

Everything in Charleston is smaller than what she recalls; the houses seem to have shrunk. The vine-covered cottage that was once her home is a lean-to shanty; the backyard which used to sprawl so spaciously before her father's rocking chair, is only a fenced-in bit of earth, barely larger than Estelle's living room. Miss Odessa is dead, Miss Addie has moved down to Florida to live with relatives—Seminole Indians.

She stays with Miss Rosalinda for a few days, grateful to be around those who know show business. Mister Bones now allows no one to call him anything but Mister Johnson because he is an elder in the church. Rosalinda makes Cora tell about Bessie Smith and other entertainers seen in her travels. Mr. Johnson advises her to keep one eye open for a couple called "Butterbeans and Susie".

"That's a team a master comedians." He goes to great trouble to round up a jug of quality corn liquor because South

Carolina is dry as a bone and only a doctor's prescription can get bottled-in-bond. Miss Rosalinda has a good time pining for her lost career.

"I'm sorry we didn't stay with Rabbit Ears."

"No, baby," Mister Johnson disagrees, "you'da had to shake and shimmy for a livin—that ain't atall becomin to you."

"But I'd be better off shakin on the road than slowly turnin to dust on a Charleston piazza." She chips ice to make Whistle-and-lemon highballs and the trio gets high on show business stories. When Johnson must leave to visit a sick lodge brother, Cora and Rosalinda get the chance to talk some down-to-earth woman talk—the story of the Garvey trip to Cuba, the shacking she is now doing with Nappy, the falling out and making up with Cecil.

"We are on-and-off kinda folks. When I see him and he sees me, it's love all the way. But we can't stick it out. One of us gotta leave, till next time. It's just on and off; can't stay together and won't make that clean break. He's not gonna do right and I'm not either. Lovin and fightin, that's how it goes."

"That's all right. Stay free, Cora. Let people talk. They're jealous of free people—women in particular."

"But don't get me wrong, Miss Rosalinda. I want to settle down to true love, the kind you read about in storybooks, the kind you and Mister Johnson have."

Rosalinda makes another light round of Whistle-and-lemon. "Storybook love is written for foolish women. Of course, I dearly love Mister Johnson, but I advise you to *stay free*. Let Kojie arrange the divorce so you can be a grass widow, and don't look for a husband if you can make your own money. These men of today are either trying to be less than nothing, or trying to put on airs and imitate the meanest kind of white folk. None know how to be themselves. You have that gift. Keep it and don't ever think of giving it up."

"But I don't want to be lonely."

"There are worse things than 'lonely'."

"Let's 'Whistle' to that."

Kojie tries to persuade her to come to his house to talk over the business of untying the knot.

"No, my friend, let's keep walkin."

"It's hot out here."

"Talk will go faster. Is there an ice cream parlor?"

"Nothing but hole-in-the-wall places where roustabouts hang out. Maybe I'll have to open one and show these dumb niggers how to really do it. Come to my house and have a taste of bottled-in-bond."

"I don't drink, Kojie."

"Shall we walk along the battery?"

"No, let's stroll through Squeeze-gut Alley."

"It's even lower than it used to be and that was underneath bottom."

They walk where Cora wants to walk. The alley has lost what little style it had when Aunt Looli and Cecil lived there. Children run about, their legs bent by hard times in a forward arc from knee to ankle. People call it "razor legs"; some are simply bowlegged, or both. Their mothers went through pregnancy on grits, bacon grease and flour gravy. The children laugh happily and play—jokes are the salve for heartaches. "How I gon have *mo*-lasses when I ain had *no* lasses yet!"

"Cora, I don't know why you want to look at misery, ignorance and neglected darkie children laughing their asses off."

"They're puttin up a damn good fight. They're alive, walkin and givin death a boot in the behind. Lettum laugh for awhile before they find out that they're gonna be punished for bein born in this alley, for havin bent legs and black skin."

Kojie is troubled by hostile stares from door fronts. "Let's move along. These rough niggers don't like well-dressed people giving them the once over. They're mean enough to cut your heart out with a dull knife. Not long ago, one killed another with a razor over an argument about a dollar and a quarter. All he got was five years hard labor. Judge won't give much time for one nigger killing another—makes a Negro life mighty cheap."

"Oh, they'll respect my mournin dress and veil."

"Shoot, they don't care about that."

A pregnant woman sits on the steps of a shack; her rags expose much of her breasts. She eats raw lumps of starch from a blue-and-white cardboard box.

"Lady, can you tell me where Miss Looli lives?" Cora asks.

"No, Ma'am, I can't."

"She's a cousin of mine, also my baby's godmother."

The alley falls quiet, children stop playing, men look up from sidewalk checkers. People lean further out of windows. Kojie's sideburns flicker with annoyance and his brown skin turns maroon. Cora places one hand on her hip, one foot on the steps and looks very much at home in spite of the crepe veil hanging down her back to the hem of the dress, which is just below the knee. Her stance is a fond greeting from all the dancing girls in traveling shows. The woman flashes a starch-filled smile.

"Darlin, Looli moved to New Yawk some years back. She sent me a pitcher of the Flat Iron Buildin. I still got it, but there's no address. She was a friend-girl of mine."

"Thank you kindly, Ma'am."

Faces glow with smiles as they leave the alley. Children tag along behind them and Cora makes Kojie give away nickels and pennies. She waves and waves goodbye.

"Woman, good thing nobody asked you in for lunch. You sure woulda gone."

"And why not?"

"Cause a few weeks back they arrested a fellow selling skinned cats for rabbits. He cut the heads and tails off and the fools didn't know the difference. Nobody but a dumb nigger would believe he could buy a dressed rabbit for twenty-five cents."

"Maybe they needed to believe it, Kojie; just *had* to believe it. Carolina sun is now bakin my head off. Let's go to your house and take care of business."

Kojie has made many improvements. The house is freshly painted—white outside and in. The kitchen linoleum is new and he has a table with an enamel top. The bathroom is equipped with plumbing. He opens the icebox, now painted white, unwraps wet paper and chips ice. He longs to "get a little bit of love" since, after all, they are still married and she did mistreat him, but he doesn't want to risk losing her cooperation on the divorce. She will not accept any of his bottled-in-bond, so he is forced to soberly pass a bit of time before getting down to facts.

"Kojie, tell me about your bride to be."

He waves one hand at the subject as if it were no matter of importance. "Catharine is a nice person and has a good business head. She sells a new line of beauty products for the race, also does hair dressing in her own home. You've heard of this Madam C. J. Walker hair-straightening method? She went out of town to take the course. Colored women all crazy to get them naps straight and shiny. The church doesn't like it but the world goes on and women want to look good, right?"

"Fryin hair is big business."

"She also carries side products from other companies—bleach cream, pomades, tetter salve, special face powders.

But what they're standing on line for is that hot comb and curling irons. The harder times get, the busier Catharine gets. She says they're throwing money at her. One woman has to try and keep up with the next, right?"

"I tried it once. Has to be done over and over, wash your hair and it all comes out. It doesn't last."

"That's what makes it a dependable moneymaker." He moves his chair closer and tinkles the ice in his glass.

"Here's to you and me, darlin. What's wrong with us gettin some just one last time, for old time's sake? Ain't no sin, the knot's still tied."

She removes his hand from her bosom. "I'm not interested, Kojie, and I'm not afraid of you. If you jump me I'll take that cleaver off the wall and show you what 'death do part' can mean."

"You still cold-natured, huh?"

"As a icicle hangin on the North Pole."

"Okay, you win, I'll explain the deal." He knows a lawyer in Delaware. She can go there and file for divorce. He will not contest the case and will sign papers to that effect. The law says she must live there for at least a year, but all she will do is give a Delaware address, go about her business, then return at the end of the year for the hearing; after which she will be given papers and send him a copy.

"And you, Kojie, all you'll have to do is sit on your rump and wait for the end result."

"I did get the dirty end of the stick when you ran off. I'll meet a part of the expense but I can't leave my job; half of the expense. . . ."

"I don't want any small shit offa you, Kojie."

"For a pretty woman, you sure got a ugly mouth."

"I've earned it." She leans back in his new kitchen chair, feeling sorry for Catharine and glad for herself. "I'll pay it all, Kojie, and I'll break the law by lyin that I've lived in

Delaware. I'll make both trips in and out—and stand up in court for the no-contest divorce."

His face lights up with disbelief as she goes on. "Do you know why, Kojie? Because I'll be gettin the best of the bargain."

"Well, if you ever get in a pinch, let me know."

"Me? I'll never be in a pinch for the resta my life." She reaches for his bottled-in-bond and pours a hooker such as he's never seen, more than one-third up the side of a large water glass. She offers a toast as she refuses a water chaser.

"Here's to you and Catharine. May she get to straighten every head of hair in South Carolina. I also hope you continue to work in a jail for the resta your life and may your new toilet never fail to flush down alla the shit you keep puttin out. Now give me that lawyer's name and let's start movin." She downs her drink. He swallows his anger and writes out the information.

"Cora, I didn't mean for you to pay anything. I thought maybe Cecil might want to do you that honor."

"Be careful whose name you roll on your tongue. Learn to respect your betters." She privately curses Cecil along with Kojie; after all, the narrow little black sonofabitch could give her something besides a baby. Kojie makes a move and she stops him.

"Don't move the bottle, Kojie, I'm not through with it yet."

Twenty

The train creaks and groans its way along the cinderbed railroad track. Cora, Looli, Chalk, the dancing girls and boys while away the time playing tonk, reading pulp love stories, some just sleeping. All are hot as the Fourth of July. Most windows are jammed tight on the Jim Crow train which they had to board in Washington, D.C. They couldn't ride it out of New York, they had to change in Washington to cross the Mason and Dixon Line, leaving the land of "equal" for that of "separate but equal" via a backbreaking ride to Georgia. Cora and Looli sit aside, to themselves, as befits management. They figure ways to catch up on paying back-salaries and giving out advances in Savannah and Atlanta. Looli is great at painting good pictures of the future and wresting the best out of the present.

"Girl, you've run this show into a goin thing all by your lonesome, depression or no."

"Thank you, Looli."

"These pince-nez eyeglasses givin me a headache all over."

"But they make you look like a million dollars, with the gold chain and hairpin stuck in your bun."

"Thank you. If the bun falls off I'll die from turnin purple."

"No need to feel shame in this cattle car. Shoulda left my double redfox fur in my trunk. Looks strange carryin fur in summer. But it is so very hot—I mean the scarf is hot, not the weather—you know, hot goods."

"It is?"

"Smokin." They examine the two foxes. Springs join them together by mouth; one bites the other. The fur is thick and fine, the best. Looli says, "Sometimes they say it's hot just to make you buy it—believe it's a bargain."

"This is hot. Can't get two perfect-matched undyed foxes for forty-nine dollars. Only one who gets em for less is the fox himself."

"Cora, have you been to the hole on this coach? No water in the washbasin, no soap and no toilet paper. I got some in my purse if you need it."

"Me too, but it's a cryin shame. Chalk! Raise up some a these windows—I'm dyin!"

The piano player's hair is solid patent leather, shinier than his new shoes. He leaves the tonk game to pit his strength against the Southern Railroad and manages to raise one window. Soot and cinders fly in. Smokestack and roadbed ruin any hint of fresh air. A dancing girl announces to the coach in general, "No drinkin water in any of the tanks, and no paper cups."

There are others beside showfolk in the coach, but they just shrug their shoulders and dig deeper into box lunches of fried chicken, hard-boiled eggs and fruit. Looli nudges Cora as the door between trains open.

"Looka this, another dick gone to waste."

The tall, stout waiter enters to offer weak coffee from a large, dingy, metal-spouted can. He glumly shouts, "Sam-mitches! Hot cawfee! Ham sammitches, fifty cent. Cheese sammitch, forty. Coffee, twenny-fi'."

"Cora, why these old timers always look mad?"

He struggles along under the weight of a large traybasket on one arm, darting scornful looks at the passengers, looks that say, "Awright, niggers, it's eatin time." Looli tries to put him down by glaring at his bunioned feet. Both of his heels push outward, bending the backs of his shoes out of shape. He surveys the Jim Crow coach disgustedly, hating his job. A few cars behind him the diner is freshly made up with gleaming silver service and white linen, ready to serve well-to-do white folk. The very thought gladdens his heart. The coffee man envies the young, sleek-looking, brown-skinned dining car waiters dressed in navy blue pants, vest and white starched coats—writing out orders, filling out papers, showing off their college educations, talking down to him when he passes.

"Hey there, Rufus."

"Whatcha say, Rufe."

He had never had the looks, education or bearing to make dining car, but he secretly yearns to be a part of first-class table service, to hang out and joke with waiters who are far above and beyond most of the ones they serve. He hates himself for fawning and catering to the upper help, but each time he returns from a trip to the "cattle car" he can't help but shake his head while catching some young waiter's eye.

"Whoo, man, you don't know." He says it with an injured air, as though he is someone once dedicated to the service of the downtrodden, but now weary of the sacrifice. "Whoo, it's too much."

The waiters respond with casual laughter, vaguely looking in another direction. "Take it easy, Rufe." They don't get too close because social lines are sharply drawn. When the train pulls into a city for overnight stopover, the waiters go in one direction, the porters and restroom attendants in another.

Across the aisle is a minister and his wife. Through every mile of discomfort, they ride erect and unflinching, representing the race. They are so very dignified, they seldom speak to each other, and when they do it is in hushed tones and the manner of undertakers speaking to the bereaved.

"They're doin without water and toilet paper just like us but wanta show the world how well some coloreds can take what's laid on us," Looli says. She stops the coffee man and registers her complaint: "Listen; no water and no toilet paper. What can you do bout that?"

His eyes open wide in bloodshot hauteur. "That's *not* my department. I'm connected with dinin car services."

Looli lays it on him hard. "Nigger, get some water, paper cups and a music roll before I walk inta that dinin car and break bad. Meanwhile, hand over them paper napkins."

"Um not suppose to do that. Git me in bad with the company." He hesitates, looks at the ceiling as he waits and hints for a tip. "Yall want somethin? Some cawfee?"

Cora turns away from the landscape. "What's your name?"

"Er . . . Mr. Jackson. What's yours?"

"I mean your first name, the one white folks use."

"Oh, well, first name is Rufus."

"Rufus, tell me what's on the menu for us colored folk—the dinner menu." He hands a printed sheet to Cora and Looli, another to the minister and his wife. "Only one meal listed for this coach, and you gotta eat it in your seat. Cornbeef hash, mash potatoe, cream beets, bread and pie. Cost two and a quarter, no service after six."

Cora crumples the paper in her hand. "I don't care for cornbeef hash, Rufus. What about diner service?"

"Only one table for . . . us. If you sit there, they gon have to draw the green curtain so the others don't have to look at you—that's the law."

"No curtain, Rufus. Tell the steward to set me up a table when the whites have finished the last dinner call. Tell them two 'shortcoats' demand some service."

"Shortcoats?"

"Ain't that what you train niggers call Negro women? The white ladies are 'longcoats' and we're the 'shortcoats'. I also want a copy of the *New York Times* and the *Chicago Defender*. Tell the porter it's for Miss Cora Anderson and Madam Looli Deveaux."

"This train don't provide 'last service for colored' like some."

Her smile grows sweeter, her tone softer and harsher. "Rufus. Don't give me trouble, else I'll turn this coach into Lindberg's airship and run it nonstop from here to Paris. Now, get goin."

He backs away. "I'll tell em." He takes the minister's order for two hash dinners.

Cora rises and addresses her company and the coach at large: "Who wants to go with us to the diner?" None do. Chalk and the dancing girls have a good laugh.

"All right, Miss Anderson, don't start a riot."

"Cora, you too crazy."

They smoke their gold-tipped Melachrino cigarettes and sip Napoleon brandy, after complimenting the waiter on the Kennebec salmon and roast duckling.

He bows from the waist. "My pleasure, ladies. I caught Miss Anderson's performance last year in St. Louis. Grand, truly grand."

"Thank you. Yall were bout to catch another if I didn't get me some service."

The train glides through the night. The dining coach rides smoother than Jim Crow, and crisp linen and silver service is soothing to the nerves. The headwaiter speaks caressingly, "You ladies are the guests of the railroad. Of course, railroad doesn't know that. Your money can't spend tonight. We like to do this once in awhile.

"Thank you, sir, you are gentlemen and scholars."

"And graduates of Tuskeegee, with nowhere to go. Don't hurry, just take your time while we set up for breakfast."

Looli rocks with the train lullaby. "I'm glad aplenty that I left Broadway maid service to come on the road with you, even if it did make Cecil uneasy. After all, Delta is my grandniece, and you and me related some kinda way—all family."

"I think I ate too much, Looli. However, most of this waistline is my moneybelt. I'm carryin enough greenbacks to cushion my soul."

"Oughta put it in the bank."

"Not ater Franklin Delano Roosevelt stole my money. I wouldn't trust a bank no kinda way. 'Bank Holiday', what kinda shit is that?"

"He's gonna pay some of it back after he straightens out the government."

"When I put it in I was led to expect *all* of my money back, with interest. Damn bank wouldn't even let me in the door to ask about it. Had guards and policemen holdin everybody back at gunpoint. Two thousand is a helluva lotta money to lose. It was for Delta to go to college like Sugar. I was left with nothin but the drawers I was standin in. All I sacrificed to save just snatched away. I planned to stay home with Delta for awhile. Not good to leave a child too much. The bank failure made me have a tough year—startin all over from scratch."

"Them millionaires jump out office windows bout losin their money."

"I could give em lessons in how to endure. I lock down; I hold on."

She puts out a cigarette, fingers the golden tip, remembering that hard, bitter winter. The railroad men had stopped coming to Estelle's as they were laid off or fired. She tried housework, but it was too hard and paid too little. Once she had gone up to the Bronx to see about a job and saw a familiar figure standing in the street near the Third Avenue Elevated. Laverne was leaning against a wall and holding a brown paper bag. "Countess, what are you doing here?"

"Good God, Cora, what you doin in the Bronx slave market?"

"Slave market?"

"That's what it's called, just for sport."

Negro women stood in groups on every corner, out in the middle of the avenue, underneath the El pillars, holding brown paper bags full of work clothes. Several white women approached and talked to members of the group.

"What is this?"

Laverne shrugged. "Day's work. You stand here until somebody talks to you about doing their housework. Going rate is twenty-five cents an hour; bring your own lunch and work clothes. Sometimes you run into luck—one who pays thirty-five cents, lunch and ten cents carfare. It's hard work but you have some cash in hand by nightfall." Warm weather chases sweat down her face; she mops the water with a balled-up handkerchief.

Cora leads her away from the group. "Laverne, come away from the slave market. You can help me take care of my little girl, help my poor, weary cousin Estelle. You must be family with us, sit down when you're tired, eat when you're hungry—we can share together. You're a countess, remember?"

"You have money?"

"I did, but the bank failed."

"I know. One time I saved up eighty dollars, but had to spend it for emergency."

"I'm goin on the road again; there'll be money comin in."

"Thank you darlin."

The train rocks onward and the crystal ashtray contains several gold-tipped cigarette butts. "Cora, wake up, they're ready to close the diner." She opens her eyes and returns to show business.

"Vaudeville is dying, Looli—movies have taken over. Money's short and my bones have had enough jouncin over hard roads. The goddam managers cancel out in the middle of the week. Now colored sits up in the Jim Crow balcony to watch white shows. I'm callin this my last trip."

"What'll the rest of us do?"

"Whatever you were doin before."

"Marie, the littlest dancer, she used to be a 'mat girl'."

"What's that?"

"At some bigshot parties, youngsters put on a kind of naughty floor show. Put down a mat on the floor. Buck-naked fellas and girls take positions like havin sex. They get the watchers all excited so they can pair off and do what they see. At first it was only make believe, but after hard times hit, they now want things truly done."

"They use boyfriend and girlfriend couples?"

"Strangers, even; you hit the mat with whoever might be workin that night."

"That's low."

"Well-to-do people like to watch, and they pay."

"It's low."

"Cora, you what they call a square. Some will do anything people can think up for money."

"I don't want that to stay true."

Hands out of control, Looli winds and unwinds her silk scarf. "You been in shelter all your days, so you think it's hardship when you gotta do a time-step. You know I know about trick-turnin and such. I know you know cause Cecil has told you his guts. What do you think trick-turnin is about?"

"Bein a prostitute."

Looli fights for the continuation of the show. "It's more than dressin fancy and smilin in a tomcat's face. You ask him *how* he wants it, and he tells you. Might say, 'Down on your knees, that's how.' What do you think it feels like to turn thirty-two-dollar tricks in one night?"

"Sore, very sore."

"That's right."

"But Looli, I can't kill myself to make employment. Can't give up my daughter."

"I crawled out of a cathouse early in the mornin. Used to hire a car driver to come haul me home. I'd say, 'Drive easy, driver, been a hard night'."

"You're not ever goin back to that."

"No, I just want you to know how lucky you are. What you got is like fresh, clean water from a country spring. We workin with some pride. You run this show, Cora. Run it till it won't run any longer. Delta is okay with Estelle. Forget Cecil; he's mine but he's always broker than the last go-round. Marie—all of us—dependin on you to. . . ."

"You more worried about Marie than yourself."

"I care about her, didn't you know?"

"No, I didn't—thought she was your friend-girl."

"More like girlfriend."

"Delta comes first with me; I don't want other people to raise her."

"Make it through the season and you might feel a change of mind."

"We'll see."

Twenty-One

Cora has the best room in the Joplin, Missouri rooming house. It is clean but smells of damp mold. Plaster walls are clammy, the bed sheets humidly moist. She lies across the bed, her eyes tracing flower designs on the rusted tin ceiling. Twilight turns to dark. Days off make her yearn to move on and be doing, rehearsing a new song or dance—anything except standing still, marking time and thinking of Delta—and Cecil. The door creaks open. Light from the hall falls on a sleek, shining head of hair.

"Come on in, Chalk." He pulls on the dresser lamps, two kewpie dolls with feather shades growing out of their heads. He sits on the foot of her bed. He is wearing a blue velvet smoking jacket. "Chalk, why didn't you go to the party with the others?"

"Sicka partyin."

"Me too."

"I been wantin to tell you somethin for a long time."

"Tell it."

"Kill me if you want, laugh or chop my head off, but I go for you—got a crush on you so bad till I dn't sleep easy. Cora, you stay in my head alla time. When I'm playin piano and you on stage in that rose-color dress—oh, my love comes tumblin down."

"I'm almost old enough to be your mother. I also know your mother."

He claps his hands together and loosens the top button of his jacket. "I'm edgin on to twenty-three. I may be young, but I'm a man. I've loved and been loved by more women than you can count in a basement sale. I don't go for chippie girls. I like women. Don't hold it against me cause I was a kid when we first met. Think like this—wasn't for me providin the matches you wouldn't have been able to find Estelle's mailbox when you come to New York. I go for women, particularly for you, cause you just so fine."

"Chalk, do you want money?"

"Anybody can use money, but I'm talkin bout you . . . y-o-u."

"Do you want money, Chalk?"

He falls silent, turns his head away. He does go for her and he does like money and he has heard that she has plenty of it and some to spare. He figures that a good-looking businesswoman with a pocket full of greenbacks is a hard combination to beat. He can't get but so far on his own and he'd like to have Cora in his corner smoothing the kinks out of his life. Older women can be good to and for a young man. But it is uncomfortable to have her talk money first thing. "Really, Cora, that was not uppermost in my mind. You been lookin so lonesome . . . I wantcha to know I truly care about you."

"I am lonesome. I also know you're a smooth liar and a womanizer. You leave a string of broken hearts in every town we visit. Looli says you are known as a cocksman."

"That's terrible. People sure like to talk."

"Chalk, lock the door and take my emptiness away. I may's well buy what I need—and you, my dear, may's well work for what you want." She throws back the coverlet and makes room for him to climb in beside her. He strips down to the lean brown as she laughs about the monogrammed blue silk shorts which he carefully folds and hangs over the back of a chair.

"Baby, here I am. Cora, you so fine."

She strokes his patent leather hair and breathes in the baby talcum smell on his chest.

"Chalk, are you clean? I don't mean *bath* clean, I mean *clean* clean. Don't bring me anything I didn't have when you walked in."

"Clean as the board a health. Why you ask me that?"

"I am practical."

"Lord, Lord, how I'm gonna make love to a businesswoman. Sweet Cora, where's your romance?"

"You got it, give it to me."

He works for his money and receives more than he thought might be coming.

"Here you are, Jack Rabbit, and remember, nobody owes anybody anything. Once in a while I get one on the house for bein a good girl."

"Anytime, baby—again right now, if you say."

The next few towns are easier, but even professional love doesn't make the road acceptable to Cora. Only on stage do lights, gels and music make magic. Backstage she jives and argues and plays "pitting wits" with theater managers. So there had to come a day of enough.

Busses are no better than trains where time schedules are concerned. One evening they arrive late and must dash directly to the theatre, getting in just as the audience is arriving. A big crowd is glad news and they hurry through the stage door to be met by the worried manager.

"Shake a leg, girls, it's a packed house."

The dancers are looking for dressing space. The stage manager directs them to the basement because "the dressing room toilet's stopped up". Cora grabs the fleeing manager while Looli goes down to unpack costumes which have arrived the day before.

"No, Cora, I won't pay half in advance."

"You promised."

"Even worse news. It's a short week. Tonight, Saturday and Sunday. Week-time shows are out. Not pullin in a dime here during the week—gotta run movies."

"What's all this dressin in basements? I want privacy!"

"You got it. Clean up man strung a curtain down there so nobody can watch you dress. There's a toilet room the workman uses to store pail and mops—the sink is outside for washin. Yall can make do."

He gives her a friendly pat on the backside. "Shake a leg, your crowd's waitin."

She goes down and inspects cracked mirrors, broken chairs, a row of nails on the walls for clothing, a black iron sink half-filled with stagnant water, a smelly, brown-crusted toilet in a three-by-four room lit by a twenty-five watt bulb. The chorus members dress sullenly on either side of a length of unbleached muslin draped over a sagging clothesline. In one corner, three yards of brown flowered chintz marks off

Cora's space, which is furnished with a broken-runged chair and a battered kitchen table.

The chorus shares a long, narrow shelf covered with green windowshade. The stage manager yells down a dark corridor, "Fifteen minutes and you're on!" Cora starts back upstairs and Chalk blocks her way. "I know this is no time to talk, honey, but a telegram was waitin for me. They want me to tour with the Silas Green Minstrel—for a lot more than I'm gettin here. What do you think?"

She pinches his cheek just a bit too hard. "Go, baby, take it. Let nothin stand in your way—take it."

"But I thought we had somethin goin."

"Sex without love is exercise. Now move so I can take care a business." She goes straight to upstairs dressing rooms and tries the doors only to find them locked. She slams her weight against one door with a star on it; nothing moves. She strides down to the manager's office, flings open first one door and then another which reveals a clean washroom. She confronts the manager as he hurries to meet her in the hall.

"Cora, goddamit, get ready. You're on in ten!"

"Why are dressin rooms locked?"

"It's the law. We must have separate facilities. You know I do white shows. But I try to bring in colored as much as I can."

Rage makes veins throb and stand out on her forehead. "You tryin to give me a stroke, you bastard!"

She places her hands on her hips, sees in him Mountain Seeley grabbing her breast . . . boys tearing into Cecil's lip, their voices taunting . . . the eyes of Kojie peeping at her private parts by lamplight. . . .

"I'm not goin on!"

"Cora, don't do this to me. The house is packed!"

The stage manager steps in to help the manager persuade her. "You have less than five minutes to get your costume on and hit the stage. Save all talk until after the final curtain!"

"Get the fuck outta my way!"

Cora's not bluffing. The manager's voice changes to a wheedle; he seems about to cry. "I'm begging you, have mercy. Do you want me to sit up and beg like a dog? I'm begging."

She paces and fans her perspiring face with a horsehair hat; she kicks over a fire bucket and sends sand pouring out on the floor. "Bossman, I don't care if you shit bullets and cry blood! Cora Anderson's not goin on till you give me that goddam star dressin room with the star painted on the door—and open up all them other rooms for the chorus!"

"It's the law—separate facilities."

"I want a clean, star toilet so I can pee in peace, and a clean washbasin with runnin water."

"This is Georgia, there are laws!"

"Fuck Georgia law, I ain't made it! And if you don't pay my advance, I'm gonna run my mothafuckin right foot so far up your ass a doctor's gonna have to saw my leg off at the knee to separate us!"

"You can have the dressing rooms for tomorrow!"

"Now! And I ain't goin on without advance money. Call the police if you wanta. Lettum come. Throw me in jail, lynch me—I'm ready to die! This is my last stop on the Jim Crow line! Pay up and open the dressin rooms, you white-ass, cheatin sonofabitch, *or I ain't goin on!*"

The stage manager goes out and tells the audience the show will go on a bit late because of "a delay in transportation". Chalk stalls for time at piano by entertaining them with the new boogie-woogie beat. The audience claps and dances in the aisles, while Cora sits in the star dressing room, recovers from a crying spell, and eases into her Rosalinda dress with gold lace. Looli holds the ribboned tambourine, and comforts: "It's a shame to make anybody as mad as he made you. What come over you, honey?"

"He made me feel like a mat girl. This business has no respect for me. It's humiliation."

They did such a rousing good show the audience wouldn't let them leave without four encores. The manager had to give a begrudging smile and let them finish out the week.

Twenty-Two

Cecil's old cheap-rent apartment is always filled with homeless men who come for free coffee and cinnamon buns. They are often hungry, but manage to chip in enough to buy Mission Bell muscatel by the pint, or a twenty-nine cent bottle of half-and-half—port and sherry mixed. One or two always need a night's shelter. They hungrily drink in knowledge along with the wine. Cecil brings great men, past and present, alive to the room—Hannibal and Toussaint and Nat Turner and Garvey, and Pushkin and Dumas and Captain Cudjoe and Garvey, and Frederick Douglass and Bill Trotter and Garvey, and Harrison and DuBois and Woodson and Muhammad and Garvey; and the topics of socialism, communism, nationalism, the Falasha Jews, Rastafari—and Garvey. They spread the word all over Harlem, stopping young men on the street and challenging them to discussions of "things you won't find in the damn history book cause they don't want them known."

Cecil now leads them away from calling themselves Negroes. "You are Blacks, or Afro-Americans. Do not accept terms slave masters have given to you." He tries to talk them away from the wine bottles: "Those Mission Bells don't ring, and half-and-half will divide your mind in half. Keep a clear head. Knowledge is power."

Some cannot function with a clear head. Sober, they would be forced to revolt, take their own lives or run screaming through the streets. One man, who suffered shell shock in the World War, had been put away for running down Lenox Avenue shouting, "The Second World War is coming! Germany again! Another war!" then pretending to remove the pin from an imaginary hand grenade and toss it into crowds. Cecil is healing him, giving hope. "Mr. Warren, what you say is true, but try and keep it to yourself. People don't care to hear about the terrible things that await them in the future." Mr. Warren becomes Cecil's right-hand man whenever he takes to the step ladder with a nationalist flag on one side and an American flag on the other.

"Brother Green, why you put up the American? Red, black and green is good enough for me."

"Because it is the law. The American flag must be displayed or I am subject to arrest."

Crowds gather when Cecil speaks. His men set up huge display pictures of Africans, Rastafari and Southern workmen, and Garvey. Little children watch, listen and giggle. The old warriors reprimand, "Laughin at yourself. The pictures are your mirror. When you look at them you only see yourself."

Right off One Hundred Twenty-fifth Street and Fifth Avenue is a beautiful park named Mount Morris. It is wild with greenery. Footpaths and stone steps lead upward to the very top of a stony mountain, from which most of the city can be seen. At that peak is where Cora and Delta enjoy close moments and grow to understand and misunderstand each other better, to quarrel and wonder at their differences.

"Mama, I don't like to see Daddy with those people on street corners."

"You don't have to. He comes to see you."

"Only once in a while."

"He doesn't like to come empty-handed."

"Last time he brought six dollars—before you came back. Cousin Estelle put some with it for my Easter."

"That's all he had. If there was more, he'd give it."

"But he buys food for those bums."

"Don't call people bums. We all start out the same—fresh new little babies, just goin to see what the end will be."

"Hard to believe when you look at em."

The wind whips across the unsheltered rock. Cora holds Delta close to her. "Life is short and we must try to be kind to one another."

"Seems long to me, Mama."

"Time is a trickster, Delta. He makes us think we will be young forever, but while I sleep he sprinkles gray in my hair and draws little lines in my face. He also steals people's eyesight, bit by bit."

"Mama, you don't talk at all like the street corner people. How did you meet and decide to marry Daddy?"

"We were childhood sweethearts—and loved each other—and, well, one thing just led to another."

"One time, after school, I was goin to the ten cent store. This girl from my school—her name is Lenore—was with me. Daddy was talking on the street corner, standing on his ladder. Lenore laughed and said, 'That's a lotta poor, dumb ignorance.' I defended him and said he had a right to say what he pleases."

"Honey, I'm glad you did."

"But I didn't tell her he was my father. I turned my head so he wouldn't see me. I was ashamed to tell her; now I feel ashamed that I felt that way. I started to tell her the next day but was afraid it might make bad feelings between us."

"Do you like Lenore?"

"Yes, Ma'am."

"Then tell her."

That topmost place in Mount Morris Park brought out their innermost thoughts. When Delta was nine she asked her mother to "hold Catechism" and see if she had properly memorized the prayers and answers she must recite by the next day: the Act of Contrition, the Apostles Creed, a general flood of words strange to Cora.

"Bless me Father, for I have sinned . . . through my fault, through my fault, through my most grievous fault. I detest all my sins because I dread the loss of heaven and the pains of hell, but most of all because they offend thee, my God, who art all good and deserving. . . ."

Cora closes the book. "Yes, you know it. But I think it's time for me to take you to a Wednesday night testimonial meetin at Salem or Metropolitan or Abyssinia, to some black place. I want you to know it all."

Twenty-Three

I look around at Cecil's broken-down apartment—just like Cohen's Charleston bookshop. I try to stop recallin those sweet days of love when we walked the battery and counted our ships. I have to live for now. He strokes my cheek the way I like him to do and says, "Here's one I heard from a fella: Some people get caught in a box and fight their way out; others hang up curtains and call it home.'"

I wonder why this tenement does not strike him as bein caught in a box. He cannot see himself at all as I see him. I can't picture myself through his eyes. My head always grows weary of tryin to follow his thinking.

"This white fellow said to me, 'If I were you, instead of fighting against the advantage I have, I'd live to show me what a fine and wonderful human being you can become even at a disadvantage.' He is saying, if I were you, I'd be me, up to a certain point."

"Up to what point, Cecil?"

"Up to the point of faint imitation—not to becoming competition. Wants me to advance beyond my brothers and sisters, but not up to or beyond him."

"Cecil, it was smart of you to say, 'If I were you, I'd be me!'"

"But it's a lie. If he were me, he'd be me. I, in his place, would be he. We don't see others except according to our own circumstances."

"Man, you're so smart, why ain't you rich?"

"Cora, everyone knows how to ask that, but someday you must ask this question of a very wealthy man, 'If you're so rich, why ain't you smart?'"

I wonder what I will tell Delta about stayin out all night.

"Mama, where were you?"

"Stayed over at a lady's house, because it was too late to come home alone."

Estelle won't ask a thing because she knows where I am when I don't come in—the times I drop by to wrestle a little money from Cecil's short supply because the bread his money buys tastes sweeter. The distance between us grows greater, but we cling. I love him still—and might not if he were other than himself. He is the box where I have hung my curtains. I have named him "home".

I spend the night in his arms, love him, then listen to him speakin against those who dare try to stop brave men from tryin. My love brightens his eyes again, and he makes plans to write a book for youngsters: "Great Black Men of Determination." I feel so womanly as Cecil's plans for a book turns to plans for us.

"By next year I'll have some money together . . . we'll have a home here or go to Africa or South America—some place where they are used to seeing people of color." He always starts off with "next year". I remember to take the four dollars from his dresser. A man oughta do something for his family, no matter what.

A depression can break some people, but none that I know. I never told Cecil about Roosevelt losin my bank money cause I hadn't let him know I had a stash. Roosevelt's doin some good now, makin plans with a lot of initials for things—WPA and NRA. The biggest thing goin is home relief and surplus food. Well, we can't get the relief thing because we're not correctly related. Nothin we have is considered an immediate family. Estelle can't collect as long as Looli, Delta and I are with her. Cousins and friends must live apart and make their own family household. This only makes the welfare pay out six rents instead a one.

Estelle says, "How the hell a lotta ex-slaves gonna be set up family-wise like the DAR? Them Daughters of American Revolution, all of em suppose to trace theirself back to the very beginnin of the U.S.A. Seems they the only ones entitle to collect relief."

We are the DAS, Daughters of American Slaves. Investigators question the soul out of you for a birth certificate with information about your parents and all such. Lookin around Harlem and seein the different colors of complexion everywhere, I'm thinkin it'll set the country flat on its back if we ever give out the real story on where we all come from. You could starve to death while fillin out forms.

I got investigated by a social worker, but nothin seems to work fast enough to do any good. I had to lie and say that only me and Delta live here.

God bless Looli, our friends and neighbors, cause we learned how to share, puttin what we have together to make some kinda meal. Back apartment might bring their rice to go along with the front apartment's beans, while downstairs apartment would show up with meatballs or cabbage. The surplus food program hurt some people's pride cause they didn't wanta go stand on line to collect what was bein given at the food station—didn't want other people to see they were out on the turf, collectin. Some friends gave their food tickets to us.

We go collect at a garage. Looli holds one ticket and I got the other. We get doubles on beans, prunes, sides of bacon, apples, celery and potatoes. We also make Cecil meet us to help haul the stuff home. For weeks we ate baked beans and apple pie.

Another help is the place between East One Hundred Sixteenth and One Hundred Tenth streets called "Under The Bridge"—six double blocks of pushcarts. We walk there with our shoppin bags and buy porgies at five pounds for a dime; they three for a dime if the man cleans em, but we get five.

One weekend, Laverne, Estelle and I clean and fry forty pounds of fish. Holdin us a house-rent party to pay the landlord. We're chargin twenty-five cents a head for entrance fee; food is thirty-five cents a plate. That ungrateful, leechin Chalk is in town so I have him come in to play piano for tips and dinner. We clear rent and some extra to go on, but I don't care to have that kind of party again. Not until the day of the affair did I see one of the tickets Looli had printed.

> If you don't dance, if you can't sing
> Come anyhow and shake that thing!
> At Cora's social house-rent party

I sent Delta and Sugar down to May's house to spend the night. Cards like that handed out on the street, with the address and apartment number on the back, brings in a lot of trash. You can't refuse em because chargin to enter your home is against the damn law in the first place. They will sic the cops on you or else batter down the door.

The place is packed and I don't know half the faces. A far cry from Pullman days. The bathtub is fulla sodas and bottles a beer with big ice chunks. Looli serves the hard stuff across an ironin board at the kitchen door. Estelle dishes food and I make change. Cecil gives us a hand movin crates and liftin heavy pots and pans. Looli said she told him, "Garvey's banished from the U.S.A. and West Indies, so you just better use some time to come round and help do for your own."

He isn't doin much smilin, but good thing he came. Some unknown nigger wants to fight a man who doesn't care to have his girlfriend dance with a stranger. He pulls out a gun and it takes Cecil and two of his buddies to talk the weapon out of his hand. They give the man his quarter back while everyone is screamin, then walk him out and clean over to Lenox Avenue. Keep pattin his back and tellin him what a fine fellow he is to be "big" about it. By the time they get back, the other fella is tryin to beat on his girl for drinkin too much and laughin with an unknown.

"Bitch, you came with me! You laugh with me!"

Looli handles him off to one side, talkin his talk and actin like she's his relative. "Shame on you, brother, you don't have to be jealous a nobody. Good-lookin guy like you. Darlin, her mind couldn't be on nobody else but you." He tones down and goes to pinchin Looli's arm. Estelle cried cause six people slipped out when the gun was pulled, without payin for their dinners. The last soul doesn't leave until sunup and Cecil has to half carry him down to the street.

Two hours after the big ruckus, a cop came upstairs to make us turn off the phonograph because of noise complaint. I turned it off. Looli gave him three dollars and he said to turn the music back on. Most folks had a good time but I'll not associate myself with another pay party. It is risky, and it's best to live legal, with honor. Cecil works so hard, cleans up the cans and fish bones, sees that every ashtray is empty, puts all furniture back in place, but he is aggravated and sad about the affair.

Depression means that people get evicted, put out on the sidewalk for nonpayment. Always somebody's furniture is piled on the pavement by the city marshall. Neighbors take in the kids and serve turns watchin the stuff until people find someplace to take their things. Folks from the Communist Party come around after the marshall leaves, knock the lock off the apartment door and move the people back into their place. Makes the landlord mad cause he has to pay the marshall each time for puttin things out. The neighbors chip in and buy containers of beer for the Communist Party and also bring odds and ends of food to make up a "welcome home" party for the evicted. Someone brought a can of home-relief veal to a party—that veal is enough to set your teeth on edge. I put it in the cat's dish and the cat backed away from it, even though his poor little ribs were showin. A lady told us how she learned to doctor it, so it could be eaten, with tomatoes, pepper sauce and a pound of chopped meat. A Communist told me the veal was a little calf that had died of hardship in a place called the "dustbowl." That's why it tastes so strange. All I know is it'll make a cat back up if it's served plain. Most likely that's why it's surplus.

Hard times will make a monkey eat red pepper. Winter's the worst. Estelle has a part-time, but it only pays thirty-five an hour. Looli is makin fifteen a week for dressin another Broadway leadin lady. She's in clover compared to the rest of us. Now and then I go with her to serve at cocktail parties given by theater people. They are crazy about Looli. If they're sporty, she tells them I'm a number one poker dealer. We pocket some good cuts from house pots but, believe it or not, the house always takes their cut, no matter how well-off the people might be. Money makes everybody smile. At one party there was a old, prosperous-lookin white man named Mr. Simeon. He watched me all night long, followed my every play and smiled with admiration when I stuck two wild cards on my bosom. I have twice as much bosom now as when Delta was born, so cards are easy to stick on my lowcut cocktail uniform.

Simeon's skin is white, his hair yellowy white, a diamond ring set in platinum sparkles on his pinky. He wears a diamond stickpin in his tie. Looks like the interlocutor of a first-class minstrel show. He's wise to every play I call, but doesn't get in the game.

While lookin at me, he gives Looli his business card and says I should call him on a strictly business matter. I'm now on the other side of young, trim and beautiful, so maybe it isn't monkey business—but just maybe. He told her I was a handsome and talented woman who could be an asset to a high class business. I notice how white folks always call a colored woman "handsome," like she's a man. We only call men handsome; we say attractive women, who are less than pretty, are fine-lookin.

Whatever he has in mind I plan to look the other way—to now live with honor. Looli is tired of my shilly-shally ways. She says, "Cora, a prosperous white friend in your corner is like ready money in the bank. Cecil is my heart, but you did not have to marry him when you got out of the knot with Kojie. Why marry somebody who can't hand you anything? Little love now and then is all right, but that's enough of it. If you not gonna live with a cat, what's the marryin about?"

"Papers, Looli. I wanted proper papers for Delta. Not fair to keep callin her Green when the last name is Anderson. I didn't do it for me. I got legal papers for her sake. These white folks give you a hard time if you don't have those papers. It's the same person, with or without papers, but the one *with* will win out every time. That's the law."

If you smile, don't complain and dress fairly decent; everybody thinks you rich. I let them think it. I like how it feels for people to think I'm rich—at least "nigger rich", which is just a wee bit more than you absolutely need at the moment—two months ahead of the sheriff. But, truth be told, the winter is hard, and folks are writin to me from Edisto and hintin for money, boat fare or train fare to somewhere else than where they are so they can change their luck with a new scene. A woman once asked to borrow three hundred dollars when I didn't have but eighty to my name. I just said I couldn't do it, because I sure didn't want her to spread any poor-mouth stories about me. I gotta look prosperous even if they hate me for it. Thank you, Mary Baker Eddy.

Sugar got a part scholarship to get in Lincoln for her nurse's trainin, but there is some expense attached to the thing anyway. Estelle didn't really want her to be a nurse, wanted her to latch on to a professional husband and be comfortable like most a these white women do. I want Delta to go South to college. I'm thinkin more like Estelle, as time goes by. Poor Estelle is now takin some kinda radiation treatment for stomach trouble, to shrink a tumor. Doctor says it's too dangerous to operate, plus she also has the diabetes, but she locks down and brightly goes on.

Laverne is so sweet, keeps house nicely for us, but we don't have enough cash to put in her hand regular. She's working for nothin but room and board. Looli's cocktail parties now comin fewer and farther between. Big shots don't even party like they used to. People also think the well-to-do got more than they got. Poor Looli had two flop shows in a row. We put our minds to it and learned to make fancy little sandwiches and canapes so we could do full caterin for the parties. Looli somehow got hold a this West Indian fella named Marion—he was dresser for a male star. He's heavyset but very ladylike and easy to get along with. He's middle-aged, but says, "I'm still lookin for somebody to be my sponsor-friend, to see me through this badass world." He's a fine bartender, knows how to jolly folks along, to make em feel good when they oughta feel bad.

Yes indeed, hard times will make a monkey eat red pepper. We now put little metal boxes outside the window to keep our food cold in the winter and save on buyin ice. But the iceman gets his revenge when the weather turns extra cold or extra warm; then the food supply is wiped out. We spend too damn much on carfare, what with hospital visits and lookin for work.

Estelle burns "job incense" to help us find work. Some voodoo woman told her it works. Looli lights up green candles to draw green money to the house. Me, I just close my eyes mornin and night and say, "I am God's perfect child and there is employment for me." Estelle does not read her science books like she used to, but me, I try everything. Cecil looks to the sky and shakes his head about me, but damn if I don't get hold a more cash than he does. Yes indeed, I am God's perfect child and there is employment for me.

The Depression makes big changes, like what's goin on with May and Apolinario. When he lost his restaurant job it made his disposition very abrupt. He spends a lot of time at home and several Filipino guys hang around and talk politics. They all wear black shirts. Every now and then they go down to City Hall and raise hell about gettin jobs, until the police hit them with billyclubs or make arrests. They call themselves "blackshirts" and have street speakers just like Garveyites and Communists. May is worried about it because someone told her they are Fascists. There are Italians in it, Spanish, what they call Latins. I don't like the sound of it, and she's dead afraid that Apolinario might wind up in jail.

The ones that hang around like to speak their foreign language except for when they use the word *nigger* or say "the bum Americano". All this is distressful to May. I asked Cecil to tell me exactly what is *fascist*. He says they're a bunch of racist bastards and have plans to conquer the world. I hated to tell May, but I did—softenin the blow by explainin that Cecil sure doesn't know everything and might well be wrong. May has a very gentle nature, so these things hit her hard. I'm learnin a few extra things bout white women. Looli and I served a fine party for a woman on Seventy-second Street—woman got a four-room penthouse lookin out over the whole city. Her bigshot boyfriend was to pay the tab for the party, but he didn't show up and skipped town bout owin somebody some money. Left her holdin the bag, owin us, the liquor dealer, and two months' back rent. Poor soul cried herself sick, but did try to do right. She gave Looli a set a luggage made in France; she gave me a beaded evenin bag and a filigree dresser set—comb, brush and mirror. Just goes to show. I thought white women always got treated nice, except for May. You never can tell.

Apolinario will not apply for relief. The Fascists don't go for that. Somehow, by hook or crook, he raises rent and food, mostly by crook. One night May calls Estelle and me down to share a bounty. The blackshirts have delivered *cases* of sardines and condensed milk, pounds and pounds of sliced ham and cheese, the same of roast beef, forty packages of butter and all manner of canned goods. Apolinario and three other blackshirts had brought it all on a truck, then they had to move on to leave the balance at other apartments. He told May to share some of the loot with us. She didn't want to keep any of it in her place. Estelle asks not one word about where the great harvest came from, but hastily kisses a can toward heaven and thanks God for his generosity. May is heartsick. We all *have* to know the stuff must be stolen goods;

but look at it this way: didn't the bank shut down with my money?

"May, accept a windfall with grace."

"Cora," she says, "this is evil. One of them takes a job in a store as a helper; a few days later he empties out the place with the help of his friends, and, of course, he never returns to the job. All the boss has is his false name and address. It's sin, thievery, robbery."

"I don't believe it," Estelle says, as she prepares to drag our share home. "And, God be my witness, if this is fascist, then it can't be such an awful thing."

May breaks into tears. "I can't go to confession anymore. Apolinario says I must not confess it to the priest. But if I don't, I can't take communion." I try to console her while Estelle fills another shoppin bag.

"Look, May, just confess this to God and no one else."

Estelle agrees. "Yeah, talk direct. You don't need a go-between to carry a message to God. That's my quarrel with the Catholic Church. Why tell mortal man? Tell God. He knows more about this Depression than the Pope."

She is still afraid. We stay with her until Apolinario returns and explains. "It is only right to feed the hungry. When Jesus picked corn on the Sabbath to feed his disciples, whose cornfield was it?" None of us could say. "It is only right to feed the hungry." Apolinario knows how to prove it.

Talk about Depression. When push comes to shove we had to hit the street and hunt down something to do. Laverne and I heard about the downtown garment district round Thirty-sixth Street. You walk and look for cardboard signs hangin out front of factories: "OPERATORS WANTED" or "FINISHERS WANTED", "HAND HEMMERS", "BUTTON HOLERS", and like that. They say now and then they might teach you how to do it, but most signs read "experienced only". We see one place with a good sign: "FINISHERS—BEGINNERS OKAY". We turn in to see about it. All of a sudden comes these yells—"Scabs! Dirty, lousy scabs!" Lotta girls are walkin up and down with signs: "STRIKE FOR UNION WAGES".

The sign carriers actin nasty and screechin and screamin. One big woman holds another who's ready to jump off the line and hit me. I say, "Come on, bitch!" And make ready to ram my pocketbook through her face. Laverne says how maybe we shouldn't cross the line cause *scab* means a sore, somethin that feeds and lives off a peoples' misery. There's bout thirty girls on the line and only one black—a meek, silent creeper. Why the hell should I help them when they don't give a damn bout me? "You white bitches got white men to give you everything in the world! Yall own it, so rare back and enjoy it!" The silent creeper keeps creepin. A old, white-headed biddy hollers, "Goddam, lousy, scab bastards!"

I can holler, too. "You white, stringy-haired, hungry-ass daughter of a starvin bitch!" She's most purple with rage, but, she can't outrage me. I got me a child to take care of. "You big-behinded monster!"

I grab Laverne's hand and we go runnin past them and up the two flights of stairs. Arrows on the wall pointin: "DOLLY DIMPLE DARLING DRESSES". We huff and puff all the way in to a large machine shop, Laverne near collapses. There's about ten Negro women workin at machines. A black boy is steam-pressin dresses. He sings "Sly Mongoose" with a fake West Indian accent and hits the steam pedal with the rhythm:

Sly mongoose, the dogs know your name . . . whoosh!
Sly mongoose, it sho is a shame . . . whoosh!

Fella comes over and says, "I'm floor manager. You get forty cents an hour till you're able to go on piece-work. Our good piece-workers can take home twenty-five a week, once they get the hang." He calls a woman over to show us how to sew hooks and eyes and make belt loops. Once the floor manager moves on, she drops the news, "They'll settle with the union soon, then let us go and take back the ones who walked out."

At lunch time, Laverne and I leave and don't go back. Lotta other signs are out, but when we go up the steps they tell us come back another time because they're full at the moment. Some colored boys who load trucks save us walkin by tellin how there's really no jobs, but bosses need a list a names on call in case a more strikes by the Ladies' Garment Union. We grab the uptown subway and treat ourselves to a meal at the Father Divine Restaurant. It's on Lenox Avenue, down in a basement. Eatin food is our one reward. If I don't eat or drink then where is the black reward? A good meal seems my only consolation.

The dinin room is clean as a pin, with a nice bowl a paper flowers on each table and white oilcloth covers. Overhead an electric fan is nicely turnin. Our own people cookin and servin. A blackboard on the wall tells the menu:

> Pot roast dinner—15 cents———Fried chicken—15 cents
> Fried fish dinner—8 cents———Buttermilk—10 cents qt.
> Peas, rice, greens, salad and pie with all orders.

We take pot roast and get much more than we can possibly eat. "Thank you, Ma'am," Laverne tells the waitress. She is corrected. "Say thank Father."

I say, "Thank Father." Woman behind the counter looks glad and says, "Father Divine is God." I once heard somebody say they would not eat at a Divine place because he thinks they must put somethin in the food to make people believe in him so. He does have a lot of followers who're workin for him free. They get free room and board, work for each other, and don't have to hit the street to seek a job in this cruel world. After all, that's enough to make folks believe and follow. Man at the next table is dressed in the Muslim get-up so many now wearin. He's eatin his fish and sayin "thank Father" like the rest. We're gettin more outta Father Divine than Estelle's gettin outta workin for the Democratic Party. All over Harlem people workin for Democrats or Republicans. Both parties promise to give jobs to those who help get party members in government and keep them there. Only thing is, they don't have as many jobs as they have helpers. For a time, Estelle was also helpin the Communist Party cause they've been so good about movin her friends back in their apartments; also will go to court with them. She kept askin me to come along and go to a Communist "cell" meetin with her. I sure wanted to see a cell, so I went.

My heart was beatin like a triphammer. But, damn, a cell turned out to be nothin but somebody's flat. Was a white woman's place, but there were at least half Negro out of ten people there. The woman reads from a book and tells how capitalism is racist and greedy. She uses such big, dry words—proletarian, socio-economic crisis—never uses one little word where six big ones will do. Every time a Negro speaks, a certain white makes a gentle, kindly correction. "Comrade, what you are trying to say is. . . ."

One Negro got very annoyed and said, "Comrade, I'm not *tryin* to say a damn thing. I done said it." Then all have a discussion about how the white comrade is too high-handed in his ways—called white chauvinism. Seems to me like the white women and black men have all kindsa patience with each other, but kinda tight on black women. They lost me when they went to talkin bout the "woman question". They had a couple of booklets for sale: *The Woman Question* and *The*

Negro Question. I asked why was the word *question* in it at all. They couldn't handle the answer too well. I know the question must ask, Can women and Negroes have their rights? But there should be *no question* that I can see.

They talk bout doin first things first. Seems employment comes before Negro and woman questions. However, I notice it's not called "The Employment Question"—it's just "employment". I hate to pick at everything too much because capitalism sure is a greedy sonofabitch and I know how it did in Garvey, who now can't enter the U.S.A. or the British West Indies. Coolidge was the one who let him outta Atlanta Federal Prison so he could be put clean out the country and never return.

Looli said, "Yall leave them Communist alone. All they wanta do is *use* our people." I said, "What the hell you think the Republicans and the Democrats doin with us?" She fell out laughin. "Yeah," I said. "They can show Communists what usin is all about!"

I take Delta to church for Wednesday night testimonial. Mostly women there like always—not too many young ones, just those of us beginnin to look life and age in the face. Instead a prayin I find myself wonderin where church women find so many funny-lookin hats. We can't quite make our peace with hats. Cecil says, years back, down in New Orleans, durin slave days, they had a law which forbid any slave woman to wear a hat—had to be a kerchief. Explanation was: so they could tell white women from mixed bloods who looked white. Lotta mean-ass laws. Right now, down in Mississippi, if a white man marries a colored woman both can be fined ten thousand dollars each and be put in jail for ten years. If they just sleep together, with no marriage, that only calls for thirty days' hard labor and a scoldin. The black man will be lynched for mixin. Strange laws and lawmakers.

I'm thinkin a hat is a silly idea, with flowers, ribbons and bows. It's the law of the church that women cover their heads and men uncover theirs. I think it's different with Jews, but there's some other kinda law that applies in their case. Well, I am here, wearin a ugly hat and uncomfortable shoes like the rest, lookin forward to hearin hardship stories and very ready to agree out loud when one happens to touch on me.

Nobody pokes fun or laughs at anybody's Wednesday night testimony. A sister rises wearin a hat that's a size too small; she has cut the back open and connected the loose ends with a strip of black elastic.

She prays, "Lord, God, be my witness this evenin. My rent was due, one son was in the house of detention and my daughter in the lonesome hospital givin birth. And wasn't no man there to see her through. Life had me backed in a corner, don'tcha know. I fell on my knees and asked Jesus to help my grief!"

"Talk, sister! We hear you!"

"Lord have mercy!"

"I know so well!"

We rally to her and she takes us to the success endin of answered prayer. The son came home, a part-time job came through and the landlord accepted a little at a time until the back rent was paid up.

"Hallelujah! Bless his holy name!" We shout for her celebration. Then another speaks about not yet bein able to see the light—nothin but a dark street of trouble. She asks our prayers.

One old man is full of regrets and tries to pray his way free. "Lord, Oh, Lord!"

A woman next to Delta jumps up and wildly slings her purse around.

"Mama, she scares me."

"Don't fear, darlin," I say, "that's whatcha call emotion, feelins. You can't stay alive without expressin feelins." She is big-eyed with wonder as the meetin rocks, specially when I am moved to testify—to ask for prayer for all the down-home women who can't even read and write, and for those like me who can just barely do it. I talk up for our need to be loved, cryin from the depths of my mother's watery grave. I even pray for the white witch who called me "scab" and beg pardon for what I called her. I ask the Lord to bless my daughter and keep her feet on the right path. I pray for Estelle, Sugar, Looli, May, Apolinario and Cecil. I ask God to give guidance and change wicked hearts and put a stop to lynchin. The church basement is alive with my sound as all fly higher and higher on the wings of my prayer. I pray for the well-to-do who are unhappy and cannot find peace and lock themselves out of paradise. They don't follow all of my words, but they follow my heart. When the shoutin is done, I see through my own tears. Delta weeps along with the rest of us. I hug her and tell her, "It's good to sometime express to the bottom of your soul. We'll never be full women till we're able to face our feelins."

It's late when meetin lets out, but we decide to walk home and save our carfare for tomorrow. We feel closer. We enjoy lookin in dimly-lit shop windows now closed for the night. A man is behind us. He fits the mean description put out on all Negro criminals: big, black and burly. I steer Delta across the street; he also crosses.

"Mama," she says, "I think he's following." We cross again to the side we just left. He trails behind, no matter what we do. As we turn into our block, I look around for a stick or a milk bottle, some sorta weapon to do battle.

"Mama, I'm scared."

It is dark. One of the streetlights is burned out. Halfway down the block I turn around and pull her along with me.

I walk straight up to him and he backs up. "Mister," I say, "what is your name?" His mouth gaps open showin stained teeth. "Er . . . er . . . Tommy." I smile pleasantly. "Well, Mister Tommy, my name is Cora and this is my daughter, Delta. We're from South Carolina and I feel scared cause bad things sometime happen in this neighborhood. Will you please protect us and see us home?" He shifts from foot to foot. "Whatcha mean?" I take his arm. "Will you kindly walk us to the door and stand at the foot of the stairs till we get safely up?"

He grumbles, "Okay."

I nudge Delta. "This gentleman will take good care of us," I say. He walks us to the stoop and stands by the stair until we get up and I call down. "Thank you, Mr. Tommy." He calls back "You welcome!" and then he's gone. I like to think he didn't bother anybody else.

I'm undressed for bed. Delta comes in to say good night with a kiss. "Oh, Mama you were so fine. I believe that man would have harmed us if you hadn't thought what to do."

"You see, Delta, if we expect decency from people, they often deliver, live up to our fine expectations. But I must say, it's best not to count on it."

After she goes to bed, Laverne brings me news that May's been by to say Apolinario's arrested. It's now eleven, so I'll see her first thing come morning. Religion is upon me! I say a prayer for the prisoner husband. In the middle of the night I am awakened by the voice of my father: "Cora, wake up." I turn on the lamp. The clock says two a.m. I try to go back to sleep, but I feel uneasy. I put on my wrapper and go down to May's. There is a strong smell of gas in the hall. I call her name and bang on the door. Neighbors come to help; we break the door down. May is on the kitchen floor, with her head in the oven. A froth of bubbles is on her lips. The ambulance comes. She still breathes. They take her to

Harlem Hospital. Praise the Lord, she still breathes.

She is ashamed and turns her pale face to the wall. The priest talks to her about how precious a life is and how no one has a right to take it. Across the hospital bed, I study the face of her mother. She, too, is pale and quiet, but I know her accordin to her letters. She leans over May, makes lovin sounds—"My baby"—she's ready to forgive now that Apolinario is in jail. She pats May's hand and promises to come again tomorrow.

I follow her into the hall and say I'm May's friend. She gives me a distant smile, and I take it off her face.

"May still loves him and he loves her, so leave them alone. She wanted to die because of your letters, not because of jail."

She turns to the white nurse and they exchange looks of sympathy. The colored nurse watches them go off down the corridor, then says, "Why care what they do? There's plenty of our own to worry about. I could hardly get in here for nurse's training. Why work yourself up over them?" I look at her pretty, dark face and wonder how to explain.

"I know what you go through, but she's my friend. I love her for good and sufficient reason. It's not ever easy, but I try to accept people just as they come wrapped."

"But do they accept you?"

"Not often. But I treat white folks accordin to how they act, not by how they look."

Twenty-Four

Best thing I know is don't run yourself crazy tryin to find the exact right answer. One thing, my Christmas comes through groovy. May goes to the Regent movie house on One Hundred and Sixteenth Street every Tuesday evenin. They give way a piece of china so you can make up a set of dishes. She went for a year at forty-five cents a go, then gave me the whole set. That's better than most presents, cause I know she wanted the dishes for herself.

She is now able to receive what the social worker calls "interim help" because Apolinario is in prison and she has tried to do herself in. If he had been law-abidin she wouldn't be able to get anything due to the fact that he's able-bodied even though unemployed.

I tried to get a job in the Federal Theater under the Works Project plan, which was started by Franklin Delano Roosevelt to help unemployed actors. However, you have to get on Welfare first, then apply and show clippins of newspaper write-ups to prove that you've been in legitimate shows. First time I knew that vaudeville is illegitimate. Somebody told me about a printer who'll print you some write-ups that look like reviews out of *The Graphic* or *The Daily Mirror*. Where the hell is there room for honor? Not enough just to need assistance or be willin to work.

I go to all these different offices but they keep you comin back for weeks, then they ask how come you didn't stay home until the investigator called. Estelle heard that you can't even become an *investigator* without gettin on welfare first. In my case, they want me to put the finger on Cecil, and then they'll make him come in for questionin. The investigator told me it would help if Delta and I lived alone, without relatives, then just report that Cecil abandoned us. I wouldn't want a job as investigator, lookin into people's hearts, minds and clothes-closets. They don't want you to own a radio 'cause that means you're not destitute. That kinda shit gets on my nerves. But Christmas came through groovy.

Three weeks before the holidays I got me a lovely job, but it was only for three weeks. A newspaper man from Chicago, name of Mister Abbot, has this idea to sell and promote a new line called "colored dolls". Some fellas thought up these dark-faced dolls and say how a doll should look like the little girl who owns it. They're really white dolls painted brown. They have black wigs instead of red or blonde and they're cute. The dresses and bonnets are pink or blue, trimmed with lots of frills and lace; all wear black socks and babydoll shoes. Mister Abbot interviewed me and gave me the job, outta ten people. He liked my attitude about race pride. Some people don't like such dolls and they can't hide their feelins. They think it's some kinda Jim Crow to have special dolls for Negroes. Lotsa people now sayin "black" instead a "Negro"; others don't like it. We call the dolls "colored" because most people would rather own a "colored" doll than one that is called "Negro" or "black" or "Afro-American", even though they're lookin at the same doll. A doll's name is important.

Some children hate the colored dolls—the ones who are old enough to be used to havin white dolls. The littlest children love them; they get a lot of attention and questions about their colored doll. Two or three days before Christmas we have to close shop because of runnin out of merchandise. What started as a curiosity turned into a big deal. One thing: Cecil brought every Black Nationalist into the shop, and they had to stand on line and wait their turn to place orders. Trouble is the shop rental, doll processin, mailin and salaries, all add up to barely makin any profit out of the boom. Hard to understand. The colored doll must cost more than the white, just to break even. I bought two small ones to go on the dresser top for Delta and Sugar.

It's such a merry Christmas. All of our friends and some of the old Pullman crowd comin together laden with goodies. Marion, Looli's cocktail waiter, brought in a big turkey and a fruitcake, given to him by some "high ups" he had worked a party for. Marion is just crazy about rich white people. He says, "Honey, there's no other kind I'd speak to—none other comes up to my level, baby." They also gave him two pounds a lobster meat. He glazed the turkey to a shiny brown and stuffed it with chestnut dressin. Marion cooked for at least twenty-five people, with a Hungarian goulash on the side in case we run short on turkey. I always believed sissies are delicate and lady-lookin. Marion has a pot belly, but he is light on his feet and whirls through a kitchen like it's a dance hall. Hard to help him because he shoos you away. "I love it, darlin. Puttin on the dog makes me glad all over." He brought a large piece of pink fringed silk to use for our tablecloth. "Sugar pie, I stripped my bed naked so we can do Christmas in style. Style, ladies, there's nothin like style!"

Looli made hot rolls and stringbeans boiled with Virginia

ham. A real surprise. Looli does not believe in givin things away. She can hold onto a penny until the Indian screams. Looli looks out for Looli first, but she can be awfully kind when her mind moves in that direction. May brought homemade Irish soda bread. Laverne cooked meat patties and peas and rice with grated coconut. The Pullman men brought champagne and port. "Lord, Estelle," I said, "this would be a bad day for an investigator to call on anybody cause I do believe there's a great comin together goin on all over Harlem." Delta and Sugar have brown-soaped the house spic-and-span, from stem to stern—even have mistletoe hangin from the ceilin light. Cecil came with the Christmas tree, put it up and placed the little candles only on the outer branches so we don't have a tree fire like many do. We only light the thing for a minute or so on Christmas, then blow every candle out.

Everybody is happy. Nobody knows how to have a ball like those who have seen bad turns. We sing, joke and laugh, sometimes laugh when no joke has been told and no funny thing has happened. We just look at each other and feel good.

I pass through the hall, on the way to the kitchen, and meet Cecil bringin the star for the top of our tree. He opens his arms and I walk in. He kisses me. "Cora, reach in my shirt pocket and take what's there."

Two ten-dollar bills and a five. I kiss his eyes and that place on his lip. I am happy.

"Tell Delta it is from the two of us."

The Democratic block captain drops by for a drop of cheer. He has brought a leftover shoppin bag from the distribution to the poor. It has chicken, celery, onions and all kindsa odds and ends from the ward leader. It's for Estelle cause she helped him get people to join the Democratic club. He gives us an Irish toast. "Here's a hundred-proof she-lay-lee to knock out your troubles! Down the hatch!" He drinks his neat three fingers. Estelle and Looli dare him to do it again. He does.

The bell rings and it's Nappy, sleek as a whistle, with a redheaded English girl on his arm. The sight of him with another woman makes Cecil feel good. And I, for one, am glad there's no hard feelin on this Christmas day. Chalk comes over with his mother and I feel sorta uneasy, but it's nicely Christmas all the way.

Looli nudges me and says, "Girl, you got so many a your men showin up, we gonna run outta chairs."

We start off Christmas Eve and make it on through into Christmas night. When people get tired they doze awhile, then start all over again. Some go home and come back—oh, such a going and comin back and forth. I look out the window, down to the street where children play. The Lord has popped his fingers and sent snow to make Harlem pretty. I feel sorry for everyone who is not as happy as I am—with love goin on all around. Thank you, Lord.

On Christmas evening, the white Communist man who corrects people comes in with the Negro comrade who will not be corrected. They bring guitars and sing worksongs . . . causes Marion to groan and raise his eyes heavenward. After three in a row, Looli teaches them some backwater blues. They try to put social meaning to the blues. Looli corrects them. "The song got meanin in the first place."

Estelle sings a spiritual to put them all out of business. Marion turns her off by puttin on a record and makin me show them the Lindy Hop and Black Bottom. He holds up another record and says, "Now, when all the squares leave, I'll play my Josephine Baker." The squares want to hear it, so he plays "Two Loves Have I". Baker sings it in French and English. On the flip side is a French song about a Japanese girl named Tonky somebody. Delta plays it over and over. Such a lovely Christmas.

Twenty-Five

A crowd has gathered on the corner of One Hundred Twenty-fifth Street and Eighth Avenue. They surround a green city bus and will not allow it to pass. May and I come out of the market and see Cecil, his arms loaded with signs on sticks: "Jobs for all". A policeman is sayin, "Move on, move on." What's happenin is Cecil's waitin for more pickets to come and carry signs up and down in front of stores between Seventh and Eighth Avenue.

"Cora, go home, it's serious out here."

"What's happenin with the bus?"

"Every driver is white, and not another goddam one will get through until they hire some black. None a these stores hiring black, not even the five-and-dime—no kinda job. Where we to get money to buy what they sellin us?"

A man bystander says, "We gotta open our own business, brother, not to look to them for a job."

Cecil says, "Oh, yeah? They won't rent us store space

nowhere on the main street; you can't even rent upstairs office space except further East, between Lenox and Fifth. Then you must know somebody and pay graft under the table. Bastards."

The lone policeman looks up and down the street for help. People are pickin up the signs. I take one and May takes another. We walk in front of a dress shop with Cecil and tell people not to go in and spend money where they're not allowed to work.

"Cecil, is this the work of UNIA?"

"No, it's mostly Harlem Labor Union, but we can't let them walk it alone. White man is sellin to us but keepin all the jobs for hisself. He got the land, buildings. . . ."

There is a victory shout from the corner crowd. They pull a driver from the bus and chase him down the street. Another bus pulls up behind the first; it, too, is taken. The policeman crosses to the other side of the street and stands in front of the bank, waitin for help.

Cecil shouts to the crowd, "We don't have but one black policeman, and he's directing traffic at One Hundred Twenty-fifth Street and Lenox! We not hired to put out a fire, to clean streets, or to teach school. Selfish bastards keepin all the jobs, makin thieves and criminals out of our children!"

May's face matches my excitement. It's feelin to me like time to take over the world. We move down to a dress shop and carry our signs back and forth. Bet the place is filled with Dolly Dimple Darlin Dresses. I shout out, "Pass on by, folks, don't throw money where you can't work! Black help in exchange for black money!"

May shouts along, "We want jobs!" The people not only pass on by, but repeat behind us and shout, "That's right!" "Buy nothin! Close em out!"

Suddenly the pickets turn and run from the clatter of

horses' hoofs. Mounted police drive the horses over the sidewalk. One gallops between us. "May!" I scream. She is pinned against the display window. I can't see over or under the horses.

"Run, May, run away!"

The police have blocked in even those who were only passin by. We all push and shove to get away, but the police keep closin off the escape. There is shoutin, the horses raise their hoofs high and clatter them down on the sidewalk. A woman stands screamin at the top of her lungs, scream after scream. There is a man in a light gray hat; blood pours out from underneath it—the front of his face shinin wet with blood. A horse moves. I see May still huddled against the window. She moves away, just in time, as someone sends a brick smashin through the glass; it rains glass. The bleedin man laughs and holds out his bloody hands to catch the shower. Cecil is on his way to me. The paddywagon shows up, and cops herd the people inside. They have May; now Cecil; I can't reach them. A policeman swings his stick splittin a cut over Cecil's eye. They drive off with him, May, and the laughin bleeder. In a while, the crowd is gone. A store owner comes out to sweep glass.

Looli helps me to go through every pocketbook I have in the house, before we find the business card of that white man, Mister Simeon. He lends me lots of bail money. I must say you couldn't ask to meet a finer gentleman.

Twenty-Six

Praise the Lord, I have found a way to face middle age with some measure of security. I have two apartments here at Seventh Avenue and One Hundred Fifteenth Street; one is on ground floor and the other one flight above. We live downstairs and I do business on the upper level. Estelle still hangs onto her old flat because we never can tell. Mister Simeon is a generous business partner—he's also gettin older every day and, if the grim reaper cuts him down, we'll be left in a bind.

Simeon took this lease in my name, so if he backs out of the picture, the rent falls on me. But, on the plus side, since it's in my name, I can't be put out. That's security. These two six-room apartments are beautiful and spacious. New furniture throughout, overstuffed with goose down. I have Oriental carpets, soundproof walls, gold-framed mirrors—classy. Upstairs, the private club is for members only. We have two gamblin tables, one dinin room, and a private office for

Simeon. The livin room has a crystal chandelier and an electric champagne fountain.

There's a big picture of Mona Lisa in my foyer. Estelle says she has a smile just like mine. Mona's my favorite, along with *The Last Supper*. I have lots of pictures all over. We look well fixed. Downstairs there's plenty of room for Looli droppin in and out, also Estelle, and whenever Sugar's in from nurse's trainin. Delta's fixed nicely with bird's-eye maple and her own private bath with shower. Sugar's time is spent at Lincoln Hospital. Delta's doin freshman year down south at Bennett, so it's good that all she has to do is get in for a quick visit, then go right on back to where she's gettin some first-class lessons in ladyhood. She's glad to be there because she's kinda picky and critical about from whence comes her good fortune.

I live with my heart in my mouth. God knows, gamblin is illegal. Mr. Simeon pays off to top-law just as regular as he pays rent. But he keeps his guard up. Nobody gets to be a club member unless they pay membership and get a card. All games are played with chips, so we don't handle money on tables. Chips not only look better, but they make people spend more freely cause chips don't seem the same as money in your hand. Our chips are red, white and blue, like the American flag that hangs on Simeon's wall.

We do good business and Marion runs us a first-class dinin room. When people want special dinner they have to give two days' notice. Showfolk from Broadway come, also bigtime gamblers. No huge crowds, either. Gamblers fly in from Chicago, Florida, Boston, Atlantic City to make a top game and play for two days straight. Some nights the house cuts two or three thousand, but that's just once in a while.

I got a set of door chimes that play "Sweet Georgia Brown" and a peephole on the door to see that whoever is there really belongs to the club, or is comin in with a member. Business keeps my nerves jumpy, but I could do worse. There's no dope sellin and we don't run any smalltime number wheel. If somebody wants to play a figure for ten dollars or over, that's all right. I've seen Simeon pay off a ten thousand dollar hit, like a gentleman, with a smile and a handshake. He is a good sport; however, too many a those big ones give him diarrhea for a week.

That Cecil doesn't put his foot in here and talks down to me bout how I'm not showin a shred of race pride. He was spendin a little time with some white woman who is active in what is called "The Woman's Movement". Seems like a lotta white women now join up together to fight for the right to work. I fell out laughin when he told me that.

I said, "Let her ask me about it. I've had that right all my life, just haven't been free to do it where she can!" Me, I need to fight for the right to *stop* workin. Cecil was tellin me how their friendship is called "platonic". I know what platonic is and they are not that. Simeon and I are platonic—not Cecil and the socialist-woman. I laughed right in his face and told him that I plan to walk into a nationalist meetin and interrupt one of his speeches and preach on the "*White* woman question". I'm not against race mixin at all, but I don't need black men to keep their white women way off in the background while they try to lead and tell me what all to do, what to call myself, how to conduct myself and all like that. He asked me to go to a nationalist dinner with him, to sit on the dais! I said, "No, baby, you take Goldilocks. Let them know who you cuttin down to the Village to see."

I'll not give him a divorce, either. Married him for better or *worse*, so that Delta could be Green in a legal way; that's all I ever got out of it. I told him to put his mouth where his mind is. Let Goldilocks sit on the dais! Cecil gets to laughin one minute and cussin the next bout how I have no social conscience. I got enough to see that whoever he picks up with, black or white, he comes on back to me every time.

I'm the one who's sendin Delta to school. I offered to help Cecil have a legal little business sellin soda, newspapers, candy and shoeshines, but he got nothin on his mind but some kinda freedom movement. And he is never on the winnin side! Dammit, they never gonna let him win. Not only got the scar on his lip, but eight stitches over his left eye from havin a hard head. Almost got me and May killed followin behind him. His ass would be under the jail if not for Simeon.

"The Civil War is not yet over," Cecil says, hintin that I've moved back on the old slave plantation because I work for Mister Simeon. He won't come here, but now and then we get together on the outside, whenever I feel weak in the head. My nerves get so tight from keepin in touch with Delta, and also remindin Estelle to keep up her doctor visits after the radiation treatment. Laverne stays over at Estelle's and is *forgetful.* Went out, left a pot on the stove, burned a hole in it and smoked up the house till the fire department had to come. I can't depend on Looli the way I used to cause she mostly stays with show business by bein the lady's maid, after ropin me into this operation by throwin Simeon at me. He was ready for some monkey business but I got that straightened from the jump. I don't feel like workin *and* bein a bed companion—one or the other maybe, but not both. I'm almost too much of a companion as it is.

He sits there in his red leather chair and slowly runs the addin machine, so more figures show up on paper. He drinks brandy—Remy Martin—says it's good for his heart condition. Drinks it out of a glass called a "pony". He looks up through cigar smoke and smiles, cause Enrico Caruso is hittin a high note on the record player. He might hear all the rest, but he only looks up on those high notes. I put that record on, "Pagliacci", whenever Simeon seems done-in. Some days the door chimes keep our heads tore up, specially if it's around election time.

Lowdown politicians switch loyalty when new people bout to put out the old guard. The "ins" will pull a surprise raid so they can get their pictures in the paper, like they're cleanin out crime. Some are decent enough to say in advance they'll do a bust, so we can clear the place of anything that's too hot to be here and also to give time to notify his lawyer.

In an emergency we don't have much to do but clear away money and chips. Marion, he'll haul our stash-pile over to Estelle's old place or sit it out at May's until the air cools. If he gets taken downtown he knows Simeon will see him through I've been down twice—out in three hours but sick as a dog for the next two days. I don't like bein arrested, sittin there wonderin if maybe nobody'll show. I try to look cool, calm and collected, even if my heart's goin like a hailstorm. Never show your hole card. Some stranger finally comes in with the bail money and a lawyer. Out in the street, we part company and I hop me a cab back home. We all lay low and keep quiet until Simeon finds how best to deal with the new politicians. He shouldn't have to figure shit—after all, he gives to both parties, by messenger.

When I get home, I go to the refrigerator and eat some of everything that's not movin. I got one of the biggest gas refrigerators they sell—and *two* of them upstairs. Everywhere I go somebody is showin off ice cubes. Niggers didn't have what to eat, but they'd say, "Have a glass a ice water?" Then they'd show off their cubes. These days you're nobody at all if you still chippin ice, or folks see a iceman comin in your door with a wooden tub on his shoulder. I now have cubes, praise God—never did like chippin ice and wet newspapers wrapped around.

And I got more than ice cubes. Looli did five weeks on the road and picked up a fine dark mink for six hundred. Sold it to me for seven, so I have accomplished that. It's gettin old from just hangin in the closet, but on special days I take it out and make an appearance so folks can see I'm not as far back on the bus as I used to be. Simeon also put me in the way of gettin a diamond brooch cause some fella had to straighten out a debt real fast. That's also how he got his own star sapphire ring. He loves that ring—I can tell by the way he holds his finger while sippin from the pony glass.

"Cora, there'll be a few live ones in town next weekend. Treat em right. Nothin but the best, and don't charge for food or drink."

I stand up for myself when I must. After all, I live in this place like a prisoner, and he goes off to spend time with his wife and children. There's no twenty-four-hours-a-day on his clock.

"Simeon, next Saturday I'm takin off to see the Hamilton Ball at the Rockland Palace."

"Why go to a sissy ball?"

"Marion is takin part in the grand costume parade. He's been tryin to win a prize for four years runnin."

"Dressed like a woman?"

"What else? That's what the grand parade is—men in ladies' clothes. A white fella from Chicago wins first prize every year. A chauffeured limousine goes to meet him at the airport."

"Well, if you and Marion are off to the faggot's ball, who's gonna cook and run the place?"

"Looli and Apolinario."

"Okay, you deserve a change, but don't you think it would be nice to ask me?"

"It'd be real nice, but if you said no, I was goin anyway."

"You are straightforward."

I put on Enrico Caruso and pour him another pony. I'm not straightforward enough to tell him I loaned Marion two hundred and fifty dollars to buy an outfit to wear to the Hamilton. I myself never paid a hundred dollars for a dress; he's havin one made to order. I told him, "Marion, you crazy? You big as all outdoors and there'll be fellas there lookin like movie stars. How the hell you gonna win?"

"I am grander, Cora—I have class, to the manner born. First-class people come in all kindsa packages. I am big . . . and first-class. You may take the money out of my future salary."

"You been drawin on future salary ever since you've been here."

"But I deliver, don't I. Well worth the risk."

"Sure do. A brown-skin cook and an Oriental waiter. You and Apolinario make us uptown's finest. The Cotton Club and the Savoy got nothin on us."

When Simeon stops listening to Caruso's high spots and twirling his cigar band, that shows he's restless. I turn down the music and he reaches for his Marcus Aurelius book. "Shall I read, Cora, or will you?" He opens the page. With closed eyes, he runs his hands down the page, then looks where his finger stops. "Hear this, 'Be like the cliff against which the waves continually break; but it stands firm and tames the fury of the water around it.' Oh, that Marcus Aurelius."

He waves the cigar in time to Caruso. This man so much admires what is refined. I think of a Marcus I once knew—Garvey. I don't tell Simeon. Some secrets are not to be shared. He doesn't tell me all. I know little about the wife who is always goin off somewhere. Well, he likes her to be gone—she likes to go. They both carry a white flag.

One night, after the place clears, I put on his Caruso and ask him about his younger years. He tells this and that and how he once visited some relatives in South Carolina. I change the subject. Accordin to his age, it crosses my mind that he could be my first father, the man who loved and left first mother. No such thing, of course, but the very thought of it makes me mad.

We often take each other's measure in a testin way. When he returned from the last Florida trip, I said, "You got so dark, you look like one of us." Once he said to me, "As you came through the door, you reminded me of an Italian woman I met in Rome when my wife and I visited for the summer." In that way we hit on each other, as if to say, "you oughtta look more like me". May and Apolinario crossed their bridge, but I can't cross over. Looli always swears that Simeon is in love with me. How can that be? Gettin so that I'm built like a postcard mammy.

Looli says, "Some men want comfort and kindness. They could roll in the hay with some gorgeous Gussie for a lifetime, and never find it. You know, honey, when a baby is fretful, the mama holds it to her breast, humming so the sound goes into the baby's head and through his little body. She rocks him and peace is declare in that child's soul. It knows somebody's lovin and nothin more need be said about it. That's what some full grown men want from a woman."

One night I was sittin on the foot of the couch. He left the leather chair and sat down beside me. "Cora, don't you care for me at all?"

"Indeed so, no doubt about it."

"Have you ever loved a white man?"

"No. I care for you more than any I've ever met, but no."

"Why can't you love me?"

"White men have not been very nice to my people . . . to me."

"All white men?"

"No, not all. I see differences, Simeon. I can't give all of myself away, got to hold somethin back; that's the best I can explain."

"Stay up here with me tonight; it would make me happy."

He has been good to me. And yet, I fight back the sight of bloody fish-hooks, dirty words comin at me, policeman chasin my papa out the park, the minstrel show fight, theater manager—the line is very long. I try to remember Looli's advice: "Means nothin, honey. It's somethin they want, that you can give. Why let 'squeamish' hold you back in life. What's all this goin on bout *love*? Explain it to me? Love? What's that? Learn to be good to people who are good to you. Nobody can take nooky away; when he's through, you still got it, right? It's the one thing you can sell and still keep. No sense in bein stingy with something you can't lose." Sounds so reasonable. Who deserves more peace, comfort and rest in my arms? We open the couch and soon bare our bodies which have seen better days. I decide to comfort him, to say "thanks" for the hard times he has seen me through. What's wrong with sleepin with the enemy color? I've known nationalists who—oh, well. I stroke his white hair, he is grateful.

"Cora, do that again." He kisses my workworn hands. It feels good and restful, but I really don't want to.

He knows.

We just keep ramblin and talkin and caressin. I act the right way. There are tears in my eyes and I pray in my heart. Lord knows I want to do this thing for the dearest Mister Interlocutor there ever was. Tambourines jingle in my head. *"Cora! Be seated!" I see myself jiggin across a stage with a glass a water on my head—and then I am Ross-a-jass, cuttin carrots and onions in the big pot while Chief Boo-Roo holds his bleedin face and dear Papa smiles and bows to strangers—"Which way to Sam Johnson?"* Tear drops on Simeon's hands—it means something to me, no matter what Looli says. "Cora, you just grit your teeth and that's all there is to it." I can't grit my teeth.

He knows.

I don't preach on the street corner, but my nationalism is right here in this room. I love Simeon, but I can't give myself. I try to think of Cecil with that woman . . . maybe the thought will push me on. I can't, no matter what that Cecil does or doesn't do, no matter what Simeon would like. It's out of my hands. God moves in a mysterious way.

He knows.

"Cora, I'm not as young as I used to be. . . ."

"Oh, you're just tired."

Twenty-Seven

It's next to impossible to get tickets for a Hamilton Ball. Thousands can fit into the Rockland Palace, but you have to know someone to get a ticket. I know Marion. May and I are here as Marion's guests in a center box. He has all kinds of food and liquor, even brought his own silverware. No paper forks and spoons for him.

The hall is decorated with golden bells. Waiters are dressed as footmen like in Cinderella, purple satin suits and white wigs. Marion points out well-to-do bigshots who have come from all over the country. Marion looks calm and collected in a plain tuxedo. I can't wait to see his dress. It's in the dressing room and he won't show it until the grand parade.

So many I think are women are really not, but men and women fill all the boxes, eager to see the show. If any came to laugh they are soon overcome by wonder. The gowns worn by these men are not to be matched anywhere in the world.

There are three orchestras; one in full dress, another in

gold suits, and one in Mexican costume. Everybody keeps jumpin up and down to see if some celebrity came in and they're all on the watch for the special fella from Chicago. A story goes through the hall that the Prince of Wales has come to see the parade. People almost fall out of boxes tryin to see. Marion is makin a big hit with his two lady guests of honor. Maybe some think May and I are men wearin disguises, but I guess they know we're not cause our clothes look like nothin in this crowd. I have to exclaim over the gowns, particularly one of silver cloth.

"May, isn't that beautiful?"

Marion flips his hand in the air and says, "Lawdy, how gaudy. Loud but not proud. Shinin with no linin. I'll have to put you out of my box, Cora, if you're gonna rave over the wrong thing. Alla your taste is in your mouth." He leaves us to go dress.

May can't get over the scene. "Just think, there are so many lonely women and these men are not interested." A girl from the next box brings us glasses of champagne: "Heidsick 28, ladies," and then "she" rushes off to join the parade.

When the grand march starts, lights change, stars whirl and spin across ceilings, walls, floors . . . red, green and golden spots of light fall on our faces. A smooth, handsome cat in a full dress suit comes out to stand in front of the band. He's rugged, handsome and well put-together. I have to laugh out loud and clap my hands because at last I'm lookin at a black interlocutor. He is black as shinola polish, with straightened hair slicker than Valentino ever had. His job is to announce the paraders. He calls them in a most serious manner: The Queen of Sheba and Cleopatra and Marie Antoinette and Mae West and Josephine Baker and the Duchess of Elba and Medea and Madame de Pompadour and on and on with the most famous names and costumes. But, of course, the crowd is waitin for the fella from Chicago who wins first prize every year. People in the next box tell how last year he came as the Statue of Liberty—wore a gold spiked crown. In one hand he had carried a sequin lawbook, and in the other, a red lamp that flashed on and off with each step.

The announcer calls out: "The Peacock from Chicago, Illinois!" When he walks on, the crowd goes screamin crazy, people almost faint. He is tall and slender as a Georgia pine. Looks like someone has sewed him up in a brown velvet sheath. He wears a purple wig with about twenty peacock feathers risin straight up and out, makin him look nine feet tall. Rhinestone earrings, a foot long, fall from his ears and rest on his bosom. He wears a train of peacock feathers, stretchin out straight behind him, one layer on top of another. Must be three hundred feathers he's trailin across the floor, as if purple and gold will never end. He wears gold slippers and golden gloves with rhinestones climbing from each finger up past the elbows. Two attendants in lavender tights go before him bearin gold bowls from which they sprinkle a carpet of rose petals as he slowly struts around the floor.

The hall's gone wild. Men rush out and strew flowers in his path, women raise champagne glasses and follow behind him. He will not smile, just moves ahead lookin superior to what the world might think of him. He reminds me of something I've long tried to do—rise above it, above everything that's tryin to hold us back.

"Well," May says, "glad to see a man who wants to be a woman. It must stand for some kind of admiration."

"Guess so," I say, "but I'm worried bout Marion. Nothin he bought could stand up to this. The Peacock has stolen the show."

People keep screaming long after he's gone, but he's so much the peacock that he won't even return to take a bow.

The Peacock has come and gone and that's that. He was far grander than the ball. Finally all quiets down enough for the parade to go on. There is Queen Elizabeth and the African Rain Queen—all kindsa costumes. But where is Marion? At long last, the announcer calls, "Madame Marion, dark womanhood!" Here comes this portly figure along the runway, wearin a plain black-velvet evenin gown, a floor-length black-velvet stole, a black wig mixed with silver, black-velvet shoes and gloves. Only one touch of color: he carries a corsage of bright red American Beauty Roses. Hefty and middle-aged, he wears a proud, patient look on his face. He pauses, fingers the single strand of pearls which reaches to his waist. He looks out at the crowd, kindly, with love. One woman calls out from a box, "Mother!" Someone titters, then is hushed by others. Marion walks forward, almost timidly. People begin to clap in time to his stride. He shakes the band leader's hand. He bows to our box and waves, breaks off a rose and merely lifts it in our direction. He is what he claims to be—a representative of that spirit which is seen and felt at Wednesday testimonial. The spirit of those who've been through some rough trials.

When he leaves, they call him back time and time again. They like him better than the Peacock. He quietly wins first prize after five years of not even honorable mention. The Peacock is second after four years of first prize, and Mae West is third after three years of second. Marion wins the golden loving cup. He steps to the microphone. "I thank all of you. In particular I wish to thank my dear friend, Mrs. Cora Anderson Green. She is not only a great lady but is also my inspiration."

He lifts the rose to me again and sings. I didn't know Marion could sing! The place turns into church meetin. "I'm on my journey now, Mount Zion, on my journey, Lord! Wouldn't take nothin for my journey now . . . Mount Zion!

You can talk about me just as much as you please, but I'll talk about you . . . when I get on my knees, Mount Zion!" Everybody can't help but join along, clappin, singin, cryin.

He gives me his first prize. I've had four outstandin presents: my father's lodge cup, the Garvey trip, May's set a dishes, and now Marion's prize. I've never been so honored and recognized in public. People congratulate me as well as Marion. He introduces us to the Peacock and Mae West.

"Marion, I'm proud of you."

He makes me say it again. "Are you? Did I come through?"

"You were magnificent."

He hugs me with fierce strength. May says, "Don't forget me! Hug me, too."

"Thanks ladies. I won't ever need to win again. This once has sent my soul."

As we leave the place, I almost plummet down the stairs. The floor rushes up to knock me in the face. I grab the bannister and Marion's arm.

"What's the matter love, had one too many?"

"No, just dizzy."

Twenty-Eight

Delta has a hard time living in the apartment, knowing what goes on overhead; but since no one told her to quit school and return home, she endures and plans and tries to stay out of arguments with her mother. Cora doesn't like the girl spending so much time at the serviceman's canteen. She constantly drops hints about army and navy men not really looking for Coca Cola, sandwiches, or dance partners.

"Mama, a canteen is there to give our boys in the service . . . encouragement. Hitler would love your attitude."

"The hell with Hitler and what he loves. Those fellas are hard up and they're lookin for relief. They'll all be movin out soon and none will be hangin around to give a kitty bout what happens to you. They're always ready for another free lunch."

"Mama, don't judge everybody by the men you've met."

"Come up in my face and say that again! Sass me again, Miss Woman! You need to be knocked down and I'm the one who can do it!"

"Like you knock everybody down, Mama? Go on, roll over us all, roll over the world!"

Cora grabs the girl and snatches at the front of her blouse; it rips. She shoves her into a corner.

Marion separates them. "No, no, not two people I love. This is not the way."

Delta sobs and talks back all the while. "I didn't do anything wrong! Mama, where do you get such evil thoughts? You don't trust me from here to the corner."

"I'm ready, willin and able to pay your way back to any college you can get into. My God, didn't I let priests and nuns mess up your head so you could learn gentleness and good manners? Now you jump up in my face and compare me to Hitler. Do it again, so I can kill you!"

"I'll run away. You can't watch and control me forever."

"I say it again: No! I will not sign consent papers for you to go in the Waves or the Wacs. I'm not gonna sign, Miss Mouth!"

"I didn't ask to be born!"

"Neither did I! Now, what next?"

Marion tries to make peace. "Only people who love each other behave this way, say such things. Now, that's enough. Stop! Delta, your mother is not well and you must not drive her pressure up higher. She's also got blood sugar—the doctor says no excitement."

"It's not my fault she won't stay on a diet. Mama, you know I'm sorry, but you've lived your life the way you want; now you wanta live mine, too."

"Listen to her. 'You've lived your life.' She's ready to turn her back and bury me for the sake a the army and navy!"

"Ladies, if Mister Simeon could only see you now," Marion tries to make peace. "Good thing he's in the hospital. This would give him another heart attack."

"I'm going to tell him," Cora says.

"Me wanting to join the national defense is none of his business."

"I'm gonna tell him how you treat me."

Marion continues to work on the case; finally Cora is willing to let Delta go in the service, providing Cecil agrees. "After all, he may be a jackass in some ways but your father knows the rundown on every government in the world, particularly this one."

Delta grabs at a straw, to turn off the venom of the moment. "I'd go ask, if I knew where to find him. Would hate to have to ask at the Black Nationalist Hall."

"Be fair, Cora," Marion says.

"Good enough," Cora grabs *her* straw. "This is Thursday, so we know he'll be at Lenox Avenue and One Hundred Twenty-sixth street—on a stepladder."

"Yes, telling everyone how to save the world while his own have to battle life on their lonesome."

"Respect your father, Delta."

"Why don't you? You don't swallow what he's putting down, so don't try to make me do it."

"Girl, I'm tryin to save you from your hard-headed, stubborn self."

"Wonder where I get it from?"

He stands on the fourth rung of the ladder. The American flag ripples in the evening breeze. The faithful gather close to the front, the curious linger in the background. Cecil, lean as ever, hangs on to the battle of life with bulldog determination, afire with zeal for the ever-bright cause. He mentally counts heads and spots strangers, eager to catch the ear of those who may well chart the future—perhaps some new Garvey, someone young, with a flashlight mind that will never burn out, someone to carry out the beautiful rebellion.

He sees Cora standing with Delta, on the fringes, with the other doubters. The girl is taller than either of her parents and far prettier than Cora ever was. She lacks her mother's flair, her style, that way of holding her head ready for defiance. But the girl is softly lovely, a dark, regal . . . stranger. He wonders why they have come. Has someone died? What terrible thing could have happened? Their faces don't tell of any urgency. He decides to preach for them, to try to win over all doubters. His subject is "Who Am I?" The good disciples have surrounded his ladder with weather-beaten posters of noble Africans—Berbers, Fulani and Masai, one Rastafarian, and Garvey. He stretches his arms to the gathering crowd; many murmur fond recognition. "Man, that's Cecil Green."

He gives them the hope of present knowledge and future triumph. They urge him on with a smattering of applause. A Jamaican calls out, "Speak, Green! Preach!"

There is more applause and he speaks . . . to the girl.

"Sisters and brothers, some say we are Negroes, some say Afro-Americans. . . ."

A spectator shouts, "No, we are black men!"

A drunk rocks back and forth on his heels, angry with himself and this speaker who wears a threadbare suit, whose black and gray hair needs a barber's attention, who has the nerve to stand arrogant and kingly in his rundown heels and limp, well-worn necktie. The drunk snorts disdain and laughs.

Cecil goes on confidently, "Brothers and sisters, don't hurry past here to go to the movies and see a Western, to watch the Indian catch a hard time. I am presenting an 'Eastern'. You've never seen an 'Eastern', have you? Nor a 'Southern' or a 'Northern'. That's because they have our brains locked down on Western. Behold, I am your Eastern, and any or all other directions in which your mind wants to travel. My topic tonight: 'Who Am I!'"

The drunk shouts angrily, "You a nigga, that's what—a dumb nigga!"

Cecil smiles as if the fellow had paid a compliment. "Nigger? My friend, that's the last thorny word I've pulled from my heart. You forget the others; there's more. We are Kaffir, native, mulatto, quadroon, buck, snowball, coon, spook, jig, octaroon, high-yaller, high-brown, monkey-chaser, boy, uncle, dinge, burrhead, cannonball, mammy, smoke, Jemima, Tom—on and on they go, all well known Anglo-Saxon words, don'tcha know! But, I found out! I found out! I found out!"

"Tell it, Green!"

"I found out that *anything* a disrespectful person calls me is a insult, even if it's 'dearly beloved'. We all worrying if we're too dark or too yaller or too *whatever* might be too much this week. But let me tell you, it ain't how we look that's makin trouble, or even what we're called, it's how we're *treated*—there and only there is the trouble. It's how they treat us, plus how we treat each other. If you can't face that, stay lost!"

Cora feels that sense of pride she takes in Cecil whenever she lets herself fully listen to him speak. Delta tries not to believe his sermon; it disturbs the soothing vision of the future which she finds in white movie stars who give her glimpses of a life she's never known—a perfect life filled with unlimited chance for careers, wealth, homes, and first-class travel by plane, train and cruising ships—the strong, firm belief in endless possibility, dreams now shaping her every decision. The first move: to break out of the restraint of Harlem and "special" schools—to search for and find a fresh, new place.

Cecil reads renegade minds. "You may want to turn yourself into a one hundred percent American, but massa's great grandson won't have it! So now you not African, not American, not one thing or another—just a little a this and a dab of that—and a whole lot of mental confusion!"

The audience is growing and enjoying the show. Delta notices that one of her father's shirtcuffs has lost a button and dangles limply from his coatsleeve. He is so elevated by his topic that a ragged sleeve can't stand in the way of his vision or the better future. He has learned to throw in some humor—good jokes that can move his listeners further up the road—victory jokes.

"Fortunately, I get along with Africans, Afro-Americans, colored people, Negroes, blacks—and even some niggers—cause it's in my best interest to do so!"

The audience applauds. A man does a quick little whirl of a celebration dance, another walks away and heads homeward. Laughter comes to a stop as Cecil holds up a hand to direct sound and mood traffic. For the better part of an hour, he outlines programs to force the white-owned Harlem businesses to hire blacks, to force the real estate owners to rent desirable property to black business. He explains the use of boycott and reprimands those who buy from places where they cannot get jobs. He urges them to buy "race" books and products—records, statues and pictures. "Read J. A. Rogers!"

When he gets to the part about signing petitions and going to City Hall and knocking on doors and handing out leaflets, the crowd thins down to the faithful few, plus a few more. Delta has no hope that he will say yes for her mother to sign the consent for service; she knows now that he will not. He thinks they came for money and is glad he has fifteen dollars to hand the child. People are now beginning to buy the black books he sells from door to door—books that enlighten. For him, there can be no greater success than to see profit from good works.

The faithful bear away the stepladder. Cecil is free to walk his ladies up to Henry's Ice Cream Parlor to buy treats and hand his daughter some money.

"No, I'll not give consent. Army and navy—that's for men. Servicemen call such girls 'Government-inspected meat'. I can take no pride in your doing this."

"But I'm to take pride in you and Mama not living together, each going opposite ways?"

"War is for killing, not about our problems."

"I won't be killing."

"Then why go?"

"To get out of here and be somewhere else."

"Go down home and visit your cousins."

"They're dead."

"Go back to school."

"I know what to do. I'll wait awhile until I am old enough not to need consent."

He puts them on the double-decker bus and cautions Cora, "Take care, try to do whatever your doctor says, watch the diet, take the medicine. I'll see you . . . soon."

Delta breaks the silence as they ride along. "Mama, when you were young, didn't you ever long to do something important to you, that others would not allow?"

The question is Cora's undoing. "Yes, I wanted to be a cabin girl on a ship. I was dyin to get away. My life mighta took another direction if I'd been able to leave and go away on my own. You have to belong to yourself at the beginnin, not wait till the very end. As it is, I've had to be linked to first one person, then another. I've never yet known the full meanin of independence."

"Mama, I would call you a very independent person."

"Looks can deceive. I don't want you to go because I don't want to see you hurt. This World War Two is no different from the other called 'One'. It's a white folks' fight—and both sides are united against us, on both sides of the line. Why should we care?"

"You care about May and Mister Simeon."

"They're different."

"Well, I trust that there are *more* different ones; they can't be alone."

"Why should you care?"

"Mama, such as it is, this country belongs to me as much as it does to anyone else. I want to make it better, too."

"By beatin on your chest and sayin, 'through my fault, through my most grievous fault', and goin off to war?"

"Mama, no way you can save me from livin for myself. After all, what is life all about?"

"My father said it's a short walk."

"And what do you say?"

"I say it's a damned first-class minstrel show . . . and I been sittin front row center all the way."

"If you had it to do all over again, is there anything you'd change?"

"Yes, Delta, and I'm goin to do that right now. I'll sign the consent paper."

"You will?"

"Yes. There's some progress in that. My daughter can now be a cabin girl, in a manner of speakin, wherein I could not. So be it."

Twenty-Nine

Delta in the service, Roosevelt dead, the peace near . . . the girl regularly sends home little fold-over airmail letters from the same navy address, no matter where she might be. Harlem streets have lost any semblance of geniality. Bigshot white folks don't come up to Harlem the way they used to. The atmosphere is mean in spite of welfare checks.

Cora changes doctors, but the new one says the same as the old, doing no good and taking her money.

"Mrs. Green, you should be hospitalized."

"I feel all right."

"Your blood pressure is too high. I don't see how you're walking around. You're spilling sugar and your heart is enlarged."

"Your medicine isn't doin me any good."

"Medicine can only do so much."

"Change the medicine. I don't trust hospitals."

She goes to see Laverne over at Rockland County where she is getting "mental care". Took three visits before she got to see the physician in charge.

"Miss Washington's general health is fine, but she does have memory blackouts and well . . . er . . . delusions of grandeur."

"What is 'delusions of grandeur'?"

"She thinks she's a countess, some kind of royalty."

"She is royalty. I was her lady in waiting."

The doctor's eyes open wide. Cora explains fast before he can decide to keep her also. Anybody would need a delusion to live in Rockland.

"I understand now, Mrs. Green, but she can't be released except in the care of a responsible party."

"I'll take her whenever she's released."

"And not related? That's very kind."

"Well, I am her lady in waiting, as I said."

The doctor in charge looks uncomfortable again.

"Anyway," Cora adds, "we're close friends."

A group of people mill around in front of a five-and-dime on One Hundred Twenty-fifth Street, arguing with a policeman and the store manager. More gather as the argument intensifies. People come running across the street from the Apollo Theater on the opposite corner. Cora hurries along toward the elevated train before any mounted police gallop onto the scene. She wanted to buy shoes from Wise, but the sight of a mob now sends her in the opposite direction. Confusion and danger make her dizzy. A group of young men running across Eighth Avenue almost knock her down. A hurrying woman gives her instruction, "Get home, honey, trouble's brewin."

"What happened?"

"They say a boy stole candy at the five-and-dime . . . say the manager beat him. This crowd is mad about it."

"Did you see the boy?"

"I didn't see nothin. Me, I'm gone."

She takes a cab instead of the El and is glad to get inside her apartment with the three locks and police bar in place. That One Hundred Twenty-fifth is fast becoming a place to stay away from.

Cora is tired but proud of her meal service for working men—and no liquor served, strictly legal. Marion is still there to help nicely and share half and half, after expenses. He calls it "sweat work for third-class trade". After frying eight chickens and baking three deep-dish apples, he declares, "Lawdy, Lawd, Miss Cora, there's no shade in a cotton-field—and since Mister Simeon died we do have us a *field.*"

"Don't leave me, Marion."

"I'm here, love, to the bitter end."

They sit down and feed themselves before customers arrive. Fried chicken, pig feet and potato salad with pepper sauce . . . and iced champagne.

"Cora, didn't the doctor tell you to let up?"

"Don't smoke, don't eat—damn, I'm not even makin any love!"

"Sorry I can't help you on that, big Mama."

"Have to give up everything? What must I do, sit here and quiver?"

"Maybe you should smoke reefers."

"That stink stuff? Anyway, I'm legal these days."

"Yes, darlin, and it's killin both a us. Well, someday my ship will come in, and you can rear back and help me enjoy my penthouse."

"Say the word. I'll be there, with the ace a hearts stickin to my forehead."

Midnight, she stretches out in bed reading a snatch of Simeon's Marcus Aurelius, sipping brandy-good-for-the-heart from his pony glass. The phone rings and it's Cecil's voice. "God, I'm glad you're home. Have you been out?"

"Not since early today."

"It's a riot, Harlem is a shambles. The stores smashed, looted—clothing, food, liquor. There's fighting,af30shooting, arrests—busted open Herbert's Home of Blue-White Diamonds. Turn on your radio and stay in the house."

"Where are you?"

"I'm at home, Cora. This is none of my doing. While I'm working with honor, they've run on past me to do it the wild way."

"Cecil, I thank you for callin. Have you heard from Delta?"

"She sent me the picture of herself in uniform. I felt proud of her—beautiful in the white hat and blue uniform. Said her group is protesting discrimination."

"The branch doesn't fall far from the tree."

"I wish we could get closer together—for her sake . . . for ourselves."

"Good to hear you say it."

The place jumped on New Year's Eve night. Looli came in to give a hand, and all that was left of the old gang gathered, loving each other with less criticism than they used to. Now, New Year's Day belongs to her and to Cecil. All evidence of the night before has been cleaned away except for the H-A-P-P-Y N-E-W Y-E-A-R letters strung across the wall. Cora has a resolution. From now on there'll be time for herself, time for Cecil, time for love.

She has invited him over and will do the quiet business thing she has long planned to do, what with the way these doctors talk and the way she no longer trusts banks.

The mantle over her fireplace looks like an altar with candles burning—red for love, green for money, yellow for health and white for purity—for the new, legal life. In the center of the mantle is her father's crystal lodge cup with the golden emblem. It is for Delta, so she can feel pride. She closes a fat envelope and ties it with a red ribbon, writes *Cecil* across the front.

Marion, in the kitchen, hastily puts away the last of the dishes from the night before so he can go to a very special party in Brooklyn. The phone rings twice, then there's the lady's voice. "I don't wanta hear that shit!"

Long silence.

He goes to the living room door. She is on the couch, surrounded by aging brocade and tasseled pillows.

"Oh, love, what now?"

"That nigger, Cecil Green, is not comin over. He's goin to some sorta goddam *coalition* meetin."

"What's the emergency?"

"Marion, there's no man anywhere in this world has ever loved me as hard as I know how to love back. All my life I've wanted to be loved, deep-down and no jive. I'm scared. I might die without ever knowin what it feels like. That sonofabitch, Cecil has never loved me!"

"Not true—don't say it, lady. Christmas, didn't he bring you a three-diamond Bulova watch, ring and necklace set from Busch?"

"Five dollars down and fifty cents a week! You made fun of it."

"All I said was how I don't like *sets* of anything. But if a square like Cecil sends a set, celebrate! When a broke man buys you something, he loves you."

"Look at the surprise I have for him!"

He examines the mantle. "Looks like a voodoo ceremony." She tears open an envelope and spills out money—fifty halves of one hundred dollar bills!

"Wow! The hell you say! But why are they cut in half?"

"So he'll have half of each bill; the other parts I put in the safety deposit box for Delta. They'll have to meet together to match and divide and . . . well, it's my way of makin a will, of bringin them closer."

"But you not fixin to die yet!"

"Sicka havin money stashed under the mattress and the closet floorboard . . . and will never trust another bank. I want Cecil and Delta to take over and take charge. Tired a bein strong—I quit."

He helps her gather the money and put it back in the envelope. "Marion, I'm just a goddam old workhorse like every colored woman that's ever had to stand squarefooted and make her own way. The more I do, the more falls on me to do."

"Your money looks very frilly and delicate."

"Cause I cut the bills in half with my pinkin shears."

"Stop cryin."

"I can't. I'm thinkin bout gettin older and bein sick and people goin crazy—and about dyin. I'm facin the first day of a new year all alone and I'm runnin scared with nothin but a deuce in the hole. Anybody can beat that. I don't wanta be alone tonight."

Marion lays out the plan. "Put on your best outfit. Do it up grand. I'll go to my party, present my regrets, and meet you on the corner of Forty-second Street and Broadway at eight

P.M. Being the first day of the year, we oughta be able to get a good show ticket. Let's hang out together?"

"I gotta say yes. I hate to, but I must. I need you."

"After the show I'll take you to the Turf Club. We'll have iced champagne in a silver server and, I'll tell you how much Cecil loves you so you'll never doubt him again. Sometimes love walks in chains . . . I know."

She comes up out of the subway, tipping along in black satin shoes with rhinestone heels. The weather is crisp, but she lets the mink fall loose, because it doesn't fit well when buttoned. The corset is too tight, but it makes the black silk jersey dress fit smoother. Her hat is a mass of black ostrich feathers; gloves and purse are gold leather. A man turns as she rests at the top of the stairs.

"Yeah, tip it, pretty mama."

Ten minutes early. She spends time in a souvenir shop. No longer angry with Cecil, she selects a comic postcard with a big fat black woman standing in front of an outhouse. Underneath is printed, *I Love You No Matter Where I Am!* She addresses it to him and signs the back—*Cora.* The clerk also sells her a stamp. Out in the street, the wind snatches the card from her hand and flips it along the sidewalk. She reaches for it, misses, then reaches again. A woman stops it with her foot, picks it up for her. Across the way she sees Marion. The sidewalk lifts and she staggers. A man takes her arm. "All right, lady?" A couple of youngsters blow last night's horns in her face. They think she is drunk. The mailbox is only a few steps away. She must get there. Her foot drags; she has broken one rhinestone heel.

The mailbox moves further away as she tries to reach it. An impatient man behind her takes the card and drops it through the opening. "Come on, lady, don't take all night."

She wants to call out to Marion, but she's on the ground, looking up at faces which look down while the ship's whistle blows. A boys says, "Call an ambulance." A woman pulls down Cora's dress to cover the glimpse of thigh which spills over the top of her stocking. Another hand places her purse on her stomach. Again she hears the noisy blast of the ship's whistle. The captains in their white coats lean over her and lift her toward the gangplank—"Oh, Joy!"